The Arasmith Certainty Principle

Russ Colson

DOUBLE DRAGON PUBLISHING

Double Dragon Press

An Imprint of
Double Dragon Publishing
PO Box 54016
1-5762 Highway 7 East
Markham, Ontario L3P 7Y4 Canada
http://www.double-dragon-ebooks.com
http://www.double-dragon-publishing.com

ISBN-13: 9781729160794

A DDP First Edition October 23th, 2018
Book Layout and
Cover Art by Deron Douglas

Acknowledgements

I am indebted to many people for the insights and ideas that made this book possible, including former students, teachers, family, and friends (and probably even enemies!) I would like to particularly thank my parents who gave me the courage to try all things, my wife, Mary, who read many drafts and found the right mix of encouragement and honest critique, my Anticipation critique group who gave lots of good advice and feedback on many writing efforts, particularly Sara Card and Ann Dulhanty who beta-read full novel manuscripts for me, and, finally and especially, my editors Erin Colson and Laurie Sand who pointed out--with great detail and sometimes-sarcastic firmness--what wasn't working.

Prologue

Kar-Tur sat on the hard stone watching the flames. He did not note the sting of smoke in his nostrils, or the black soot darkening his rough dwelling. Although he hadn't moved for nearly two days, his back and legs rested comfortably from long practice at stillness. He gazed patiently, waiting for the understanding he knew must come. He didn't look at the fire, but into it, searching, as he had yesterday and the day before, and last year and the year before. As he would continue to do until at last he understood.

Or until his tribe lost patience and would no longer share food and water or repair his house and clothes.

This was a good year, better than many. Meat was plentiful. His tribe didn't resent his absence on the hunt as they had in some years.

They didn't truly understand his quest. But his former quests, and things he'd done for them after those long vigils, made them trust in the value of this one. Especially in times of plenty. Even now, meat from the great hairy elephants rotted by the cliff, a wastefulness he would have cautioned against had he not been so focused on his task.

The fire danced. He could see it had Power. When he looked deep, he could sense its *Material*. Power and Material made up all things. But there must be more to this magical essence that lived and died so differently from human or animal. With a mere twenty-six cycles of seasons behind him, and being among the pampered of his tribe, he surely had much time yet to search.

Seasons passed, and, one day, insight came to him. His inner eye found a new and deeper character to the flames, a deeper essence to Power and Material. As understanding expanded, he realized that this deeper essence was found not only in the flame, but in the great sloths and beetles of the forest. It was in the spirit that moved the grasses of the prairie in great sweeping waves and in the stones that lay unpresuming on the slopes of the hills. It was even in his own mind.

It was so clear, so complete! *All things were possible.* The wonder of the new understanding took his breath away and he moved his eyes at last from the familiar flames where they'd rested for so long. The blue images burned onto his eyes by the comforting fire left him almost blind in his dark room, and he felt a moment of fear brush through his thoughts.

With the fear came a new realization. All things were possible, but that meant bad as well as good. Evil could come. Evil from the stars. Evil from the past. Evil from himself or his tribe. It could overwhelm them.

He must warn them. Tell them of both the wonder and the terror, of potential and danger.

He rose to leave his fire at last, casting a glance back at this glowing companion who had taught him the secrets of existence, of truth, of knowledge and faith. His vigil had once again born fruit. And he must tell his tribe. But would they bless him or curse him? Would they even understand?

He left his dwelling, immersed suddenly in the less familiar world with its green woods by the stream and the sweeping expanse of grass stretching forever out to where the empty rock and cold ice began. He cast his eye upward at the sky, nervous at what might be there, or who, and whether they saw him or cared. He looked inward again, dwelling on the wonderful, but also testing the terrible, feeling it for what it was, realizing that it would even be possible to...

In that moment, silently and without moving the gentle grass or casting an image that any eye of his tribe could have seen were one looking, Kar-Tur unexpectedly winked from existence.

Chapter 1

I fussed at my hair instead of working with it, turning this way and that in the mirror and finally choosing to believe it was fine. Brown could only be brown and straight was only straight. I pulled my peach sweater over my shoulders. It was a nice complement to my hair and skin, and I chose to wear it even in the warm southern California air. It might, after all, get cool tonight at the open-air restaurant Jonathan had invited me to. In any case, I wasn't entirely at ease in the shoulder-baring evening gown I'd summoned the courage to wear.

A date, for crying out loud. Why a date? If we just went out together like graduate school buddies it would be fine. His quaint insistence on paying my way tonight completely transformed the experience.

I liked Jonathan and felt excited to see him for the first time since he took the faculty position at Burns College. But he was a friend, nothing more. I considered whether I should tell him as much tonight but was afraid he might be hurt. Even more afraid our date really was just buddies reuniting after a time apart, and I'd look ridiculous.

Probing my feeling a bit deeper, I wondered if I resisted telling him because he was an important professional contact for me, having already taken a first job, while I still had a year--hopefully no more--to go on my Ph.D.

I hoped I wasn't that cynical yet.

But I really didn't want a date. I was uncomfortable mixing friendship and romance. One was sure to end up losing both.

I heard his knock at the door and bounded from my chair, hoping to jump-start my inner enthusiasm with outward buoyancy. A flash drive containing my day's calculations lay on the table, and I grabbed it to drop off at my lab in the geology building on the way to the restaurant. I always kept a non-cloud backup separate from my computer, but I wondered briefly if I really needed to make that extra stop at the geology building or if I used my work as a way to polish the sharp edges off my nervousness.

"Humph" I said aloud to no one but me. "You're nervous and should just quit obsessing about it." And, listening to myself almost none at all, I met Jonathan at the door.

***

The restaurant he picked truly was delightful and the night lovely. I found myself seduced to an inner quiet by the bright stars and the susurration of the waves about fifty yards from our table. Jonathan didn't seem hurried to talk. I imagined that perhaps the evening would pass in good company and few words. I relaxed a bit more at the prospect.

His eyes drifted away from the shoreline, which was just making its final disappearance into the gathering gloom of night, and toward a loud and slightly intoxicated group of people at a nearby table.

"Do you ever wonder what other people, ones you don't know, are happy about?" he asked.

I looked at my friend of four years with new interest. I did think about such things. It surprised me that he did.

I smiled and nodded, feeling no need to speak, perhaps a bit afraid that if I encouraged intimate conversation it might stir whatever motives he had for asking me on a date. I wondered for a moment if I should be interested in him as more than friend. With his fit 5'10" frame, dark hair and eyes, he wasn't unhandsome, although that seemed rather feeble praise for a friend to grant. He looked sufficiently distinguished when not wearing his quaint and goofy field hat—the one I teased him about when we did field work together. And he was certainly intelligent.

But I felt no overwhelming romantic urges. I wondered if you were supposed to feel some irresistible impulse toward the person you were meant for.

"What do you think about alien visitors?" He turned his fierce gaze on me, catching my eyes into his.

I smiled at his effort to start a conversation. He always spoke forthrightly and often abruptly of what he thought, which always made me believe he had no hidden agendas, no secret plots for how to use people.

"Do you mean, aliens, like from outer space?" I raised my brows.

"Sure," he said noncommittally, inviting me to choose my own interpretation.

"Aha." I paused a bit, sipping from the tea I had ordered as we awaited our dinner.

"As a geology professional, I think there must be no other intelligent beings in the universe." I grinned, letting him know I was being silly with the geology professional bit. "Or perhaps it's simply impossible for intelligent beings to travel the stars. Either way, there are no aliens visiting us here on Earth. If there were other beings, intelligent beings able to traverse space, the Earth's rocks would be filled with evidence of their presence here. A million years is only a moment to the universe, but an eternity to the expansion and advance of a technologically intelligent race. All the universe should have long since filled up with them. The Earth would not only bear the mark of their exploration, but of their colonization. They would be here, and not us.

"And," I continued, "By the same measure, there will never be time travel. Otherwise the rocks of the age of dinosaurs would be filled with the petrified refuse from an eternity of time-tourists."

I paused for his response. This was one of the more enjoyable aspects of graduate school, the expansion of ideas and testing of reasoning that took place in half jesting, half serious intellectual sparring over supper, or in a stairwell, or in a lab late at night. I wondered if Jonathan missed it.

Jonathan didn't answer immediately. He seemed rather more sober than he had as grad student when he had been quick to leap into the verbal fray. He started to speak, but stopped as though unsure what to say or, perhaps, whether he really wanted to say it. I wondered if my somewhat silly intellectualism had turned him off.

Our meal arrived, and Jonathan turned to it with such delight that I thought he must be relieved at the interruption.

Jonathan relaxed with the meal. We reminisced about our grad school days. They were still very present for me, but Jonathan seemed to have already developed a melancholy attachment to their memory, although he'd only finished last spring. When conversation lapsed, we watched the stars, enjoying each other's company and the universe we'd chosen to study.

We took a walk along the beach behind the restaurant, finding a few shells tossed up by the recent windstorms, shells that the endless swarms of beach-goers had somehow left untouched for a day or two. A grove of palms stood near where the restaurant property went down to the sea, and we lingered there for a while.

Our casual conversation lapsed occasionally as we listened to the waves. Several times, Jonathan became sober again, as he'd been before our meal was served, and he seemed about to share something that was weighing heavily on his thoughts. Each time, something else came out, or he turned his eyes back to the sea and fell quiet, allowing both his sudden intake of air and intense look at me to simply breathe away. By evening's end I was quite curious about his behavior.

I felt somewhat awkward, fearing that I knew what he wanted to talk about. I thought seriously of preempting it, by commenting, perhaps, how glad I was that we were friends with no romantic entanglements with each other. But I didn't, hoping that the problem would just go away.

"Jen," he began as we leaned on a palm tree watching the waves sparkle in the light of the just-risen Moon, "I didn't bring you here just to socialize or to maintain our friendship, which is certainly valuable to me. I have an ulterior motive. I think I need your help, as both a friend and geologist. Your advice at least, and maybe your collaboration."

My heart crossed from a mysterious combination of hope and fear to relief as Jonathan spoke. I especially breathed a sigh of relief that I had not presumed too much and announced uninvited that I was only interested in him as a friend. I realized with chagrin that I was unsure whether I felt happy or disappointed that my fears of his romantic interest in me proved unfounded.

"What kind of help?" I asked.

"My question earlier about aliens wasn't a casual one." He paused for a long moment searching out into the sea for his words. "I've found something."

"At your field area in Wyoming?" I knew he was working in Quaternary rock, much too young for my interests.

He nodded. "Suppose I were to tell you that I've found evidence of ancient alien visitation. Or found something unusual anyway. Something not ordinary in the rock.

"I haven't told anyone else yet. I'm not sure if I'm afraid the CalTech folks will steal my thunder, or if I'm just afraid everyone will think I'm a nut. But I don't know what to do with it. I think I'm even a little scared of it. Does that make sense? It's really not even in my field. I'm no anthropologist."

"What have you found?" I prompted when he said no more.

"I've found something...odd. A human skeleton in partially lithified shale, in the Atosoka Formation. I, well, I measured several bones in the skull and found that the dimensions are almost modern. It's a woman, apparently quite old when she died."

"Why is that odd?" I brushed a wayward lock of hair from my eyes. "Late Pleistocene, I'd expect the skeleton to be of modern appearance, at least within the variability common to our species."

"I found it in the Atosoka Formation." he repeated. "And the skeleton seems to be *buried* there, not deposited naturally. There are—" he paused again, "belongings with it."

I remembered that the Atosoka Formation was a lake deposit, not a typical place for a burial. And with an age of nearly forty thousand years, it was also a bit early for humans in North America, especially ones who buried their dead. My eyes were just beginning to widen with comprehension when he added, clearly delighted with himself, or on the border of hysteria.

"And, the old-time radio I found buried with the skeleton was a bit odd too."

Chapter 2

Susan was busy (what else was new?) and Cynthia, hesitant to interrupt her, slipped into the windowless room quietly. She wondered if Susan remembered that they were supposed to meet for lunch today. In those not-uncommon moments when Susan forgot their dates, she was usually in her office or some other accessible location where Cynthia could find her. So, she'd never seen her sister's lab before.

Cynthia looked around. It was a bit disappointing for a science lab. She'd expected more chrome, or blinking lights, or whirring sounds. It looked instead more like, well, like a basement storage room converted temporarily to a laboratory for a new faculty member.

Even Susan's equipment disappointed. No sleek, shiny surfaces, no blinking lights. It was mainly wires, and boxes, and computers like some of the old stuff she and Mike had at home. Her son, Adam, who liked to call himself the science geek, had electronics that looked more impressive.

Cynthia ambled around the room, waiting for Susan to notice her in her own time. It surely couldn't be too long. The room was only about twenty-five foot square, although the mysterious vertical cylinders towering in the middle hid her from Susan once she stepped away from the doorway.

She suspected she shouldn't touch anything. Who knew which items might be poisonous or radioactive or something? But Cynthia couldn't help herself. She liked to touch. She ran her hand over the top of a smooth, metal box with a digital keypad and a couple of lights. It seemed out of place, looking far too scientific—translate: sleek and shiny--compared to the other gadgets in the room. She smiled to herself, wondering what Susan would think of her impression.

She continued her exploration until a turn around a table piled high with more stuff--which Cynthia suspected was just empty boxes--brought her up beside her sister.

"You need to keep a cleaner ship, I think Susan," she said with a smile.

Susan gave a start, apparently having still been unaware of Cynthia even though they stood side by side. Susan straightened, stiffly, as though she'd been bent over her work for some time.

"I'm sorry. I forgot. What time is it?

"It's a little after noon."

"I'll just be a minute more here, I'm almost done."

Cynthia nodded and continued her journey around the room's perimeter.

Big, heavy-duty bus bars clung to the wall on this side of the room. Cynthia wondered what kind of experiments required such large quantities of direct current. "What are you working on, Susan?" she asked.

"My research deals with the Heisenberg Uncertainty Principle," Susan answered absently, scarcely glanced up from the instrument she seemed to be adjusting.

Cynthia waited a moment to see if her sister would say more, then responded playfully, "Well, I'm glad to hear that you scientists have some humility after all. You always seem so *arrogant*, you know."

Susan looked up at that. "What do you mean?" she asked blankly.

"The uncertainly principle," Cynthia said, smiling. "I didn't realize you could do things uncertainly."

"No, no, Cynth. *Uncertainty* Principle, not *uncertainly*." Susan's attention went back to her instrument. "It deals with the prediction that we can't measure both a particle's momentum and its location at the same time. One of them has to be uncertain."

Cynthia grimaced, knowing Susan couldn't see, being turned away from her. She started to explain she was just joking, but then realized Susan would probably think she was trying to cover up for being confused.

Her sister really needed to take herself less seriously. Maybe get a boyfriend. Recognize the presence of other people and not treat her own thoughts with such religious solemnity.

Cynthia recalled with a wince the last time she suggested Susan should get married. "I'm a complete person," she had said with sudden fury. "And I don't need to ride a big dumb ox to get where I'm going!"

"Mike's not..." Cynthia had begun, but couldn't finish, simply turning to leave. Susan had immediately apologized, her anger dissipated by the hurt in Cynthia's face, calling after her in tears. But Cynthia had not wanted to hear it, and they hadn't spoken for a month afterward.

Cynthia, glad that misunderstanding was cleared away, wasn't interested in a repeat performance. She finished the last quarter of her tour, which took her along a bench supporting a couple of computers connected by cables to the towers in the middle of the room. With her eyes on the puzzling towers, her foot hit something that skittered across the floor to end with a bump against the wall by the door. Hoping she hadn't broken something important, she scampered to retrieve it. She looked around for a moment before finding a small cell phone behind the door, the flip-phone kind that Cynthia hadn't seen in years. So very Susan.

She wiped the dust from it, hoping that action erased any harm her blow did to the electronics, and returned it to the bench by the computers.

Susan came to join her then. "All done. What was that sound?"

"I'm afraid I kicked your phone into the wall," Cynthia replied. "It must have fallen to the floor."

Susan picked the phone up and looked at it, obviously puzzled. "It's not mine. I don't keep one with me, certainly not at work."

Cynthia raised her eyebrows. Even Susan, private as she was, needed a cell phone. "Who else works here in the lab?" Cynthia asked. "Might they have left it?"

"Well, no one is supposed to, right now. I have a graduate student, but he's on vacation in Maine. Some of the cleaning staff must have left it."

Despite her words, Susan didn't look convinced by her own argument, proceeding to open the phone and poke at some buttons.

"Requires a pass key," she said. "Odd."

"Why odd?" Cynthia came up beside her.

"No one should be in this lab. Not without me knowing. Why would they be here?" Susan's eyes drifted to the tangle of wires and boxes that housed her research project and held there a moment, considering.

"Well, let's go," Susan said, returning the phone to the bench. "I am hungry."

Chapter 3

Jonathan expected my astonishment, but I don't think he expected my disbelief. I suppose it *was* uncharitable to disregard our friendship so by not giving him the benefit of the doubt. Friendship should be a trusting relationship. But in this instance, Jonathan seemed far too trusting. I thought at first he was joking. But neither going along with the joke in a caricatured, conspiratorial tone, nor teasing him about the absurdity of his statement drew the response I expected. He was too serious. He wasn't joking.

He truly believed he had a forty thousand year-old radio.

Then, all I could think of was "hoax," either his, or someone else's. Science, particularly anthropological science, had a long history of such "jokes" on its practitioners. And the old-time radio, one of the frequency-scanning types from perhaps three decades past, was a bit too much to take seriously.

Nevertheless, I was packing for Wyoming. Who wouldn't? It was worth it even for a hoax. As long as it was a well-done hoax.

I packed mostly field clothes and not many of them. Given the few days I planned to be gone, I didn't need to over-pack. Even after adding toiletries, substantial room remained in my small travel bag.

Hmmm. I didn't want to waste that space. I might have a chance to attend church, or we might drive into town for supper or other activities some evening. I tossed in a dressier outfit and a nice pair of shoes. I planned to wear my comfortable field shoes on the plane, so that bulkier item didn't need to go in the bag.

I still had my camping gear to get together, but I decided to take a break by putting my apartment in order. I rolled up my sleeves and set in to wash the giant pile of dirty dishes in the sink. I hated to come back from a trip to a mess in the kitchen. Of course, I didn't mind letting messy dishes accumulate for a few days when I was home, hoping the bugs would help me clean them. The bugs had missed some spots, I noticed.

I straightened things up in general and vacuumed the carpet. That's better, I thought. Now I had a comfortable place to return to. Somehow, the journey ahead felt less intimidating.

I put my camping gear together quickly, following a routine that was familiar after my recent field work. I had a separate duffle to hold my tent, mess kit, sleeping bag and pad, and other things I'd need in camp.

I paused, considering if I had everything. Almost. I tossed a deck of cards into my clothes bag. There might be opportunity to play. I liked cards, I think because it left talking as an option but not a necessity. One could be companionably quiet.

My bags packed, I stepped in front of the mirror to ensure I was presentable to the world. I groaned a bit in remembering my mis-anticipation of Jonathan's interest in me last night. I resisted acknowledging what this betrayed about myself that I didn't want to think about. At twenty-four, I had not spent very long unmarried; I had unmarried friends of thirty. But it *seemed* like a long time.

I wondered if there might be some reason I wasn't married. Despite my effort to overcome it intellectually, I couldn't help but worry that I might not be attractive enough. And here I was fretting about it again. I wasn't unattractive, I encouraged myself. I was quite sure, for example, that I had the right number of heads. I checked the mirror again to be sure. Yes, a perfectly fine number of heads for a human. I smiled at my humor, aimed at diverting vanity as well as insecurity. The right number of heads, and a nice figure.

I laughed and shook my head. I definitely needed more to do. That ought to be easy once I got started on a new project. I loved becoming immersed in new challenges. My own field work was mostly completed, and I hadn't quite summoned forth the discipline to start writing yet. Jonathan's project, hoax or not, would be good for me.

Chapter 4

Professor Jack Myrvik clenched his hands into fists, unsure whether to be frustrated or irritated, and turned his steps toward the university and the corner office he kept there as physics department Chair. The streets around the stone administrative building where he'd met the President and Chief of Staff were quiet this late in the evening but both foot traffic and cars picked up as he neared the university.

The government team hadn't really been interested in his work, despite requesting the interview, although they did have significant questions about his research. And they listened politely when he pontificated about the need to develop a broad surveillance system using applications of his breakthroughs in quantum sensors. It would, as he had argued, completely transform both military and civilian surveillance.

But their casual questions about Susan's work, just before they finished talking to him, betrayed their true interests. They had tried to make their interest casual and polite, asking general questions, and not over-pursuing his answers, but he was not easily misdirected. The questions themselves revealed their focus. Susan's work was not published, not even complete. There was no reason they should even know about it, let alone be asking questions.

The two other people int he room, the man and woman he'd thought might be secret service, had perked up and even asked a couple questions at that point. Who were they? They certainly weren't security people, given the type of questions they were able to ask. The male in particular seemed more than merely science-literate.

The presence of the President and military Chief of Staff had certainly caught his attention, and he answered their questions about Susan's work as best he could. But he knew of nothing so significant as to draw such high-level attention.

What had he missed about Susan's work?

Youth suffered from inexperience, but it also found new ideas and insights that older scientists were too biased by precedent and expectation to see. He remembered his own days as a new scientist, a young Turk taking the world by storm. His early work was some of his most innovative, vaulting him to prominence in his field and a position here at Cal Tech before he was thirty.

Just like Susan, he thought.

He berated himself for underestimating her potential. He would have to look into Susan's work more closely. There must be something she was doing other than this Heisenberg nonsense. He needed to find out what it was. He remembered that she had asked for department volunteers for something she planned to do this fall and that she had already started vetting volunteers from the community. That was a place to start.

Chapter 5

Susan liked reading mystery stories. Agatha Christie's Hercule Poirot was a favorite. The observations were so carefully made, the solutions so elegant and logical as to make her participation as reader delightful. The mysteries were like science puzzles, she thought. The detective, in the fashion of a scientist, wove together a coherent fabric of ideas and conclusions from seemingly disparate threads of observation and reasoning. Only the application differed from science.

So much better than modern mysteries, where the emphasis on incomprehensible and erratic human character took away much of the element of deduction, substituting intuition and luck.

Susan put her book down and glanced at the clock. One o'clock. The afternoon was young. She didn't want to read the day away, and experience told her that going back into work was unwise. She needed a break to provide time for the creative well to refill.

Some company would be nice. She didn't want to get too cozy of course, just a good group for some noise and companionship.

She wondered if it was too late to put together a bowling party for this afternoon. Who could she ask? She knew several people at the lab, both faculty and technicians, who would probably have few plans for the afternoon. And, she could call Cynthia.

Of course, calling Cynthia meant inviting Mike too. That didn't sound so appealing.

Then Susan remembered that Mike worked until six in the evening on Saturday. Perfect!

Leaping from the couch, she started calling. She only needed six or so for a fun group.

In thirty minutes, she had her group and a plan to meet at the bowling alley at three.

Grabbing an umbrella in the very unlikely event of rain-- she prided herself in her preparation--Susan set off to hike the four miles to the bowling alley. The prospect of a good walk brightened her spirits almost as much as the prospect of company at the end of it.

It also provided an opportunity to assemble in her mind the research chores that needed to be done next week.

The paradox of the uncertainty principle always intrigued her. Something intrinsically immeasurable went contrary to her intuition. The implication that the location of something was undefined defied her sense of the universe. If she measured a particle's momentum, how could its location be unknown? Wasn't there a box of space somewhere, of some size, she could put it in? Of course there was, she knew, depending on how well she measured the momentum. But what about the theoretical limits: What if she measured its momentum *exactly*? Wasn't there *still* some box the particle must exist in? It must exist somewhere, and if somewhere, then it must be definable. If not by the laws of physics, then by something else.

Otherwise, the macro-world of common human experience must ultimately crumble into the unknowable as well, at least over some time-scale. Crumble into a mathematical world where concrete sense collapsed into nonsense. The macro-world, after all, was comprised of the Heisenberg-uncertainty world, like solid objects were made of atoms. Something had to give the uncertain location a real value, whether or not people were able to measure it. Something had to give that location solidity, certainty, just like there were principles and processes that gave solidity to a group of atoms, which were themselves made mostly of nothingness.

She felt uncomfortable at an intuitive level with using the wave nature of matter as a fudge-factor to correct for blurry knowledge of where a particle lay. The whole mystery of whether matter was particle or wave seemed to her to reflect a missing key somewhere.

Paradox permeated existence, or at least human understanding of it, and enlightenment often depended on grappling with that paradox. She found the mysteries implicit in this paradox fascinating, but unlikely to succumb to the simple experiments she'd designed. For this reason, she'd hesitated to risk her research-time on it prior to taking a permanent position. Now, with a tenure-track position in hand, her fascination would not be restrained.

She found it most intriguing that it was her sentient knowledge of the momentum, her measurement of it, that rendered the position immeasurable. It was this idea that gave her at least a tiny hope for her experiments.

Susan had been somewhat surprised when Dr. Jack Myrvik volunteered to participate in her first study set, but she truly appreciated it, despite her impulse toward suspicion when people appeared a bit too altruistic. Jack understood science well enough to know what to expect from her experiments—part of her control group. It was the results from other participants who would have no expectations other than those she gave them that she found herself most interested in. Walter Roden, an older gentleman in need of some extra money, certainly fit the mold of a non-scientist with no preconceived notions. Hopefully she could hire a few more.

The cell phone that Cynthia had found in her lab continued to trouble her. It was gone when they returned from lunch. Who had been in her lab, and why? Maybe it was only a custodial worker. It was odd if anyone thought they had to sneak around to see her work. Her lab was free to anyone. She had no secrets.

She arrived at the bowling alley in plenty of time. It was one of those with electronic score-keeping and cute little videos of frightened pins being devoured by dinosaurian bowling balls.

She enjoyed the bustle and noise of people and the companionship of cheering each other on. She also enjoyed conversation in small doses, and so, once the others all arrived, she touched base with each of them for a few minutes.

She was pleased when Craig Hedlund, one of the physics faculty close to her own age, and a resident at Cal Tech for only three or four years, plopped down beside her to chat. True to form, he talked about his vegetable garden, and she talked about mystery books. Conversation had drifted briefly to work, when he asked her about her research.

"Do you think it's a good project to be working on here at the start of your career?" he asked. "You do have to face tenure application."

Good question, Susan thought. Ironic that she had thought about that very thing on the walk here.

"Well, I can't help myself," she said smiling. "And I do have other projects in the queue."

He shrugged, as though doubtful, but nodded in understanding, and rose for his turn at bowling.

They ended up playing two games before breaking up around five o'clock. Several of the group, including Susan and Cynthia, walked across the street for an early supper at a Chinese place. Susan had eaten there before and knew the food was good.

She found herself seated across from Craig, and quickly leaped into conversation. Susan was not aware she was talking so much about work until he interrupted her with a laugh.

"Sue, you really are too straight-laced! Lighten up and have some fun!"

Susan tried to smile back but her face felt stiff. She'd planned today's get-together. Didn't that count as light and fun? Although, she had to admit, she did talk a lot about work. Maybe she should let people see more of her light and fun side.

The waitress arrived to take their orders and Craig ordered wonton soup.

"Oh. *Waun-taun!*" Susan exclaimed loudly enough to halt various conversations at the table. "I always thought it was pronounced *"wanton,"* and thinking it was something bad, I never tried any."

The group looked at her, puzzled, before carrying on with their conversations.

But Cynthia, sitting at her left, kept her eyes on her.

"Susan! she whispered. "Was that a joke?"

Susan smiled wanly. "Well, sort of. It's the best I can do."

"It was really funny," Cynthia whispered back and gave her sister's hand a squeeze under the table.

***

Susan returned to her apartment energized by the outing with friends. The walkway lights in the quadrangle outside blinked on as night advanced. There was still some light in the sky, but her apartment was shrouded in darkness. A gentle breeze stirred the tree outside her second story apartment window.

She lay in bed awake for a time, watching the moving leaf-shadows dance across her ceiling. Like the shadows, her mind danced with plans for her work.

Four of her colleagues agreed now to be present for the first set of experiments. She could get those set up and done in a week or two easily, before fall classes started. She planned the second—and more interesting--set to follow as soon as possible. She still needed to hire a couple more participants for the second set, but she had taken steps in that direction.

Susan puzzled again over her unknown lab visitor. It was so odd. Had there been more than one visit? What was he looking for? Who was it? And how could she find out?

She had some ideas, and thought through what she could do. But she was too tired to do anything tonight. Tomorrow or Monday would be soon enough. If these visits were a regular thing, and if they occurred again, she'd be ready.

Chapter 6

The San Bernardino Mountains fell away below them as the plane to Denver rose to cruising altitude, the valleys and peaks diminishing to crinkles and crevices on the shrinking map of the world. How small and insignificant would that landscape look to an alien arriving from another star, Jonathan wondered. Or from another galaxy? Or another time?

He appreciated that Jennifer didn't expect constant chatter. The quiet gave him a chance to sort his thoughts and explore his own puzzlement at his find in Wyoming. Jen's insistence on skeptical inquiry made her collaboration valuable, but he waited eagerly for the moment that Jen saw the skeleton and its accoutrements with her own eyes. When *she knew it was no hoax*, and joined him in this new reality where the horizons of possibility enlarged suddenly beyond the hills, and reached past stars and time toward the limits of the imagination. He wondered if she would find gazing into that vastness as exciting and as frightening as he did.

He pulled his travel bag from under the seat in front of him and took out two rocks, both fine grained shale. He hefted the first stone in his left hand, turning it slightly to look at it from multiple perspectives. The fine laminations were marked by thin layers of dark and light, together giving the stone the uniform blue-grey look typical of low-organic lake shales.

The patterning of the second stone looked quite different, although of similar color. The laminations were missing and instead the stone appeared blotchy, as though made of the same shale, but broken up into many small blocks and chunks by some disturbance.

As though someone had dug in the mud long ago before it became stone, churning it into the mottled mixture he saw now. Perhaps digging a grave.

But why dig a grave in the bottom of a lake? How had the woman come to be there, and with all the things she had with her? For a moment, Jonathan imagined a long funeral procession crossing the bare landscape of the Pleistocene hills, gathering along the shore in solemn quiet, and watching as she was lowered to her final rest in the lake.

"What're those?" Jennifer asked, leaning over to look at the two stones.

Jonathan stuffed the stones back into his bag, not wanting to bias her interpretations of the deposit. "Just some rocks I chopped out of the Atosoka."

They played cards for a while, then Jonathan took up a copy of *Nature* that he'd brought to read on the flight. He soon found his mind wandering to yesterday's conversation with Linda Thi, an anthropologist at Cal Tech from whom he'd taken several classes in pre-historic archaeology.

She'd listened politely while he described his skeleton buried in 40000 year-old sediments, and was condescendingly gentle in her explanation that there was little evidence for such an early settling of North America. She mentioned some 12000+ year-old human remains in South America, which must imply people migrated through North America even earlier, but her tone said clearly "not that early."

Jonathan had not intended to tell Dr. Thi about the belongings buried with the skeleton, but he needed to ask if such elaborate burials were common from that time (they weren't), and before he knew it, he'd babbled more than intended. Fortunately, he did not mention the radio, but he did talk about some of the other items indicative of a much more modern origin.

Dr. Thi hadn't said much after that.

***

After taking the jumper flight from Denver to Laramie, they picked up their rental car and headed northwest. Jonathan wondered why rental cars were always white. They must not be intended for geologists. Of course, he had no intention of telling the clerk at the rental office what kind of roads he'd be on. And that was just the places that had roads. As long as he washed it before returning it, they'd never know. *Hopefully* they'd never know. Although, there was that time he broke the Jeep axle...

As the mountains to his left and rear grew more distant, the land yawning toward the horizon alternated between shrubland and grass, the grass colored brown and gold with late summer. Only a couple of hours road-time divided them from his site, although the last few miles, with no road at all, would take another hour. That put them into camp about dusk, he estimated.

After chatting through the first thirty minutes they settled into the comforting sounds of the tires beating at the road and the wind whistling past. The grass gave way to scattered pine as they turned toward the Laramie Mountains northeast of Medicine Bow. The place where Quaternary stream and lake deposits nestled among the Mesozoic rocks of the dinosaurs. Jen, he noticed, had dozed off and didn't see when they left the paved road.

Jen awoke before they encountered the first cattle gate. She opened it to let them pass, closing it behind. Fortunately, much of the land was open range, and there weren't many gates. He had called the landowners to let them know he would be in today, so there was no concern with trespassing. They started down a rutty pasture pathway through the open trees and grassland.

Deep ruts cut into the hard soil by summer storms made the road rough. He drove slowly, avoiding the exposed rocks and mini-canyons. Eventually the road opened onto a grassy mesa that sloped toward the tree-capped mountains ahead.

The land here was dissected by gullies and stream-channels winding down from higher elevations. He came to a stop at the edge of one of the gullies.

"This is as far as the car can go," Jonathan said. "We can camp here and hike on in tomorrow morning."

The sun was just setting, partly hidden by trees to the west, and the air was already growing cool as they set up camp. The surrounding grass was too dry to risk a fire, so they enjoyed a late supper of fruit and sandwiches from the cooler Jonathan brought.

They talked in the darkness for a while, but with no fire to keep warm by, they soon went to bed. Jonathan lay in his tent listening to the crick-crick of the crickets hiding in the grass and to the wind murmuring through the pines that sprouted sporadically on the grassy slope. He could hear Jen shuffling around in her tent, getting ready for bed. He felt glad that she felt safe here alone with him. With some poor romantic choices behind him, he appreciated that trust and was of a mind to look for friends, not lovers.

Not that there wasn't a bit of sexual tension between them now and then. People were wired that way. But, at some level, he knew that he had to cling to the platonic nature of their relationship. If he did not, if he allowed his honest friendship with Jen to dissolve into just another of his flings, he suspected that he would never find a real friend.

Or real love. And, at twenty-nine, real love was starting to look more appealing.

***

A storm swept off the plain from the southwest later in the night, rousing him from sleep. The wind pounded at his tent, threatening to collapse it to the ground, though he was confident his stakes would hold. The lightning show and thunder were impressive, but only a few raindrops--big round ones that fell with a thump like hailstones--splashed against his tent wall. It should prove no threat to his excavation, but he was glad the site was safely covered by a tarp.

Long before morning, the storm was gone.

***

They ate breakfast and left camp early. Jonathan devoured the rough landscape with long strides. He noticed that his friend easily kept pace.

There was no gentle route to the lake deposit, as it was well entrenched in a cleft between the mountains. The deposit hailed from a time when this valley was blocked by landslide and subsequently flooded with rainwater and snowmelt from above. The ephemeral dam that formed the lake, ephemeral at least on geological time scales, provided an opportunity for silt and clay washing down the mountains to accumulate for ages, to become part of the Atosoka Formation. The sediment accumulated to tens of meters thickness in the quiet standing water of the valley lake, protected from the erosive power of the swift mountain stream.

It was here, searching for stories of geologically-recent uplift and subsidence, and for tales of climatic warming and cooling ancient by human standards, that he found what he had not even thought to look for. A human skeleton. A human skeleton from a time and place where they were virtually unknown.

Jonathan spotted the flapping blue tarp long before they reached the site. He'd thought he anchored it better than that with stones at the corners. But the important part of the dig was still protected.

He removed the tarp and watched Jen's face as she fell to her knees beside the skeleton. He had exposed enough of the skeleton to identify it as female, and to take some measurements of bones. The other items, the small wooden cross and the broach, protruded from the sediment near it. Only enough was exposed to reveal what each was. A depression in the stone marked where he had already removed the radio. Each of the other items remained imbedded in the soft stone, as he had intended. He wanted a witness to the fact that the bones and artifacts were not *float*, materials idly drifting with the whims of surface weathering and divorced from their link to the rocks. They were *in-place*.

Jonathan let Jen stare for a while, enjoying her astonishment as she puzzled over the paradox. How could it be real? Yet, how could it not be? No one could artificially embed those artifacts in rock.

"Look here, Jen." Jonathan directed her attention to a wider area of the short cliff he had excavated. Most of the area was laminated silt and clay, thin layers of shale of slightly differing colors. These laminae extended both laterally away from the skeleton as well as vertically above it. However, an area around the skeleton, about 2 feet deep and three feet wide, seemed disrupted. Here the sediment contained small blobs and pieces of the different colored material floating in suspension in the overall rock, as though the layers had been chopped up when the sediment was still soft. The laminae sometimes deformed into loops and curves, further indicating soft-sediment deformation.

"You see," Jonathan said. "This skeleton didn't settle here in death. If it had, the laminae would simply continue through it. It was *buried* here. A hole was dug in the sediment. It must have been dug in the mud at the bottom of the lake long before the mud was rock. Does that make sense?"

"Why would anyone do that?" Jen asked. "It couldn't be easy to dig a hole in a lake bottom. The saturated mud would slide right back in as fast as they dug."

Jonathan shrugged. Any answers weren't to be found in speculation, but in the site itself. They began to set up a grid from which to excavate the find.

"The metal in the broach is interesting," Jen said. "I agree with you that it looks very modern. It certainly isn't stone-age, since it isn't, uh, stone.

"But I can make a polished section and examine it under a microscope. By looking at the shape and orientation of the different species of metal crystals, their texture, we can learn a lot about the metallurgical technique used. If it's modern, we'll know it. If it's not from Earth, we might know that too.

"With chemistry, we can constrain it further," she continued. "The type and amount of both impurities and complementary components in the metal reveal a lot about where and when it was made."

"We want to make sure we nail the age down," Jonathan said.

Jen nodded. "The wooden cross should give us a carbon-14 age, although there's always the chance that the cross was made of a long-dead tree and wouldn't reflect the age of the burial.

"I noticed a bentonite layer here above the bones a few feet." She pointed to a whiter layer a half-inch or so thick, slightly yellowed from weathering.

"The volcanic ash in that may give us a constraint on the age as well. Although the half-life used to date the ash is much longer than carbon-14, and this deposit may be too young for an accurate date."

"Maybe get a date from the organics in the bone?" Jonathan asked.

Jen nodded without comment.

Jonathan didn't know much about interpreting bone. He suspected Jen didn't either. It wasn't in their field. They would need to get help with that.

He did know that trace elements and stable isotopes of carbon and nitrogen in the bone could reveal diet and general health. Forensic analysis might give clues to how she died, or what diseases she suffered. It could also reveal her age at death, although, based on the condition of the vertebrae and sutures in the skull, she was not young. Jen agreed with him that the woman was quite old when she died, even by modern standards, and certainly by ancient ones.

What did it mean to have a cross and old-fashioned radio buried here, Jonathan wondered. They were not only odd objects for a 40000-year-old site, but they were *obviously* odd objects, clearly not set in their own time. Why pick these objects for burial? Was it just a burial of personal objects, ones that meant something to her, and leaving them with her in death gave her companions comfort?

Or was this a deliberate effort to send a message through the ages? Were these peculiar objects *intended* to attract attention?

Jonathan found himself wondering not only what this find meant for him here and now, whether it confirmed travel through time, or travel from the stars, but he wondered what it revealed about the life this woman must have lived, for her to come to be buried in this place 40000 years ago. Who was she?

***

About ten o'clock, they finished the last of Jonathan's emergency granola bars that he kept in his backpack, but they were too engrossed to head back to the car for lunch. By noon they were both famished from struggling against the wind and from the steady work. Jen discovered a bag of potato chips, left from one of Jonathan's previous trips to the site, washed into the gully by rain or wind.

She picked it up with obvious excitement. "I do love chips," she said, dusting off the ants with a puff of air. "Fortunately, there's still some left!"

This was so like Jen that Jonathan wasn't too surprised. Before they reached the car he was quite hungry and thinking that maybe he should have shared.

Chapter 7

Susan enjoyed sharing dinner with Cynthia and her family, something she did a couple of times each month. It was a noisy place, with a teenager and an almost-teen. But there was an inner quiet as well, a peacefulness the source for which she couldn't quite identify. Everything seemed *right*.

Mike smiled when she came in, but continued reading the paper. He'd stopped trying to talk these past few months. Their views of practically everything always differed so stridently. At least he was friendly. Susan feared that maybe she was the one who wasn't always friendly, but his views really set her off.

She went into the kitchen to help Cynthia with any remaining preparations. Adam, the teenager, was overseeing his Mom's cooking. "No, you don't want to add the sauce until the stir-fry is done," he said. "Otherwise the vegetables don't cook right."

"I think it will be ok, Adam," Cynthia responded, catching Susan's eye with a smile and shrug as she came in.

"It's a mistake," Adam concluded, seeming almost angry about it somehow. He glanced at Susan then looked away as though embarrassed.

Susan remembered being like that herself. So caught up in the dawning realization that she owned her own thoughts and could disagree with adults that she became convinced disagreeing was a sign of maturity. Yet at the same time she was not quite able to separate her ideas from her person, and became defensive. When she thought about it, she wasn't so much different now. She took Adam's seeming-arrogance as a sign of intellect and strong character. She liked him.

Being assured that there was nothing she could help with in the kitchen, Susan joined Erin, who was reading in the living room. With a few minutes free, Susan took her computer from its carry bag and keyed up the video captured last night by the surveillance system she set up in her lab.

She'd used a motion detector and camera from one of the activity-based introductory physics labs to monitor both the entryway to her lab and her computer. Last night, movement in the lab had activated the camera. The video was sent to her office computer, so an intruder couldn't simply delete it. But, she had only gotten about two minutes of feed before it had ended, presumably when the intruder discovered the camera. In those two minutes, a stranger entered her lab and sat down at her computer.

Before the video cut off, she saw something else in the image. Beside the man seated at the computer shimmered a flash of color, like the rainbow reflection off an oil slick.

Only a single image captured the shimmer, and she paused the video to examine that one image more closely. The shimmer had the shape and size of a person, although quite transparent. Maybe it was a reflection of someone else in the room. But no one else had entered. In any case, what could the image be reflecting from?

Susan resumed the video and watched to the end when the intruder spotted the camera and rose to shut it off. She knew from the keystroke record on the computer that the intruder didn't leave after he found the camera. Instead, he accessed all files connected to her Uncertainty project, including her personal notes.

Clearly, the intruder knew he had been seen. Perhaps he hadn't guessed that she would be able to review his keystrokes at the computer. Or perhaps he hadn't cared and thought he might as well get what he came for.

Why would anyone break into her lab to look at her research notes? If anyone had sent her a message asking for files from her work, she'd have been flattered to send them.

✳✳✳

Dinner went well. Susan talked mostly to Erin and Adam. Erin asked her a question about science, religion and human destiny which was quite sophisticated for a twelve-year old. In her answer, Susan made the mistake of referring to evolution. She didn't even refer to biological evolution, but rather the evolution of scientific thought.

Even so, Mike's face darkened with the reference to evolution and she dreaded another creationist argument. When Mike said nothing, she felt compelled to invite it, unsure whether she was being falsely noble, being masochistic, or secretly hoping Mike would embarrass himself with his misunderstanding of the kind of evolution she referred to. "What do you think, Mike?" she asked.

Mike squirmed a bit, as though he would rather say nothing. "About evolution?　Well, OK, I can accept maybe God could make things however He wanted.　And the Bible isn't supposed to be a science book.　But I disagree with the whole idea of evolution."

And I disagree with gravity, Susan thought to herself with a surge of condescension. I think we should just float around in the air. But she kept her face frozen in interested non-judgment.

"Evolution's all about survival," Mike continued.　"It's about preserving your own life.　But the purpose of existence is not to preserve life.　It's to *use* life.　Use it as best we can.　Use it so it isn't all just selfish.　That makes all the difference.　Life is about how you live and what you *do*, not survival and theoretical ideas."

Well, my life is about ideas, Susan thought. Otherwise I wouldn't know what to do or believe in. *Just like you don't.* She bit her tongue and didn't say it out loud.

With supper completed, Mike drifted into the living room to watch TV, while Susan and Cynthia cleared the table and started washing the dishes.

"I see nothing has really changed in the world," Susan commented dryly. "The women still doing the dishes while the men sit and stare at the TV."

Cynthia looked at her reproachfully. "I wouldn't have it any other way, Susan," she said. "It's when we can talk. I think Mike even envies it a bit. I do have a dishwasher you know. I don't have to do this."

"Cynth," Susan said after a few moments. "You could have done better."

"You mean maybe I could have married, like, maybe even a scientist?" Cynthia answered, a trifle sarcastically. "Susan, Mike is very loyal to his friends, including me. He's faithful to me, and kind.

When you can say as much of one you love, and know for certain it is true, as I do, then maybe you can give me advice. Until then, please try to like my husband."

Chapter 8

The week in Wyoming went more quickly than I thought possible. The whirlwind trip already seemed surreal, and the incredible things I now believed true made it seem even more so.

I sent off samples of wood, bone, and bentonite from the university post office to a colleague in Chicago for isotopic analysis. But I expected the results to simply confirm what Jonathan and I already knew. The dates might vary slightly one way or another, but the site was clearly in the Atosoka Formation, and it couldn't vary by much.

I returned to the rock prep lab, picked up the metal sample where I'd left it in the cabinet by the doorway, and then headed toward the back where we kept the polishing table. The sample prep lab was always a bit cluttered, and I had to wind my way through the rock saws. The smell of cutting oil suffused the room with its characteristic odor. Sitting down at the large polishing table where I had set out the glass plate and polishing compounds, I started to grind at the tiny sample of metal from the broach, mounted in a block of epoxy. Although I had access to an automated polisher, I preferred hand grinding down to fifteen-micron grit size to minimize the potential for damaging the sample. Secrets of its manufacture were no doubt imbedded in the microstructure of the metal, clues to when and where it was made.

But the most significant clues required no microscopic analysis. Stone age humans didn't manufacture it. My main curiosity concerned whether the metal would reflect a modern metallurgical process that had been developed on Earth since the time of the burial, or if the process was foreign to Earth, or at least foreign to our time. Somehow, I suspected the former. The broach looked like something I could go to a rather upscale store and buy today.

I considered the harder questions, ones that I was unsure the samples we had taken could address.

Why was a burial made in a mountain lake?

The people who buried the elderly woman, presuming of course that they were indeed people, had to dive into a lake in order to excavate a grave for her. This was not a very easy or convenient burial. The saturated mud would persistently slough back into the grave. Diggers would need to continuously swim back to the surface for air. The body might not even cooperate by settling down into the grave once it was dug, preferring to bob back up to the surface. What made it worthwhile? What was their purpose?

I was much better at thorough thinking in the quiet of my own lab than at quick thinking on my feet in the field. The purpose of fieldwork was to gather observations and samples for analysis. But my more substantial mental efforts happened over longer periods of time as I digested those observations, and the results of sample analyses.

I turned my thoughts to the puzzle of the objects buried with her. Were they simply her personal treasures with no greater meaning than that? Or was their purpose to carry a message through the ages? As Jonathan noted, the objects were not only peculiar, but blatantly so, as though intended to draw attention.

If they were intended as a message to us, what prediction would that hypothesis imply that I could test?

Of course, the ultimate test would be to find the message. But, the hypothesis did fit some of the other peculiar observations. If the intent was to convey a message, then those who buried her would have *planned for the burial to be discovered thousands of years later*! That could explain both the unusual items included with the body and why so much effort was made to bury her in lake mud. If those who buried her understood that a lake bed was an area of rapid deposition, protected from erosion, where a body might be preserved for thousands or tens of thousands of years, and if they understood that a mountain lake was geologically ephemeral, soon to vanish with renewed erosional excavation and re-expose the grave, then they would see the lake bed as a time vault that would reveal its contents at the appointed time.

Given the possibility that the skeleton was intended to convey a message to the future, then her people did not bury her simply for reasons of sanitation, nor to address their sense of community or religion. They buried her so she would be found. And they chose to include items with her that would draw attention.

Crazy as it sounded, maybe the grave did indeed represent a message to our world, our time. But, if so, I needed to find the message. I wondered what that might be.

I became aware of my heart pounding in my chest. I could scarcely wait to talk to Jonathan.

Chapter 9

Jack stared at the computer, annoyed. Not only did he think Susan's Uncertainty experiment was scientific nonsense, but, as near as he could tell, his presence in her lab during the experiment was pointless. Everything was automated. Susan simply wanted him to record by hand the results that the computer reported to him. With Craig's presence in the lab also, doing the same task as he, their presence was doubly useless. What a waste of time.

It did, however, give him opportunity to search Susan's lab computer for clues to her true purpose. Susan insisted on being absent, for reasons that escaped him, and Craig was on the other side of the room, hidden by the big vacuum chambers rising up between them. Jack casually searched through her computer directories, reading files that looked interesting, searching for deleted or hidden files that might reveal something important.

He paused a moment to record the most recent result. "No particle in box," he wrote, next to the line that read "particle split number 500".

He looked up at the 499 other entries of "No particle in box." He wasn't sure what she expected. It was impossible to know the location of the particle. Since she was measuring very accurately the momentum of the particle--by capturing and measuring the energy of the companion particle created at the same moment and hurtling in another direction by a recoil-like effect--the location was undefined. Why did she think it would appear in that particular small space occupied by the box?

Even were it possible to measure the particle's position, the likelihood of it being in that box was very low. If he weren't busy snooping through her computer, he would have indulged in the decadent pleasure of calculating the infinitesimally low probability that the particle might actually appear in the box.

He did have to admit that her method for detecting the particle's presence in the box was innovative. He wouldn't have thought of it. By observing the frequency behavior a single helium atom held in the same box, she could infer the particle's presence in the vicinity without actually measuring its location.

He knew the results of experiments overseen by the other two volunteer faculty members, one who sat here yesterday and one the day before. The experimental results from them were a combined 2000 lines with "No particle in box." Surprise, surprise.

Susan, for reasons incomprehensible, asked the other two faculty members to waste their time one by one, rather than as a pair like he and Craig. He and Craig were wasting their time much more efficiently. He snorted a laugh.

He set in with renewed vigor to learn what she was really doing. There must be some clue here.

Unfortunately, the experiment reached its completion without him finding anything on her computer that might reveal her true purpose.

Susan returned shortly after the experiment ended, and he and Craig each gave her their list of 1000 "No particle in box."

"What's this for, Sue?" Craig asked, clearly as puzzled as he.

Jack was more blunt, not waiting for Susan's response. "Of course there was nothing in the box. It's impossible to measure, and, even if it weren't, the particle could by anywhere in the known universe. It's not likely to be in that box."

Jack considered adding that thinking of the experiment in terms of particles rather than waves was not even consistent with uncertainty mathematics, but Susan certainly knew that as well as he. Even better, since this was her area of specialty.

"I hope you see that these experiments are a waste of time. You need to look into doing something else." In this last, he was fishing, hoping she'd reveal something of her real purpose.

But Susan only said, "Thank you both so much. I'll send you the results when it's all done."

Chapter 10

Jonathan stopped by in the evening a couple of days after I had my initial thoughts about the lake burial but before any of the lab results had come back. I told him my hypothesis for why the burial took place in a lake bed and how the presence of the burial in a location likely to be preserved and discovered 40000 years later supported our idea that the burial communicated something to us.

My ideas excited Jonathan, as they had me, but he wasn't convinced. "I don't understand how they could expect it to be found," he said. "Few such burials would be preserved even in a lake bed, and fewer still would be found."

I puzzled for a minute as I recognized Jonathan's point. "But what sense would it make to bury her in such an inaccessible place unless the purpose was to make preservation and discovery more probable?" I asked.

"Since when do people worry about making sense?" Jonathan laughed. "Especially making sense to a culture that wouldn't exist for 40000 years?"

"So you don't think the burial site supports the idea that there's a message in it for us?" I asked.

"Actually, I do," Jonathan said. "The burial objects already suggested an effort to draw our attention. And your reasoning supports that idea, although it doesn't prove it. But what kind of communication could it be? It's hard for me to conclude that the purpose of the burial is to carry a message to us when there's no message. Does that make sense?"

It did. Regardless of how much evidence I might assemble that the burial was a message to our time, that conclusion was undermined by the absence of any message.

"Maybe the message is more general," I said. "Maybe it's simply a statement to us that time travel, or star travel, or something we haven't anticipated is possible."

"Hmmm." Jonathan nodded. "Maybe."

Jonathan had his own news for me, and he left off thinking about my ideas rather more quickly than I wished. "Jen, I got an email last week from a physicist at CalTech who's interested in our find. At least she's interested in some aspects of it. She's interested in its *unusualness.*"

"How did she learn of it? I thought you hadn't told anyone."

"Well, I don't know." Jonathan thought for a moment. "Maybe she heard about it from Dr. Thi, one of the anthropologists at CalTech. I talked to Dr. Thi about my odd find before our trip to Wyoming.

"Anyway," he continued, "Dr. Arasmith's own work--she's the physicist--led her on a search for unexpected or seemingly impossible events. Hearing of this find struck her as opportune. I've scheduled a time for us to meet with her and talk about our work."

"Oh." I wasn't sure I liked having to share our discovery. "I'll look forward to meeting her."

"I've already met with her once," Jonathan said. "Susan's really bright and interesting. Dedicated to her work and excited about it. I think you'll like her."

The dedicated scientist focused on her work seemed more like Jonathan's type than mine. Jonathan was always so intensely focused on his research, while my mind followed rabbit trails, like our present project, that seduced me from my own work. Jonathan's behavior made me wonder how old this 'Susan' was. And how attractive.

"Well," I said, laughing, "you seem quite smitten with her."

I intended to tease Jonathan, but my voice came out more plaintive than teasing. Voices, I thought, ought to do what they're told and not provide their own commentary.

***

Fall classes had begun, and, although my coursework was completed, I taught two lab sections and an undergraduate discussion session as part of my teaching assistantship. That, plus writing my dissertation, should have kept me busy, although I still procrastinated on starting my writing. It always took significant activation energy for me to commence something new. However, once I got started on a task, I held to it tenaciously, driven to complete it. I still held on to the mystery of the lost skeleton, as I flippantly termed it. Or it held me. As students filed out of my classroom, my mind turned to the skeleton and the radio.

Ideally, in any decent science fiction story, the radio would be composed of mysterious and exotic elements unknown on Earth, which resisted decay and were still in working order. In that story, I would accidentally stumble onto the 'on' switch, providing a sudden and unexpected radio-link across the emptiness of space or time to an alien race. But, alas, the far-more ordinary components of the radio were long since deteriorated beyond use.

But, I still thought that there must be *some* message. If someone from a technologically advanced society either in the future or from elsewhere in the universe intended to send a message, they would surely have included a written message or other type of symbolic communication. Such a message, I realized, could have been on either the cross or the broach. Neither Jonathan nor I had noticed anything that looked like writing. But writing from another time or place need not resemble what *we* knew as writing. And, in any case, figures or symbols sketched into the wood or metal might be nearly worn away over the years by chemical reactions with impurities in the interstitial water in the sediment. Of the two, cross and broach, I thought a message on the broach more likely to be preserved, but I resolved to check both for writing that Jonathan and I may have missed seeing.

Impatient to test my idea, I hurried from class to the lab where I kept the broach and cross locked in a secure cabinet. I took them out and looked them over.

I had already examined them with all the intensity that astonished curiosity provides, as had Jonathan. But I hadn't examined them with the specific intent of looking for writing. Observations right in front of one's eyes were often invisible until the moment one thought to look for them. Sometimes, even the careful scientist needed to imagine possibility first.

So I looked closely again. Wearing disposable gloves to prevent oils from my skin contaminating the wood, I turned the cross over and over in my hand. There were dark scratches and streaks abundant on the wooden arms, remnants of the carving process that created it. But I could find no pattern to those streaks.

But what kind of patterned forms might alien writing take? Would I recognize it as pattern at all? I didn't know.

I realized that finding similar patterns on the broach and cross would indicate the scratches weren't random. Remembering as much as I could of the streaks and scratches on the cross, and the shapes they took, I lifted the broach from the cabinet and examined it as well. It was no longer shiny with the polish it must have once had. Tiny scratches from years of dust and handling gave it a frosted appearance. Bigger scratches here and there reflected contact with particles of sand, the quartz and feldspar of the sand being much harder than the metal. Chemical corrosion from interstitial water in the sediment had damaged the finish as well.

I turned the broach over in my hands, looking at each spot to see if scratches there made any consistent pattern. Aha! There were, I saw to the accelerating music of the drum in my chest, coherent scratches on the flat metal back of the broach. Tiny, thin ones seemingly cut by a stone tool, but nearly obliterated by time and burial. I examined them closer under the low-power zooming binoc scope. They were patterned and made shapes I could recognize. Under the magnification of the microscope, I made them out one letter at a time.

It read in English, "Be a Friend."

I sat back, startled. How could any message be in English? My former suspicions of a hoax resurfaced, despite my certainty that the broach had been imbedded in stone.

The words, "Be a Friend," rang of those that might be inscribed on a gift. But the scratches were far too rough to be engravings included as part of the broach's manufacture or more formally added later.

They might be scratchings of a child. But the broach was not one a child would give as a gift to anyone. Nor was it one likely to be given to a child, given its apparent expense and elegance. Perhaps I was biased because I had predicted the presence of the message, but I still believed that this was a message sent to us, sent deliberately with a purpose it behooved us to learn.

"Be a Friend." What did that mean? Why would that be a message to pass through the millennia? Why would anyone go to such extensive effort to communicate such a generic platitude?

Or was there some specific person, or instance of friendship, to which the message referred? Some place in particular where friendship was needed?

Needed for what purpose? To accomplish what goal?

A new thought struck me, along with a tingle of fear. Or, needed to *prevent* what events? What might the message warn us of?

How could I possibly know what was meant? Or whom it was for? Or even when it was directed?

Chapter 11

One man crumpled to the floor with a look of astonishment. A second man, standing over the body holding the gun he'd pulled from his desk drawer, wheezed a bit, perhaps in shock at his own actions or in disdain for the disbelief frozen in the other man's eyes, the last look they'd ever register. No doubt, the dead man felt betrayed.

The gunman knew he was the one truly betrayed. He needed people loyal to him. People who trusted his leadership.

He didn't need someone to question his plans, or threaten to reveal them too soon.

He'd tried to be patient and explain. He'd tried everything. Pity that Carter hadn't seen the big picture. Then he would have understood that the stakes were too high for one life to matter. Even the life of a friend.

The whole world and the whole future were at stake. The needs of the many outweighed the needs of the few. And he was the one best able to know and understand the true needs of the many.

Humanity needed protection from violence and anger--he winced at the burden of his own memories. They needed protection from each other and protection from themselves. He had to make the hard decisions. He needed his friends to trust those decisions.

His foolish friend had bled on the carpet, he noticed. Well, no matter. Who would think to take a sample of blood here for a murder he would ensure occurred somewhere else? A good shampooing and no one would notice unless they knew to look.

He knew they wouldn't look. He had only to focus on politeness at the right moment, with a bit of misinformation or withheld information. *Negotiation* he called it in polite company. He remembered in grade school getting other kids to trade him their oranges at lunch. They would trade him a small orange and a big orange for his two medium oranges. They never figured out that the volume of the oranges increased as the *cube* of their size, making the small and big much larger than the sum of two medium. He doubted they knew it still. They stumbled through life with no clue how to negotiate for a better deal.

They needed a leader, someone who understood how to deal with life. They needed a leader to marshal them behind goals of greater importance. Despite his youth, he was that leader.

These recent discoveries would propel him into that role. Discoveries that the world had yet to learn of, discoveries into which he alone had a unique and chance insight. He was fortunate indeed to have stumbled upon the events taking place in Los Angeles. *The events yet to take place.* He must move swiftly to capitalize on them and secure his control over their result. Already, the President was working for *his* goals, albeit unknowingly.

He was glad of his new allies from Los Angeles.

He was equally glad that his new allies, due to their unique limitations, could not know what he did or planned in Washington D.C.

Allies were very valuable. Especially when they didn't really know what was going on.

Chapter 12

Susan Arasmith lived in an apartment complex just south of the university. Jonathan had once rented a room in a nearby district when he was a student at Cal Tech, so he had no problem finding the correct address after picking Jen up at her place.

Meeting at Dr. Arasmith's apartment promised a relaxing conversation, a less formal atmosphere than when he had visited at her office on campus. She had impressed him then. So many scientists, particularly young ones, tended toward ritual posturing to establish their stature and credentials among colleagues, asserting the importance and success of their research, hinting at how hard and long they worked, and dropping names of important people they knew. To Jonathan, this seemed more like reveling in their insecurities.

Dr. Arasmith didn't posture. She was frank and enthusiastic. She seemed honestly interested in his work, and excited at the prospect of learning more. He delighted in her refreshing lack of pretension.

Her apartment complex was a nice one. Mature trees bordered the walkway wending through the well-maintained yards. The early afternoon sun glinted off the water in several artificial pools. Jen pointed, having spotted Dr. Arasmith's apartment number. They walked up the metal steps to her door and knocked. Dr. Arasmith answered the door promptly.

She waved them into her living room and then stepped into the kitchen to round up some tea. Jonathan settled into one of her well-stuffed chairs. Certainly much more comfortable and personable than meeting in her office. One side of her apartment overlooked the street, while the other opened into the secluded quadrangle interior to the apartment complex. A bookcase sat against the wall opposite the kitchen, displaying a couple of books and some old calculators and a tape players, reminiscent of the curios he'd seen at her office.

Jonathan watched Susan cross the room with the tea, handing

them each cup before taking the chair opposite the couch where he and Jen were seated. He liked the movement of her body, like water flowing smoothly over stones. His eyes turned to her face and, by old habit, he noted her features. Her nose and mouth were crisp and well-formed, highlighted by high cheekbones and clear blue eyes. Blonde hair fell in a gentle wave, cut to fall just to her shoulders, one wayward lock curling across her forehead toward her eyebrows. Jonathan felt his heart rate quicken just a notch.

Without preamble, Dr. Arasmith launched directly into her research.

"Since I was an undergraduate," she began, "I've been uncomfortable with the idea that aspects of the universe might be intrinsically undefined. Unmeasurable. It seems to me that everything must have an actual value, a true definition, even if we don't know what that value or definition is.

"Thus, the Heisenberg Uncertainty Principle is a troubling incongruity to me. How can a particle not have a defined location? How can our measurement of it affect what is defined or undefined?

"Considering the fact that our measurements can affect a particle's location, I began to wonder if our measurements, our knowledge, even our *expectations*, might somehow influence other aspects of our reality as well. Perhaps our expectations could explain how a particle can have an undefined location when reason suggests that it must be *somewhere*.

"I came to the thought that a significant part of our understanding of reality might be found in considering the influence of what we expect and what we do not expect. That's why your discovery of the skeleton interests me. It's so very unexpected."

"I don't know much about the Heisenberg Uncertainty Principle," Jen said, "but isn't the undefined location of a particle simply a reflection of its wave character? A consequence of the fact that a wave really does occupy a region and not a spot?"

"Yes, but even so, the measurement by an intelligent being still must influence the size of the region occupied," Susan replied. "The influence of measurement and intellect is what intrigues me."

Susan and Jen talked in math-ese for a while, which he couldn't follow. The connection between her work and the discovery in Wyoming was still a bit murky to his mind, but he supposed that 'uncertainty' and 'unexpected' must have some relationship to each other.

Jonathan participated more once the conversation turned to the find in Wyoming. He described the skeleton and its geological setting. Susan probed his thinking with questions.

"How can you be sure that someone didn't just leave the seemingly-modern objects nearby during a picnic, and they got washed into the sediment with the skeleton later?" she asked.

"The rock around them is lithified," Jonathan said. "Meaning that it's stone, not loose sediment. It couldn't just 'wash in'. Also the context of the stone, the layers in it and the fabric of it, prove that it's part of the bedrock, not loose float washing downhill. Does that make sense?"

Susan nodded. "But then how did the modern objects get there? If it results from time travel or space travel, why don't we see more unusual objects buried in rocks around the world? Neither time travel nor space travel is likely to have happened only once. And people have been searching the rocks for thousands of years. Why hasn't anything been found until now? Why has no one but you found something like this?"

Jonathan shrugged, unsure whether he needed to defend himself or puff up a bit at his accomplishment.

"This is where I get interested," Susan continued. "It's *unexpected*, a discovery at the juncture between human preconception and the unknown. How can this discovery be so different from everything else that makes sense in our world?"

Jonathan looked at Jen. They had no answer to that. He shrugged again. This time, Jen joined him.

"We have done some testing," Jen said. She told Susan about the work already done on the artifacts and tests still in progress whose primary purpose was to confirm what they already suspected. She talked about the ancient age of the skeleton and whether the composition and texture of the artifacts confirmed their origin in the present time.

By the time they finished talking through the odd objects found with the skeleton, the implications of the skeleton's geological setting, and the message on the broach, several hours had passed and the dinner hour was approaching. Even so, Jonathan didn't want to leave. The afternoon had been so fun. They didn't get any instant revelations, but examining the puzzling observations from different perspectives had proved fruitful. They at least understood the questions better, even if they didn't yet have answers.

Dr. Arasmith had seemed to enjoy the time as well. At least Jonathan thought she wasn't too eager to shuffle them along to the door as they rose to leave. Some part of him hoped that was so.

She started to say something more, but hesitated, perhaps considering whether to speak or not. "You might think carefully about whether you want to get mixed up with my work. I had an intruder in my lab a couple weeks ago. Associating with me might not be entirely safe." She held up a finger. "Wait a minute. I have something to show you."

She headed off to her bedroom and returned with a small tablet computer. She sat down between them on the couch and provided some commentary as she played a video. "This guy broke into my lab and sifted through my research notes," Susan said. "And notice this odd glimmer or reflection here beside him."

They watched the video a couple of times, but neither Jonathan nor Jen recognized the intruder nor could they explain the cause of the odd reflection.

If Susan thought to dissuade them from her project with this news and her warning, she failed. It served only to intrigue Jonathan more.

"Listen," Susan said as they again prepared to leave, "I'm going bowling with my sister and her family this evening. Why don't you come along and we can continue our conversation?"

Jonathan cocked an eyebrow at this abrupt invitation. They'd hit it off well, but he'd only met Susan a few days ago. He slanted a look at Jen who also seemed taken aback.

"I don't think we want to intrude," he said.

"I'd like for you to," Susan said. "My sister and her husband and kids make a nice little family unit, and I always feel a bit like a fifth wheel. It'd be nice to have some friends with me. Also I don't..."

She hesitated and seemed to change what she was about to say.

"Anyway," she continued, "Why don't we go out for a bite to eat, and you can decide if you want to stay for bowling. Everyone who knows me has to go bowling with me sooner or later!"

Jonathan glanced at Jen and she nodded in agreement. Jen was far more perceptive and sensitive to people than he. If Jen liked Dr. Arasmith, then he took that as a good sign.

Dinner with Susan Arasmith was fun. She told jokes and stories from her graduate school days at Harvard. Jonathan contributed his part to the conversation, and even Jen, normally quiet with new people, participated.

"So why bowling?" Jonathan asked.

She looked at him, long and deep as though she could see through him and know his thoughts.

"Do you really want to know?" She frowned as though doubting it.

"Of course I want to know," Jonathan replied, somewhat miffed. "That's why I asked."

"I'm sorry," she said, "but so many people ask questions only for a way to make conversation flow, not looking for a serious answer. That doesn't work with me."

There were a few moments silence before she continued. "I'm good enough at bowling to enjoy exercising my skill, but not so good that I always win, or have to win. I like that. Plus, if you go with other people, there's lots of time to talk. I like that, too."

She rose from her seat. "Well, we should be going, if we want to have time for a couple of games." She gave his shoulder a playful punch. "That's assuming you have enough muscle in there to hold a bowling ball!"

Jonathan grinned and stood, glancing down to hide his embarrassment at the slight awkwardness. It might have been a worse kind of embarrassment had his recent weightlifting program not arrested the slow decline in his physique. "I suppose we could try out the bowling alley. Although, I have to warn you, I'm probably not very good despite my powerful muscles!"

Susan introduced them to Cynthia and her family as friends she met through work, a presumption of friendship that Jonathan found pleasing. Jen usually didn't talk much, but he noticed she had a lot to say to Cynthia. Jen seemed to like Cynthia's kids too, whose names, at the moment, escaped him.

Jonathan enjoyed the evening a great deal. Like Jen, he enjoyed more than only Susan's company. He particularly liked talking to Mike. He discovered that they had hunting in common. Jonathan told him of his expeditions hunting pronghorn in Wyoming. Mike in turn shared some of his trips elk hunting in the Blue Mountains of Northeast Oregon. Mike seemed like a really nice guy.

***

Susan brought Jonathan and Jen back to her apartment, where Jonathan's car was parked. Susan was pointing up at her living room window among all the many windows in the building visible from the street, when they noticed the bobbing light in her apartment.

"Should someone be in there?" Jen asked.

"No," Susan said. "No one has a key, not even Cynthia."

They parked the car and slipped up the steps to her apartment, unsure whether to be quiet so the intruder would be caught off-guard, or to make sufficient noise to scare him off. They chose the silent route.

Susan opened the door, and Jonathan went in first. He heard someone rustling in the next room. He stepped in at the same moment that Susan flipped on the overhead lights. The man wore all black, his white face plainly visible. It was without question the same man whose picture Susan captured in her lab. The intruder ran straight at them, attempting to knock them aside to reach the doorway.

Jonathan set himself to block the charge, planting his feet firmly, leaning slightly forward. Unfortunately, the intruder was far more skilled at this type of burglar football than he was. The man seemed about to slip to his right, and Jonathan moved in that direction, but when he shifted from his braced stance the man drove straight into his stomach. Jonathan collapsed to the floor. By the time he staggered back to his feet, the intruder was gone, and Susan was already calling the police.

Chapter 13

Walt Roden enjoyed the week spent learning about the lab and the experimental procedures. When he had spotted the ad in the classifieds for *research assistant, no science training preferred,* he knew this was a job for him. He also liked Dr. Arasmith. She was a patient and thorough instructor.

The job itself seemed ridiculously easy, and Walt wondered why the week of training was even necessary. Maybe Dr. Arasmith thought she couldn't get any takers for the ad if at least a week of work wasn't involved. That was probably true in his case. A week was just what he was looking for.

Four of them had gone through the training. Omar was here for today's experiment--Walt wasn't sure what the other two were doing.

Dr. Arasmith had explained that she couldn't be here for the experiment itself, and so he and Omar needed to be very careful. Walt hoped they didn't mess up somewhere.

The computer flashed a message, and Walt carefully wrote "No particle in box" on his sheet next to the line that read "Particle split number 400". He supposed that Omar, on the other side of the room, was making a similar notation.

Looking down the list of results left Walt concerned. Dr. Arasmith had explained during their training that once particles formed in the split, the momentum of each was determined by measuring the value for only one. The particles lined up so that, as they shot apart from each other, one particle traveled across a vacuum to either pass through or appear within a small box. Walt wasn't sure exactly how the particle reached this box, or what the box actually was. Dr. Arasmith explained it as a box, but not one made of matter. That part puzzled him, but he understood the image of a box, so he held on to that.

Few of the particles appeared in the box--or so the computer reported--which concerned him. From his list, he estimated that only about half of the entries were "Particle appears in box". The remaining said "No particle in box."

Half in the box was just random, right? Like flipping a coin, half the time it's heads, half the time it's tails. Yet from their training, Walt expected the particle to appear in the box most if not all of the time. He hoped he and Omar weren't doing something wrong.

Dr. Arasmith had emphasized that this particular experiment could not be repeated. It was a one-shot deal. She said the results of the first experiment might change the results of any subsequent experiments. Walt didn't really understand that part either.

The computer beeped at him, and Walt conscientiously wrote "Particle appears in box" on the next line. All he could do was his best, he thought. Maybe the results would improve with time.

As the monotony of recording the results the computer reported to him dragged on, Walt's thoughts wandered to his nephew, Jerry. Walt had heard only this morning that Carter, one of Jerry's childhood friends, had died. He hadn't seen the young man for years, but the news hit him hard and came with a vague sense of unease.

He remembered how important Carter had been to Jerry's efforts to overcome his difficult childhood. Walt felt a kinship with his nephew. Like his nephew, he also knew the desire to protect himself and others from a violent father, the intense longing to get some kind of control. Will, Walt's brother and Jerry's father, had not been able to escape the cycle of violence and fear, instead passing it on to his son.

Walt had tried to show his nephew the kinder potential of life but was unsure of his success. Jerry still seemed driven by the need to seek connections that gave him power over his universe. That was, Walt knew, very different from being beckoned to relationships by the warmer emotions, like he'd learned from his wife, Karen. Even so, his nephew was successful in his present work, and Walt hoped he was rid of the anger and violence that could destroy generations.

But he didn't know. He'd had little contact with Jerry since Will's suicide. He frowned to himself, troubled anew by the loss of Jerry's best friend. Perhaps he should contact Jerry now.

***

Nearly all one thousand of the readings were done. Walt wrote his entry for particle split 986. The results *had* improved, he thought, if only slightly. Slightly more than half the particles now showed up in the box. He hoped that was good enough for Dr. Arasmith.

Chapter 14

The results from the second set of experiments left her stunned. Susan stared again at the neat tables her temporary research assistants had provided her. Her heart pounded whenever she looked over the results, even though she must have looked at them a hundred times already.

The reports from the first two participants, who each monitored and recorded the results while alone in the lab, showed only a combined three entries of "particle appears in box" for their 2000 observations. Even that was cause for astonishment. As Jack insisted on reminding her, there was no reason that any of the particles should appear in the box. Yet between 0.1% and 0.2% of the particles had appeared there. This contrasted strikingly with the results from her departmental colleagues where, in 3000 trials, not a single particle appeared in the box.

But the truly astounding results occurred when she paired two of her temporary research assistants in the lab. They reported over 50% of the particles appearing in the box. This was an incredible result. An impossible result. One she had hoped for at some deep, intuitive level, but which her analytical mind had refused to anticipate.

Even the deep and intuitive part of her mind never expected a result so unambiguous.

Clearly the results of her uncertainty experiments were strongly biased by participant expectation. But the participants only recorded what the *machine* observed. How could the machine be biased by the human participants' expectations?

Susan was careful not to lie to the participants. She told the four participants from the second set only that the particles should appear in the box some of the time, which was technically true. Her repetition of it, and focus on it, led them to expect a more frequent appearance in the box.

But how could her honesty or lack thereof be responsible for the results? That the particles appeared in the box, even though she had no reason to expect it, made any suggestion to her participants that the particles would appear in the box perfectly true.

She reassessed what she knew, searching for some pattern, some reasoning that made sense of it. The premise of her study was the theoretical idea that a particle with exactly defined momentum had completely undefined location and could be anywhere in the universe. At an intuitive level, she perceived that as an absurd idea. *Anywhere* meant a transcendence not only of space, but of time, because the limitations of light-speed travel would be compromised.

Yet the laws of physics that she knew mandated that once the momentum of a particle was perfectly defined, that particle's location was undefined. It had equal probabilities of being anywhere in general and therefore an infinitesimal probability of being anywhere in particular.

Of course, nature was not obliged to obey the laws of nature as humans phrased them. Suppose this principle were true, that a particle's momentum and location could not be simultaneously measured by any method within the laws of nature. Then what power or law chose where a particle *actually was* once its momentum was measured?

If a particle's location was undefined by the laws of nature, did that mean that intellect was free to choose its location? Could it be that its location, although an unknown parameter in nature, became a known, fixed value based on the expectations of a measuring intellect?

Could parameters of the known universe, at the level of the uncertainty principle, be altered by belief or choice? And going further, since these principles underpinned the entirety of existence, could the macro-world be influenced by this choice?

This felt too heady for one sitting. She paused to reestablish what she knew, not what she speculated. Certainly, her experiments implied a fundamental relationship between the wave character of matter and intelligent thought. It implied that events, at least under the controlled conditions of her experiments, were strongly influenced by the beliefs and expectations of the experimenters. It implied that the influence of that expectation was amplified exponentially as the number of people involved increased from one to two. Both ideas she'd considered in designing her experiment.

What she hadn't counted on was such a profound and significant effect. Such significance should have been noticed in experiments done long before her own. That it hadn't been meant that there was something unique about her experiments she hadn't yet identified. Given her method for detecting the particles' presence in a box, and the intrinsically non-particle nature of the "particles," she needed to think harder about what her results *really* meant, conceptually and mathematically. She needed a mathematical way to express this profound influence of thought on the character of scientific results. A mathematical expression, she knew, provided the prediction that other researchers could then test with new experiments.

She needed to talk it through with someone. Not necessarily with someone who could help with the math, but someone who could help hone conceptual ideas as they developed.

Maybe she could talk it through with Jonathan and Jen, but she cringed at the thought of meeting them again. Her resistance to seeing them, her embarrassment, was her own fault.

She couldn't believe that she'd flirted like that. Jonathan probably thought she was a complete fruitcake.

She hoped not. Although, for all she knew, Jonathan was already attached, maybe even to Jen. Her behavior in that case would not only be embarrassing, but rude.

There was nothing to do but pick up the pieces where she'd scattered them and try to put a reasonably professional relationship back together. That, or simply avoid Jonathan and Jen altogether.

Which she might have considered if not for the fact she wasn't a hider. And she had a perfectly reasonable reason to talk to them—the police had identified her intruder.

Susan had turned in the image of the intruder from the video camera in her lab, although she held back the more puzzling image of the shimmering light. The detective in charge told her the man was a mercenary, a soldier for hire, with training both in the U.S. military and later from foreign terrorist groups. He was a known political assassin working under the alias "Raven."

What did such a man want with her? Or, more likely, with her work?

Susan began to comprehend that her research could have implications far beyond her small lab or sub-field of physics. For the first time, she understood why someone wanting to learn about her work might do so in secrecy. Her work had implications for nations good and bad, and for individuals honorable and criminal. What nation or individual wouldn't want to control aspects of our natural world that nature itself left open to choice? Aspects that make up the very foundation of existence?

But *she* hadn't realized the potentially Earth-changing implications of her research until now. This was not some small tweak to existing physics, as she'd thought possible in a long-shot, but wholesale reconstruction. How could anyone have known the outcome and significance of her work before she did? Who could have known the significance of her experiments *before they were even done*?

She decided to give Jonathan a call.

The phone rang four times with no answer, and she almost hung up to avoid his answering service. He answered before the fifth ring. Then she wished she hadn't called at all.

Just keep it professional.

"Hi, Jonathan," she said. "This is Susan Arasmith from CalTech. I have some new results and wondered if you'd like to get together tonight to talk about them? Maybe we could go for supper someplace."

His "Sure, Susan" sounded honestly interested, she thought. Not just polite. She wondered why she was micro-analyzing a simple two-word sentence.

"I can pick you up in fifteen minutes," she said.

They drove to a steak house downtown. After they took a seat by the windows and opened their menus, Susan launched into the results from the lab, especially from Walt and Omar, without so much as glancing at the open menu.

"I mean, I imagined these results, even hoped for them, or I wouldn't have done the experiments," she said. "But I never imaged the scope of it, and to actually see it happen, see the expectation of observers influence the results so profoundly, still takes my breath away."

"Sounds important," Jonathan said. "Astonishing actually."

"It is." Susan nodded, pleased with his interest. "Who'd have thought that such a discovery could fall to me?"

"Why not?" Jonathan asked. "Your dissertation must have been pretty good too, or you wouldn't be at CalTech."

"I work hard, and do good work, but this is one of those shots in the dark that take a lot of luck as well as insight. Many people brighter than me have looked for a lifetime and never stumbled onto something like this."

The waitress arrived to take their order. Jonathan ordered steak, medium-well, with a baked potato. Susan substituted rice for the potato.

Susan talked more of her research. Jonathan's questions, while lacking in specialized knowledge, provided a new perspective and nice reflection of her thoughts as she examined her results again.

Once Susan had spent her first blush of enthusiasm, she paused to catch her breath. Jonathan changed the subject, rather abruptly she thought. "Have you noticed," he said, "how the hostess always brings guests first to that table near the work area used by the waiters? It's really a poor spot with the clatter of dirty dishes and waiters always going in and out. The first four groups she offered it to declined the table, but she finally got someone to take it. I wonder why she takes people to that undesirable place first?"

"Maybe she wants to make sure that the restaurant doesn't fill up and then have a group that won't take the table when there aren't any other options," Susan said.

"So they give the undesirable table to the least assertive customers?" Jonathan shook his head in disapproval. "That seems kind of manipulative."

Susan hadn't noticed the little drama until Jonathan brought it to her attention. It didn't really seem all that important. She wondered if he distracted her from her research because it bored him.

"I hope you don't mind my calling you to get together tonight?"

Susan asked. "And my ranting about my new results?"

"I like your intensity, your interest in your research." Jonathan returned his attention to her from his private theater. "Are you always this focused on your work? Or is this the race to tenure?"

The implication that she cared more for job security than science offended her.

"What do you mean?" She felt the defensive irritation start to leak into her voice and tried to tamp it down. "I like doing a good job. Is there something wrong with that?"

"Don't get prickly," Jonathan said, laughing. "I didn't mean it in a negative way. I like your--if I may label it--your task-oriented perfectionism. At Burns, my research is fun and important to me, but less crucial to my tenure than teaching is. So I can work hard on my research because I like to, not because I have to. My bet was that you are that way too. Does that make sense?"

"I'm sorry. I *am* a bit prickly, I suppose. That's the second time with you, too. I guess I'm used to people being less frank than you are. The motives of the men in my life haven't always been that transparent."

"Openness begins with oneself," Jonathan said. "Not everyone knows it when they're not being open."

Susan wondered what he meant by that, and what it revealed of his past. And she wondered what prompted her own confessional about the men in her life. She breathed a sigh of relief when their meals arrived to preempt any further pursuit of the topic.

Conversation lightened as they ate their meal. Susan managed to introduce a few topics other than her research, a contribution to the conversation of which she was quite proud. She told Jonathan about reading Agatha Christie mysteries. He told her about hunting Pronghorn in Wyoming.

About eleven o'clock the manager asked them how they had liked the meal. It was wonderful, of course. At eleven-fifteen he stopped by again to ask them if they would like anything more. They didn't, they were just fine.

On his third visit, Susan finally realized he probably wanted them to leave so he could close before morning.

"I guess we better go," she said, embarrassed.

Jonathan nodded.

They split the bill, and returned to her car.

On the drive to drop Jonathan at his place, Susan commented, "We should do this again."

"Yeah." Jonathan kept his eyes on the road ahead. "I'd like that."

Chapter 15

Three and a half weeks had passed since our outing with Susan at the bowling alley, and I only now, finally, had the isotope work back from Chicago. I clutched my computer under my arm as I walked up the stone pathway to Cynthia's blue-gray rambler with flower boxes under the windows—a home straight out of a storybook. Cynthia and I had struck up a friendship since we met at the bowling alley. We'd met for tea last week, and afterward she let me relax and get some work done at her place. I looked forward to more good conversation followed by some quiet time with my data.

It felt nice to have a new and growing friendship, especially given my recent unease with Jonathan. After Cynthia and I sat down with our steaming cups, and while we waited for the tea to cool enough to drink, Cynthia asked me about him.

"Jonathan and my sister sure seem to be spending a lot of time together," she said. I could feel her eyes watching me and knew she must have guessed some of my conflicted feelings.

"Yeah, they've been out bowling a couple more times, and I think they've been meeting to talk about research nearly every day." I swirled my tea a couple times in my cup and then took a quick sip off the top. I didn't mention that I'd been at a couple of those meetings that dealt especially with the Wyoming skeleton and Susan's research.

Cynthia smiled. "I haven't seen Susan having so much fun with anything but physics for years."

I nodded, forcing my eyes up to Cynthia's. "Jonathan too. I think I've been a bit jealous that his mind seems more on Susan than our collaboration with the Wyoming research." I laughed, hoping that my laugh conveyed the idea that I wasn't too jealous.

But, Jonathan talked about Susan all the time now. I wondered how she had insinuated herself into his life so completely in only a few weeks time. I'd known him for years!

Even so, Susan was a wonderful, brilliant, beautiful woman. I liked her too. Jonathan could find no one better with whom to fall in love. I just needed to set aside my own feelings of being a bit forsaken and be happy for him.

"How's that work in Wyoming going?" Cynthia asked after a moment of silence.

I settled a bit deeper in my chair, glad of the change in topic. "Well, not much movement for a while, although the micro-texture of the broach matches modern metallurgical practice, as we half-expected it would. I got some additional data back from a colleague this morning and am hoping to go through it today--if you'll let me hang out again?"

Cynthia laughed. "Of course. It's nice to have you around. The house seems a bit empty with Mike at work and the kids at school."

Our conversation continued comfortably for another thirty minutes, until our tea was gone.

"How'd you like to meet at Arroyo Park next week?" Cynthia asked as we both rose to carry our cups to the kitchen. "It's quiet and we can talk or not as you like."

I nodded. "That would be fun."

She did understand me, knowing that I liked my friendships small and quiet. I thought that perhaps she also liked companionship without the need for too much talking. She, like me, preferred intimate friends to big social groups. I liked that idea of close friends who shared a life together rather than casual friends who waxed and waned with time, as though addicted to the intoxication of new relationships.

After depositing my cup in the sink, I retired to the living room and sat down with my computer in the overstuffed chair by the fireplace. There was no fire, but Cynthia had set a vase of flowers in the firebox, strawflowers with mums and baby's breath.

I began my analysis of the new data by first considering the numbers for the wooden cross sample. C-14 counts were low, near the limit of sensitivity. Perfectly consistent with its placement in the Atosoka formation. Given uncertainties, the age came out between 30 and 50 thousand years, the rather large uncertainty due to the low C-14 concentration and small size of the sample.

The C-14 in the organic sample I'd pulled from the bone gave similar results. What caught my attention more than the C-14 values in the wood and bone was the concentrations of other isotopes in the tooth sample.

There were clear elevations of Ba-137 and Zr-90 relative to expectations for a tooth from 40000 years ago. I knew that Ba-137 and Zr-90 were daughter isotopes from the radioactive decay of Cs-137 and Sr-90. Cs-137 and Sr-90 were products of nuclear fission. Elevated concentrations of the daughter isotopes suggested that the formation of the tooth had to post-date the nuclear age. Thus, the tooth would have to be younger than 70 years, even though other evidence confirmed the skeleton as nearly 40000 years old. Interestingly, there was no detectable Cs-137 or Sr-90 in the bone, which, given their short half-lives of about 30 years, is what one would expect for a skeleton 40000 years old.

Bone that formed less than 70 years ago and yet had been aged for 40000 years—what did that mean? There seemed to be only one possibility, and that possibility wasn't possible.

I met Jonathan later that afternoon and told him my results. He nodded, reacting less to the conflicting results than I might have expected. He had his own results to report.

"I've taken a look at the guts of the radio," he said. "Combination of X-ray tomography and cutting out some samples for scope work. It's just like a modern radio, maybe vintage of 40 or 50 years ago. Even the electronic circuitry is the same, like the old scanner radios. So, my results confirm yours. It's both very old and very young at the same time."

We talked around the paradox a bit longer, but avoided stating its obvious implications--that we had a time-travel event on our hands--although we both understood what our results meant. I did find the courage to ask Jonathan about Susan, still obsessing a bit about how it might affect our relationship.

"You and Susan are sure becoming good friends," I said.

Jonathan looked at me a moment before responding. "Yes, I think we are. And you and Cynthia seem to have hit it off too. Kind of amazing how meetings and events we couldn't have planned have such a big impact on our lives, isn't it?"

I nodded and smiled. Jonathan's observation was just what I needed to hear. I needed to quit obsessing over what I feared I might lose and focus on what I might gain. Even though the deeply introspective portion of my being was a powerful tool in improving my own behavior and setting my own course, I needed to remember that I didn't want to spiral into a recursive internal evaluation from which I couldn't escape.

Chapter 16

Susan enjoyed her monthly bowling outing with Cynthia and Mike more than she had for a long time. Perhaps her frequent and pleasant outings with Jonathan the past couple of weeks had mellowed her. The kids were absent today, and so she couldn't hide from Mike by talking to them. As a consequence, she and Mike even enjoyed a short chat, without much disagreement.

Tonight, Susan found the familiar sights and sounds of the bowling alley particularly enjoyable. She liked the clattering noise of falling pins and the shouts of patrons elated or disappointed with their bowling. And she enjoyed the companionship without expectation.

A perfect evening.

Susan watched as Cynthia rose to pick her ball from the return rack, a light-weight purple one. Cynthia glanced over her shoulder to the horseshoe benches that wrapped around the end of their lane where Susan and Mike sat. Cynthia's eyes went first to Susan, a faint smile warming her lips, no doubt pleased that she and Mike were getting along so well. Susan returned the smile. When Cynthia's eyes went to Mike they warmed a bit more, and her smile changed, almost as if to say to Mike, "See, I told you she'd do ok in the end."

Cynthia stepped to her spot in the lane and began her throw, but another motion caught Susan's attention, two lanes over, half-way down toward the pins. At first it was just a hint of moving color, shimmering in the empty lane, a few feet above the polished hardwood. It flickered like an image from an old, failing film projector, blinking in and out as though not quite sure whether to exist or not. As she watched, the image began to resolve into something like the shape of a person.

Susan might have wondered if she were seeing things, an hallucination, except she noticed that everyone else was watching too, eyes riveted on the shimmering being now hovering in mid-air.

It had stopped flickering. Cynthia's throw went awry as she spotted the apparition. The clatter of her ball down the gutter was followed by a surreal silence as everyone in the bowling alley fell quiet.

She could now make out arms on the being, and she let her eyes follow the arms to a pipe like object held in what she supposed must be the creature's hands. The way the being held it, bringing it slowly around, reminded her of how someone would hold a rifle.

A weapon.

Slowly the weapon swung around, passing over several of the stunned bowlers, and came to rest on her.

A part of her knew she should be terrified, but she felt oddly calm, as though another part of her brain refused to accept the scene as real. A third part felt curiosity. What was this creature? Where did it come from? And why did it so much resemble the shimmer in the video from her lab that she had thought to be some odd reflection?

The figure of the being was now quite well resolved, and she saw a finger wrap around a flange on the weapon like a finger on a trigger. She should move, fall down, do something. But she felt frozen in place.

From the corner of her eye she saw that Mike was not frozen. His body hurtled toward her, and a moment later she felt his weight slam against her side, tackling her hard to the floor. She saw a flash of light and felt a burst of heat in the air above where she and Mike lay on the wood boards of the alley. The flash was accompanied by a crack like thunder.

Suddenly the surreal moment of fearlessness was over, and the world seemed very, very real. Terror surged up in her throat, almost choking her.

Mike was still moving. He rose and ran straight at the being. It swung the weapon toward him, trying to track his movement. But the being's motions seemed sluggish and Mike dodged from side to side, not making an easy target.

Mike ducked his head and drove one shoulder straight for the center of the shimmering being. As his shoulder made contact, Susan, watching from where she still lay on her stomach on the floor, expected the impact to send the being flying toward the pins at the back of the alley. Instead, an explosion raced outward from the point of impact, accompanied by a flash so bright that Susan had to momentarily close her eyes.

When she opened her eyes again, the shimmering being was gone. Mike lay in a heap on the floor, half in one lane and half in another, one leg turned at an impossible angle and his head twisted in a way she knew it should not be. She saw a streak of blood on the wood boards where Mike had skidded before coming to rest.

Susan pushed herself up from the floor, events swirling around her in a blur. Cynthia ran to Mike, collapsing over him and screaming for help. A few other people were screaming, their eyes darting around looking for attackers, but most were silent, staring in shocked horror. Her own stomach churned, and she felt frozen. For the first time, she questioned not carrying a phone of her own, but soon saw that others were already calling for help. She looked around for something to do and finally decided to go be with Cynthia.

She felt only partially aware when the police came, or the ambulance. Once they arrived, she simply floated along with them, riding their professionalism and hoping.

***

They sat in the hospital waiting room for hours, scattered around it like their own scattered thoughts and fears. For Susan, there to support Cynthia and the kids, worrying about Mike took precedence over wondering about the shimmering being or the meaning of the surreal events at the bowling alley. Waiting for news about Mike felt nearly as surreal as the events at the bowling alley.

Normally she didn't pay much attention to what people were doing around her, but, in the quiet tension of the waiting room, she felt almost painfully aware. Adam seemed to have reverted from teenager to something younger as he poked at his seat with a pen, ignoring his mother's requests that he stop. Erin, younger than Adam, had simply shut down and stared blankly at nothing. Cynthia's distress was perhaps the most profound, if less obvious. She looked aimlessly around her, as though searching desperately for evidence that none of it was real. Every once in a while she took a large breath in prelude to a sigh, only to hold it and let it out inconspicuously, perhaps suddenly aware of herself and her children. She seemed too numb to cry, and too exhausted not to, so that her face was scrunched up as though she wept without tears.

Susan didn't know what to do, and she had nothing to say.

She rose and sat by Cynthia on the couch, hoping her action carried the love and empathy she could not convey with words. After a moment, Adam left his pen-perforated chair and joined them. She put her arm around his shoulders, and he wept. It was, she decided, a sign that silence was just fine.

***

Mike died about 2 o'clock that morning. The detective had kindly waited until their vigil was ended to question them about what had happened. Susan answered as best she could remember, but she wasn't sure how helpful police could be in tracking down a killer like the one at the bowling alley. The detective didn't show much skepticism at their story, surreal and unlikely as it seemed— he'd probably already heard the same story from others. He kept his interview to a brief ten minutes and let them go home, saying they'd talk more later.

Susan thought she should have gone home with Cynthia. Cynth wouldn't sleep, and a dark, empty home filled with Mike and memories was no place for her and the kids to be alone tonight. But Cynthia insisted she was all right and that Susan should be in her own home.

Susan walked up the steps to her apartment, unlocked the door, and stepped inside without bothering to turn on the light. There was a bit of yellow glow streaming in the window from the streetlights outside. She opened the window for a breath of fresh, if damp, air and then sat down on her couch and gazed into the darkness for a while.

She had almost died today.

It felt odd to be saved by the loyalty and courage of someone she'd thought beneath her, even disliked. He certainly must have known that she disliked him. Yet he hadn't hesitated to put his life at risk for her.

She had misjudged him. Hadn't understood what he offered.

Hadn't even tried to learn. She wanted to tell him. She wanted another chance to talk to him and see if maybe they could be friends. She wanted to try again, share experiences and ideas, remembering this new feeling toward him.

In the quiet of her dark room, she cried.

Chapter 17

I noticed things in Cynthia's yard as I walked up to her house: a wheelbarrow half full of dirt parked beside a flower bed, a pile of boulders that seemed to be waiting for a home around the base of a small palm tree, a propane grill along the side fence going toward the back yard. The things of a busy life brought suddenly to a halt. The afternoon sun cast shadows across the yard, making everything seem both ordinary and strange. There was something in the air that made me think of coming fall but I couldn't quite identify it, perhaps the scent of the sea had strengthened with the shifting winds.

I reached the door and had to encourage myself that this was the right thing to do. Cynthia needed time alone during this black period in her life, but she also needed friends to care about her.

I wasn't part of Cynthia's family or group of long-term friends, and she might see my visit as presumptuous and intrusive. But caring is always better than indifference. At worst, she'd have a few uncomfortable minutes of company that she had hoped to spend alone. An unwelcome visit from an acquaintance was much less painful than unwelcome loneliness because a friend *failed* to visit.

I knocked on her door, standing straight. She opened the door and her eyes filled with delight and then with tears. I stepped in and she hugged me tight.

Cynthia served some herbal tea, and we sat in her small, homey living room and talked about Mike, and her children, and what she planned to do now.

"Is there insurance?" I asked.

"Enough for a few months." Cynthia looked down at her hands, clamped around her cup of tea. "Then, I guess I need to find a job. Adam might be old enough to help some, but..." she trailed off.

I waited, not wanting to press. After a minute, Cynthia continued.

"Maybe I can get a writing job. I'd planned to go into journalism before the kids came along. Got my degree." Her voice strengthened as she talked.

"That sounds like something you'd enjoy," I said.

She nodded. "I think so."

We talked more. And sometimes we just sat in silence together.

After an hour or so, Cynthia rose to take the cups to the kitchen, and asked, her voice tentative, "I don't reckon you brought some work with you and would want to spend the afternoon?"

I had my phone with me but not my computer. Work hadn't really been on my mind lately. Even the time travelling body in the shale in Wyoming seemed to have paled as events unfolded.

"Of course," I said. "I'd love to stay."

I took the overstuffed chair by the fireplace. Cynthia bustled around for a while before settling in to read a kindle book in the chair opposite. I tried to get some writing done on my dissertation, but the phone was quite cumbersome for the job and my mind wasn't on it anyway. Instead I set about to make a list of "stuff we knew."

We knew that there was a skeleton in Wyoming of a modern woman who died 40000 years ago.

We knew that a strange glimmer appeared in a video in Susan's office and a glimmering being tried to kill her at the bowling alley. The glimmering being had killed Mike. It wasn't clear how much help the police could be with this event. I hoped that agencies beyond the police were being brought in.

We knew that Susan had discovered something about the uncertainty principle that exceeded what she'd anticipated—an influence of human expectation more pronounced than previous observation would seem to allow, almost as though her very discovery of it had somehow made the effect stronger. I wondered about my own faith and how the idea of faith played into Susan's idea of expectation. Certainly, faith involved a type of expectation.

What we didn't know was the connection between the different strange things that we knew, or even if a connection existed. The break-in at Susan's office, the glimmering being, and Susan's discoveries all had Susan in common. The uncertainty principle itself was a bit of a spooky thing, like the shimmering beings, making a connection between them seem more reasonable. But what connection could there be to the skeleton in Wyoming?

Maybe none except for the chance way that it brought Jonathan and me into Susan's circle.

On the other hand, two such extraordinary things happening at nearly the same moment in time seemed unlikely to be pure chance.

The sky was growing dusky with evening when Cynthia rose up from her chair and stepped toward the big picture window that looked toward the mountains across the small park behind their house.

"Someone was watching us with binoculars," she said. "There, from behind the restrooms in the park."

"Are you sure?" I rose to stand beside her, doubting that additional strange events could follow so soon upon those we'd already been through. "Why would they be watching us?"

"I don't know," she said.

I heard the fear in her voice. Hadn't her husband just been killed by some strange being whose purpose she couldn't understand?

My own fear rose up in my throat as we stood at the window looking into the darkening park where Cynthia thought a stranger spied on us. How was I to understand these strange events, intruders in Susan's lab, murders by beings who seemed not human? I felt overwhelmed by what was happening, out of control of my life.

The recent events had made the world seem to withdraw into unreality, become a place where enemies lurked around every corner and any oddity hid something sinister. It must be even worse for Cynthia, trying to understand and deal with Mike's death. But I also knew rationally that allowing paranoia to take root would consume us.

Was there really someone out there watching Cynthia? In my old world, I would have thought it unlikely at best, but now anything seemed possible. The safest thing to do might be to call the police and let them check the area, and the two of us could remain safely here. And yet, whatever was going on was more related to science than to traditional detective work. Even more than that, I simply couldn't stand the thought of huddling in a corner, waiting for the police to take care of things that they didn't understand any better than I did, when the unknown danger might already be closing around us. I felt in my gut that now was a time to be brave, not timid.

I took a breath and turned to Cynthia. "Let's go see if anyone is there," I suggested. "Maybe it's nothing. Maybe someone is bird watching in the park."

Cynthia looked uncertain, but agreed to come with me. Anyone skulking around in the park was likely gone by now, slithering into the darkness to avoid us. But maybe he left something behind.

If, on the other hand, Cynthia's overwrought imagination simply created the watcher, we wouldn't find anything at all.

We searched all around the area where Cynthia thought she saw the man. I wasn't sure what I expected to find, and, sure enough, we found nothing, not even a cigarette butt. That didn't really prove anything, --negative evidence was so very unsatisfying—but, I hoped it would set Cynthia's mind at ease.

However, as we returned to the house, Cynthia seemed even more uneasy. I knew fear could play tricks on the mind, but Cynthia didn't seem overly panicked or irrational, and her certainty about seeing someone made me inclined to believe she hadn't imagined it. Despite my earlier doubts about the police, they might pick up something we'd missed and at the very least they'd help keep any villains at bay. Cynthia did have two children to consider.

"Why don't we still call the police?" I encouraged. "They can check around and make sure it's safe."

Cynthia agreed, and shortly the police came and talked to us. They searched the park and drove up the cul-de-sac, but found nothing.

I left Cynthia's a half-hour or so after the police left. I'd parked my car at the far end of the cul-de-sac. The night was cool and, after the unsettling evening and lack of resolution, I let myself be calmed by the sound of cicadas in the trees. The sky still held enough light to hide the dimmer stars. A splash of deep red streaked across the heavens where the sun glanced off a high cirrus cloud perched on the western horizon.

Focused as I was on the falling night, I was late in registering the sound of quick footsteps behind me. Too late, I started to turn. Rough arms circled me, pulling back my head and forcing a cloth over my nose and mouth. I had a moment of dizziness, confusion, without quite enough time to register what was happening. Mercifully, neither was there quite enough time to be afraid.

And then the world dissolved into blankness.

Chapter 18

Susan gave the carpet a quick go with the vacuum and then dropped her plate and cup from last night's supper in the sink. Not that she really cared that her place looked clean for the detective, but she expected Jonathan and Cynthia too, and the routine gave her something to do other than worry about Jen's disappearance.

She had to force herself to work through the exhaustion after being up most of the night. She still had a whole day of classes to teach.

She could do this. She flopped into a chair to wait for the detective whom she expected at eight.

The knot of tension in her gut refused to unwind. At least they knew Jen was in trouble. If Cynthia hadn't worried about her and tried to call, no one would even know she was missing. When Cynthia couldn't get ahold of Jen, she'd called Susan about midnight and then Jonathan. Neither of them had heard from Jen, so Cynthia called the police. The police found her car still parked in the cul-de-sac at the end of Cynthia's street, but Jen was nowhere to be found.

Why Jen? Even if someone was after Susan's own research, how did that bear on Jen? Susan could find no pattern, no reason for why any of this was occurring.

Jonathan and Cynthia arrived a little before the detective and the detective came promptly at eight. Susan felt glad she at least didn't have to go down to the station. Life seemed disrupted enough even in her own home.

The detective, the same one who had talked to them the night Mike died, put them at ease, suggesting they all sit in her living area. He introduced himself as Detective Raumin, then chatted a bit, presumably to set a mood for harder questions. He seemed like a nice guy. Probably the type with a wife and two kids at home, although she noticed that he wasn't wearing a wedding band. A good, solid citizen, but probably little experience with murder and kidnapping and none at all with scientific espionage, or whatever was going on here.

Nice really wasn't what she hoped for. Capable would be better. And tough. Of course, a person didn't have to be nasty to be competent. Hercule Poirot didn't have the tough-guy image that heroes of other detective stories sported, and he was perfectly competent.

"So, Dr. Arasmith, you told me that someone left a phone in your lab. Do you still have it?"

Susan shrugged. "I left it in the lab, and it was gone when I got back. I didn't really consider it important at the time."

"Yes, it's not there now." The detective made it sound as much accusation as question, at least in Susan's ears.

"The guy must have taken it when he broke in again." Susan's felt her voice get a bit sharp.

"What makes you think it was the same person?"

"Well, I guess I don't know, but it's not like I expect hordes of people to be breaking into my lab. Most likely one person broke in twice."

"And then broke into your apartment. This apartment."

Susan nodded. "Yes."

"I was there that night," Jonathan added. "He was a big guy. Strong."

"Hmm." The detective referred to some notes on his phone. "So, we have a break in at your lab, a break in at your apartment, and an attack at the bowling alley. We've connected your description of the man here at your apartment with the man in the surveillance video, an agent called Raven. But what makes you think those break-ins are related to the bowling alley attack?"

Susan paused. She'd already been through this. "The shimmering...being...that killed Mike, I saw something like that in my surveillance video at the lab. I think they have to be connected."

"Connected by what?"

"As I explained to you before, I think it might have something to do with my research. I got some startling results for some experiments with the uncertainty principle and I think somebody might want those results."

"But the man broke into your lab before you had those results, isn't that right?"

Susan nodded. She had to admit, it all seemed far-fetched.

"And how does this relate to Jennifer Hewitt?"

Susan shrugged. "I don't know."

Jonathan cleared his throat. "There might be a connection with something that Jennifer and I are both working on, a skeleton we found in rock in Wyoming which appears to be both ancient and recent."

"Ancient and recent," the detective repeated. It sounded so ridiculous when he said it.

"Kind of." Jonathan outlined their recent discoveries of the old radio from a burial in Wyoming, and the mismatches among the ages of the skeleton, rock, and belongings.

The detective frowned. "Why didn't you tell me this before?"

Jonathan gave an exasperated snort. "It didn't seem to be connected. I still don't see how it can be connected. Although, I'm not so sure now."

The detective rose from his chair, paced back and forth a couple of times, and then hovered over them. "What else aren't you telling me?"

They looked at each other. Susan spoke first. "Nothing. We don't know any more."

"You do know that what you're telling me is preposterous?"

"Of course we know." Susan really wanted to add, *And, are you equipped to investigate the preposterous* but bit her tongue. Even so, the detective's skepticism had increased his competence in her eyes.

The detective turned his attention to Cynthia, asking about the man she saw watching through the window, about the exact time that Jen left her house, and anything else she might have noticed. He focused a couple of questions on the binoculars. Cynth had to acknowledge she really just assumed they were binoculars.

The interview took about 30 minutes. Before he left, the detective said, "I'm sure you realized that this case is a bit out of my wheelhouse. Out of anyone's wheel house. It's a dangerous situation and you'd be wise to not take any foolish chances and try not to be alone. We'll be watching you as best we can, but you are your own best bodyguard. Use common sense."

As though guessing their unspoken concerns about his abilities, he added, "I have no idea what to do with your shimmering being, and the old skeleton that's also new still seems like someone's hoax to me. Right now, I'm just trying to see all the pieces of the puzzle and not worry too much about where they fit. But your friend's disappearance is something I can deal with. I have twenty years of experience in this business, including many cases of violent crime. I know my job, and I'm good at it. I have every hope that we can find your friend, if she's still alive, and catch this guy before he does more harm."

Cynthia left shortly after the detective. She asked Susan to stop by her house in the afternoon. Her almost pleading tone made Susan wince. She should have been there before now. But she was so busy at work, beckoned by both the fall term and research.

"I'll try, Cynth," she said.

Jonathan hung around for a while longer. "Are you going to make it over to Cynthia's?" he asked.

Susan shook her head. "I doubt it. I'm teaching this morning and early afternoon. Then I have to drop some manuscripts off at the post office for overnight delivery. That has to be done by early afternoon. I have to send in hard-copies of reviews that are due tomorrow. And I have some banking and grocery errands to run as well. I'm not sure when I can find time."

"Why don't you let me take care of some of those errands, Susan. I have time between classes. You should spend that time with your sister."

"No, I can take care of it." She knew she spoke too quickly. She didn't want someone else to help with what was clearly her responsibility. She didn't even know what Jonathan's motives were.

Jonathan didn't speak for a while, and neither did she.

"Why can't you trust me, Susan?" Jonathan asked. "At least enough to lean on me when you need to?"

Hearing the hurt in Jonathan's voice, Susan looked down at her feet.

"It's hard for me to trust people. People aren't trustworthy. Deep down, they're manipulative."

Susan glanced up to see Jonathan watching her, looking into her, and felt uncomfortable. He was looking into places even she didn't look. Places she didn't want to look.

"Why do you think that?" he said at last.

Susan didn't want to answer, didn't want to think about the answer. But she had to. She felt answers tumbling toward her mouth like water pressing to burst from corroded, aging pipes.

"I lived with someone. In college and afterward. A political science major, older than me. He seemed nice, caring. But, over time I came to see that he used people. He used me. He was good at it though. It took me two years to understand what was going on."

"Where is he now?" Jonathan asked.

"In the U.S. Senate. He's a brilliant man. The kind who stirs a sense of loyalty in everyone who knows him. When we were together, I always felt a sense of pride that someone like him wanted me. When he was first elected, he was the youngest member of the Senate by many years."

Jonathan fell quiet for a while, apparently giving her time to sort out the thoughts that must be parading across her face. Then he asked, "What did you see in him? You lived with him. You must have loved him."

Susan thought about that for a while. What had she seen in him? He'd risen above hardship in his early life. He seemed to have overcome it. She respected that.

And she respected his brilliant intellect, equal or superior to her own.

But what had she *loved*?

That he cared for her. He seemed so sincere at first, with no pretenses or posturing. It took years to realize he was just more skilled at pretense and posturing than anyone she'd known before. He had a nearly perfect façade of caring. He used it to get people to follow him and to support his goals. She'd done that for years. People were his tools. If he wanted fire, they were wood.

"He seemed to love me," Susan said finally. "And I couldn't help but love him back.

"But I think I was just the appearance of success to him. A woman to hang on his arm."

Susan reflected a moment, forced to self-honesty. "And maybe I had some of the same motives. I was ambitious. I wanted a successful man to match my own success. It made me look even more accomplished."

Jonathan nodded. He seemed to understand. Susan wondered if he had some bad choices of his own to reflect on.

"How did you come to realize he wasn't right for you? What did he do to you?"

"He never did anything violent, if that's what you mean," Susan answered. "His abuse was with words, but not the kind with a raised voice or swearing. Words that weren't true. Words that got me to stick by him, or back something he wanted to do, but over the long haul failed to match his actions. Words that gained my support of him, but never provided any support for me.

"I didn't want to hear what his actions told me, so it took me a long time to figure it out. I don't remember many of the things he did early on, because I thought forgiveness was noble and meant ignoring and forgetting character flaws. But one thing happened later on that I remember, when I began to see our relationship as a dysfunctional one. We made plans for a vacation together. I planned it into my work and had time off. He broke our plans because he had a chance to meet with the governor, a political opportunity he couldn't miss. He said that he knew I didn't want to be selfish and keep him from making such an important contact. Afterward, he assured me how much he loved me and told me all the things he planned to do with me to make it up. Romantic evenings. Camping trips in the mountains. Everything he knew I liked. I believe he really meant it when he said it. That's what made him such a great liar. He always really meant what he said, in that moment. But then, a better opportunity would come up, or he would just forget, and it never happened."

Susan fell quiet, thinking about those years she had thrust from her mind for so long. There was still pain there. Still bitterness she had yet to sort through. And guilt that she'd expected him to put her ahead of his career.

"He told me how he was just a simple, honest man from a poor background, his heart an open book," she said. "Then a business trip I didn't expect, or a late night at work he supposedly hadn't anticipated came up preempting something we planned. Or I found a personal letter to a friend of his that I'd never heard of, talking about important things he'd never told me. And I realized he wasn't as simple or open as he appeared. He was always sincerely apologetic, *Oh, yes I meant to tell you...*

"He told me how he hated his own father's violence and would never hurt me. That was true, physically at least. He never struck me or threatened me that way. He never even raised his voice against me. I believe that was a battle he fought in himself and won. But I think that one consuming effort used up all his strength of character."

Susan wasn't sure why she told all this to Jonathan, a stranger just a short time ago. She, of all people, should know better than to make herself vulnerable. But she felt driven to trust him. Something about his frank questions, his simple interaction with her, struck her as real. She could only hope that her trust was not misplaced.

Chapter 19

When I opened my eyes, I discovered red alligator clips, attached to wires, laying on my chest, looking like little...alligators. A variety of needles lay in a tray on a small stand at my left and gleaming machines surrounded me on all sides. Strange white creatures drifted in and out of my rather myopic vision.

Everything seemed straight out of an alien abduction movie, and I should have been terrified. But somehow the scene felt too much like a movie—or a dream--to be as frightening as it should have been. A part of me knew I must be drugged, but the conscious part of me didn't care.

Motion caught my attention as one of the white creatures took something from the tray and bent over me. I noticed a needle moving toward a bare arm laying on the hospital bed beside me—an arm that I suspected must be mine since it seemed to be attached to my body. I recalled in a distant sort of way that I was scared to death of needles, but I felt not the slightest glimmer of concern for my arm. I felt a faint prick as the needle struck, and dutifully noted that that observation confirmed the arm must be mine.

I let my eyes wander over my surroundings. Such odd-looking creatures, these white beings. Oodles of arms. Some hanging limp and others with strangely-shaped hands on the ends. I squinted, and realized that what I'd taken for hands were tools of some kind. I wondered what the extra limp arms were for, hanging from the creatures' waists down toward their knees.

Maybe the extra arms were props for the movie. I remembered an old gangster film where the goons would drug people, steal their kidneys to sell on the black market, then abandon them in a tub of ice water with a note saying that they really should get some medical attention soon. I really hoped that wasn't happening to me.

Especially if there was going to be a party after the movie. I didn't like parties very much, but I *really* didn't like to be left out of parties.

I shook my head, trying to clear away the fog. I knew this wasn't a party. I shouldn't be here. I tried to pull myself more upright on the bed, but my body didn't respond. My thinking slipped back toward the party. My parents had always advised against parties like this but had allowed me the choice of whether to take their advice or not.

I tried again to focus. I needed to be afraid. I needed to try to escape. The white creatures were putting me in a tube, all strapped down. I didn't know why they strapped me down. I couldn't move anyway, and even if I could, why would I? It felt so pleasant just floating along.

I lost consciousness again.

***

My head was clearing. I could keep my attention focused for longer now. I noticed the scent in the air for the first time, stagnate with a touch of mold. The room was warm, with little circulation other than the faint drafts stirred by the white beings moving around me.

The beings rolled me into a room with a computer and a monitor. They connected the alligator clips and wires to the sides of my face and then left me there, looking at the blank screen. If I could have reached the alligator clips, I would have pulled them off, but the movement of my arms was limited by flat, webbed cords to which my wrists were attached. My impatience with the blank screen signaled that drug-induced lethargy continued to lift.

Puzzles appeared on the computer monitor, patterns and shapes I was expected to group into like and unlike categories. I quickly learned that a wrong answer, or no answer at all, resulted in painful shocks. Unlike the needles from earlier, I definitely cared about the shocks.

I did the puzzles and quickly reduced the shocks to nearly none.

But, the sadistic interrogators weren't done yet. They gave me some new drug. This time I was alert and the needle terrified me. Actually, it was the needle's contents, being injected into my body where I was quite sure it didn't belong, that terrified me.

I had to find something funny in it. Otherwise, I feared I'd start screaming and not be able to stop. It occurred to me that a very proper person would insist that humor was quite inappropriate in this situation.

The drug did not inhibit my thinking this time, at least my memories were clear and intact. But I didn't seem to have access to my thought-editor. Whatever popped into my head, popped out my mouth. Before it even occurred to me to test it, or evaluate it, or rethink it, I blabbed it. Therefore, a lot of what I said was wrong.

Truth serum, I supposed. My first experience with it. Ironic that truth serum stirred one to talk without thinking and thus undermined one's ability to actually tell the truth. But of course, the objective was to prevent me from *withholding* truth, not to ensure that what I said was, in fact, true. It did succeed prolifically at that, much to their chagrin I imagined.

Someone, or *something*, hidden from me, asked questions. The questions were in perfectly good English, the voice deep like a male. That did *not* prove they weren't aliens, I thought. I possessed, after all, a 40000 year-old artifact with writing in English. Wouldn't they be surprised at that! But they didn't ask about the artifact.

Instead, they pried out all my most precious secrets of youth-- stuff of clear interest to secret organizations and aliens. I told them about our family vacations, and playing the piano, what time we ate supper, and my favorite TV show. I told them about judo lessons, playing scrabble by the fireplace, Sunday mornings in spring when the windows were left open for church service and the breezes stirred the curtains during worship, and my brother who died of leukemia when I was fifteen. They asked about my faith and my schooling and what my parents were like and how they raised me. They kept asking the last part over and over. I suppose they were sorely disappointed with the lack of juicy details of family discord. A functional family must seem rather unrealistic and boring to sadistic interrogators from evil secret societies.

They asked and asked. Then the needle came back. I was still talking about their last question and was too busy to watch the needle. I did happen to notice, as the white being with the needle approached me, that the extra white arms I saw earlier were only the ends of an untied belt of a lab coat, dangling free. Aha.

I was still talking when blank unconsciousness engulfed me again.

Chapter 20

The woman, he knew, was as important a figure as the man. That is what the being, the *Shimera*, told him. He had to wait for the man to arrive, of course. But the woman he could examine now.

NMR, Cat scans, brain chemistry, blood chemistry, metabolism, hormone chemistry, family history. He found nothing out of the ordinary. Her intelligence was indeed very high. In the top two percent of the general population. But then, his own intellect was higher than that. It wasn't intellect that made her special.

What did she have that that gave her such potential? More importantly, how could he get it?

He saw nothing in the tests of her physiology or intellect to give him a clue. But perhaps, as he continued to watch her and gather more data, he would make new connections.

Of course, he had to let her go, at least until she grew too dangerous. Watching her when she thought she was free would give him opportunity to learn about her power, where it came from, and what was destined to awaken it within her.

He needed some way to make her feel safe from surveillance. A belief that she was no longer watched. He thought on that for a minute before reaching a decision.

Then he thought of the longer term and bigger picture. At some point, he must discontinue this woman. He couldn't bring himself to use the word *kill*. He was no killer. He only did what was right for all people.

His duty was clear. This power was too great, too important, to relegate to a simple citizen. A leader such as he must harness it. Harness it for the good of all.

He needed this power. Power to shape nations. Power to shape the future.

With it, he could protect the world. With it, he would be safe from the world.

Unfortunate that he had lost his contact with the Shimera. Given the location of the explosion in the bowling alley where they met, he knew that the Shimera who died must certainly have been his contact. The contact could be in no other place, after all. Perhaps he could find and make contact with another Shimera.

Or perhaps he could persuade Susan to help him. Her research involved her deeply in these events. Her insight into her work might give him the understanding he needed.

The fact that they shared both a romantic past and a connection to the events about to unfold was not truly coincidence if what the Shimera said was true. But Susan didn't know yet what was happening to her. And by the time she did know, it would be too late. Too late for either of them.

She had loved him once. And he still loved her. Loved her and missed her. Why had she rejected him? He'd never understood that. Sometimes, he knew, people just drifted apart. But it was wrong of her to reject him. She shouldn't have done that. Old anger and hurt welled up again.

No, reaching out to Susan now might not be a good idea. He didn't need his judgement impaired by emotion at this critical juncture, and she didn't yet understand the implications of her own work anyway.

Instead, he had to focus on the man's arrival. He needed to develop some operatives to work with him in the Los Angeles area to capture the man once he arrived. That one *must not* escape him.

His uncle's message was timely. He remembered his uncle with fondness. Astonishing that his uncle was, in the irony of life, involved in these events. Again, if the Shimera were to be believed, it might not be as much coincidence as it seemed. He'd not thought before to respond to the message, but his uncle might be able to help with the man who was soon to arrive. Perhaps a bit of family courtesy was in order.

There was another who was an even better bet to start building a network. That one would be flattered to serve him. Although, of course, he wouldn't know it.

He was not completely satisfied with that. He wanted people to serve him from the same noble faith in the rightness of this course that he had, not from ignorance. *To act because they believed in him.* He needed them to need him. To respect him. To implement his vision because they delighted to do so. He needed the little people to need their shepherd.

But if they wouldn't willingly, then for their own sake, he would make them. He cared for them in a way that only one who had not been cared for himself could understand. He would save them, not only from the dangers that lay ahead, but, if need be, even from themselves.

Chapter 21

Jack Myrvik waved his two guests toward the chairs he kept in his office for students and took his own seat behind the small oak desk cluttered with papers and half-assembled electronics. The two guests just about filled up the room, both because of the small size of his university office and because of the big size of the one guy's personality.

Jack recognized them both. One was the younger of the two US Senators from California. The other had been with the President in that meeting about his and Susan's research, the man that Jack had thought was more than science-literate. Clearly an important man. An influential one.

"The United States needs your help," the Senator with the big personality said.

Jack Myrvik decided that was a very fine attaboy indeed. Happiness, he thought, was keeping his ego satisfied. In academia, accolades were uncommon, and certainly not expected. To have his value acknowledged in this way, being called upon to serve, was high honor.

"What can I do?" he asked.

"It's an issue of national security," the Senator explained. "The work of one of your colleagues, Dr. Arasmith, is potentially destructive in the wrong hands. We need your help to keep it in the right hands.

"For now, we simply need copies of her notes. And any thoughts about her work that she shares with you. We need to know what experiments she has completed and their results."

"Not a problem," Myrvik said. He already knew her results. And he could get her notes. At least any she kept on the computer.

"We have reason to believe that other people may try to get this information," the Senator continued. "They may go to extreme lengths to get it. When the time comes, we may need your help to get people to safe houses, or perhaps to take some into custody.

"Here's the name and address of someone I expect to cooperate with us." The senator handed Jack a piece of paper with a name on it. "I plan to ask him to provide a place of safety to individuals who need it."

Jack glanced at the paper. Walter Roden. The name felt vaguely familiar, although he couldn't remember where he'd seen it before.

"Everyone here in the physics department knows of Susan's work," Jack said. "And she's been collaborating with a geologist on campus. Is there any danger of this work getting into the wrong hands through these people?"

"Right now, her work is not classified," the Senator said. "Since it's done by a civilian scientist, it's public knowledge. But, that may not be a good thing. Depending on how it develops, we may need to suppress some parts of it. Can we count on you?"

Jack wasn't sure what "counting on him" entailed, but his own research had significant implications for military applications, and he had learned that, for some things, the traditional openness of scientific inquiry had to be compromised. Certainly, if national security was at risk, Susan needed to know to screen her results.

"Of course," he said.

The Senator rose, extending his hand to shake Jack's. "Thank you." His handshake was confident and warm. "The support and integrity of people like you is what makes this a great nation."

The Senator and the other man left Jack's office. With them left a certain feeling of life and power. Jack understood why this man was a Senator at such a young age. He was a man you could believe in.

Jack considered going directly to Susan with the Senator's concerns. He admitted to himself that he was a little astonished. He thought Susan's experiments were nonsense. But clearly there was something about them he didn't understand.

He should alert Susan to the risk of the results getting into the wrong hands. Warn her about the possible risks to her own safety.

But, on second thought, maybe he shouldn't talk to her. The Senator had entrusted *him* with this knowledge, not Susan. He felt a little guilty keeping it from her, but experience told him he shouldn't tell anyone more than necessary. It just stirred up trouble and depleted one's own arsenal of future options.

In any case, this information really wasn't his to tell. Although the Senator had not instructed him to keep it secret, the situation implied that their conversation took place in confidence. Keeping it secret from Susan was his duty.

Chapter 22

Jonathan gripped the steering wheel a bit tighter as he changed lanes on the way to his meeting with Detective Raumin at the police station. The fall monsoons were late in arriving and the sky remained clear, quite contrary to his cloudy thoughts.

The intruder had escaped at Susan's apartment because he relaxed his guard for a moment. He was determined not to fail again. Not with Jen.

Although, he really didn't know what to do except try to motivate the detective to greater effort. He thought through what he understood of the situation, hoping for an idea he could take action on. It seemed too much coincidence for the break-in at Susan's apartment and Jen's kidnapping to not be linked, which meant that someone knew the connection between the four of them. Whoever broke into Susan's apartment was after information, so it was a safe bet that Jen's kidnappers were after information too. If they thought Jen had what they wanted, that should keep Jen safe for a while, although, so far as he knew, neither he nor Jen knew any more about what was going on than the kidnappers.

The kidnappers might always kill to protect their anonymity, but Jonathan couldn't let himself think in that direction., Instead, he considered where the kidnappers might leave her once they were done with their questions. The hospital, maybe, if the interrogation was rough? He winced, not letting his mind go there.

Or maybe Jen's apartment. The kidnappers might think no one knew about the kidnapping yet—not expecting Cynthia's suspicion and concern—and an apartment drop-off would keep the kidnapping low-profile.

Maybe the police should stake out her apartment and the hospital.

Jonathan pulled into the police parking lot and went inside. The receptionist directed him back to Raumin's office.

When Jonathan entered, Detective Raumin rose from his seat to shake his hand.

"Thank you for seeing me," Jonathan said.

The detective nodded and waved him to a chair, retaking his own.

The detective looked a bit stern. He probably didn't appreciate Jonathan's amateur help, but Jonathan felt he had to do something. He couldn't just sit and worry.

"I had an idea that maybe you should watch Jen's apartment," he said, "and maybe the hospital."

Raumin offered a faint smile, somewhere between gracious and condescending. "I'll put a team on it, if it makes you feel better. In fact, I already have, but, we're not likely to catch anyone that way. It's like throwing coins at the carnival, a lot more random than it looks."

At Raumin's words, Jonathan felt silly. It was pretty obvious stuff, and, clearly, the detective had already thought of keeping an eye on the apartment and hospital. But that suggestion wasn't really what had brought him here.

"Do you have something that I can do?" he asked, a faint desperation in his voice. "I can't just do nothing."

Raumin eyed him for a moment. "I can't have civilians getting involved, putting themselves, Ms. Hewitt, and everyone else at risk. But I do have a question for you. One of the neighbors in the cul-de-sac where your friend was taken remembered seeing an unfamiliar car that night. A Porsche Starway, not an easy car to forget. None of the residents along the street claimed it. I've got some people checking out registrations, but I'm wondering if you might know anyone with a car like that?"

Jonathan shook his head, relieved that the detective actually had a lead, but frustrated at the question.

"Why would you think I'd know the kidnappers? I mean, it seems obvious we're dealing with professionals and...non-humans. How many alien professional kidnapper-killers do you think I might know?" Some of his exasperation came out in his voice.

Raumin waved a calming hand. "Take it easy. I just needed to check. In my experience, it's always real people behind crimes, however odd the crimes might seem at first."

"However," he continued, "I'm wondering how you know it was a professional kidnapping?"

Jonathan felt flustered at the question, like he was being accused of something. He fumbled out a few stray words before finally saying, "The way they took her when she was on the way home, when it was likely no one would check on her for a while. And then I guess when you told us about the Raven guy, who broke into Susan's apartment, he was a pro..." Jonathan trailed off.

"Hmm," Raumin grunted and stood up. "Ok. Let us know if you remember anyone who drives a Porsche Starway."

A clear dismissal. Jonathan rose and found his way out in a fog of disappointment. The conversation with Raumin had been too brief, too embarrassing, and ended with no invitation for his help.

He continued to feel antsy on the drive back to his apartment. He had to at least try to help. He thought about driving around Los Angeles looking for a Starway. But the Starway was a popular car, the Porsche for the poor man they called it. That meant the city was full of them.

Most of the new Starways were equipped with StarNav positioning and mapping, one of the newest systems. That was something he knew about. He had worked for StarNav out of college for a few years before going back to grad school. The car accessed the standard satellite GPS for its location, but it also accessed the StarNav computers via the phone system.

Somewhere in the StarNav computers was the knowledge of the location of every StarNav system in town. He still had a friend, Barry, working at StarNav. He wondered if Barry would grant him system privileges long enough to find the location of just one.

He pulled off the freeway at the next exit and headed back toward the StarNav building. He could at least ask.

He found Barry tucked away in the clutter of his back office next to the servers at the rear of the building. Pieces of computers, hard drives, and replacement boards lay strewn around his office, just like old times. Jonathan chose the direct approach, and told him about Jen's kidnapping and the Porsche Starway spotted at the scene. "Do you think you could get me access to the location records?" As he asked it, he realized allowing access to those records by anyone but authorized company employees was likely contrary to company policy, maybe not even legal. It could probably get Barry fired.

Barry gave a pained grimace. "Uh, can you tell me why it isn't the police asking?"

Jonathan stretched his lips in a sheepish half-grin. "Because the police would need a warrant and I don't want to wait that long?"

"I see." Barry took a breath. "Well, I'll do it for your friend. It does seem like a reasonable use of the data. You seem as guileless as always. If you ever become a crook, you've got a good line."

"Thanks, Barry." Jonathan let his appreciation and relief come through in his voice.

Barry called up the StarNav accounts. Of the 150000 or so accounts StarNav kept in the LA area, only about 1000 were Starways. As quickly as he could, Jonathan scanned through the locations of the Starways, displayed on a map of the city. He was aware of Barry hovering beside him, perhaps curious about kidnappings or merely impatient to continue his real work of the day.

It took only a few minutes to identify one Starway located apart from the main cluster in an unlikely area of town, a seedy district with few residences and a large number of abandoned buildings and warehouses. That was, Jonathan thought, an odd place for a Porsche. That *didn't* make sense.

He zoomed in on the satellite photo of the area in question, overlain by text naming buildings and streets. The only building left in the old railway district at the southeastern corner of town was a three-story building abandoned years ago and currently used for storage by a furniture company. The Starway had been parked there for at least the preceding two hours, two hours being the maximum time retained in the computer records. But it had just left. It was heading east on the San Bernadino Freeway.

Jonathan couldn't be sure this was the Starway that had been sighted when Jen disappeared. He couldn't even be sure the Starway parked there that evening was related to Jen's kidnapping. But a Starway was the only lead he had. And this was the most suspicious Starway in town.

Jonathan thanked Barry and left. His only choice now was

whether to pursue where the car was *going*, or to check out where it *left*.

Jonathan chose to check out where it left. There was a possibility that Jen might still be there, and trying to chase the Starway to who knew where seemed less likely to work out.

Traffic diminished to almost none as he approached the area where the Porsche had been parked. The late fall sun fell warmly on the empty pavement, contrasting with the cool breeze that swirled the summer dust into snakes that slithered across the vacant streets.

He pulled to a stop beside the lone building. Several of its windows were missing, and blackened bricks indicated a fire at some point in the past. The obvious signs of disrepair and lack of upkeep made Jonathan nervous. Even if it were used only for furniture storage, wouldn't keeping good windows in the building be justified by better protection of their furniture?

Jonathan got out of the car and peered in the lower story windows. Couches and beds were stacked everywhere. He tried a couple of doors, finding each locked. There weren't any missing windows on the lower floors, but a fire escape led up to a broken window on the second floor.

Leaping up, he caught the bottom section of the fire escape and lowered it to the ground. As he stepped up on the first metal step, it groaned under his weight. Hoping to limit the noise, he pressed himself close to the wall and walked quickly up to the second floor. He slipped through the broken window, managing to avoid cuts, but sharp edges of broken glass still clinging to the window frame clutched at his clothes.

It was dark. Streaks of light from the windows stretched across the immense, empty floor space. There was no furniture on this floor.

He heard footsteps echoing from the floor below. For the first time, he realized he was trespassing and might be caught.

He softened his footsteps and looked around for a stairway down. He spotted a door with a sign saying 'stairs' above it, the sign unlit and barely visible in the dim light inside the building. The large metal door creaked horribly as he swung it open. Oh well. He was committed now.

He rushed through and ran down the stairs, watching for a place to slip into if or *when* someone came to check out the creaking door. There was no place to hide in the stairwell, but he emerged onto the lower floor safely and stepped out among the stored furniture.

He heard the sound of light footsteps, startlingly close, and ducked behind a sheet-covered couch. It might just be an employee come to pick up some wares. Or a thug with secrets to protect. He felt his heart hammering and took a couple of slow breaths to try to calm down.

The footsteps came up on the far side of the couch and paused. He held his breath, listening for the steps to resume. When they did, he noticed they sounded soft, like the pat-pat of bare feet rather than the sharper ping of shoes.

He peered through the gap underneath the couch, trying to catch sight of the retreating feet. He spotted them, walking away at a slight angle, bare as he had guessed. And, brushing the floor around the feet swept the gossamer fabric of a hospital gown.

Jonathan crept to the end of the couch, doing his best to make no sound, and peeked around for a better look. He followed the feet upward, past the hospital gown, up to the head full of somewhat wild hair, the exact color and length of...

"Jen?" he whispered.

She paused but didn't turn.

Jonathan rose to his feet and hurried to her. Taking her by the shoulders, he turned her to look at him. It was indeed Jen, but there was no sign of recognition in her face. She stared right through him, unseeing, or perhaps seeing some other world invisible to him.

"Jen," he said again, but she didn't seem to hear.

Taking the cover from one of the couches, he sat her down.

"Stay here," he said. "I need to find a way out."

He found several doors out onto the street where he was parked, but most were padlocked. He finally found one that could be opened from the inside.

He guided Jen to the car and took her directly to the hospital. He called Susan and Cynthia and they arrived in separate cars about thirty minutes later. Jen was already sleeping, having been given a sedative, and Jonathan explained to Susan and Cynthia where he found her.

Detective Raumin arrived soon after. He nodded and frowned as Jonathan re-explained for a second time.

"Well," Raumin said. "I'm glad it turned out ok."

"I should've called you," Jonathan admitted.

Raumin didn't answer, either to agree or commend him for what he'd accomplished, and instead said, "I do have some news. We caught someone in Ms. Hewitt's apartment. He was attempting to hide a wireless surveillance camera and a mike."

Jonathan nodded, a bit too overwhelmed by events to react to this new information. "Did you learn anything about who's behind this?"

The detective shook his head, his face scrunching in puzzled frustration. "Whoever kidnapped your friend is no amateur and must have known the apartment would be watched. But then this guy gets caught, almost like it was on purpose, and he doesn't seem to know anything. Says some out-of-towners hired him."

"So, he's just a fall guy to put us off the scent." Relief at finding Jen kept Jonathan from too much disappointment, but he did feel an undercurrent of concern. Whoever was behind Jen's kidnapping had resources and skill. Maybe more resources and skill than Raumin.

"So it would seem," Raumin said.

Raumin left, promising to return once Jen awoke. Cynthia and Susan joined Jonathan in Jen's room.

"We need to talk through this, once Jen is better," Susan said. "To think about who knows of our research, and why it might be important to them. I'll set up a time in the next couple of days. I have some new ideas about my research that might be important. But I need to think on it more."

"We do need to talk about our research," Jonathan agreed, "but we also need to talk about how to stay safe. It's fortunate the police caught the guy before he put the camera in Jen's apartment. Maybe she's safe there from prying eyes. But where else might they be watching? What else might they do?"

Jonathan walked out to the parking lot with Susan. With so much uncertainty, it felt good to have her with him. He felt grateful for her friendship and for what might be starting to be something more.

As she reached her car, he laid a gentle hand on her back. "We'll get through this," he said.

She turned at his touch, taking his forearm in her hand with a desperate ferocity. We'll find her," she said. "Won't we?"

Jonathan nodded and almost took her into his arms. But, after all the false boldness of his prior flings, he wasn't quite sure what real love was supposed to look like. Although, he was learning. And what was love but a learning process, never completely realized but always a journey?

***

Jonathan visited Jen the next day in the hospital. She was to be released tomorrow. She still looked weak and exhausted, but her mind seemed to have recovered. He stayed for an hour, mainly offering her the support of his company.

As he drove back to his own place, his thoughts wandered through what had happened. One component of their experience came to mind in particular. A component so astonishingly unusual as to cry out for examination. A component which, in the turmoil of the last few days, they had not had time to consider fully and which detective Raumin either didn't believe or interpreted as a hoax.

What was the strange shimmer that killed Mike? Was it the same shimmer that appeared in Susan's video of her lab?

How could he find out?

Chapter 23

The events of the last weeks troubled Susan, but they couldn't keep her completely from her research. She was, to a significant degree, defined by her work. Although, her recent interactions with Jonathan were slowly awakening her from that.

She was falling in love with him. She recognized the terror. It was an old feeling, much more frightening than intruders and kidnappings.

The turbulent concerns of the past weeks, and her growing relationship with Jonathan, fought for her mental time. But the safety of all of them, including Jonathan, might rest on understanding the implications of her experiments. She needed to explore those implications, understand them. That was what she could contribute to easing the turmoil and danger around them. That was *her* role.

She unconsciously rose from her chair, her whole mind focused on the Puzzle. Pacing helped her focus. Or perhaps it was a manifestation of her focus. Sometimes, when deep in thought, she'd find herself blocks from her lab, startled to realize she had no memory of the journey.

"So what prevents chaos?" she whispered quietly. This time, she didn't walk far, but kept to her office. Her hands busied themselves of their own accord, returning a folder to the file cabinet, wiping dust from the shelf where she kept the pictures of her sister and parents. Without a second thought, she wiped her dust-coated fingers on her pants.

But her mind went with ever-narrowing focus toward the one thing it sought to enlighten, determined to either reveal it or be devoured by it. Equations danced across the visual screen in her mind, but each one gradually resolved into a far more conceptual question, one more accessible to her mystical side than her analytical one. One not easily put on a graph, and one she suspected no graph could address.

"What prevents Chaos?" This time she spoke louder as though to demand answers of the universe itself.

The ordered universe was an idea her science had both assumed and confirmed for centuries. The cornerstone of her beliefs. The very name *Cosmos* implied a harmony, a *rationality*, to existence. Yet her experiments suggested that there was no foundation for that order. That it was built on nothing more than the capricious winds of intellect itself.

How could there be order?

There must be some power of consensus, something that dilutes the minority and emphasizes the majority. Something that keeps every random thought and its thinker from dominating its own reality, keeping beings from being gods in their own private universe. Something that made every being subject to a greater reality than its own beliefs or whims.

"But still, if two humans are agreed together..." She corrected herself, "Or rather, two sentient beings are agreed together, then..." Her thoughts leaped to their inevitable conclusion, "Then, *anything is possible*! They could even..."

Her hand was busy straightening the items that made her space *her space*, darting here and there among her books, the steel balls that bounced back and forth on little swings, preserving momentum but seeming to start and stop like magic, and the old scanner radio she'd taken pride in keeping in working order, part of her collection of old electronics. Her mind, far away in the world of ideas, had caught upon one. And in the next moment, Susan Arasmith, reader of mystery stories, bowler with friends, and twenty-nine year old physicist at Cal Tech, vanished from existence.

Chapter 24

I felt better now that we were taking action. I didn't know what we could do, but doing *something* gave me a certain sense of control. The four of us could surely come up with some plan. Susan's office seemed like a safe place to meet--public, but not too public.

I saw Dr. Myrvik in his office as I walked down the empty hallway. I wasn't surprised to see him here, even on a Saturday. He seemed very dedicated to his work.

I'd seen him on previous trips to the physics building to meet with Susan and Jonathan. Susan had introduced us. His warm handshake seemed genuine, although his eyes wandered over me in a way that left me uncomfortable. I wondered if he had no family, that he would work so much of the time and seem so lonely.

As though cued by the concept of loneliness, memory of my kidnapping and interrogation swept into my mind. Ever since Jonathan had found me, it had been happening off and on. I would think I was doing fine one moment, and the next I would be trembling uncontrollably, my mind generating images from memory as vivid as my immediate reality.

I was finally beginning to comprehend my experience. My mind had protected me from the pain and confusion of it at first, feeding memories to me in small doses as I recovered in the hospital. It still felt like an ethereal dream. A nightmare of fear and fighting with fear.

I knew now that I couldn't have saved myself. In my stupor, I couldn't even have gotten myself out of the warehouse onto the street to find help—a humbling realization.

Just expressing my relief in seeing Jonathan had not been possible with my drugged emotions still lost in the sunbeams and dust of the old building. I hadn't even been sure that Jonathan was really there. It had all seemed like dream.

It still seemed unreal. To be so fully violated left me doubting the very fabric of my society, my world. How could such a thing happen? Were secret hospitals sequestered in other cities, with armies of secret doctors waiting to devour ordinary citizens? I didn't know how I could ever regain any sense of security.

I felt weak from my ordeal, and a deep fear shivered up from my belly, more fear than I remembered ever having before. I knew I should have talked things through with Cynthia. I should have explored with her this new fear, this feeling of deep violation. She had asked me if I wanted to talk. But I wasn't sure I wanted anyone to hear what I felt. I wasn't sure that I *knew* what I felt.

I needed to sort things out myself before I talked about them. And Cynthia had enough burdens without sharing mine.

I reached the hallway outside Susan's office. Cynthia and Jonathan hadn't arrived yet. Strangely, Susan wasn't at her desk, which I could see through the window in her office door. The window was small, but it looked directly over her desk. I was sure Susan had arranged to meet us here at her office. I checked my watch to confirm it was the correct hour.

Susan was always prompt. She didn't want her time wasted, and she didn't waste that of others.

Cautiously, I pushed open the door. As I had suspected, Susan wasn't there. That alone, with everything I'd gone through, stirred a deep sense of unease. However, what really made my heart pound was the half-naked man standing in the middle of her office.

His clothing looked primitive, like something from a Tarzan movie. He stared back at me from dark eyes that slanted upward at the corners.

I should have turned to run. The last few days had taught me how dangerous strangers can be and this stranger definitely did not belong in Susan's office. And the way he stared at me steadily, without the social grace to either glance away or speak, left me unnerved.

Something held me back. Maybe it was the fact that he'd made no aggressive move. Maybe it was the mixture of curiosity and startled fear I saw in his eyes.

"Who are you?" I asked.

He said nothing.

Strange. If he was an agent sent to learn more about Susan and her work, his attire seemed an odd choice. And why had he not immediately fled?

And where was Susan? I felt my skin grow chill, as though from the passing of a cold breeze. My eyes swept the room again, looking this time for the dark mass of a still body. Fear gripped at my throat at the thought, but to my relief, the floor was clear. My gaze returned to the stranger.

"What are you doing here?" I asked with rising intensity. "What have you done with Susan?"

The strange man still hadn't moved or responded to my questions. He wasn't large for a man, probably five-foot seven or so. But he looked strong. Of course, that might simply be my perception because all of the muscles in his upper body were exposed for my examination. I forced my eyes from the corded muscles to his face, which looked equally strong.

He stared at me. I stared back, trying to pin him with my gaze. This man had done something to Susan or she wouldn't have missed our appointment. I was sure of it. Perhaps, even, he was the very same man who had captured and interrogated me. A shiver ran up my spine at the thought, although I realized at the same moment that I had no real evidence that this man was my own captor, and it was not completely rational to think he might have taken Susan and then returned to her empty office to be captured himself. Even so, I felt surge of anger well up against him, stronger than either fear or reason.

My gaze wasn't much to immobilize him with, and I hoped he didn't challenge that gaze, but I kept my eyes on him and moved slowly toward Susan's desk phone. I picked it up and called 911.

The man still didn't move, as though mesmerized.

I whispered into the phone, hoping my quiet voice would not break the man's odd trance and let him escape or, worse, harm me. I knew full well that he could hear every word, but, still possessed with the strange burning anger, I didn't care. "I'm in Susan Arasmith's office in the physics building at CalTech, with an intruder who's broken in," I said. "Susan is missing and this man may have done something to her. I need help."

I held onto the phone and heard the dispatcher quiz me further, a thin, tinny voice emerging from the phone. I could see that the intruder heard it too, as his eyes left mine and went to the phone. However, I said no more, and he had no further reaction. Hopefully, they'd send someone quickly.

Chapter 25

His step didn't fall on the soft turf of the prairie. It fell instead on a surface hard like stone, in a place where the sky and the moving-spirit within it were both vanished. Kar-Tur stopped utterly for a moment, his thought of an instant before dissolved into nothing. How had he come from his fire to this place?

Everywhere around he saw only strangely-textured stone, and tools whose purpose he could not fathom. There was no land or grass or tree. It was as though he were in a cave, or dwelling, though none such as he had ever seen or heard of. He reasoned that this must be some type of constructed room, although certainly more permanent and elaborate than the wood and hide structures of his people's summer homes.

Within moments, a woman entered the room through an opening that suddenly appeared on one wall. The woman stood as tall as he, who was tall among his tribe and certainly taller than any woman. Her skin shone fairer than his own, and her hair was brown, not black, glinting red in places like the evening sun. He'd never seen anyone like her. She was beautiful, godlike. Her dress looked odd to him, but he knew that other tribes often kept different traditions concerning dress, sometimes covering different amounts and parts of their bodies or using a variety of furs to draw attention and achieve various artistic effects. He'd never imagined any garb quite as different as this thin, smooth clothing that resembled the pelt of no creature he knew of. It fit closely to her, highlighting her femininity even as it covered her whole body.

He hoped this woman knew how to behave in this incomprehensible place. He certainly did not. She watched him, seeming to will him to be still. Perhaps she was trying to warn him that any other action would be unsafe. He wasn't able to discern what was safe or not in this strange world. He could only trust that this woman knew. She wasn't *tribe*, but that couldn't be helped. Waiting for her action seemed his only choice.

She raised some device to her head. Since it was no plant, animal, or stone he knew of, he inferred it must be a tool. She spoke into it softly, and he heard the tool speak back to her even more softly. He understood nothing of what either said.

Shortly, other men arrived, dressed in garb as strange as the woman.

These new people treated him rather roughly, putting a hard, silver cord on his wrists, tying them together. He did not like being treated as a captive, but there seemed no choice but to trust the woman who knew this place better than he and had looked into his eyes with such deep rapport. The new people took him and the woman out through the opening that appeared in the wall. They traveled through long, enclosed pathways before coming out under the sky.

He felt comforted by the sky. It, at least, was familiar. But he knew little else around him. Great dwellings such as he had never imagined towered around him, hiding much of the sky. A strange, smooth stone lay in ordered patterns over the whole earth. Patches of trees and a strange grass that seemed too green for the drought implied by its short height were scattered sparsely here and there.

The men with him gave no time to examine and explore this amazing place. They hustled him and the woman along one of the stone pathways. He wished he could tell them he was a seeker, the one who looks and thinks, the one who sees the world beyond the world. Then perhaps they would slow down so he could see and learn.

Although he told them this, they didn't respond to it properly. His words seemed to make them angry. They pushed him harshly into a small, shiny house that sat on round legs. He banged his head on the top of it. Then he began to grow angry too.

He told them he was growing angry. Asked them what they were doing and why. They ignored him.

The house was filled with seats. The woman took a seat in front of him. They were all saying things, but he could not understand. He wished the woman would tell these people to go slower so he could study this world and not bump his head. He tried to speak to her, this only person in a strange world whom he felt might help him, but she didn't turn around to listen. She must not understand him any more than he understood her.

The tiny house was moving. He could see the world sliding past through the clear stone walls of the house. He reached across the man beside him to tap his fingers on these amazing partitions that he could see through. It looked like ice, but didn't melt in the warm air.

There were people everywhere, more people than he had ever seen or imagined to see. There were many of the moving houses. He saw the small faces of other people within their mouths.

They traveled faster than Kar-Tur thought possible, sometimes even faster than the great cats that hunted and scavenged the plains of his tribe. After a time, they came into a grove of buildings towering like a great forest around them. Kar-Tur craned to see out the clear walls, fascinated by these mighty constructs, clearly built by a tribe with great power and knowledge. They stopped beside a smaller building and disembarked from the shiny house that Kar-Tur realized must be some type of incredible tool to aid *traveling*.

Although they'd come a great distance, Kar-Tur saw nothing familiar on the journey. No part of his beloved prairie came into view, nor any of his tribe, nor even any of the people with whom his tribe sometimes traded or warred. Nor did he see the rocky mountains at the edge of the great grassland, nor the ice-mountains that crept out of the north.

His own tribe might be a great distance away. Perhaps farther than he could ever travel.

A dawning new fear grew in him. A fear of not finding his own people again. For a searcher and learner, a mystic such as he, there was usually a *joy* in the unknown. But to be divided from his people, his tribe, was a terror with no joy. The roots of tribe-contact reached deep with his people. Never would one be willingly separated for extended periods of time. Only death was acceptable parting.

Many of the men and women in this new building wore clothing with a blue color and patterned one like another. Their clothing differed from the woman's clothing. He wondered if this pattern designated a particular tribe. Perhaps these people were not of the woman's tribe. Perhaps she was alone as much as he.

They talked to the woman for a time and tried to talk to Kar-Tur, but he couldn't understand them. Nor did they seem to understand his response. Then they placed his fingers on a flat, clear rock, and suddenly pictures of the ends of his fingers appeared on one of their mysterious tools. He examined the picture, intrigued by the lines and patterns made by his fingers. He had never thought before to examine his fingers this way. This tribe seemed to know many things he had not yet thought of. He hoped they could teach him.

They tried to separate him from the woman. She moved towards the door they'd entered, while two men held him and pulled him deeper into the building.

Didn't they understand they shouldn't separate him from the woman? The woman was the only one he'd contacted here. It wasn't tribe-contact, true. But it was all he had. Clearly his contact with the woman was too significant to allow forced parting. Particularly since he had no tribe here, and perhaps she did not as well. What manner of people were these that they would force *parting* on a stranger? A stranger recently torn from his tribe. And the woman also seemed of a different tribe than the others.

He couldn't allow this parting.

Although his hands were still bound by the shiny cord, he broke easily away from the two men. They seemed slow and weak. His own strength and speed were below-average for his tribe, since he spent so much of his time in meditation and study. Although, given his size, he suspected he would be stronger than most had he spent more time on the hunt.

Perhaps the people of this tribe were all engaged in meditation and study, even more than he. That would explain their weak strength and speed. Their wonderful moving devices and immense buildings implied great thought, supporting that idea.

Or perhaps their devices for moving, and their great buildings, had made strength less needed and it atrophied. In any case, he was stronger than they.

He leaped easily past another pair that moved to intercept him and landed at the side of the woman with the magical brown hair glinting red. Given the slow reflexes of this tribe, he knew he could escape with the woman back out under the sky. Perhaps she would know where to go from there.

But the woman fled from him, as though in fear, and he stopped, confused. Hadn't she felt the bond between them?

But, of course not. He was the one cut off from his tribe and alone, not her. He felt an affinity for her simply because he had no one else. These others, the ones that would part them, were her people, perhaps even tribefriends or more. She had summoned them with the talking tool in the house where he first found himself.

He was the stranger here. He was the one who had no one. These people were breaking no codes against forced parting simply because he had no tribe-bonds to be parted. He had reacted too quickly, too impetuously. That was always a failing with him, his passion too near the surface and too quick to anger.

These people had great knowledge. Surely they also had great wisdom. Perhaps he could trust them to help him find his way back to his people.

Kar-Tur relaxed body and mind and let himself be taken and led into the deeper parts of this strange building in a strange world he both feared and delighted to explore.

Chapter 26

Jonathan arrived at the physics building in time to see a group of
police cars breaking up and driving away. It wasn't until he checked
Susan's office and found Cynthia there alone that he thought to
wonder what police were doing at the building. Cynthia had also just
arrived, and after a few minutes waiting, they grew worried. Under
normal circumstances, they might have been less concerned. But
events of the past days and weeks were not normal circumstances.

They chatted sporadically about their growing concerns, serving
both to comfort each other that all was well, and to stir up additional
fears that neither could have formulated alone. Why were the police
here? Why were both Jen and Susan *not* here? It reached a pitch of
nervous concern that demanded resolution, and the only question
was what to do first.

"Susan would be here unless something happened," Cynthia said.
"So calling her won't help, and she doesn't keep a phone with her
anyway. Maybe the police caught the intruder who's been bothering
Susan. That would explain the police being here but no ambulance.
Susan and Jen may be at the police station, waiting for us. Why don't
we just go see?"

"Shall we go together?" Jonathan asked.

"Sure."

They took Jonathan's car. The trip to the local police station was
short in distance, but long in worry. Jonathan tried to call Jen a couple
of times but got no answer. Each stoplight seemed interminable.
The shortest route took them past a high-rise apartment complex,
which would not be congested normally, but a construction zone
slowed traffic.

They didn't talk much. He realized that Cynthia, with her
husband newly buried, shouldn't have to bear another emotional
blow so soon. He should encourage her. Comfort her with the
likelihood that Susan was perfectly safe. But he felt a terrible fear

growing in his gut that this smart, fun, lovely woman he had come to love has not going to be waiting for them at the police station, and, overcome by his own fear, he stayed silent.

Cynthia laid a hand on his shoulder as he sat at a traffic light. "I know how hard it is to lose someone you love. But Susan is going to be ok, and Jen will be too. So many tragedies couldn't come so close together."

Jonathan appreciated her support, even as he didn't believe her. When a coherent force, something unseen, was *causing* those tragedies, then *of course* they could occur close together. But maybe, maybe Susan was safe. If Susan was safe, then had something happened to Jen? He didn't think he could bear to lose either of them.

Cynthia squeezed his shoulder and then withdrew her hand. "If Jen or Susan were injured or killed, the office would have been cordoned off. Police would still be there. I think they're ok."

This time Cynthia's reasoning convinced him more. Indeed, the police wouldn't have left so quickly from the scene of a crime. And, if someone were injured, why did neither of them see an ambulance?

"That makes sense," he said.

Maybe he and Cynthia, made fearful by recent events, were simply letting their imaginations run away from them. There were, after all, many possible reasons for Susan and Jen to miss their appointment, and for the police to be on campus, other than tragedy or murder. Hadn't he only recently reasoned that whoever was watching them sought information rather than something more deadly?

Or was he rationalizing away real danger? Letting hope construct imaginary realities that recent events rendered unlikely?

His mind was still tangled up in hope and fear when they approached the police station. As they pulled up to the curb to park, his eyes turned to the entrance in time to see Jen just coming out. He felt himself sag with relief—she was all right after all. However, as he watched, the door swung closed behind her. She was alone. No Susan.

Jen looked up and saw them and headed in their direction. As she got close, Jonathan took in her face for the first time. Her mouth was pressed into a hard line, her eyes a blazing mingle of fury and fear. She opened the door and got in the back seat.

"Is Susan here, too?" Jonathan asked. "Should we wait for her?"

Jen shook her head sharply. "No. She wasn't at her office when I got there. I don't know where she is."

Jonathan saw Cynthia's shoulders slump. She stared out the windshield in blank silence.

"It's not like Susan to miss an appointment." Jonathan said, pulling away from the curb. "Where can she be?"

"There was a man in her office when I got there." Jen described her encounter in Susan's office. "I'm afraid he may have taken her. Maybe killed her. A violent, frightening man. I think he must be the one who kidnapped and interrogated me. He's that type."

Jonathan glanced back at Jen, raising his eyebrows. Not like Jen to be so quick with judgment. She couldn't possibly know this man was the one who kidnapped her. He worried how the ordeal of her recent kidnapping might have affected her thinking and behavior. He also wondered what type of man this was, to frighten and anger her so.

"What did he do?" Jonathan asked. "Where is he now?"

"The police have him." Jen shivered, like a dog trying to throw off muddy water. "He was quiet at first, almost too quiet. Then suddenly, he just snapped and attacked me. Or acted like he was going to attack me anyway. I've no doubt he's capable of attacking Susan as well."

Jonathan felt desperate to find Susan. But, between Cynthia's discouraged silence and Jen's irrational anger, he doubted they were in any condition to help him. They could help later. For now, he'd have to look for Susan on his own.

Jonathan dropped Jen and Cynthia off at their cars parked near the physics building, but didn't continue on to his own home. Instead, he parked his own car nearby and slipped down the concrete steps to the outside door that led to Susan's basement lab which was in the same building as her office but in the basement two stories lower.

Despite Jen's anger-tainted arguments, he was skeptical that the man in Susan's office had taken or killed her. If he'd taken Susan somewhere, why was he still in her office? If he killed her, where was the body? It didn't make sense.

He had a different idea of where to look.

A light glowed from Susan's lab windows. A sudden hope overcame him that she might be there, somehow oblivious to the turmoil in her office. Susan was very dependable and punctual for professional meetings. Sometimes she was more forgetful of personal ones. Maybe she forgot their meeting, or lost track of the time.

He ran the last several yards to her door. As her lab came into view through the window, Jonathan saw Professor Myrvik working at Susan's computer.

Disappointment transformed quickly to suspicion. What right had this man to be messing in Susan's lab while she was missing? Then he realized that Dr. Myrvik might not even know she'd disappeared. He might have missed the bustle of police. Maybe he came down here to Susan's lab before the police arrived.

Dr. Myrvik gave a start and looked up with a guilty expression when he opened the door, making Jonathan suspect he really had little honest business at her computer. He wondered what part the professor might play in recent events.

Dr. Myrvik recovered quickly and smiled. "I'm sorry for jumping like that, but I really don't have Susan's permission to be snooping on her computer. I thought you might be her. I need to get some of her results and notes off the computer for a departmental report that's due Monday."

"Susan is missing." Jonathan offered no preamble or explanation.

Dr. Myrvik looked blank for a moment. "Missing? I saw her just an hour or two ago in her office upstairs."

"She's missing now. And the police caught some guy in her office."

Jonathan watched Dr. Myrvik's response. It seemed unlikely that he would sneak around in Susan's lab if he weren't involved with her disappearance. However, the professor looked genuinely startled, gasping a bit like a landed fish.

"Surely, she'll turn up," he said. However, from the doubtful look on his face, Dr. Myrvik knew as well as he that Susan wouldn't miss an appointment or disappear without alerting friends. He made a little sweeping motion with his hand, as though trying, subconsciously perhaps, to get Jonathan out the door. But if Myrvik wanted additional private access to Susan' computer he wasn't going to get it. Jonathan held his ground.

When Jonathan made no move to leave, the professor returned his attention to the computer, apparently sending something, then rose. He looked at Jonathan as though to speak.

Jonathan spoke first. "I'll lock the door when I leave."

He had something to check that might relate to Susan's disappearance. He was in no mood to beg permission to stay and in no mood to be forced to leave before concluding his business.

Dr. Myrvik hesitated, perhaps weighing his own apparent eagerness to be gone, the wisdom of leaving Jonathan alone in Susan's lab, and the awkward fact that Jonathan caught him snooping on Susan's computer. At last he shrugged.

"Sure," he said, and left.

Surprising that he left Susan's computer available. Maybe he thought Jonathan couldn't find what he had been looking for. Or maybe Dr. Myrvik deleted whatever he took from the computer so no one else, Jonathan included, could find it.

It didn't matter. He wasn't interested in the computer or in whatever Dr. Myrvik took from it.

Although, the computer *was* his point of reference in Susan's lab. The shimmer in her video occurred beside the computer.

He wanted to talk to that shimmer, that *being*, from the video. The shimmering beings were involved in these puzzling events. They might be the Rosetta Stone that gave the babble of events meaning.

Although he had to be careful. A shimmering being killed Mike. Clearly, they were dangerous.

He stood by the area where the shimmer appeared in the video, and called out.

At first he wasn't sure it was anything, a glimmer at the edge of his vision. Then a colorful patch began to materialize in the air, with the rainbow appearance of sunlight on oily film in a parking lot. As near as he could tell, it was in the very same location as in Susan's video.

It wasn't a voice he heard. More like a *communing*. A sense in his mind.

"What do you wish?" it asked.

"I want to know what you've done with Susan Arasmith." Jonathan spoke aloud, hoping this being could hear it.

"Is she the one who traveled?" the being thought in his mind.

Jonathan had no idea what this meant. A kidnap victim did 'travel' of sorts, he supposed.

"Yes," he said.

The being said nothing for perhaps a minute. Jonathan grew uneasy, but judged it wise to wait. If these beings took Susan, his only chance to get her back might lie in patience. The being hovered a few feet in the air, not quite touching the ground. Its humanoid form shimmered in and out of view. He saw arms and legs now and then, although, often, only a central glow was visible.

It communed again. "Is this one your friend?"

"Yes. She's my friend. I love her."

Again there was a long silence before the shimmer spoke. "This one, your friend, has done great harm. And your kind, through her, have done great harm."

The shimmering was starting to fade. What did it mean, "done great harm"? What could Susan do to these beings?

The shimmer spoke again. "We allow movement in thinking, not wanting to judge unfairly. But as we go, we decide what is to be done."

The shimmer began to disappear, fading toward oblivion. Jonathan cried out frantically. "What do you mean *decide what is to be done?* Tell me where she is!"

But he was shouting at empty space. The shimmer was already gone.

Chapter 27

Cynthia listened as Jen ranted about the man she caught in Susan's office. She'd never heard such hostility in Jen's voice before. It seemed unlike her, at least unlike who she was prior to the kidnapping.

She knew Jen still suffered the effects of her kidnapping. What Jen had told her of it was horrific. But Jen never talked about how she *felt* about it; she only described what *happened*. And she often joked about that, evading its gravity. Although, her anger about it came through more and more often.

"We don't know this man did anything to Susan, Jen." Cynthia said, washing the last spoon. "Jonathan thinks the shimmering beings are involved. The shimmering beings like the one….." She left her sentence unfinished and focused on a bit of potato dried to the spoon.

"You didn't see how he leaped at me at the police station," Jen said. "He was so powerful—he tore himself free from two police officers holding him like they were nothing. He could have probably escaped outside, but he went after me instead. He wanted to intimidate me. He wanted me to know he could do anything to me he wanted.

"And you didn't see him there in Susan's office," Jen continued. "Half naked. Staring at me. Daring me to call the police. I...I don't know, his strength when he so easily broke away from the police was...all I can think about is when someone came up behind me, and put their arms around me, really strong arms, and..." she faded away with a shiver. "And what gets me is that he wasn't afraid. Not of the police, or facing justice. Just like the man who kidnapped me." Her hands tightened around her ceramic cup.

Cynthia looked away to give her a moment of privacy. She checked the table again to see if she'd left anything. Some part of her thought the dishes weren't done yet. It still seemed strange to have so few dishes when she had a guest for dinner. Astonishing that she could notice just one plate missing.

"Jen," Cynthia said, "He does sound frightening, and he has to be involved somehow. But we don't know he took Susan. Or kidnapped you. Why was he still in Susan's office? Why would he pretend to not understand English?"

She paused a moment. "Would you want to talk about what happened? When you were kidnapped?"

"There's nothing to tell that I haven't told already," Jen dried the last dish and set it in the cupboard. "And with so much new happening, it doesn't make sense to talk about what's already washed down the river."

Cynthia nodded. "Let's go sit down in the living room. We can talk there."

She felt frustrated by Jen's reticence. Jen needed to talk. Something was eating her up inside. Fear, or anger, or hate, or *something*. Something clouding her judgment and darkening her personality. Cynthia hoped Jen had other friends she could talk to about it, but she thought that unlikely. Jen showed all the signs of bottling a problem, one carefully preserved, fermented, waiting to explode.

All she could do was invite. She couldn't force Jen to share with her. Cynthia felt embarrassed remembering how open she was with Jen when Mike died. She'd poured out her heart. She had to. She needed someone, and Jen was there. But clearly, Jen believed sharing was a kind of weakness. She wasn't going to share, only invite others to it.

They talked about general things, the evening, the kids and their school activities. They even talked about Susan some more, wondering, hoping.

"Jonathan's taking it very hard," Cynthia said. "He and Susan grew very close."

"Yes, I'm very glad for them," Jen replied.

An awkward silence fell, which Cynthia saw Jen pretending to ignore.

"Jen, did Jonathan liking Susan bother you?"

Jen smiled and ran her fingers along the fabric of the overstuffed chair. "Of course not. Why should it? I'd be a poor friend if I wasn't delighted for him."

"Human feelings are complex things," Cynthia said. "Sometimes talking about them helps us understand them."

"Well, my feelings aren't very complex." Jen exaggerated a sigh. "I guess I'm just a feelings-simpleton." She laughed. "Why don't you tell me how *you* are, Cynth. How are things going for you and the kids? When you lose someone, it's always harder after all the crowds of sympathizers go home, and you're alone."

Cynthia didn't laugh when Jen did. Her lips tightened, and she tried for a time to restrain her anger. But Jen's clumsy effort to divert attention from her own problems and feelings was too much. She rose from the couch and headed to the kitchen, hoping to hide her feelings. But Jen was sensitive that way. She knew.

"Cynth, what's wrong?" Jen's voice, filled with concern, followed her into the kitchen. Cynthia wondered suddenly how much of that concern was real. How much of Jen was real? And how much was just a façade?

She turned back to Jen. There was nothing to do now but say the truth. Maybe it would heal things. Maybe it would let them know their friendship had no further to go. Either way, it had to be done.

"Why'd you pick me as a friend, Jen?" Cynthia asked.

Jen fidgeted, clearly uncomfortable with the sudden turn in the conversation.

Of *course* she was uncomfortable, Cynthia thought. She always avoided what was hard.

"I was ready for a friend, I think." Jen was standing, apparently unsure whether to chase her toward the kitchen or stay with the overstuffed chair. "You seemed introspective, like me. We both liked walking, and the quiet. We didn't always have to talk. Sometimes just being together was enough. I liked that."

Jen paused. Her eyes were full of tears. That was all it took for tears to spring into Cynthia's own eyes.

Jen continued. "Even though you have a bright mind, you're centered more on people and relationships than ideas. I wanted a friend like that."

Jen couldn't meet her eyes and returned to her chair where she sat fidgeting. Cynthia cringed at Jen's discomfort. Clearly, she'd rather be anywhere, doing anything other than conversing with her. Jen didn't want the stress, the pouring emotions. But Cynthia had to say what had to be said. And she was still angry. Fire flashed through her tears.

"Our friendship has come quickly, Jen. I needed a friend. Someone to talk to. You were there for me. Friendships are often like that.

"But I don't know you, Jen. It's hard to know you. You hide from people. You hide behind humor. You hide behind your interest in other people. You divert every conversation away from yourself, like you just did when I asked about your feelings for Jonathan.

"You're a good listener, and I like that. But you hide too much of your own feelings and thoughts. I don't know what you're like inside. I tell you everything about me, share my pain over Mike and now Susan. But what do you tell me of your inner world? People who can listen are rare and wonderful, Jen. And I value it. But you can't only listen. You have to share too."

Cynthia paused, her breathing heavy. Whatever was done, was done now.

The tears in Jen's eyes had burst their dam and trickled down her cheeks, leaving windy, shiny paths. Cynthia wondered what churned in her mind behind those teary eyes, wondered who she kept locked up secret inside her. Jen's inner world was a complex one, Cynthia knew. Complex inner worlds were so fraught with evolving character and deep feeling. Cynthia knew how hard it was to identify deep feeling, let alone share it. She knew because she too fought that battle to know in her own mind what she felt or thought.

Jen apologized over and over, pleading for forgiveness. But Cynthia was looking for openness, not apologies.

Somehow, Jen must have perceived that, and stopped apologizing.

"It's very hard for me, Cynth," she managed.

With this try at openness, Cynthia's anger melted away. She realized she was being unfair. She'd been under a great strain as well as Jen. She wasn't herself.

"I'm sorry, Jen. I'm distraught. So much has happened."

"No, you're right," Jen said through tears. "To be a friend, to ask my friends to share their life, I have to share mine. And I do want your friendship. But, can you give me time to work on it?"

"Of course," Cynthia said, flooded with relief that she hadn't cut the wings of a fledgling friendship before it learned to fly.

Chapter 28

The Senator from California stood at his window and gazed out over L.A. It was a dirty little city. But it was his city. He would watch over it.

His people were ready. Even now, his private army prepared in the East Indies, ready for whatever he called them to do. And with the President's backing, he'd control the U.S. military as well.

His domestic machine also pleased him. His man on Susan did well, checking on her work, her contacts, her friends. Unfortunate that Raven had been caught on a video cam. Clever Susan. He'd have to send Raven back to the East Indies. He'd be valuable again once war broke out and domestic security waned.

Each day brought crisper operation from his people. The operation with the woman, and her testing, had been conducted perfectly. No one would ever trace the people or the facility.

Only losing his contact with the Shimera still disappointed him. But maybe that wasn't so great a loss as he thought at first. The Shimera that died, his contact, wasn't as all-knowing as he claimed. Not everything happened as the being predicted. Despite his arrogance, the strange being provided only partial knowledge.

And now he was dead. No doubt another oversight on his part.

The Shimera had seemed angry throughout their interactions. Angry and in great sorrow. Anger and sorrow that no doubt clouded its judgment. That even godlike beings fell when they failed to submit emotion to self-interest intrigued the Senator.

Whatever the being's shortcomings, it had managed to cue the Senator in to the great events unfolding in L.A. The Senator turned his thoughts to the man taken into custody by the police and how he might gain access to him. The police wouldn't be able to identify him of course. And no crime could be tied to him. Eventually they'd have to free him or deport him. But he had no native country. Where would they send him?

If the Shimera was right at least on this one point, the man was one of two people crucial to gaining power in this present age. He needed to get to him unobtrusively. Perhaps he should simply await his release. He could call in a few favors to ensure the man wasn't deported, or incarcerated for too long.

The CalTech professor still promised to be an important cog in the machine. He had done well acquiring Susan's data and a few notes, not really a necessary task, but a good test of the man's loyalty and ability. The notes weren't too extensive anyway, as he already knew from Raven. Apparently, Susan kept many of her notes in her head.

He'd looked over the experimental results, with no great insights yet. He would have to continue to consider them. He now held in his hands two pieces of the three-piece puzzle, those two being Susan's experiments and Jen Hewitt's background and mental profile. Now he had only to get what he needed out of the man from the past.

The President still backed him. Such a weak man, scarcely seeing the imperative to seize the greatest opportunity in all of human history. Never before had such a conjunction of stars arisen in the sky of human destiny. And never would such arise again.

This was opportunity not simply to play king with nations and people. These next weeks and months offered opportunity to shape the destiny of humanity for all time and to transform the very fabric of reality that humanity would live within.

Of course, he hadn't really explained that to the President. Yet. He would reveal it in his own time.

Eventually, stronger minds would see that the President wasn't his own man. They would hear the Senator's voice in his. The Senator needed to gain more extensive backing in preparation for that inevitability. He needed the support of the whole nation behind him.

He must find a means to gain that support. Some opportunity would arise, he simply needed to be ready. Something would happen. Something always did.

The Senator cast one last look across the city, the sea lying to his left, the hills to the right. He could almost make out his uncle's house right between the two, nestled on the north side of town. His uncle had appreciated the short letter he'd sent. Now it was time to give his uncle a call.

He sat down at his desk, propping his feet up on the edge, and pulled out his phone. He placed the call and waited for his uncle's hello.

"Hi Walt," he said. "It's me, Jerry. How have you been?"

He listened politely as Walt talked about something or other. When Walt's words had run their course, he made his request.

"Say, Walt, I've got a guy, a refugee of sorts, that I'm trying give a safe place to stay. I was wondering if you might be able to help me out."

Chapter 29

Kar-Tur still could not understand what his jailors told him, but the words no longer sounded so alien. He recognized the edges of the words, where each began and ended. He thought he understood the words for simple things like food and water.

His room wasn't unpleasant. He might have even called it elegant by his own standards. But the finest home was only a hovel when one couldn't leave.

He wasn't yet impatient with his imprisonment. He spent the first few days in the jail examining all the amazing tools in it, delighting to infer the purpose for each. He felt the fabrics of the bed, and the magical material that made the walls and bars themselves. He couldn't fathom the skill that could make such things.

The clothes he wore fascinated him. The clothes differed in color from what the guards wore, being more like those of the woman he met first. They felt soft on his skin. They were thin, yet amazingly strong. He wondered how so much strength could be packed into such thin material.

After a few days of examining what he found inside his prison, he turned his attention to the guards. He watched them, hoping to learn the ways of this tribe. Slowly, he became familiar with their tools. Some were for eating and drinking. Some manipulated other tools, such as opening doors or keeping the thin white leaves with funny pictures on them organized. All of the people of this tribe carried little boxes that they drew pictures on, or examined carefully, or talked into. These must store their thoughts and traditions, as his own tribe used pictures on stone. Sometimes, they took instructions from these boxes, and he wondered if the boxes were more than tools. Their behavior made him wonder if, in some way, the strange little boxes were fellow tribesmen to these people.

Many people came to his jail-room to talk to him. None understood him.

After a time, he realized that the pattern of speech for each differed from the speech of those who guarded him. Perhaps there were many languages known to this tribe. He knew that other tribes often spoke differently from his own. Sometimes, in trading with other tribes, someone who knew the language of both tribes interpreted between them. Perhaps this tribe searched for someone who spoke the language of Kar-Tur's people, so they might communicate together.

But he understood none of them. There were commonalities among all the languages he knew of. Similarities between patterns of speech. But he found no such commonality between his own tongue and any of those he heard here.

Indeed, an immense distance must lie between this place and his people to cause the language to differ so much. He began to despair that he would ever see his tribe again.

Kar-Tur wondered who these magical people were who made beds so soft and walls so hard.

He wondered if they were gods.

Searching for the gods was new to his people. Kar-Tur's own father first began that search. Kar-Tur continued that tradition as the *seeker* of his tribe.

As seeker, he sought higher beings who watched or cared or participated. Beings as much greater than he as he was greater than the ants so proud of their granaries and cities.

As seeker, he wondered if he were *made*. Made, like one made a spear. The spear was organized and held purpose. It was not haphazard. Likewise, *he* was organized with purpose. It implied intellect and order in the world. If order and intellect existed beyond his own ability to create them, didn't that prove there must be gods?

But a natural order existed that did not demand the gods' participation. He knew that the behavior of the universe could be *understood*, and in being understood, controlled. Harnessing the power of stone, wood, and fire came from that understanding. *Understanding* the world seemed more immediately effective and reliable than appealing to the gods for intervention. Through his understanding, Kar-Tur had aided his tribe in the hunt, making spear throwing more efficient, and spear points more effective. That required no unnatural intervention from the gods.

But if gods made the natural world, why should he expect their participation in it to appear unnatural? Wouldn't the gods' participation fit seamlessly into their creation, embedded in the very natural behavior of it?

Many in his tribe worshipped gods. Sometimes they worshipped hoping to control their gods, and, through them, their world. And sometimes they worshiped just to bring all the tribe together into one purpose.

But Kar-Tur wondered if gods existed who were *real*. If they were real, were they like these powerful beings who built houses to the sky and moved faster than the spirit of the air?

Kar-Tur thought not. Real gods must be higher than human in origin, perhaps from realms not seen with one's eyes. Otherwise, they would not be gods, only members of a more powerful tribe or race.

This tribe that held him prisoner did seem powerful. What, if anything, reached beyond their capabilities? Was there a limit to their power and understanding?

But power was not enough to make them gods.

Considering the limits to human power reminded Kar-Tur of his long vigil at the fire, and the terrible, wonderful insight that had sent him to his present situation. There, in his vigil, he saw possibility for greater human power in the universe than even this tribe exhibited. There existed a deep part of the universe that would bend to human will. A place where humans could go and touch the very essence of existence. In that place, he saw potential for great creation or great destruction. Somehow, he had tapped that potential and come to this new world.

But there was still a part that humans could *not* control. This new power was for the asking, not for the dictating. He sensed in the nature of what he saw during his vigil that he could not *control*, so much as *choose*. To gain authority over this power, he must learn to understand that distinction between controlling and choosing.

He puzzled over that part of existence that humans could not control. An order and intellect existed in the universe that humans did not create, to which they were subject. Yet order and intellect surely must originate from *sentience*. Did that prove there were gods who made that order? Or were there other explanations?

The immense universe teemed with grand mysteries seething like living things just beneath the surface of a restless sea. His place as seeker gave him a secure place in the tribe, and he enjoyed seeking the gods and guiding his tribe in that search. It was a task not likely to be soon completed.

He felt confident that his discovery of this powerful tribe did not complete his search. They were not gods.

***

Kar-Tur couldn't see the sun, so he didn't know how much time had passed since his captors brought him to this place. But assuming this tribe's eating patterns related to the morning and evening, he had been here a few more days than he had fingers. That meant the time past was about half the time for the Moon to disappear and return.

One day they brought a new person to see him. This one wore clothes more like Kar-Tur's own new clothes, or the woman's. He came with three guards. Unlike his former visitors, this one did not attempt to talk to him. Rather, he spent much time arguing with the guards he came with. He showed them some of the funny little pictures on his personal little box, after which one of the guards came to the barred door of Kar-Tur's room and opened it.

Kar-Tur rose smoothly from the bed where he was seated. His eyes watched them alertly. Were they releasing him? Or did they have some less pleasant plan?

The guard beckoned him from the cell and he slipped out quickly, glad to be free from the small room. He scanned this outer room checking for exits he might use to escape, but all he found were more rooms and doorways of a building large beyond his previous experience.

They led him toward the room he had first entered half a moon ago. From that room, only a single doorway separated him from the outside. Kar-Tur knew he could escape from that room.

He considered whether he wanted to escape. This world held

mysteries foreign to him. He understood little of it. This tribe still might be his best hope for safety and finding a means to return to his people.

But they had shown little inclination to help him thus far. Perhaps they didn't even know how. They could not yet talk to him, proving their limitations. It seemed, then, that his best hope lay in escape and seeking his own way.

As they came into the outer room, Kar-Tur's quick eyes spotted both the doorway to the outside and the distribution of men and women around the room. He knew they were too slow to stop him.

He shrugged off the grip of the guards who held him, and slipped quickly toward the door. He'd taken only a couple of steps when he felt a bee sting him in the neck. His hand reached reflexively to swat it away, but his hand seemed sluggish. He felt himself falling, his legs disobediently collapsing beneath him. As he fell, he turned, and saw the visitor above him, a stick-like device in his hand.

Then Kar-Tur lost consciousness.

Chapter 30

The highway stretched nearly empty ahead as Jack drove to the police station. Seven o'clock on a Sunday morning was often quiet. The sabbath-resters read the newspaper, or fished, or curled up with a book. The church-goers bustled around preparing for a morning of worship, not yet gone from the house. The partiers slept, at last.

So, it was quiet. The downtown skyscrapers rose above the horizon like tombstones. The vacant expanse of roadway reached toward the tombstones like a life reaching toward its vacant end.

Jack Myrvik had felt the vacancy of his life of late. His wife's infidelity had hit him hard, and when she took the kids he'd realized how much they had embodied his sense of purpose. A successful career was never quite good enough to compensate for the chance to make a more direct difference in people's lives. So, it pleased him to participate in the Senator's work. He believed in it. It made him feel needed and valued again.

The Senator's letter had astounded him, asking him to pick up a man *from the past* at the police station. A man from the past? What did that mean? Time travel? What did it have to do with Susan or her experiments?

He believed in this Senator and his plan. The power to *travel in time* certainly bore too great an impact on humanity to leave in the hands of chance, or an individual. If ever a time came for government intervention in ordinary lives, or a time for government compromise of ordinary liberties, this was such a time.

The state had clear interest in the safety of this man, both to protect him from the world, and to protect the world from what he knew.

To be part of such great events gave Jack a renewed sense of purpose.

He reached the police station and pulled into a parking spot. As the Senator had promised, his contact met him at the car, and

Myrvik rolled down his window as he approached.

"You Dr. Myrvik?" he asked.

Jack nodded. "Yes. And you have a passenger for me?"

"Yes indeed, but I need for you to pull over to the side door, there." He pointed to the north end of the building. "We had to sedate him."

"Uh, ok." Jack restarted the engine. "What am I supposed to do when he wakes back up?"

"The Senator says he'll be OK once he's out of custody." The man tapped Jack's car hood a couple of times as if to say 'get going.'

Jack pulled the car as close to the side door as he could get. Two police emerged with an unconscious man between them. Jack opened the rear door of the car and they tucked the man inside. He wasn't particularly notable, no sign saying "I'm a cave man" or anything. His eyes and face had a faintly Asian appearance, although not enough that Jack would have called him Asian. He wasn't particularly tall, although his clothes fit tight around a muscular build.

Muscular enough that Jack definitely hoped the Senator knew what he was doing. Seemed a bit risky to trust this guy to the custody of civilians, both for the safety of the civilians and for the safety of the man from the past.

Although, he understood why the police couldn't deal with the man. So far as formal records could reveal, he didn't exist. Police could never match his face or fingerprints to anyone. He had no dental records. He had no language they could know.

Jack felt good about having a chance to do something for someone again. This man needed refuge.

A bit odd that the Senator didn't simply take the man into government custody. That kind of thing happened. The Senator could use the fact that the man was not a citizen, not granted the same rights as others, to do whatever was necessary. Voters wouldn't care about the fate of a foreigner.

That the Senator didn't take that route made Jack suspect that more went on behind the scenes than he knew. With stakes so high, there must be many ambitious people with less noble intentions than the Senator who might try to seize this man and his power.

With the man from the past situated in the rear of the car, the police removed the cuffs they had on his hands and closed the door. "He's yours," one of them said, and they both disappeared back into the station.

Jack got back in the car and started the engine. He wondered if the police thought it odd that a man who spoke no English, and seemed involved in a possible crime, should be released into the custody of a university professor. Surprise was the nature of life, he supposed. People must get used to it. He'd certainly been surprised by his wife's affair. He'd thought they were so close.

His thoughts lingered on his wife for a moment. He wondered if his lack of awareness meant that he'd taken her for granted, hadn't paid enough attention to their relationship. He wished he could go back and try it over again.

He would never take her for granted again if he had another chance.

With a few quick taps he keyed up the map to the Roden house and backed out of the parking spot. Jack liked the man and woman who'd offered to give the time traveler sanctuary. He'd visited Walt and Karen yesterday, talking about how to get the man to their home and how to keep him hidden. They seemed kindly and gentle, able to offer a warm refuge. Jack thought with some irony that he'd like such a refuge for himself.

Jack remembered now where he'd heard Walt's name. Walt Roden was one of Susan's lab assistants for the Uncertainty experiments. How coincidental.

Chapter 31

Light rain was falling from a gray sky as I stepped out from th church. Low clouds drifted in off the sea, and intermittent showers swept the air in short bursts, each sending a spray of tiny droplets dancing over the warm asphalt. It was the first precipitation of fall, and the dusty scent of rain in the parched city was refreshing after the long, dry summer. I left my windows partly open to let in the smell of rain as I made my way across town to Cynthia's house.

I hadn't seen Cynthia in a couple weeks, although not because of our argument. My teaching had kept me busy and I'd finally found the motivation to start writing my dissertation.

I'd also stayed busy hiding from my recent troubles. Hiding from oneself took a lot of time, I discovered. All the good hiding places were already used up. The only good spots left were work-related. Thus, my prompt to start my dissertation. I decided writing was better than morbid thoughts.

So, to try to reconnect, I'd made plans to stop by Cynthia's for ice cream after church. As I walked up the sidewalk to her house, I thought about our last encounter. I knew Cynthia wanted openness from me. She took that as a sign of friendship and trust. But I didn't know how to be open.

I knew my inner self well. But it was a complex self, and character was always a moving target. I wasn't *sure* about my inner feelings, and how could I talk about myself before I really *knew* what was true?

I wanted Cynthia's friendship, but I was afraid to reveal too much for fear she wouldn't like the inner me. Maybe I could start small. Just try to share *one* thing.

Adam, as well as Cynthia, met me at the door. "Aunt Jen would let me go," he said before I was scarcely through the doorway. "Wouldn't you?" He looked at me, pleading.

"Let you go where, Adam?" I discouraged friends' children

from calling me "aunt" when I wasn't really their aunt, especially after such a short time. Was friendship somehow not sufficiently intimate so that people had to pretend genetic relationships in order to feel close? But Adam was clearly upset and his real aunt was still missing, so now wasn't the time to be critical.

"Mom won't let me go to a party," he said. "Everyone is going."

"Everyone?" I tried to find a way to lighten the mood. "That's really a lot of people."

"I mean all my friends," Adam said.

"What kind of party is it, Adam?" I asked.

"They're meeting at a quarry in the mountains. It'll be really fun."

"Ask him what time it starts," Cynthia inserted.

Adam glanced at her in irritation. "It starts at nine o'clock next Friday."

"Nine in the *evening*?" I asked, astonished. "Golly, Adam, I think I have to side with your Mom."

Adam cast another angry look at Cynthia. "Dad would've let me go."

"You don't know that, Adam." Cynthia said.

Adam tromped off up the stairs to his room. I smiled at Cynthia, conveying patience with the foibles of life, youth, and parenting.

Cynthia had mint chocolate chip ice cream, my favorite. I ate slowly, matching our conversation. We didn't say much, but it didn't feel awkward.

I finished my ice cream as Cynthia's phone rang. While Cynthia answered, I rose and took a turn around the living room. Cynthia had a nice house, filled with life and family. Pictures of Mike were on the end table by the couch and on a knick-knack shelf over the fireplace. I marveled that Cynthia kept his picture out, reminding herself of her loss. I thought that I would not handle the pain of losing a mate as well as Cynthia. But, on reflection, I decided I'd rather lose a mate than never have a mate at all.

There were other pictures on the shelf. Pictures of Erin and Adam, as well as pictures of others I didn't know. I presumed they were cousins, grandparents, aunts, and uncles.

A picture of Susan was there too.

Where was Susan? And how could we find her?

The strain in Cynthia's voice as she talked on the phone distracted me from my questions. "Are you sure, Jonathan? Why would they do that?"

A long silence followed. I looked again at the picture of Susan. Something about it troubled me. I couldn't put my finger on what. I wondered when I'd see her again.

Cynthia disconnected the call, and I rejoined her at the table. "What was that about?" I asked.

"Detective Raumin called Jonathan to tell him the man you found in Susan's office was released today. Apparently he was taken to a safe house that even the police weren't supposed to know of."

"How can they do that!" I exclaimed, immediately angry and afraid. "They can't just release him!"

Cynthia shrugged but said nothing for a minute.

"Why are you so angry at this man, Jen?" Cynthia asked. "Surely there's no evidence linking him to your kidnapping or they wouldn't have released him."

I struggled to assemble my feelings. Even if he wasn't my kidnapper, I still didn't like him. He *reminded* me of my kidnappers. He was *like* them.

"He's a dangerous man, Cynth. I'm afraid of him."

She nodded, but I could see she wasn't convinced.

"Cynth," I continued, "No one raped me when I was kidnapped, so far as I remember. But I *felt* raped. I think I'm afraid of angry, aggressive men in a way I wasn't before."

There! I thought to myself. I did it! I'd been open with Cynthia. I felt triumphant.

Cynthia reached across the table and squeezed my arm. "We aren't always as safe as we like to think we are." she said. "That's scary, too."

Yes, that was it. It wasn't only that I was attacked, but that I was forced to realize my vulnerability. I missed the comfortable safety I used feel.

"Maybe I *am* being a bit over-generous with my new-found distrust," I acknowledged.

Cynthia smiled, just a little smile that seemed to say that life is full of complexities. "Sometimes we have to do both, trust and...not trust."

***

Something troubled me as I drove home from Cynthia's. I could not quite place the source of my discomfiture, although I thought it lay in something I saw there. I searched back through the last hours for images. A picture taunted me from the edge of my consciousness. Something I'd seen at Cynthia's house.

I called to mind each of the pictures that sat on Cynthia's well-kept shelves. I settled on the photograph of Susan, taken perhaps a year ago.

Realization struck me like a physical blow. For a moment, I froze, stunned by what it meant. I didn't want it to be so. I examined my thinking again, hoping that close inspection might reveal a flaw in my reasoning, an alternative to my interpretation. I slogged through my thinking, slowed by the dread that grew as each additional part to the puzzle fell into place. The pieces fit together so well, but my mind still tried to reject them, numb and cold at the implications for my friends and me.

This changed everything. So much that had been mysterious and impossible made complete sense.

One more thought occurred to me, almost as terrible as the last.

I would have to tell Jonathan.

***

I stopped by Jonathan's place on my way home. He returned to his desk after admitting me, papers and notes spread around him.

"I've been trying to figure out how to find out more about these shimmering beings," he said, "like the one I told you about meeting. I think they must have taken Susan. If I can talk to them again, maybe I can get more information."

He was talking fast, almost excited, obviously concerned for Susan but buoyed by the possibility of getting her back. Believing it was still possible.

I hated that I was about to shatter his hopes.

He was my friend. We'd been friends for years. We'd continue to be friends. My jealousy of Susan melted away at last, as I saw how much he loved her. How much he hoped to find her. I would give her back to him in a minute, if only I could.

"Jonathan," I said, taking a deep breath to give myself courage. "I have to tell you something."

He looked up at me, seeming to be startled that I interrupted his planning to find Susan.

"I saw a picture of Susan at Cynthia's house when I was there today," I said. "You know she doesn't usually wear jewelry, but she had jewelry on in that picture. I knew there was something unusual about it, and it stuck in my head, but at first I couldn't figure out why. She was wearing a broach. Just like the one we found in the Atosoka. It's the same broach."

I paused, giving him a chance to process. He simply looked at me, his mouth slightly open.

"Jonathan, it's Susan. The skeleton we found in Wyoming has to be her."

I watched dawning understanding play out on his face.

Susan, our friend, was the one who had communicated to us through the years, *knowing with certainty that we would hear that communication.* She knew exactly where a skeleton would be preserved, because she knew already where one had been found. She knew what objects to leave, and the story they would tell. Only she could know 40000 years ago to send her message in English. She knew already, before she wrote the message, who would receive it.

It was an older version of Susan, or all that remained of her, that we had found in that ancient grave.

Jonathan gazed off at nothing for a few moments, weighing what I was telling him against all that we'd seen and done. Weighing evidence to judge whether my conclusion was speculation or certainty.

The broach could be no one's but Susan's. And there was no reason to hope that, somehow, Susan wasn't wearing it.

Then sudden sag of his shoulder, the change in the angle of his body, revealed the very moment when he accepted that Susan wasn't coming back, that she could not come back because she was already dead, long ago. His back bowed as though with a terrible weight and his eyes turned down toward the carpet between his feet.

I rested my hand gently on his knee. "I'm sorry," I said.

He put his head in his hands and wept.

Chapter 32

Officer Sarah Mendez's message arrived on Detective Raumin's phone. Raven was indeed at the airport, awaiting a flight. Mendez and Officer Williams had him under surveillance.

Raumin had little time. Raven's flight left in less than thirty minutes, and at any moment he might suspect a trap and slip away. Mendez and Williams lacked the experience to track a man of Raven's connections and skills, once he decided to escape watching eyes. He'd have too many holes to hide in.

Raumin called the airport to request a few minutes delay in the flight, in case he needed it. Requesting more than that made no sense, since Raven would grow suspicious and be gone in any case.

By the time Raumin called for backup, he was already on the way to the airport. Raven was a dangerous man. Raumin wanted an overwhelming contingent at the airport before confronting him.

With a professional killer and trained terrorist, one couldn't be too careful. And Raven was the best, or worst, in the business.

But men like that tended to underestimate everyone else. Failing to imagine that others might have the same skills and knowledge they had, they could fall into a well-laid a trap.

Raumin had learned nearly a month ago of Raven's connections with a paramilitary group in the East Indies. Since Raven's effectiveness in the States could only diminish once he was identified as the intruder in Susan Arasmith's lab, Raumin had reasoned that it was only a matter of time before Raven returned to the safety of his haven in the East Indies.

So Raumin had decided to watch for flights to the East Indies, and the people who took those flights.

Raven was no fool. He had scheduled several flight changes, hopping from country to country to confuse the very type of search Raumin implemented, changing names from flight to flight and scheduling the flights with different online travel services. But he made one mistake, scheduling the flights from the same computer address. Raumin had acquired a search warrant to monitor the thousands of flight reservations made with many online companies to find that link. But once he found it, connecting the dots from Los Angeles to the East Indies became a simple matter. Then he had only to send people to look for Raven among the passengers of the flight from L.A.

Raumin arrived at the airport about the same time as his backup--eight experienced plainclothes officers. Airport security, already notified, nodded them around the scanners with brief but careful examinations of badges and weapons. Raumin's team melted into the press of travelers.

Raumin himself quickly spotted Raven reading a magazine at his gate, seemingly at ease. Raumin hung back at a coffee kiosk, silently counting the seconds, giving his team time to get in position. Wait. Wait. Now.

Raumin walked up to Raven and showed his badge. "Please come with me," he said

Raven gave a faint start as though surprised to be stopped by police. "I'm sorry officer, is there some problem?"

His eyes flitted beyond Raumin, assessing the route back down the terminal. Raumin knew what he would see: a casually attired but completely baggage-less person at every possible point of egress. Raven even seemed to consider the big glass windows that offered views of the tarmac and taxiing planes, but unless he had a pretty hefty battering ram he wasn't going through there.

Raumin offered a faint grin. "I guess you could say that." He pulled out his cuffs. "Your hands please."

***

When Jonathan Renner and Jennifer Hewitt arrived to identify Raven, Raumin went with them to the lineup. Mendez was already in the room when they arrived.

Raumin liked Renner. Although he meddled in police affairs a bit too boldly, he actually wasn't too bad at it. He'd done well in finding Hewitt. And, he was an intelligent and friendly guy.

But Jennifer Hewitt troubled him. Not because of anything

in particular about *her*. But he wondered why so much attention should be focused on one, seemingly ordinary, young woman. Why was she kidnapped and tested? Why did she, or her friends, warrant the attentions of a man such as Raven?

Raven, predictably, had told him almost nothing in interrogation. He claimed to know nothing of Susan's disappearance and that he acted alone in breaking into her apartment. That he was only looking for money.

But he did slip up once. When Raumin asked him about Susan Arasmith, about why she was important, Raven laughed and said, "Arasmith isn't the woman that's important." He had immediately realized his error and become even less communicative.

Who else but Hewitt might he have referred to? What about Hewitt made her important to an assassin and terrorist?

As Raumin joined the two civilians and Mendez in the viewing room, Raven stood scowling in the lineup, still arrogant and self-assured even in captivity.

"Take your time, and be certain," Raumin instructed them, as they looked in on the group of rough-looking men. He hoped they'd know the man. Sometimes memories blurred in the turbulence of an attack. Or worse, memories were very clear, but wrong.

He need not have worried. Jonathan Renner and Jennifer Hewitt both identified Raven positively. They'd seen him in full light, and close up, when he charged them during his escape from Susan's apartment.

"You can feel safer now," Raumin said as he walked with them back into the police station lobby.

But he didn't really believe it, and he knew that Renner and Hewitt probably didn't either. It wasn't the open enemy who scowled at you that you needed to fear. The one to fear was the hidden enemy, the one who profoundly believed in the rightness of his actions and was willing to impose the consequences of those actions on others with warm smiles and good intentions.

Who was that enemy?

As he led Renner and Hewitt back toward the entrance to the station, Officer Williams called across the squad room.

"Hey, Noodle, did you get an ID on the guy we brought in?"

"Yeah, just now. Mendez has the computer work," he returned.

Renner looked at him with a hint of a smile. "Why do they call you 'Noodle'?"

Raumin also smiled a bit. "Well, because of my acumen, I hope." He tapped his temple, "You know, the old noodle."

Raumin continued toward the door in silence, reflecting on how much to tell them about his suspicions and the danger they might still be in. The way the man caught in Susan's office, the John Doe, was released, apparently by direction from someone higher in the government, worried him. How high up did the threat go?

He didn't think the John Doe posed a direct danger. He didn't seem to be guilty of anything, even though he spoke a language no one could identify. But his manner of release suggested a deep hidden interest, and that raised Raumin's concerns. It seemed similar to the inexplicable interest in Jennifer Hewitt. In both cases, tips and rumors were coming in not through his contacts in the criminal world, but from contacts in the government. Why was Hewitt kidnapped then released with no demands? Why was the unidentified man released to a civilian home? In neither case could any of his sources identify a reason for the interest shown the two, only suggesting that someone influential was interested in information regarding them. That interest was clearly not friendly.

He wondered about professor Jack Myrvik's role. Raumin had had the professor followed when he left the police station with the former prisoner—he'd taken the man to an ordinary house in a poorer neighborhood. Why? Peculiar.

The number of seemingly unrelated people involved in this series of crimes and odd events implied causes and consequences on a much bigger scale than Raumin was prepared to deal with as a local precinct detective. Raven's association with a paramilitary group in the East Indies also suggested that these suspicious events were not local in origin or purpose.

When they reached the entrance back out onto the street, Raumin paused, his hand resting on the push bar of the door. "I think you should both know that there appear to be elements within the government involved with your kidnapping,"—he nodded at Hewitt— "and with our mysterious John Doe. They are involved in ways that I don't understand, and I'm concerned I may not be able to keep you completely safe."

He hesitated, thinking carefully before stepping outside the bounds of police practice. Under normal circumstances, it was crazy to involve civilians in the details of his work. But these weren't normal circumstances. His gut told him to trust these two and, in the end, he had to follow his gut. "I'm thinking of getting some help from old friends in military intelligence where I worked for several years as a young man. Just something for you to know if I should get pulled off the case."

He pushed open the door for them, and they left. He watched them walk down the steps to the street. Hopefully, he'd done the right thing. At least they'd be aware and on their guard. And if things got any crazier, he might end up needing their help.

Chapter 33

Cynthia struggled to grasp the fact that Susan was dead. It seemed unfair. She couldn't assimilate so much loss at once. Susan was so young, four years younger than she was. How could her little sister be gone too? So many memories shared only with Mike, or special memories of childhood shared only with Susan, that she could never share with anyone again.

But she could find no flaw in Jen's reasoning. Jen had even brought the broach to her house, and, together, they had compared it to the one in the photograph. It was Susan's broach. The one she had bought for herself when she graduated from college as part of her curio collection.

With no reason to doubt the broach's testimony, hope ebbed from Cynthia.

Part of Cynthia saw the loss of her sister differently from her loss of Mike. Mike died still young. But Susan died after a long life. The skeleton was of an *old* woman. Both Jen and Jonathan assured her of that. Jen showed her a bit of deteriorated leather string found with the broach. Jen had speculated that Susan must have worn the broach as a necklace long after its metal clasp failed through years of use.

Susan lived many years after she vanished from the present. She lived a full life.

Cynthia hoped it had been a rich one.

Susan's burial occurred in a location difficult to reach, underwater, possibly in a place distant from where she lived. That meant something. It meant that someone cared for her a great deal. It meant she was not alone. She had loved ones. Perhaps children. Certainly friends. People willing to make great effort and take great care in her burial.

Cynthia preferred to not consider Susan vanished into the past, and now dead long ago. Instead, she imagined that Susan still lived the adventure of life, parallel to her own life, only in another time. She reckoned it as though Susan took a journey across a sea to a new country where she lived far from her former home. But Cynthia could still share *being* with her, even though a great ocean divided them.

Cynthia knew that Jonathan was working through his own grief with his plans to promote Susan's work. Like Jonathan, she also hoped that Susan's legacy would be valued and offer scientific enlightenment to the world, and that her work would turn to good and not ill.

So much *evil* lurked around Susan's work, crawling around the astounding discoveries she left behind. This darkness seemed more focused on Jen than others, but it threatened each of them. That darkness must not overwhelm what Susan had learned. Perhaps Jonathan's shepherding could guide Susan's work toward brighter outcomes.

Not being trained as a scientist, Cynthia had little to offer in refinement or publication of her sister's work.

She wasn't a scientist. But she had once been once a writer. Her own gifts lay not in the science itself, but in the public dialogue that could shape how that science was used and interpreted. Perhaps she could become a writer again. Play a part in the public examination of Susan's research. Now, with Mike gone, she needed to find work anyway. Despite the ongoing changes to journalism, writing was still writing and she could contribute.

Cynthia felt perhaps the first glimmer of enthusiasm she'd felt in many weeks. She ran her mind over names she had known way back when. Some of them, surely, were still in the business. She took up her phone to start calling.

Chapter 34

I still felt a margin of safety in my own apartment, sitting on my own couch, watching the trees move in the courtyard outside my living room window. It was raining, the fall monsoons finally arriving, if late. I watched the grey sky and the glistening wet leaves and let my fingers follow the soft curves of the broach in my hand. Susan's broach. My broach now.

I thought about the man I'd found in Susan's office. It made sense now that he had said nothing to me when I first saw him at the university. If Susan had vanished into the world of 40000 years ago, this man must have arrived from that place and time. No wonder he couldn't communicate and seemed so strange.

His appearance when she vanished linked him in some way to Susan. Susan's research, her discovery that certain unmeasurable properties of the universe could be *chosen*, must have summoned this man out of the past. Somehow, they switched places, simultaneously discovering an unknown pathway through time and space.

Since we met with Raumin at the police station, the detective had taken to letting Jonathan and I in on most of his thinking. I'd told Raumin about the broach and what it meant. His concern that the same dangers threatened this man that threatened *me* intrigued me. What about me could possibly be similar to this man from the past? Why should there be any link at all?

Raumin had pointed out that, like me, this man was linked both to Susan's experiments and Jonathan's discovery in Wyoming. His hidden assumption, of course, was that Susan's experiments were somehow the *cause* of her disappearance from the present time, an assumption that I realized I found quite believable.

I set the broach down on my coffee table and picked up the cup of tea I had sitting there, still warm enough to comfort my two hands as they wrapped around it but cool enough to drink. I took a sip.

That the stranger and I might share a common enemy should

have given me a sense of empathy with him, but it didn't. I couldn't overcome my instinctive dislike.

Many people preferred the dominant, ambitious alpha-male, choosing them for leaders, and choosing them for mates. I wasn't one of them. I valued the quiet, reflective man.

In my opinion, society greatly overrated action and extroversion and underrated reflection. I still awaited eagerly the breakfast cereal box that proclaimed in splashy, colorful letters, right underneath the picture of physicist Marie Curie:

Get *supercharged* with Cubic Puffs fortified cereal!
You too can be *thoughtful* and *introspective*!

The message on the back of the broach came to mind again. Now that I knew Susan sent it, I took it more personally. I believed Susan sent the message specifically to Jonathan and me. The brief note she sent us must be important.

"Be a Friend." But who were we meant to befriend?

In all the years that had passed for her, Susan must have learned something about the happenings here in the present time, the cause of the strange events, the purpose of the shimmering beings. She must have known of this man from the past. She'd have known his people. As a physicist, she surely investigated the forces that took her into the past and him into the future.

To whom but this man from the past could Susan's admonition to friendship refer? Her message was too generic to provide meaningful guidance unless Susan knew that the one to befriend would be *obvious*.

Somehow, this man from the past must hold the key to our future. Or perhaps Susan knew that he shouldn't fall into the wrong hands, or be alienated from the right ones.

The dangers around us, the shadowy powers that kidnapped and interrogated ordinary citizens, sought him as well as me. This man from the past, castaway on the shores of a land stranger than any he could have imagined, was far more vulnerable than me.

I had to help him.

My decision to aid this man was barely set in my mind when I found myself slipping into a vision of a place where I knew I had never been. I was walking into the kitchen of a strange house. I saw it, felt it, yet I knew I hadn't left my own apartment. Some part of me still sensed the warm cup of tea in my hands, and the soft couch on which I sat. But that real world faded further as a different reality swept over me.

The vision was realistic down to the feel of wood floors under my bare feet, and the scent of fried chicken in my nostrils. The long, narrow kitchen unfolded to my left and right. Straight ahead was a sink with a wide window above it that gazed out over an empty alleyway. A clock with gold, spiked arms radiating like a caricature of a star, hung over the sink.

Into this vision stepped the man from the past. He talked to me. The words blurred past my understanding, like words in a dream, although they seemed to be English words.

One sentence crystallized into understanding. "My tribe lived on the great grassland," he said.

The vision vanished as quickly as it came. I found myself in my apartment again, suddenly dark and silent after the brightness and conversation of my vision.

I'd never had such a vision before. I'd heard that such things sometimes signaled a brain tumor. I hoped that wasn't the case with me. I hoped it was just the weeks of stress and fear.

But the idea from the vision was a good one.

I could teach this man to speak. I could, of course, learn his language, but then he could only communicate with me. Teaching him English would allow him to communicate with many people. I could, perhaps, teach him to read as well.

Susan's message urged me to be a friend to this man that I didn't know. I wasn't sure I could do that. I couldn't be a *friend* to a stranger from the past who frightened me. But I could *teach him to speak*. And I would trust that Susan, in sending her message at such great effort, somehow knew what must be done.

Detective Raumin could tell me where the man from the past was held. I would go there and explore wherever Susan's words led me.

Chapter 35

Kar-Tur let his eyes follow the great structures up and up as they soared above him. He'd seen them before, of course, from the house on wheels, the car, that had taken him to the police station. But for two full moons, Woman JenHewitt had told him to stay in the house for safety's sake. She was upset when he left today, but he had needed to see this new world for himself, to see more than the pictures that Woman JenHewitt gave him.

The immense scale of human activity with its bustling people and great buildings no longer surprised him. Nor did the celerity of the cars. But the loud noises and strange smells surrounding him in this new world bothered him. He couldn't shake the instinct to flee the predatory roar of huge trucks on the more heavily traveled streets. He didn't care for their rancid breath stinging his nostrils with every breeze. He yearned for the quiet prairie with the wind whistling in the reeds along the river and the scent of dry grass-dust lingering in the air.

Woman JenHewitt assured him that these still existed. Not all the world was like this congested place of human habitation she called Los Angeles. He longed to go back to the prairie one day, even though the Woman had told him that his people no longer lived there.

Kar-Tur paused to pick up a small stone lying beside the pathway. At least this new world had rocks in common with the world that he knew. Woman JenHewitt said that she studied rocks and could read in them great stories of the ancient past.

Ancient, like his own past.

After the Woman recoiled from him at the police station, he had feared he might never see her again. He had felt joy and relief when she came to his house to teach him the words of her tribe. She had remained uneasy at first. But later, perhaps as she came to know him better and saw how quickly he understood, she grew more comfortable with him. She had used many methods and tools, such as motions with her hands and objects and pictures she brought with her, to help him learn.

At first, he had to work very hard to make his mouth form the proper sounds and to remember the strange little symbols that she associated with each sound, but, after many days of listening to Woman JenHewitt and connecting the sounds to pictures, understanding became easier. Now he could understand most of what she said, even when she talked with the Man or the other Woman.

On one occasion, she had shown him a map portraying mountains and sea and pointed to where she thought Kar-Tur's people once lived. He spent many hours studying it, imagining in his mind the size of this world portrayed on the map, and comparing it to the stories that travelers brought back to the tribe in his own time.

He found pleasure in the fact that the Woman had taught him not just words, but *meaning*. She pursued with him the inner purposes and causes that made things what they are. When she learned how much he delighted in this, she instructed him in things as diverse as the power that makes the cars go, and the nature of the air that made clouds grow in it. She showed him pictures, like the map, that helped him learn quickly. And she taught him to *read* her strange language as well as speak it, so he could pursue on his own his hunger to understand.

He found it gratifying to share these interests with her. His interest in the meaning of objects and ideas, and their inner reasons, was rare among his own people. He always felt alone in that pursuit. Most were concerned with what they ate, and how they lived, and their stature within their tribe, missing the wonderful insight into existence that simple curiosity afforded.

Kar-Tur inferred that the Woman wasn't typical of her people either. Her depth of knowledge of many aspects of the world was breathtaking to Kar-Tur. But from watching the box with pictures, the television, he gathered that most of her tribe didn't know as much as she. Although the kind couple who shared their home with him--Man WaltRoden and Woman KarenRoden--pursued discussion of many ideas with him, they couldn't reach as deeply into the meaning of things as the Woman.

He wondered if Woman JenHewitt was a seeker of her tribe. He resolved to ask her, when he remembered.

Kar-Tur saw many things he still couldn't identify. The short red posts at the corners of some of the street crossings, for example. Or the metal towers that rose beyond the buildings here and there. He tried to remember everything he saw to ask the Woman about each later. Or, perhaps he could pursue understanding through the small tool for communicating and computing, the little box he saw before in the jail, which she had taught him how to use.

Something about this part of the city seemed corrupt to Kar-Tur. The cheerful grass and flowers in the lawns near the Man's house were missing here. The buildings, while still impressive in size and design, decayed and crumbled in places. Kar-Tur surmised them to be less well cared for.

The people also were more furtive. The two men that followed him, darting into the shadows when he glanced toward them, didn't seem open in purpose. But Kar-Tur couldn't be sure what behaviors were normal for this tribe. Kar-Tur's clothing and appearance were like others in this world. He saw no reason that he should have drawn the attention of those who followed him.

Perhaps Woman JenHewitt was right. Perhaps he was unsafe alone in the city and should not have ignored her instruction to remain indoors. But curiosity drove him to explore more than pictures and words.

Nevertheless, he turned to retrace the branching walkways back to the house. His two shadows waited for him to pass, then turned with him. He wondered if they really thought he didn't notice them. They were far less subtle than the mice of the prairie. Perhaps, if their life depended on staying hidden from the sharp eyes of the hawk, as the mouse's did, their skills would be more finely honed.

Thoughts of the Woman's instructions concerning wandering outside the house brought to mind aspects of her that both attracted and repelled him. As their communion deepened, there were things he grew to like about her. The Woman spoke candidly about ideas and the mysteries of the whole earth and sky. She shared her time and knowledge with him. She seemed like him in her passion for understanding.

But something about the Woman also troubled Kar-Tur. He was growing uncomfortable with the distance she maintained from him, a form of detachment strange to his tribe. Although she spoke her thoughts openly, she didn't speak of her inner feelings. Kar-Tur never knew if she was happy or sad, angry or afraid. How could he gauge his behavior toward her when she kept her reactions to him secret?

Kar-Tur might have suspected that her personality was simply a quiet one without pronounced feeling, except he sometimes caught stronger reactions buried in her eyes. Like today when he decided he'd go for a walk outside despite her wishes.

He had grown impatient at his imprisonment, eager to see the sky again, and to explore a place so profoundly new to him. When the Woman told him, no, he could not go out, he had risen too quickly from his chair and sent it toppling to the floor. He *was* going out, he told her. And he did just that.

He spotted a reaction hidden in her then, as though shielded by long practice. Anger? Or fear? Or, perhaps something else?

He wished she'd be more open with him, so he could learn more quickly what was appropriate in her society. So he could learn more quickly who this Woman was.

The two men who followed him had been creeping closer for some time. Now Kar-Tur heard their footsteps rushing toward him from behind. He turned upon them just as they came within his reach. The nearer of the two held a cloth in his hand, stretched out as though to give it to him.

Kar-Tur didn't know what this cloth might be, but he was not inclined to find out. He grasped the man's wrist, wrenching it downwards until the man released the cloth to the ground. The man gasped in pain, and Kar-Tur felt the man's wrist crack beneath his grip.

By now the other was upon him as well.

"You're going down ******, whether you like it or not," the man growled. Kar-Tur didn't understand one of the words.

This one held some type of weapon. Not a gun, which the Woman had taught Kar-Tur to recognize. It looked more like a simple stick. The man held it as though to strike him. Kar-Tur dodged and the stick flailed through empty air.

Turning, Kar-Tur grabbed the stick from the man before he recovered from his swing. He twisted it away from the man's hold. With one man's wrist broken, and the other missing his weapon, the two scuttled away down the street.

Kar-Tur turned and continued his journey back to the house, tossing the stick to the ground in some nearby bushes. What an odd place, this world of the future. Even his own tribe, barbaric as this advanced tribe must think it, did not allow people to attack each other at random.

The Woman still remained at the house when Kar-Tur returned. She usually stayed until evening, but Kar-Tur feared his insistence on leaving the house might have driven her away early today. He felt glad to find her still there.

A stranger was there as well. A man he didn't know. Man WaltRoden introduced the stranger as his nephew Jerry, a Senator. Kar-Tur had not heard the word Senator before, but he understood it to mean that Man WaltRoden's nephew held a place of high prominence. The stranger offered his hand in the greeting typical of this tribe.

"Good to meet you, young man," he said. He smiled broadly, but to Kar-Tur's eye, the expression seemed practiced rather than spontaneous.

Kar-Tur responded, wary and unsure of his English. "Yes, and you also."

The stranger's friendliness continued, and Kar-Tur's distrust grew. He smiled too much. It wasn't natural that anyone should always be in the same mood. In every natural conversation there is an ebb and flow to reactions and feelings of the participants. Sometimes interest, sometimes distraction, sometimes irritation, sometimes warmth, sometimes confusion, sometimes weariness, sometimes laughter. This stranger affected a persistent outgoing pleasantness.

It didn't seem right to Kar-Tur.

But then, didn't Woman JenHewitt exhibit the same behavior? That was the very thing he didn't like about her. Maybe hiding natural emotional reactions and variations was the way of this tribe.

Chapter 36

Walt's nephew was perhaps the most handsome man I had ever met. He was tall, about four inches over six feet. His square, strong features resembled a face cut in stone.

Unlike stone, his face filled with warmth and joy as he greeted me. I understood how he had marshaled the personal support to become a Senator at so young an age. Who could dislike him?

He turned from me to give his aunt Karen a hug, and I slipped into the living room to await Kar-Tur's return. Kar-Tur shouldn't have left the house. I remained both angry *at* him and afraid *for* him. The people searching for him could be lurking outside. It wasn't safe. But, I understood his longing to get out into the world. Could I stay cooped up in a small house, without prospect of an end to it, if I found myself transported to an incredible, unimaginable world of the future? I didn't think so.

It occurred to me that perhaps I should go out with him, watch out for him. But with surveillance so pervasive, I doubted that I had the skill to keep him out of sight.

I sat on the couch and picked up a magazine to distract myself from worry. I couldn't focus on it. The pages melted away, blurred, distorted, and I felt myself slipping into another vision. It was my third of the last couple of months.

I was less surprised this time, more aware of the sensation of sliding from the tangible world. Almost it felt like I went to another *place*, as though it were real and not only a vision. Recoiling from the immensity that I felt there, I skirted its vastness and came quickly to the vision.

Smoke rose like a mist above a scene of utter desolation. The barren ground lay in wavy hummocks, like sea waves frozen in motion. Here and there, pits sunk into the ground exposed bits of concrete or steel that must once have been human-made. As far as I could see, no life softened the harsh world. There were no buildings.

There was not even any color. A fine dust resting on every exposed surface shrouded even the brown of dead earth in a gray pallor.

The hot wind blowing over the still simmering rock and earth burned at my skin. The acrid smoke veiling the landscape smelled of dead life and scorched stone.

As before, the vision vanished quickly, and its intense realism winked away into puzzled disbelief.

What were these visions? Where did they come from? Did they truly foretell future events?

My first vision, of Kar-Tur speaking in English, prompted me to teach him to speak. That vision came true. But that could simply be a self-fulfilling prophecy. The vision came true because I had the vision and *chose to make it come true*. This was quite different from the interpretation that I had a vision because it was *destined to become true*.

But even in my first vision of Kar-Tur, I saw the inside of the Rodens' house as it truly was. I'd never been in their house before then. I couldn't have known what it was like. And no one could simply guess the existence of their garish gold-star clock in the kitchen. The clock was hideous in a way that even a decorative maladroit like me wouldn't imagine.

Actually, Karen told me that a friend gave her the clock as a gift. Knowing that, and knowing that she chose to place it so prominently in her house, imputed a beauty to it that I didn't see at first.

Did my visions predict the future, or did they in some way shape the future? My experience suggested a bit of both.

I suspected that these visions related to Susan's work. Her studies revealed that certain parts of our reality could be chosen by human intellect. I didn't know the implications of that exactly, since the part of the universe we chose existed at such a profoundly fundamental level that its manifestation in the macroscopic world remained unclear to me.

But I wondered if, somehow, the consensus that such visionary insight into the future was impossible was beginning to weaken, at least among those people surrounding me. Perhaps accepted beliefs were beginning to break down among those of us who knew of

Susan's work, and somehow this altered what was possible. It was as though a part of the universe had been chosen one way for centuries, and now a new choice was possible.

However, neither Jonathan nor Cynthia reported experiencing such visions. It seemed that any such dissolution of consensus should affect them as much as me.

If my visions were true, as evidence suggested, then I had reason to worry about my second vision. It came about a week ago, as Kar-Tur and I looked at pictures in the encyclopedia, talking about words and what they meant.

In that vision, I saw Kar-Tur standing over the body of a fallen man, his feet straddling the body like a bridge. Kar-Tur beckoned to me, insistently, as though I must come.

The vision was short, but unnerving. My trust of the man from the past was uneasy at best. Only Susan's words "Be a Friend" kept me coming here.

I didn't care for his manner or treatment of me. He often called me simply "woman" to my face, which I found demeaning. I had told him my name, and he was gaining an excellent command of English structure. I was sure he knew what his words meant, and I thought he knew what he said. So I found no excuse for him to call me "woman." I presumed he brought with him from his own culture some preconception of women as property.

His sudden and unpredictable fits of emotion or anger also unsettled me. When he knocked his chair over in his determination to leave the house earlier in the day, I was actually frightened of him.

Not frightened physically, I decided. More a fright at a relationship that I couldn't predict or understand.

He no longer frightened me in a physical way as he had at first when he leaped at me in the police station. He explained that behavior to me--he thought the police were threatening me--and I believed him.

I wasn't sure I could ever call him "friend" as Susan admonished. But I no longer thought of him as "enemy" either. But what did my vision mean, with him standing over the body of a fallen man? How far would his sudden fits of anger take him?

Kar-Tur arrived in time for supper. When Karen invited me, I decided to stay for supper as well. I found Walt's nephew very interesting. I checked his hand for a ring, wondering if he were married, then scolded myself for wondering. What business was it of mine?

"Tell me, Kar-Tur," he said as Karen passed the plate of pork roast, "What was your world like?"

I was a bit surprised. I had told him Kar-Tur's name earlier, but I had been quite careful to not let out that Kar-Tur came from the past, from a different world. And I had told Kar-Tur he shouldn't tell others either. I caught Walt's eye, wondering if he had said something.

"Jerry is the one who arranged for Kar-Tur to come here," Walt said, addressing my unspoken question. "He is the one who first explained Kar-Tur's...past...to me."

"Ahh," I said, wondering how the Senator possibly knew this, but gaining a new appreciation for his efforts to protect Kar-Tur.

"My people lived where the great plain met the mountains," Kar-Tur replied. "Near the edge of the great ice."

"And your role with your people?" The Senator asked. Then, after a moment of silence, perhaps realizing that Kar-Tur might not understand, added, "What work did you do for your people?"

"I was Seeker," Kar-Tur said. "I sought out things that others might not see."

"So, did you seek out scientific understanding, like Ms. Hewitt here, or was your role more that of a person of faith, a religious man?" he asked.

"Yes," Kar-Tur said, "Understanding and faith, like Woman JenHewitt."

"I see." The Senator smiled and turned his attention to cutting his pork, but I caught a quick widening of his eyes, as though he had gained some new insight.

The Senator kept the conversation lively for the entire meal. He impressed me with his inquiries, seeming to reflect an honest interest in Kar-Tur and uncovering some things that I had never thought to ask. His conversation ranged widely and revealed an experience and curiosity about many things.

***

The next day, I went directly to the Rodens' house, as I usually did after my last class at noon. It still amazed me how different teaching my CalTech undergrads was from teaching Kar-Tur. Even the boldest discoveries of my discipline seemed to leave my students indifferent while Kar-Tur showed a deep passion even for the mundane.

A few weeks ago, I had told my Intro to Geology discussion group about the center of the Earth, a place where no human had ever been, and where no one would likely ever be within their lifetimes or the lifetimes of their great grandchildren. I told them how geologists had *listened* into the Earth and figured out what was there! What a delightful solution to a seemingly impossible puzzle.

Then today, I had told them about the Man in the Moon. No one lived when that shadowy face was painted on the Moon. Yet geologists read the tale of how it formed, recounting a vivid story of the Moon's collisions with great space rocks that exploded in a fiery cataclysm unimaginable by any modern experience. We could gaze directly into a past so ancient that no human had ever seen it. Good grief, geology was better than a time machine!

But as excited as I was, my students still gazed out the window, daydreaming about their date for the weekend, their eyelids sagging from boredom or else from sleepiness after a night on the town or maybe from weariness after a night working to pay their way through college. I realized that they probably really were tired and that I was being too hard on them. Most of them showed at least *some* interest.

But Kar-Tur clung to every word. He wasn't satisfied with knowing only language. He yearned to understand. I could relate to that. His hunger to comprehend the entirety of the universe matched my own delight in existence.

The Senator still tarried at Karen and Walt's house, having spent the night there. He greeted me with apparent delight when I arrived. Flattered by his friendliness, I stopped to talk for a few minutes before starting Kar-Tur's lessons. It took a special man, a great man, to pause from the work of a Senator to offer a kind voice to a casual acquaintance.

Kar-Tur and I retired to one of the bedrooms, both for the quiet and so we wouldn't interfere with Walt's conversation with his nephew.

Although Kar-Tur pursued many disciplines with me, geology, my own discipline, interested him particularly. Its story-telling nature pleased him, I think. His own people were story-tellers. Much of their accumulated knowledge was passed from generation to generation in the form of stories. Likewise, much of geology was simply the story of the Earth.

Perhaps, also, he realized that geology was the discipline most likely to cast light on his own time, now vanished into prehistory. Only the stories recorded in the Earth still linked Kar-Tur to his own people and time. I didn't have to plead with Kar-Tur, as I had with my students, to recognize that geology was a wonderful time machine.

I told Kar-Tur about the face in the Moon, and its formation, since that was fresh in my mind from the discussion group.

"Hummm," Kar-Tur grunted as I finished the story. "The story is interesting, Woman, but unsatisfying. It teaches no lesson.

"And, it does not explain all the evidence. Haven't you told me that scientific theory must explain all the evidence?"

Kar-Tur's face grew very grave. But, I knew him well enough by now to guess that he was teasing me, and had a story of his own he wanted to tell.

"Oh?" I replied. "And why is that? What evidence is not explained?"

"It fails to explain why the face turns upside down every morning. The face in the Moon starts the evening right-side up. But by morning, every time the Moon is full, he is standing on his head.

"Your explanation, you see, does not explain why the face should do that. My tribe has an explanation that is more complete."

Now I knew Kar-Tur was teasing. He had been quick to grasp the difference between the stories of science, and the mythical stories of his people. But he still insisted, only half-teasing, that his stories were more real than mine. His stories always had a lesson for people. He said that made them better. And in some ways, he was right. I settled in to hear his story of the face in the Moon.

"You see," Kar-Tur began, "the lesson is this. It's unwise to eat before bed, particularly if one has a mate."

"Aha," I said.

"The face in the Moon appears, of course, when the Moon grows large and full with overeating before bedtime. And while it is large, the face turns first right side up then upside down as the poor fellow tosses and turns with sleeplessness through the night. Eating just before bed, you see, results in sleeplessness because there is too little time to digest the food before the body grows still with rest.

"Sadly, the poor fellow's mate does not wish to sleep with one who tosses and turns the night away. Tossing and turning with his incomplete digestion, the poor fellow drives his mate to the other side of the bed.

"That is why the Sun always sits on the far side of the sky when the Moon is full with late eating. The Moon's mate, the Sun, grows weary of the sleeplessness. But as the Moon chooses his eating better, and slims down, the two mates grow close again, working and sleeping together. That is why, as the Moon grows thin, the Sun and Moon grow closer in the sky.

"This continues until the sad fellow forgets his lesson, and begins the cycle again.

"So you see, eating before bed is bad for union with a mate. And forgetfulness destines one to endlessly cycle the same mistakes."

I laughed at his funny story, and Kar-Tur laughed with me. He was right. His story had a truth that mine didn't have. But my story also had a lesson about our place in the universe, just one not so obviously linked to everyday life.

Chapter 37

Walt watched his nephew depart down the sidewalk. He was glad Jerry visited them at last, after not stopping by for at least a decade.

His nephew clearly needed to get away from the pressure of his work more often. He was far too tense and intense. His type of friendliness lacked the depth of real joy that could be felt in family. He needed to feel the simple flow of life for a while. Unassuming, ordinary life. Certainly, no life was more ordinary than his and Karen's. But there was a joy in that commonplace life, eating together, being together. Walt hoped his nephew enjoyed his time with them, that it was a retreat from his busy-ness into a quieter inner place where he could know himself and God.

His nephew's visit also troubled Walt. Why now? Why with these people present, Jen and Kar-Tur? His nephew had clearly been instrumental in helping Kar-Tur, releasing him from an unjust custody, perhaps protecting him from hidden dangers. But Walt had learned from Raumin, the detective who brought Jen to the house, that those hidden dangers might have backing from within the U.S. government.

Suddenly Walt wondered why his nephew remained so interested in keeping Kar-Tur here at his house. It seemed very strange indeed that Kar-Tur, an unidentified man from another time, was given refuge in his home. Professor Myrvik had mentioned Walt's connection with Susan Arasmith's experiments as though that explained why the man was brought to Walt's house. But that thin connection could not explain why Jerry had contacted him and asked if he would shelter Kar-Tur in his home. It only made sense if Jerry wished to keep Kar-Tur, and now Jennifer Hewitt, under his own personal surveillance and out of the eye of other elements of the government or law enforcement.

Walt feared his nephew might be involved in something

improper. His nephew had never been never able to completely overcome his father's violence. He never really connected with the warmth of people. Warmth was always a pretense to him, a way to achieve an outcome. He couldn't *feel* that warmth as something real.

What a terrible loss and burden that must be, to not really understand love, one thing that made life truly meaningful.

But Jerry had always understood duty. And, having suffered so much from his father, Walt's brother, he was fiercely protective of everyone around him, unwilling that they should suffer as he did.

Even if his nephew had some hidden interest in these two as part of his Senatorial responsibilities, and even if his sudden visit here was no accident, he surely had no criminal motives. Surely, Walt reasoned, Jerry couldn't be so damaged as to be involved in Miss Hewitt's abduction.

Or in the attack on Kar-Tur when he had ventured out into the city. Kar-Tur had told them about the men who attacked him on the street. Walt found it particularly troubling that it occurred just as Jerry arrived. And, as Kar-Tur described it, the cloth the one man held sounded very much like the chloroformed cloth used to abduct Jen. Jerry expressed outrage at the attack, and that outrage seemed to reflect honest anger. But was that outrage real? Or part of an act? The outrage expressed in words had not been equally expressed by any facial evidence of surprise or dismay.

Walt decided that he needed to make sure that detective Raumin knew of the attack on Kar-Tur. Kar-Tur and Jen were his guests. He must ensure that they were safe. His nephew, given his violent past and the peculiar visit of the past couple of days, would bear watching.

Walt reflected a moment on his own vulnerability and the danger he and Karen might be in. But he knew violent people. And, he had years of experience keeping safe from them. He did not worry too much.

Chapter 38

Jonathan relocked his mailbox and walked back to his apartment. The envelope from Detective Raumin felt pretty thick; he must have written a novel. Not that Jonathan was complaining. Thick was good. He'd asked for more information about the case, but given Raumin's patronizing attitude in the past, he hadn't been sure he'd get much. For one thing, Raumin probably wasn't free to discuss most aspects of the case with a civilian.

Jonathan flopped into his favorite chair, tore open the letter, and read.

> Dear Dr. Renner,
> As you requested, I'm writing to apprise you of my progress on the Arasmith-Hewitt case. I still find snail mail more secure than an encoded message splattered through airways and cyberspace, thus this note."
> I have continued my investigations of Raven. Local observers in the East Indies report that the terrorist group he is tied to has recently begun conducting exercises more typical of conventional warfare rather than terrorism. Activity has picked up in both magnitude and intensity.
> I'm not sure whether or not Raven's association with the East Indies group had any bearing on his interest in Dr. Arasmith. Raven's instructions while here in the States did not originate from the terrorist group, but rather from a contact based in D.C. This is consistent with other signals, such as the release of Kar-Tur from jail, that there is high-level government involvement (all I was told was that his release was under mandate from "higher-up" in the police bureaucracy).
> The activities in the East Indies, as well as the deeply covert and government-connected activities related to your friend Jen Hewitt, are troubling. I have trouble believing that these activities truly are embedded in our own government. But they seem to be.
> I have uncovered an even more troubling rumor, which I

am telling you in part for my own safety--if anything happens to me at least one person outside the system knows. Some former colleagues in the military intelligence community inform me of a plan to overthrow the U.S. government from *within* the U.S. They didn't know how or when. Nor is it clear if this is related to the East Indies group. But it is clear that the intelligence community takes the threat seriously.

I have connected this rumor with some of my own findings here in L.A. I have learned of an underground group forming here, political rather than criminal in nature, that goes by the name ONE. It is possible they are associated with Ms. Hewitt's kidnapping, and I will pursue it further."

Using my somewhat rusty networking skills in the military intelligence community, and trading some of what I have learned about Raven, in whom the military is also interested, I managed to learn something else that may be of particular interest to you. L.A. is not the only place where the shimmering beings have appeared. There is a report of strange, glimmering people appearing in England as well, undoubtedly the same as those you have contacted.

Unfortunately, the rumor of this contact carries with it the possibility of war. I don't know in detail why the beings contacted the British government. Nor do I know exactly what message they carried. Security on this information is as tight as the British can make it.

But, needless to say, such an incredible, high-profile event cannot be completely suppressed. One aspect is known, apparently leaked intentionally to the military intelligence community by someone with U.S. sympathies. The beings are contemplating war with the U.S. and seek British aid in that effort."

This letter probably provides a great deal more information that you were expecting from me. As you can tell, my confidence in my own superiors is somewhat shaken, and I felt the need to let someone outside the police know about this.

Relay to your friends as much of this letter as you deem relevant to their safety. I recommend that you not be careless in who you talk to since we can't be sure who is an ally and who is not.

Sincerely,
John Raumin

Jonathan felt his heart hammering in his chest--not racing as though from exertion but pounding in ominous rhythm, like deep jungle drums. Stories of a pending coup on the U.S. government was frightening enough, but the idea of war with alien beings was terrifying. What argument could creatures from another world have presented, that the British, a U.S. ally, would still be conversing with them? And why would the shimmering beings attack? What did they want?

He rose from his chair and walked to the window that overlooked the street outside his apartment. He wanted to talk again to the shimmering being he met at the University. They really needed to come up with a better name, Shimmers? Shimera? Shimera sounded good. He wanted to confront the *Shimera* and ask point blank what they planned.

The possibility of war with alien beings of unknown power, of whom most people on Earth remained ignorant, left a sick knot in the pit of his stomach. It rendered the whole day, the whole world, surreal. The clear sky full of sun seemed strangely harsh and unfamiliar to him, as though there were something new in it that he'd never seen before. He felt, perhaps, like a newborn baby opening his eyes for the first time onto the bright, harsh world outside the womb, wondering whether it harbored joy or pain. His world, his people, were born into a new universe where they were not alone. And that made all the difference in the day.

Tucking the letter into a pocket, he left his apartment and headed to his car. He had to do something.

He drove to campus and parked outside the physics building. He went down the steps to the basement and found the outside door locked. He headed to the main door, hoping to ask Professor Myrvik to let him into Susan's lab.

These shimmering beings, the Shimera, killed Mike. So perhaps their unfriendliness to humans should come as no surprise. But war? For what reason? What kind of war could it be? What kind of weapons might these creatures use?

Of complementary concern was Susan's message from the past, "Be a Friend." Who else could her message refer to but to these shimmering beings? Did Susan learn somehow, in her journey into the past, in her crossing of both time and space, that war with these beings would turn out badly? Did she know that peace was essential to survival?

Dr. Myrvik was in his office, and, to Jonathan's surprise, he seemed very willing to let Jonathan into Susan's lab. He didn't even try to pry out a reason, simply accepting Jonathan's declared need for access.

When the man left, Jonathan went to the spot where he had contacted the being before, and called out. He called again and again, with increasing desperation, but there was no response.

He stayed in the lab for nearly an hour, sometimes calling, sometimes just waiting in silence. He even read over Raumin's letter again, looking for deeper understanding.

After one last round of calling, he realized that the creature might never again appear. Maybe it didn't want to talk with him or maybe it simply was no longer here.

Jonathan turned to head for the door. But as he turned, he caught a slight shimmering in the air. As he watched, the being coalesced further, becoming more concrete than in his first meeting. He could see more pronounced limbs, arms and legs. He wondered if practice made the being more skilled at this materialization.

The being had dark hair shoulder length, a small nose turned up at the end, and an oval face. A woman. Or, at least she had features that a human would identify as feminine. That these beings resembled humans astonished him. He wondered vaguely why that should be so and what it might mean. But his mind was too focused on the prospect of war to linger long on that question.

Dilly-dallying around with pretended niceties was not in Jonathan's plan. Instead he went straight to the point. "We have heard that you plan war with us," he said. "Your people have contacted the government in England. What have we done to you that war should result from it?"

"England?" The female asked. Her question was nonverbal, the words echoing in his mind rather than his ears.

Jonathan became impatient. With war a possibility, he wanted none of this gamesmanship.

But he was, in effect, Earth's diplomatic envoy to these alien people from some unknown place in the universe. He needed to be careful with communications potentially fraught with misunderstanding. Misunderstand probably didn't even begin to capture it. Try wildly divergent views of reality.

"England, a nation, an independent state of Earth." He forced himself to stay calm. "It is on the other side of our planet from this location."

"Those may be our people," the shimmering being said. "But we can't know of them, or what they do, at so great a distance from us.

"But there are those of us here, in this place, who also contemplate war with you. Therefore, I don't doubt that those in other places do the same."

"Who are you?" Jonathan asked. "Where are you from? And what have we done to you to warrant war?"

"We are the Shimera," she said. "We share Earth with you.

Jonathan started slightly at the use of the word Shimera, which he had just made up. Odd, and seemingly coincidental, that they should call themselves by that name.

"You exist in a single time on Earth," she continued, "tied to that time, growing gradually from it. Yet, you are free to roam the Earth within that narrow time. We, on the other hand, exist in a single *place* on Earth, the place of our birth. Our minds and bodies become tied to the magnetic and gravity fields of that place and it's from that place that we gradually grow. As you grow into time, so we grow into place. We travel along a corridor of changing place, carried by the fields there, much like you drift gradually through time. Unlike you, we move easily through time, going wherever in it we choose, but always chained to our place on earth."

Jonathan stood silent before the Shimera. The idea that another race of beings shared Earth with humanity, and perhaps had *always* shared the Earth, seemed incredible to him. How astonishing that, after humans searched the heavens vainly for another race with which to share the universe, a race should be found sharing their own world.

Some things the being said simply made no sense. Jonathan picked one of them to ask about. "If you travel in time, then how can you talk to me? Talking, for me, requires the passage of time. How can you understand *my* passage of time?"

"We don't perceive time as you do," the female replied. "But when I hold myself to nearly the same time as you, walking along in time with you, I'm also moving gradually into a slightly new place, with a new pattern of gravity and magnetic waves. It's too small a move for you to see, but I feel it. My mind associates new events, new memories with that new position in space. I become a new being, place by place, just like you become a new being moment by moment.

"This is not something I control. But, like you, there comes a place where I reach the end of the changing and growing of that which is me, and I die. This place where I die is not a time, but a place I reach in the fields of Earth."

"How can I see you?" Jonathan asked.

"You've come to my *place* on Earth. That's your gift. You can go where you will. I have come to your *time* on Earth. That is *my* gift. I'm walking through time with you. If I did not walk with you in time, I would not appear to you nor you to me. We would be glimmers, disappearing before we were aware of the other."

"Why have your people attacked us?" Jonathan asked. "Why did you kill one of us? And why do you threaten war?"

"Yours was the attack," she said. "The two humans traveling in time disrupted our space, and many of us in the corridor that they traveled died. That one who attacked you was in sorrow and anger over their deaths. Those who died included his loved ones. That one thought in place, and did not taste the passage of distance, nor pause to commune with those at even greater distance.

"When the human who was to do this thing stumbled into his space of cognizance, he acted rashly. His target, the one he sought to kill, was not the one who died, but rather the woman who was to be the source of the disruption. He thought he might change events if he killed her before she traveled. But, of course, such paradoxes are not allowed.

"The one who died of your people, did so because he moved the body of the Shimera. A Shimera cannot move and live. Of our own selves, we cannot move at all beyond the life that sweeps us gradually through the fields of Earth. But you, the People of Place, can move us. And then we lose coherence, and our energy dissipates rapidly, and we die. The explosion you experienced was from this."

Jonathan puzzled over this for a moment, wondering which of the many conflicts and impossibilities he should question next. "If you can't travel, or move to a new place," he asked, "how do you even know of this event that happened miles from here? It occurred in another place, where you say you can't go."

"We're able to communicate over a certain distance," the Shimera answered. "We occupy only a finite space, and are aware of things in a small space of cognizance. But we hear of things from other places and know of them, perhaps like you hear of things from your past, your histories and traditions. These travel from one of us to another over the spaces we occupy. But in the same way that your history disappears into myth as it becomes distant in time, so our communions disintegrate into nonsense as they become distant in space. There are many of our people who remain unaware of this death we caused, or of the terrible deaths caused by your people traveling in time. There are those of my people that I don't know, and that I can never know. Just as surely, there must be beings from your past and future that you will never know.

"But there is an even greater danger to us than those who, for you, have already traveled in time. It is for this greater danger that we would go to war. There are those of your people who would continue to travel in time, harnessing it for the goals of your people. And there are those among your people who would wield other powers as well, to shape your world anew, to alter what would have otherwise been. This harms our people wherever on Earth they might be. For you, this has not yet come to be. But for my people, our way into the future is blocked by it. Many are cut off from loved ones. Many face death if this reality comes to pass."

Jonathan felt a sense of despair seeping in from all sides, like the seeping in of cold through a coat that was too thin for the weather. The power the being referred to must be that which Susan learned of in her Uncertainty experiments. Did this mean that any application of Susan's discoveries was destined to lead to war with the Shimera? Must her work vanish, as she had, into obscurity? Jonathan didn't want that. Her astonishing discoveries were all he had left of her. He wanted them to make a difference in the world, as a scientist's work should. He wanted them to make a better world.

"Can my friend Susan's work not be pursued without harming your world?" he asked. "What exactly harms you?"

"We don't understand completely what is happening," she replied. "For us, it's as though there are many ways the world can be, and it's not yet decided which will prevail. The reason we can't travel in time beyond this point is because there is no future there. That's why so many of us are lost in a place now cut off, on the other side of this gulf.

"But we do know that not all uses of this power by your people necessarily cause us harm. We know that *some* uses premeditated by your people, the leaders of your nation, will cause us harm. We don't know what makes the difference between that which harms us and that which does not.

"But we can't allow this injury to our people. We will stop you if we can. If you can't arrest the actions of those in your leadership who would do this, then we must be at war."

There was a moment of silence when Jonathan didn't know what to say or ask further. He remembered that the being had called herself *Shimera*. It seemed too coincidental that he had chosen that very name for them just minutes before. "Your name, Shimera," Jonathan said. "It's so much like the word we use to describe you, *shimmering*. Is that how you see yourselves, also? As a shimmering?"

"No," the Shimera replied. "You gave us this name, Jonathan, where you described this meeting to your friends and others."

Jonathan frowned in confusion. He'd not told anyone. He'd not even thought of the name until today. The being must be mistaken.

Then he realized that, for him, this had *yet to occur*. He *would have* named them. In fact, from his present timeline, he still would.

How did the woman know his name was Jonathan? Was he yet to give his name to a former version of her?

"I can stay no longer," the Shimera said. "It's hard to stay in one time for so much distance. Come again when you have communed with your people. We will see what can be done for peace."

Then, she vanished.

The lab felt suddenly darker and dingier than it had a moment before. Jonathan sank into Susan's chair beside her lab desk. He thought about the Shimera, about how different they were from humans, about how human actions and purposes could harm them. He realized that it was possible that their interests were so opposed to human interests that there could be no common ground, no peace. Perhaps they could only be enemies.

But Susan's message, "Be a Friend," moved him to think otherwise. Susan must have known something. There must be a way to find friendship with this race with which humanity shared the Earth.

Chapter 39

The Senator from California clamped his fingers onto the walnut window sill in his penthouse office and gnashed his teeth at his men's bungling. The spacious office, far more plush than his office in D.C., and the serene view that overlooked both the city and the sea failed to distract his fury. He'd instructed them only to watch the man from the past, to ensure he didn't escape. He hadn't authorized an attempt at capture. They deserved the broken wrist and scare that they had gotten.

Although, as it turned out, their bungling provided him with a lucky and timely warning. These two, the man from the past and Jen Hewitt, were not to be taken lightly. It wasn't just luck that events conspired in their favor so often. Somehow, he had to overcome whatever control or insight they had of future events. He had to seize that power for himself and his country.

He looked again over Susan's results, provided by the CalTech physicist, as he had done almost daily during the three months since she completed the experiments. At last, he began to understand them. And perhaps he began to see what made Jen Hewitt and the man from the past special. If so, he no longer needed them at all.

The two were alike in one aspect. They both had a spiritual bent. The possibility of power that rested in them must be related to their religious faith. His survey of the woman during her interrogation had revealed that religious proclivity. He thought nothing of it at the time, not seeing its significance until he spoke with the man from the past at his uncle's house, and learned that the man was some sort of mystic or shaman of his people. *Now* he made the connection.

But Susan's results revealed something else. Faith wasn't necessary. It must be the ability of the man and woman to *believe* the *unbelievable* that gave them their potential. Susan's results clearly showed it was expectation, not faith, that moved the particles and set them in their place. In the case of Susan's experiments, this belief was formed by Susan's own words to her researchers. She *made* them believe it, and it became true.

The Senator knew himself. He was a master at getting people to believe things. To see things as he saw them, as they truly were, or should be. Susan's results proved that, by altering what people believed, he could change what was actually true.

No wonder that leaders needed charisma, a force of personality. No wonder that leaders acted swiftly, decisively, while weaker people paused to endlessly plan and speculate. It was that very decisiveness that brought nations to agreement. And it was *agreement itself* that forged reality.

He could be the blacksmith of reality. By persuading those around him what must come to pass, he could transfigure existence itself to his will.

He no longer needed the man and the woman. They were now more threat than asset.

Although, he could use the story of them to his benefit. He needed to undermine American confidence concerning what was possible. Make people believe that *anything* was possible. Only then could his own efforts to alter the possible bear fruit. What better way to do that than with the truth? At least part of it.

The propoganda artist, he knew, didn't warp truth so much as limit it. Propaganda worked best when every word of it was technically true, just incomplete.

He worried momentarily about the Shimera. Were they truly working against him? How else could he interpret the rumors from Great Britain? What interest would England have in war with the U.S. unless they contrived to stop him from taking his rightful place? The place he *must* take if he was to protect Americans from the dangers to come. Had the Shimera revealed to them the true stakes of this war?

He must take action to maintain his safety. He would discontinue his efforts to contact the Shimera in Los Angeles. His people might be unable to contact them because the L.A. Shimera were no longer on his team. Perhaps, even, the Shimera hid themselves from his people deliberately, hoping they might lure him into contacting them directly. Then they could kill him easily. Their time travel abilities meant they might have already tried to kill his past self if he hadn't taken precautions. His foresight in not directly contacting more than the original one who died, and its companion, had proven prescient.

He thought again about the man from the past and Jen Hewitt. He needed the country to know this power should be in the hands of the government, in *his* hands, not in the hands of civilians. But for the country to agree with him on that point, they had to know about it. They had to know about the amazing events unfolding beneath their sleepy eyes.

He could use the rumor of a time traveler and a strange power over nature to initiate his plans. He didn't actually need the two of them as proof of time travel or power over nature. They could be eliminated before their power came to fruition. Before it threatened his own.

With them dead, he'd be free to shape the future as he chose. It would have to be a small, surgical operation. He couldn't afford to draw attention just yet to the scale of his plans and power. It would have to be done by someone they knew, someone they trusted.

Professor Myrvik would do just fine.

Chapter 40

It felt normal, being with friends, talking together, playing poker at the Roden's kitchen table. Cynthia felt happier than she had since Mike died. Jen, always eager for a game of cards, soon had them in a game of three-hand poker.

Cynthia could almost forget that she and Jonathan had to wait until dark to visit their friend at the Rodens' home, and that even with that precaution they had worried they might be seen or followed. She could almost forget the surreal turn life had taken and the danger they all faced.

Walt was already at work. Karen had excused herself from the game to make cookies. The warm smell of them filled the house. The man from the past, Kar-Tur, didn't play, but watched the game with the same eager fascination with which he seemed to approach everything. More like a puppy than the frightening brute Jen had originally portrayed him to be.

But one never knew what went on inside a quiet exterior. Cynthia worried about Jen's decision to help this stranger learn English. Kar-Tur was a man from an unfamiliar culture, caught up in strange events in a world alien to him. Who knew how he would act and react?

Although, Jen's reasons for befriending the man seemed sound. Susan's message to "Be a Friend" was ambiguous, and surely must refer to someone obvious. Otherwise, Susan couldn't have expected anyone to correctly interpret the message. Perhaps this was that obvious man. Then again, Cynthia knew Jonathan believed Susan's message referred to the Shimera. They couldn't both be right, could they?

"So," Jen said, peering toward Cynthia's hole cards as she prepared to bet in a hand of seven-card stud. "Do you have another queen under there?"

Cynthia fanned the three cards with her fingers, snapping them back against the table, relishing the feel of them slipping across her thumb. "I'm not sure," she said. "Which ones have the swords and which ones have the flowers? Is this a feminist deck? Do the kings have flowers?"

"The queens have the flowers, the men carry swords and axes," Jonathan said. "Like real life."

"Since when is that like real life?" Jen inserted. "Women can fight for what they believe in. And men can pursue peace."

"But there is a certain nature to men and women that make men more suited to defense," Kar-Tur added. "At least, that seemed to be so in my time."

"I don't think you have it, Cynthia," Jen said. "I call. Two pair, tens and twos."

"You lose." Cynthia grinned, turning over not a third queen, but two kings. "Two pair, kings and queens.

"Once upon a time," Cynthia said, as she scraped in her winnings, "a Queen traveled toward the town wearing a fine gown and corsage. 'Why was the town wearing a corsage?' someone asked. 'Because you never know when a Queen might drop in.' was the reply."

Cynthia caught Jen's curious smile, probably wondering where she was going with this. It *had* been a while since she engaged in her trademark grammatical humor. Certainly none since Mike died.

Cynthia stacked her winnings neatly and continued. "Another time, a King traveled toward the town with an unsheathed sword. 'Why did the town have its sword out?' someone asked. 'Because you never know when you must defend against someone who would be king."

"So you see," Cynthia concluded, "you can prepare for the King or you can prepare for the Queen. But you can't prepare for both."

"Aha," Jen said. "Sort of like us. The Shimera are coming. Do we take out our swords or our corsages?"

"My vote is for the corsage," Jonathan said. "They're not our enemies." After a moment's silence he added, "You see, Cynth, I do have a feminist deck. Sometimes I think men should carry flowers."

"I'm not so sure about a corsage for the Shimera, Jonathan," Jen said. "Whoever spied on Susan and her lab, and whoever kidnapped me, knew about Susan's work before it was even finished. Someone had foreknowledge of it. Where did that come from but the Shimera?"

"And sometimes women carry a sword." Cynthia added.

"There are many Shimera, just like there are many of us," Jonathan replied. "If one or two is against us, that's no reason to fight them all. I think we should follow Susan's advice and befriend them. Her message must have referred to the Shimera."

Mention of Susan took away some of the peaceful fun that Cynthia's forgetfulness had brought the evening. Suddenly the unreality of it punctured her pretense of normalcy. So much unreality. And unreality continued to expand, consuming an ever-growing part of her life.

"I wonder what Susan is doing tonight," Cynthia asked.

Jonathan looked puzzled for a moment, then, with a nod of understanding, said, "Or what she did in whatever evening was the equivalent evening for her."

"I wonder how it happened?" Jen asked. "How'd she end up in such a distant past?"

"She must not have been able to return," Cynthia said. "Otherwise, she'd already be back, wouldn't she?" She looked around, hoping one of her scientist friends could refute her time-travel logic.

"Or she knew it would harm the Shimera," Jonathan said. "She was a very kind person. She wouldn't hurt others, even to return to her loved ones. She didn't come back to us because traveling through time harms their world. Doesn't that make sense?"

"I miss her," Cynthia said.

"Me too." Jonathan's voice caught and he looked down at the cards.

"What did she do to make it happen?" Cynthia asked after a moment of silence. "How did she travel through time?"

Her friends just shook their heads.

"Maybe we should ask Kar-Tur," Jen said. "He must surely be the other half of Susan's experience. What did you *do*, Kar-Tur? What did you do to make it happen?"

"I didn't do anything," he responded after a moment. "I was just thinking. I was thinking about..."

Kar-Tur paused, clearly deciding against saying more. Cynthia saw his eyes flit to Jen and then look away. She wondered what he withheld, and why.

Kar-Tur continued. "Perhaps your friend did something, something that caused us both to travel. I don't know. Or, perhaps, she was only thinking, as I was."

"That seems like an important thing for us to find out," Jen said. "If by some act, or some thought, we can alter time or place, it might be better to know what it is. Maybe there's a clue in her office. That's where Kar-Tur appeared. That must be where she was when it happened. We should check there again. See if we missed something."

They pressed their questions no further, having no further answers. Cynthia perceived that her friends were as eager as she to resume the card game that had carried them for a time from the present world. They returned to play, but somewhere in her mind, Cynthia still wondered how Susan broke through the ramparts of time when no one else had done so throughout all time past and future. And she wondered why Kar-Tur held something back. And how their hidden enemy kept always one step ahead of them. And whether the Shimera were friend or foe.

They played quite late into the night. Karen, their host, went to bed about ten in the evening. But Cynthia saw her friend Jen only rarely now and was unwilling to leave too soon. She and Jonathan stayed long enough to hear the bell of a nearby church ring only a single time.

Afterward, Jonathan drove her home. He didn't drop her off, but parked the car and walked her to her door. She appreciated that. More demons filled the darkness now than she remembered at any time since becoming an adult. She wondered if the demons of childhood ever really vanished, or if adults merely grew weary of fearing them.

***

Cynthia had the TV on with the volume low as she picked up things in the living room and dusted the knick-knack shelves. She didn't watch it much, but she liked the background noise making the house less quiet. With Adam and Erin at a school ballgame, there just wasn't enough *sound* in her home. It felt too alone.

When the story about the time traveler came on at the top of the news, she grabbed the remote to increase the volume. The news anchor never mentioned Kar-Tur by name, but who else could the 'time traveler' be?

The story linked the time traveler to secret experiments. Susan's, Cynthia presumed. According to the reporter, the experiments had the potential to undermine the U.S. economy or even its government. "We have received reports from a credible source that this secret research is linked to the activities by a well-funded organization trying to unbalance the American government," the reporter said. "We only have to think of the German heavy water experiments of World War II, and the American effort to beat the Germans to the atom bomb to understand how dangerous these secret experiments are. Information leaked about the secret research imply that the law of nature itself might be subject to human control, a power that makes the atom bomb look like a firecracker."

The report continued by revealing that the anonymous source was in the government, well positioned to know about these events, and had accused two Senators from back east of working with Great Britain to suppress public control of these experiments. "Our source," the reporter said, "emphasizes the need to secure this power into the hands of our own government. The safety of the American people, and the security of our nation depend on it.

"The time traveler has a companion, a woman who is learning how to control the very fabric of nature, the weather and the earth itself. These two, above all others, must be located and watched."

Cynthia felt a flare of anger at the unjust innuendos that seemed aimed at Susan, but the last of the report alarmed her the most, more than any of the bizarre incidents of the past months. The companion referred to could only be Jen. Cynthia accepted the danger to her friend from an unknown criminal element. But how could she accept a danger to Jen from her own government?

Where was this report coming from? Why the ridiculous exaggeration of Susan's work? And why attribute such unbelievable abilities to Jen?

Most importantly, why did it impugn the characters of Kar-Tur and Jen with such implications of wrongdoing? They were not enemies of the government, or of the American people.

This was no longer a fascinating science project that Cynthia's friends stumbled upon and let her participate in. This was a deadly game, with high stakes, played on a court she knew nothing of.

Susan's experiments were not just amazing science. Her experiments impinged on the world of power and politics. The experiments transformed human understanding of reality and offered power beyond imagining to people skilled in the art of taking power for their own.

Cynthia considered calling Jen to warn her of the report, to ask what she planned to do. But Cynthia hesitated to bring attention to Jen in case her own actions were being monitored.

Normal life was disintegrating around them. Even more for Jen than for her, Cynthia realized. And it promised to disintegrate further before any new form of normalcy could evolve. Kar-Tur and Jen stayed in the open only at their peril. Whatever malevolent forces were behind this news release, they would not acknowledge that Kar-Tur and Jen had neither political ambitions nor any reasons to oppose the U.S. government. Jen and Kar-Tur had to hide from these people.

Cynthia wanted to keep in touch with them, if or when they went into hiding. The computer network, too pervasive to limit availability and too complex to be completely monitored, was the obvious choice. She could set up an anonymous email account. She'd heard it was possible to access such accounts without having your location traced, although increased scrutiny on terrorism had made it harder to set them up. Cynthia had heard of apps that could help with that. Maybe Jonathan would have some ideas.

Chapter 41

The sun prepared to rise as Kar-Tur and Woman JenHewitt crossed the Caltech campus to her office-lab. The well-tended landscape materialized slowly from the gloom, resting quietly, pregnant with possibilities. Kar-Tur knew this to be a place of learning, where the Woman gained much of her wonderful insight into existence. 'University' she called it. Universal. The place for learning everything. He wished he'd had such a place to learn.

The length of daylight, Kar-Tur noticed, grew longer again with each new day. Yet, there was no winter. Even at dawn, he and the woman were comfortably warm with only light sweaters. He wondered at this strange phenomenon. The deepest period of winter always came when days began to lengthen after a period of shortening and the sun began its trek northward.

Kar-Tur's people knew of places where winter was mild, or never came at all. Sometimes traders, returning to the tribe from a long journey of many years, told stories of places by the Great Water where winter never came. A Great Water lay near this place, Kar-Tur knew. The Woman gave him maps showing Los Angeles squatting at the edge of the immense Pacific Ocean. Although, because of the confinement at which he still chaffed, Kar-Tur had yet to see it.

"Woman, why is it so warm when the sun has traveled south?"

"It's mainly due to the ocean nearby," she confirmed. "The nature of water is such that it doesn't heat up as quickly in the sunlight, or cool off as quickly in winter. It has to do with the way the atoms bond together and absorb energy. The steady ocean temperature keeps the air temperature more regular through the year."

She'd talked of energy before, in some of their lessons. He didn't completely understand the idea yet, although he associated it with his sense of Power and Material, something deep in the *nature* of things. He marveled again at how easily the Woman could gaze into those deep places. Places he spent years looking for and could still see only dimly.

Kar-Tur reflected on all that Woman-JenHewitt had taught him and showed him of her amazing world. He accepted her days spent with him as a wonderful gift. Never had anyone given him more of their time and effort, even among his own tribe.

He felt a growing affection for her, despite their widely different ways. She was like him in her wonder and delight in learning. Clearly, she was Tribewoman to him. Why hadn't he recognized her as Tribewoman before now?

They entered the geology building, already unlocked for the morning. They had timed their visit so the Tribewoman wouldn't need to use her key card, which she said could be traced to her. Her own lab opened with an old-style metal key, which couldn't be traced.

Once in her lab, Kar-Tur waited while the Tribewoman downloaded data from her computer onto portable devices. Although she still taught her classes at the University, she had become increasingly uneasy spending time on campus since the news reports about them came out. She now did most of her work at the house of Man WaltRoden and Woman KarenRoden.

While he waited for her to finish, Kar-Tur explored the peculiarities and mysteries of her lab with fascination. There were objects and machines he didn't recognize and lacked even the comparisons to describe. His eyes skipped over the incomprehensible and alighted on several less-strange items sitting on a shelf in a cabinet with a thick glass window. One item was a gold oval with a polished green stone in the center. A wood object carved in a crude letter 'T' comprised the second.

Tribewoman JenHewitt stepped beside him as he stood there.

"We found these with Susan," she said. "They're part of why I wanted you to come with me this morning. Did you ever see anything like them in your time?"

"No," Kar-Tur replied. "Although we made wooden carvings of many sorts. The wooden 'T' could be from my era. But the other item is from your time, not mine."

"That is what Jonathan and I have concluded," the Tribewoman said. Then after a moment of thought added, "Susan's experiments imply that there are certain aspects of the universe that people can choose, or control. Somehow, that must be involved in her disappearance."

They gazed at the artifacts for a time, Kar-Tur thinking of what had brought him to this new world. And of the people lost to him.

Then the Tribewoman continued. "Do you know of anything that might explain how she disappeared?"

Kar-Tur did know something. But there was so much danger in the power that caused him and SusanArasmith to switch places. He'd been unable to control it; presumably SusanArasmith was unable to control it as well. She and he were both consumed by what they did not understand. Because of that danger, he hesitated to reveal what he knew to his Tribewoman.

Especially since his Tribewoman showed promise of far more power in that place than he could summon. Her knowledge of her inner self, together with her understanding of nature, granted great influence, great power. He knew this from his long vigil at the fire, watching the flames dance, looking into them to perceive the nature of things. Measuring well the universe and yourself gave you choice in matters outside yourself. And the better that measurement, the greater the choice in matters not measured.

But his Tribewoman didn't seem to realize her discretion in nature, nor invoke her power over it. He wondered that this advanced people didn't know of this power. The work of Tribewoman JenHewitt's friend SusanArasmith seemed to represent new discoveries, still not understood by this tribe of the future.

Kar-Tur knew that he could teach the Tribewoman to *feel* into the nature of existence in the same way she taught him to *think* into it. He could teach her to awaken that spirit within her that could *choose* the way of things.

But, in choosing, there was so much potential for evil as well as good. He hesitated to activate that power latent within her. He even hesitated to awaken his own spirit of power for fear it might do more harm, like the harm it did in bringing him unexpectedly into this future place.

She, as he, was of a thoughtful and careful nature and able to keep a disciplined mind. Their safety might lie in helping each other maintain that discipline. Perhaps they could learn together to safely harness this new authority in the cosmos. Perhaps that was the purpose that had brought them together across the impassible expanse of time and distance.

But he kept silent for now. After a few more moments, she turned from the cabinet and they left her lab.

"Let's stop by Susan's office," Tribewoman JenHewitt said as they walked back across campus toward the car where Man WaltRoden awaited them. "I want to see if there's something there that helps us understand what happened. Something I missed before."

Woman SusanArasmith's office door was locked, but they could peer into the office through the small window in the door. Officially, she was still a missing person, not dead, and her belongings were left in her room undisturbed. They could see her things in the morning light that filtered through her outside window. As he looked at her personal things, Kar-Tur wondered who this woman had been, whose life linked so intimately to his own, yet whom he would likely never meet.

"Look carefully," the Tribewoman said. "Is there something of yours there? Something that might reveal how you traveled through time?"

"No. Nothing came with me from my time, except what I was wearing."

"She kept an old radio on the book shelf over her desk," Tribewoman JenHewitt said. "One of the kind that scans the whole spectrum. I remember seeing it there. It sat beside a Newton's cradle and some other science curios. It's gone now. She took it with her."

The Tribewoman appeared to be sinking into deeper thought, and Kar-Tur remained silent, listening.

"She liked to bustle when she thought deeply," she continued. "Messing with her shelves, rearranging things, straightening them. I saw her do that sometimes when we met to talk about her work, or the excavation site.

"She must have been doing that when she disappeared. That's why she took the radio with her. She was thinking, and bustling, and she happened to have it in her hand.

"She was deep in thought, not concerned with what her hands were busy at. That would suggest," the Tribewoman concluded, "that it was not what she was *doing*, but what she was *thinking* that caused her disappearance."

She paused for a time in silence. "I want to bring her back, Kar-Tur. I want to bring her back for Jonathan. He misses her so much."

"Don't others miss her also?" Kar-Tur asked.

"Well, yes," the Tribewoman said. She seemed to struggle to say what came next. "I know it's not my fault that she disappeared. At least I hope it's not my fault." She stopped a moment, thinking. Kar-Tur presumed she reflected on her visions and what they might imply. "But I resented her close relationship with Jonathan. And now I feel guilty and would like to make that up somehow.

"Think how much could be saved if it just hadn't happened," she continued. "You would be with your people, Kar-Tur, and Susan with hers. The Shimera would not have suffered. Our enemy, whoever that might be, would probably not have learned of this power Susan discovered. And Jonathan would have the one he loves."

Kar-Tur saw a flicker of pain cross her face. "Do you wish that you might be the one he loves?" Kar-Tur asked.

The Tribewoman shook her head slightly at his question. But she didn't answer. "We better get back to Walt," she said.

Kar-Tur frowned at her diversion. Why did she share so little of her inner world?

He realized suddenly that this was why he had been so long in recognizing her as Tribewoman. She didn't have a Tribewoman's openness with him. That raised a barrier between them. Had it not been for that flaw, he'd have recognized her as Tribewoman long before now.

He knew from watching her, and listening to her impassioned explorations of creation, that her inner world was a rich one. She knew her own self, her own thoughts, and examined them deeply. Why didn't she express them? He found this frustrating. He felt that she invited him to share himself, but did not answer in kind.

"Tribewoman," he said. "Why are you so closed with your

feelings? I am not happy with that. It's not the way of my people."

She looked uncomfortable, but started to answer. "When I was in High School......." She stopped.

"I'm sorry," she said. "We really should get back before we're caught. It's not safe for you here."

It was already too late. Man JackMyrvik, the one who had picked Kar-Tur up at the jail, came down the hallway toward his own office a short distance from Woman SusanArasmith's.

"What are you doing here?" he asked when he saw them standing there.

Neither of them answered.

"Look," he said. "It's not safe for you to be seen in public. Too many people are afraid of you. You should stay out of sight."

Something about his manner left Kar-Tur uneasy. Despite the fact that this man was a friend and colleague to his Tribewoman, Kar-Tur was unsure whether he was friend for foe.

Man JackMyrvik opened his office door and entered, leaving them alone in the hallway again.

They left quickly, encountering no one else on the return to the car.

On the drive to Man WaltRoden's home, Kar-Tur thought about what he should tell the Tribewoman. Should he tell her of her potential, about *feeling* into the nature of things, of that place where such danger lurked? Her insight at Woman SusanArasmith's office, when she realized that it must have been Woman SusanArasmith's thoughts and not her actions that sent her into the past, revealed that Tribewoman JenHewitt would likely figure it out on her own anyway. He may as well tell her so they could learn together, and perhaps find greater safety in that collaboration.

But how could he be open with her, trust her with such dangerous thoughts, when she did not trust him with her simple feelings?

***

Two days later, Kar-Tur still didn't know what to say, or whether to keep silent. Tribewoman JenHewitt arrived at midday. Woman KarenRoden prepared a meal she called "fried chicken." As did most foods in this strange world, it smelled appealing but unfamiliar, a bit like cooking meat, a bit like the vegetables his tribe sometimes boiled in bear fat. Kar-Tur enjoyed talking with her about the foods, and how she prepared them. Preparations were very different from those of his people. His own people exposed food directly to fire, and had recently, through Kar-Tur's own efforts, found ways to contain and heat water for boiling vegetables and meats. But the elaborate mixtures of foods from this time, the coating of meats with crushed grass seed before cooking, and the cooking in oils, were new to him.

Kar-Tur sat at the kitchen table with the atlas, looking at Wyoming where Tribewoman Jen Hewitt told him his people once lived. He wanted to see that home of his tribe again. To assure himself his people indeed were gone from there. He wanted to see if some clue, some vestige of who they had been, remained there.

He longed for them. His people were not strong in separation. *He* was not strong in separation. He yearned to return to the prairie, even if only to share that place together with his loved ones, albeit severed by an epoch.

A possibility also existed that going there might help them understand the present dangerous events. His own journey in time began in that place. And events in the present world clearly connected to his journey.

The Tribewoman entered the room, interrupting his thoughts.

"Tribewoman," Kar-Tur began, pointing to a place in the atlas. "I would like to go here, to the place where my tribe lived on the great grassland."

Tribewoman JenHewitt paused as though startled. Kar-Tur didn't know if she reflected on his relatively new use of "Tribewoman," or if some other thought held her attention, although the fact that she had not reacted when he called her Tribewoman before suggested that latter. But, in a moment, her startle passed and she sat down with him to examine the atlas.

Soon she was as excited as he, pointing out roads and places she knew. She talked of how far it was to Wyoming, and how they might get there. They pored over the map until Man WaltRoden joined them at the table and Woman KarenRoden served their meal.

How much like his own tribe these people were, Kar-Tur thought, building community and family in meals shared together. He felt honored to be part of them.

***

After lunch, they retired to the living room for their afternoon lessons. By now, Kar-Tur's command of English was quite good and they spent less time on study of it. They still explored Tribewoman JenHewitt's world of science, and all the wonderful places of discovery. But today, their conversation turned to the shadow that lay upon them, what it meant, and when it might lift. She told him about the Shimera's conversation with Jonathan. She told him about the threat of war with the Shimera and how it related to Kar-Tur's own trek through time and space. She told him about the threat of a coup against her government and how incomprehensible that was to her.

And Kar-Tur began to tell her of his expedition into the flames.

They were submerged in discussion when the bedroom door opened and Woman-KarenRoden slipped through, closing it behind her. Her face strained with worry, and her voice was urgent.

"Another news broadcast was just on about a man who travels in time and a woman companion. This new report says they're both to be taken into custody. Walt is concerned for your safety, and thinks you should leave now. Your presence here might not be secret anymore."

Kar-Tur didn't know what to say. During the past months, the shelter of the Man and Woman's kindness and warm home lulled him into a sense of safety. Didn't he even plan a trip across the country through strange territory, thinking himself safe? Why should danger sweep upon them again so swiftly?

"Why aren't we safe here?" the Tribewoman managed to ask.

"Walt thinks his nephew's visits are odd. Before a couple months ago, he hadn't been in our house for more than a decade. It seems peculiar that he should visit now, when you're here.

"Our nephew," Karen continued, with a shrug and twisted smile that made Kar-Tur think of apologies in his tribe, "is a man with many demons.

"In any case, Walt thinks you'd be safer hiding in the building he works in. He has spare keys to the main door and most rooms on the tenth floor. He is getting those for you now."

Tribewoman JenHewitt seemed more troubled than Kar-Tur felt. This was her world. It must seem strange indeed to have her safe, predictable world suddenly transform into something strange and frightening. She struggled to comprehend these intolerable events in her tidy, normal life. Kar-Tur tried to imagine how he would have felt had his predictable life with the tribe suddenly disintegrated into the seemingly impossible.

Like the Tribewoman's, his own life *had* disintegrated into the impossible. But he could comfort himself by imagining his tribe continuing on with working and hunting as they always had, the only difference being his absence.

Man WaltRoden arrived with two small rectangular cards. He gave them to the Tribewoman. Tribewoman JenHewitt was in the kitchen gathering a packet of food to take to their hiding place, when a knock came on the door.

Man JackMyrvik, the man who had brought him to the house, stepped in. Tribewoman JenHewitt looked relieved to see it was he. Another man that Kar-Tur didn't know entered with him.

"You probably know from the news broadcast that you're no longer safe either here or at the university," the professor began. "I arranged with the geology department to have your spring classes taken by another grad student. You need to come with us to a safe place."

Kar-Tur saw the puzzlement growing in the Tribewoman's face. Something didn't seem right to her.

"But the broadcast was just now on," she said. "How'd you know ahead of time to get someone to take my classes?"

The other man, standing beside the professor, drew a pistol from his jacket. The Tribewoman's apprehension turned to fear as the man directed the gun toward her.

"What are you doing?" the professor asked in sudden confusion.

The other man took no notice. He aimed the gun at Tribewoman JenHewitt. Kar-Tur was faster and stronger than the people of this time. But he was not faster or stronger than their weapons. He couldn't cross the room to the man with the gun before he killed his Tribewoman.

But standing and doing nothing could not save her either. He launched himself toward the man, stretching out a hand as though he might knock the gun aside by power of will. Perhaps if he moved fast enough, he could draw the gun toward himself. But the man was already pulling the trigger, and it was still pointed directly at his Tribeswoman.

Kar-Tur knew he was not going to make it in time. He was too far away.

But the professor, much closer than Kar-Tur, took a step sideways, coming between the gunman and Kar-Tur's Tribeswoman just as the gun barked like nearby thunder. Before the gunman could step around the professor's falling form to try another shot, Kar-Tur reached him and brought the heel of his hand up under his chin with all his strength. The gun flew from the man's hand, landing halfway across the room. The man's head snapped back with a terrible crack, and his body fell unconscious to the floor.

Tribewoman JenHewitt rushed to the side of the fallen professor. Kar-Tur heard his words, weak, but audible. "Sorry. I thought I did right, that the government should watch you. Didn't know enough." He took a wheezing breath. "Watch out for the Senator, he's not what he seems."

Kar-Tur stood over the unconscious man who'd attempted to kill his Tribewoman. They needed to flee. There might be more people waiting to attack them. In fact, it was likely. A strategic adversary would not leave the outcome of this encounter to the chance failure of a single man.

He beckoned to Tribewoman JenHewitt, but she still knelt by the weakening professor. Kar-Tur didn't know whether the professor would live or not, but they could not wait to see.

The Tribewoman seemed paralyzed by events. No doubt her mind rejected the impossible happenings leaking into a world otherwise so reasonable. To Kar-Tur, this whole world was new and unreasonable. This part of it was no different. *He* was not paralyzed.

He beckoned more insistently. Reluctantly, she rose from Man

JackMyrvik's side and followed Kar-Tur to the back door of the house, where they raced quickly into the alley and away toward the building where Man WaltRoden had sent them to hide.

Chapter 42

Jonathan's discomfort with the situation quickened his steps along the walkway and made the shadows cast by the trees in the park seem to darken. Raumin, at his side, lengthened his stride to keep pace.

Jonathan liked the detective. And he respected his abilities in police matters a great deal. But meeting secretly in a city park smacked too much of the melodramatic. That Raumin came to him rather than higher authorities left him uneasy and hinted at dangers Jonathan wasn't sure he wanted any part of. Although he and Raumin had developed a sort of friendship, it was a young one, unready for this kind of test. The topic was one he could scarcely believe he heard correctly.

"Treason is not to be contemplated lightly," Raumin told Jonathan. "But there are those within the U.S. government who fear the President's actions are unwise. There are even those who believe the President's actions are not his own. We are organizing now and we need you with us."

Yes, Jonathan thought, he respected the detective. But the man's lack of outrage at the prospect of treason astonished him. And, in this particular instance, Jonathan agreed with his government, that this power over time--or whatever power that Kar-Tur had--should be in the hands of government, not individuals. The California Senator's speech this afternoon had moved him. If the potential existed for greater control of the world, if it could make people safer and lives better than ever before, people should seize that opportunity. It did not make sense for some private group to usurp or hide that potential. The right choice for society was to address the needs of the many, even if it infringed on the rights of the few. Didn't that make sense?

But why had Jen and Kar-Tur gone into hiding? Jen was a scientist, dedicated to the belief that knowledge was free to everyone.

Why was she now unwilling to share her insight?

If they were in danger, as Raumin now asserted, why not commit themselves into police custody? Raumin could surely protect them, and it wouldn't leave the impression they really had something to hide. It wouldn't leave the impression that they were hoarding this power for themselves and didn't want other people to share in it. The Senator's speech certainly left few people sympathetic to them. Jonathan realized that if he didn't know Jennifer, and know she must have reasons for hiding, the speech would have caused even him to distrust her.

Jonathan continued along the ridge that cut through the park. Sunbeams peeked through a few scattered high clouds painted bright yellow by the sun on the western horizon. He could just make out the glint of sunlight on the sea in the distance.

"I'm not sure I can join this group you're talking about, not like you want anyway," Jonathan replied after a good minute of thought and nearly a hundred yards of paved pathway. "I can do some things with you, to help my friends. I can be a contact with the Shimera. And I can try to protect Jen and Kar-Tur if you ask me to. But I can't commit to treason. Does that make sense? How can you be so sure of this organization? Even if it did begin locally here in L.A., it's now grown beyond that and you can't know how a shadow organization like that might behave or what they might do. In any case, how can I support a group that may try to overthrow my own country? A group which you, yourself, have only recently learned of and know little about?"

"If there's nothing wrong," Raumin added, "if the British concerns are in error, if the Shimera that you talked to was mistaken or confused, or even if the Shimera are our enemy, then ONE will make no move against the government. We're patriots. But if something *is* wrong, if the Shimera warnings are real, we'll be ready. Or at least not completely unready."

Part of Jonathan wanted Susan's work, that which she gave her life for, to matter. He didn't like the message from the Shimera hinting that it must be suppressed. The Senator's proposal to explore this power further, on a vast scale searching for beneficial uses, offered

Jonathan a way to believe in the continued pursuit of Susan's research.

The next few days or years would shape the future as far as he could see. It wouldn't do for just anyone to direct that shaping. Jonathan understood the need for society, through the arm of its government, to act for the good of all. He agreed with that ideal.

But, who were the good guys? The Shimera? The U.S. government? The British government? He didn't even know which group within the U.S. government the Shimera feared. And what about the people in this underground movement that Raumin spoke of and wanted him to join?

Sometimes, it wasn't possible to know who was good or evil. Good and evil were concepts too aloof for him, requiring that he understand the outcomes and implications of actions over a time scale too long to predict or even comprehend.

Sometimes, when good and evil couldn't be discerned, one could only know who was enemy and who was friend.

Jen was his friend. And he'd come to know Raumin reasonably well over the past few weeks and trusted him. He didn't need to know what was *ultimately* good or evil. He only had to remember his friends. If Jen fled from her own government, she must have reasons for doing so.

They reached the end of the walkway, where a bench sat on a hill overlooking the city and the sea. They stopped there for a time, watching the sunset.

"I'll think about it," Jonathan said at last.

Chapter 43

The last of the library patrons trickled out into the advancing evening as closing time approached. I tarried for a few more minutes at the computer. Drawing attention to myself by being the last to leave was probably unwise, but I wanted to check the email address that Walt gave me from Cynthia. The time elapsed since I last spoke to Cynthia seemed long to me, and I missed my friends.

I fretted at the slowness of the connection, but, at last the account appeared. It held three messages. The first was a simple greeting explaining Cynthia's hopes for maintaining contact in case I had to go into long-term hiding. She gave instruction on how to send a message back and not have it traced to the computer I sent it from. I had worried about that, which explained why I risked coming to the library to access the email rather than using the computer in Walt's small custodial office. If someone learned of the account in the future, I didn't want them using it to locate Kar-Tur and I, nor did I want Walt Roden to suffer for his risk in hiding us.

The second message offered a bleak outlook on my situation.

"Dear J,

Suspicion and opposition to you and K continues to grow, fueled by our friendly Senator, whose stature and influence increases rapidly. His argument that time travel should be regulated by the government is reasonable, as is his claim that your apparent motives are tainted by your flight. When he asks 'would innocent people run away?', people wonder. Were it not for my knowledge of your kidnapping and the later attempt on your life, I'd believe him. He says that you are planning to use some power, apparently related to Susan's experiments, to overthrow the government. Does that make any kind of sense to you? Or is that just propaganda? I'm sorry if I seem to doubt you, but his claims are so reasonable when he says them.

Stay well and safe.

Love, C."

I paused in reading. Did the capability imputed to me by the Senator relate to anything I could actually do? What kind of power did Susan's work imply? I thought about my visions, and what they might mean. Could I use that insight to help our cause on the scale suggested by the Senator? I didn't know.

I remembered what Kar-Tur told me this morning as we hid together in one of the storage rooms of Walt's building, sharing space with buckets and cleaning fluids. I had asked him how he traveled through time. Instead of answering my question, he had looked at me, hesitant, as though measuring not only me but all the world. "Tribewoman," he said--I still wasn't sure what he meant by that name—"you hold a deep faith, is that not so?"

I nodded, unsure where he was going. "I would like to think so."

"And also a deep understanding of your world."

I nodded again.

"I know only a little of what brought me to your world, your time," he said. "But I believe that you have even more power than me to reach into the deep parts of existence. You only need learn to *feel* what is there."

I didn't know what he meant, and his words frightened me. He had looked away quickly but not before I saw a shadow pass over his face. As much as his words had frightened me, telling me had also frightened him. But the idea of *not* telling me must have frightened him even more.

The third email from Cynthia offered both something to dread and something to hope for.

"Dear J,

Rumors of war are common now. Great Britain's posture toward the U.S. has become sharply harsher. No one in the general public seems to know why. They just accept it, and talk of war.

J tells me that there are rapidly expanding underground forces working in opposition to the Senator. They're in contact with Great Britain and the Shimera there. The Shimera in

Great Britain have a weapon which they promise to use if the Senator isn't stopped. The Senator, it appears, is the focus of their concerns. But they hesitate to use the weapon on us because of the wide devastation it will cause in our world. J said that, when asked if the weapon would destroy us entirely, the Shimera gave an odd response. They said, "Clearly not, we're here." What do you think that means?

There is still no open dialogue about the role of the aliens, the Shimera. J believes they should be considered friends. If the Shimera are truly behind the Great Britain opposition to the U.S. then I'm left with torn loyalties. The Senator frightens me, because of his threat to you. But he's not the United States. He's just one man. How can I oppose my entire government, or support those who oppose it, for his sake?

J plans to work with the underground, and to coordinate their contact with the Shimera here in L.A. He sends his greetings.

A. is doing well in speech competition through the school this year, and E. is playing in band. Life goes on normally for them, or at least they seem to think it's normal. But I worry for them, and for their future.

It remains unsafe for you to visit. Our house is watched constantly. J stops by now and then, just so his failure to visit won't plant seeds of suspicion about his own loyalties. But he doesn't talk with me about joining the underground for fear my house is monitored. He only writes notes, which he has me destroy. He says people can listen to us without even bugging the house, simply by watching the windows vibrate when we talk. That's scary.

Love, C."

It hurt me to see my friend's words, telling me I couldn't see her any more. But I knew she was right. My own photograph, and Kar-Tur's, published on the web news, testified that the search for us was no longer surreptitious. They searched for us openly, and, if I believed Cynthia, which I did, I had few allies in the general public.

I worried that we might be recognized even in the office building where we were hiding. However, our presence in the janitorial area provided some moderate cover. Walt was the only one on our floor using those areas. And janitorial spaces tended to be somewhat invisible to people.

I had little to tell Cynthia, other than to confirm my continued existence, and to reaffirm our friendship. But those I could do.

"Dear C,

K and I are reasonably comfortable, given the circumstances. We continue in our respective work, I on my dissertation, and he learning about a completely new world. Our contact with W keeps us sane, and not too lonely. I have taught K to play cards. We continue in the hope that these matters can be cleared up, and we can return to a normal life.

Love, J."

Darkness hid my return to the office building. Secretiveness was not my long suit, but I did my best to avoid looking furtive. Nothing made one stand out so distinctly as the obvious effort to stay hidden. I strove to appear nonchalantly uninterested in everything. It occurred to me that anyone walking through downtown L.A. at night as seemingly oblivious as I practiced to be would have to be either an idiot or live in a world without muggers.

I hoped that the night hid me well enough that I wouldn't be recognized. I didn't know how widely my photograph had been published, but I imagined that everyone could recognize me easily. For the first time, I found it comforting to recall my tendency to be self-conscious. Perhaps I was not as conspicuous as I felt.

After all, I did sport a new hairstyle that might confuse anyone's efforts to identify me. My innovative hairdo could be succinctly and accurately described as an uncut, unkempt mess. The matted strands were coiffed medusa-style in snake-like tangles. I might have expected them to crawl around my head, except they were too stiff with dirt and natural oils to wiggle.

I looked forward to thwarting the effectiveness of my unintentional disguise with a bit of water and hand soap when I got back to the ladies room.

I entered the building by the front door, just as Walt did. I tried, as much as possible, to use Walt's key just as he would, coming and going only at times when he was at work. Since I was using his card, his name would show up in the entry record. If his name appeared during periods of the day when he wasn't on duty, it might draw attention.

I was more worried about being identified on the tenth floor where I spent most of my time. Eventually, if I were seen enough times, someone would take notice of me, and wonder what my business there was. I peeked from the elevator to see if the hallway was clear before stepping out. It was empty. The advantage of being out and about at night was that not many other people were around.

The disadvantage was that I was a morning person, and really hated being up at night.

My first job of the new day was to clean my hair. Using Walt's master key, I sneaked into one of the offices to borrow a pair of scissors. With a bit of scissors-creativity, maybe I could have both clean hair, and a new hairstyle to act as disguise.

After checking for occupants in the women's bathroom, I slipped in to use the "excellent shampooing facilities" mounted there. That's what Kar-Tur called the sink when I complained about its small size. He reminded me that his people had no such convenience in washing.

Hand soap didn't work all that well to clean my hair. That's why it was in such bad shape to begin with. But after thirty minutes of cutting and washing, it was cleaner than when I started.

I cut it short. I thought it looked perky. But then, I compared it to Medusa.

I returned the scissors to the desk where I found them, and slipped back toward the small janitor's office that served as home. Walt kept a short desk and computer there where I worked on my dissertation. Working without easy access to either my data or statistical programs was inconvenient. I wasn't able to check developing ideas. But writing gave me a sense of accomplishment, and the routine provided a calm place in the midst of my life's turbulence. I liked the pretense of normalcy it furnished.

Kar-Tur sat reading on the couch when I entered. Walt wasn't there. Walt usually left us his office space, only intermittently stopping in to chat, to bring us some convenience from Karen, or to talk of world news.

Kar-Tur rose from the couch when I entered, startled by my new hair. His muscular frame rippled under one of Walt's too-small shirts, struggling to stay within its confines. "Your hair is shorter, Tribewoman," he said.

"Do you like it?" I asked.

He looked puzzled, returning to his seat on the couch. "Of course."

"Aha," I said, not quite sure why I felt disappointed. "I'm hoping it makes me less recognizable."

Kar-Tur returned to his reading, a book about architecture in the Middle Ages, and I settled in at the computer. Our space was so claustrophobically small that Kar-Tur and I were compelled to create space between us through our behavior. One of our rules was that we didn't talk much at the start of our 'day'.

The isolation and confinement seemed to suit Kar-Tur well. He seemed relaxed and even happy in our situation, untroubled by the small scope of our world and our narrow options. The inactivity and effective incarceration bothered me more. Several times, I impatiently considered if it might be better to just go to the police and take my chances with their ability to protect me.

I always believed myself to be mentally well-disciplined, with more than my share of pertinacity against duress. But Kar-Tur proved far more disciplined than I in this instance.

As our time together increased--nearly two months now since we had fled the Rodens' house--I grew to like Kar-Tur a great deal. I liked his depth of thinking, his courteous regard for our relationship, his hunger for learning. The passionate frankness that once angered me became charming as I knew him better. Most of the time, anyway. His calm tolerance of our confinement proved that my initial assessment of his character, that he was violent and unstable for example, was wildly in error. Not the first time I misunderstood someone, but I never seemed to learn *enough* humility in my ability to read people.

The sharpness of his emotional outbursts still made me uncomfortable. They startled me and made me unsure of the constancy of our relationship. I instinctively retreated from him and his open passion.

But Kar-Tur had expressed his own frustrations that I wasn't sufficiently open with my feelings. It left him uncertain about my motives or intentions.

How ironic that I tended to hide my inner self from people, as most people did, yet was drawn to those who demanded openness. Cynthia, too, had asked for greater emotional candor.

But my parents' experience made that openness difficult.

It wasn't the accusations of the police that had hurt—it was easy to dismiss the accusations of misguided strangers who didn't know them. It was the friends who remembered for the news reporters that my parents were "always a little strange and emotionally unstable." That's how their friends characterized my parents' trusting openness. No doubt, my parent's friends mainly wanted to appear perceptive and important. And they didn't want to support something evil. When my Dad was arrested for sexual assault, even his church counseled him to confess and repent. "We still love you and want to help," they said. It must be a strange kind of love that didn't *believe* in him, having known him for years. The very people we leaned on in that darkest time, had no faith in us.

People enjoyed believing ill of each other. I learned the lesson well. Don't give them any ammunition.

I'd told Kar-Tur the story a couple of days ago when he asked me why I wasn't more open with him. "I call you Tribewoman," he said, "and yet you share little of yourself with me."

That had been my first real clue what he meant by "Tribewoman." I told him of my parents and that terrible year. "I should have spent that year basking in my last carefree days at home, enjoying my family and High School," I'd said. "When the real rapist was caught and confessed, my parents' friends never really comprehended why relationships didn't return to what they were before. To them, it was all over. To my parents, a trust in community was lost forever.

"You were a stranger to me less than half a year ago," I'd continued. "I guess I'm afraid of what being open might do. Does it really lay the foundation for friendship? Or, does it lay the foundation for lost friendship and betrayal?"

It had been very hard for me to say, but Kar-Tur seemed to accept it, for a while at least.

My parents' loss of community had contributed to their decision to go into missionary work overseas, once their only daughter graduated. Funny, how humans both direct and are directed by the currents of life. Our life is neither an action on our part, nor a reaction to the world, but an *interaction*, without distinction between cause and consequence.

I eventually settled my mind back onto my dissertation and kept at it for several hours. About two in the morning, I took a break to meander through the partially-darkened hallways, peering into the vacant offices wondering what work transpired there in daylight. I used Walt's key to enter one office with a large floor-to-ceiling window partially covered by drapery. I stood behind the drapery so I wouldn't be silhouetted in the window by the hallway lights, and watched the city dreaming below me. I wondered what the past day had brought to those sleeping there, and what the new day would accomplish. I wondered about the people in the few cars still buzzing here and there on the streets like gnats lost from the swarm. Where were they going? Why were they out? Were they returning from a binge at the bar? Did they work late? Or were they returning home from visiting a friend?

I longed to be part of it again. I never realized what a blessing it is to simply be free to go and do. To be able to delight in the open sky, or a meal with a friend.

A flash of light caught my eye, and I turned my head to see a meteor streak across the sky, exploding in a burst of red and blue, seemingly just above the city. A meandering brown trail glowed after it for a few seconds, highlighting its pathway from the heavens. The falling star was just a stray, so many weeks after the passage of the Quadrantids. But it reminded me of the prodigious existence that spanned beyond my own dissertation and my own concerns.

I wondered about Susan's work. About my own place in it, my visions, the power that the Senator implied I practiced but that I knew I had not. Susan had lived many years after she perished from this present time. Surely, in all those years, she must have thought more about the implications of her work. If so, why hadn't she left it for us to find at her burial?

There must be more there, at that site in Wyoming. Something we hadn't found yet. Something that would reveal more of Susan's insights into this power over the undefined, this Certainty Principle, that she uncovered. We should return there to search for it. Kar-Tur wanted to return to Wyoming, to search for signs of his own people. Perhaps we could find a way to leave L. A. safely and return to Wyoming.

***

Kar-Tur and I went out for groceries toward morning. We kept sandwich fixings in Walt's small refrigerator and sometimes heated malt-o-meal or soup in the microwave. But we didn't have room to keep more than a couple of day's food supplies on hand.

We went to a small twenty-four hour convenience store. I still had a small amount of cash, but it ran low, and I didn't dare go to the bank for more for fear I'd be recognized there. I also didn't dare use my credit card for fear it would be traced. We checked out our groceries and paid in cash. As we prepared to leave the convenience store, a man we didn't know spotted us and approached. He marched to Kar-Tur and demanded in a too-loud voice, "Is it true, that you can travel in time?"

Kar-Tur and I glanced around the nearly empty store, hoping for help, but also hoping there was no one else there to identify us. I grasped Kar-Tur by the hand and tugged him toward the door. The man followed us, holding out a Bible, shouting, "If it's true, that you can travel in time, then swear it on this Bible."

We made it to the door, and ran outside, turning away from our intended destination, searching for a place to hide, or a way to lose our follower. But the man didn't follow us, his goal apparently accomplished. We continued for a while away from our office building hiding place, hoping to misguide anyone who might be watching, before circling back through alleyways.

***

The next evening, I read the web news on Walt's computer about the local radio minister who had proved the story of a Time Traveler to be a hoax. The time traveler, the story reported, was unable to swear on a Bible that his story was authentic.

Chapter 44

Operation National Examination, or ONE, as the underground movement was called, proceeded slowly. Doing otherwise would be irresponsible, Raumin thought, and would justify the accusations the Senator made against them. They planned, after all, to overthrow the U.S. government, should that become necessary. Two and a half centuries ago, the founding fathers warned that citizens would need to repeatedly overthrow their government to remain free, but that hadn't been necessary. Until now. The system of checks and balances established in the U.S. government proved to be even more stable than the founding architects expected.

Jane O'Hara, L. A. City Councilwoman and director of the entire California operation sat across from him, paper notes laying on the somewhat-beat-up oak table. Her dark hair, cut short and graying lightly, carried just the right mix of tough competence and experience. The meeting room, spare and bunkerlike, matched that image.

"We've got nearly half of the Army and Marines, and over half the Air Force ready to split from the President," O'Hara, told him. "They can support the British troops if needed."

That such a large operation had developed so quickly both astonished and frightened him. Long periods of quiet boredom followed by intense moments of terror—it applied to a broader sweep of life than war alone. Clearly the human race was adapted to such sudden activity. Even their own cell here in L.A. was impressive in size and quality.

Councilwoman O'Hara impressed him. She initially recruited him as he nosed around with old intelligence buddies trying to learn about the Hewitt kidnapping. ONE had existed only as an idea then. Now, in a short few months, its mycelia permeated the country.

Mycelia. Hopefully the fungal reference did not reflect badly on the purpose of their organization, Raumin thought with inner humor. Only on its pervasive and ineradicable character.

"I want you to take on oversight of Professor Myrvik as well as this new guy, the geologist, that you've brought on board," O'Hara said. "Dr. Myrvik is still in periodic contact with the Senator, and may help us ascertain his intentions. And Myrvik's knowledge of spy technologies is invaluable.

"I'm putting you in charge of our intelligence-gathering division here in L.A. You're free to develop your own protocols and do what you see fit. But keep me informed about anything you uncover. Particularly concerning the Shimera. We need to know from them when the U.S. government takes threatening actions so we can determine whether we should intervene or let events play out. On our own, we can't detect efforts to alter time or reality.

"Also, I'd like to meet the geologist before we trust him too far. Can you bring him to see me?"

***

Raumin met Dr. Myrvik in his office at the University. It was risky to meet so openly, but students and faculty were always coming and going from the professor's office with concerns about teaching, or research, or issues related to his duties as department chair. No one was likely to distinguish Raumin from one of those. Also, if anyone recognized him as a detective in the local precinct, they should know that he had reasonable business with Dr. Myrvik as he continued to follow up on the disappearance of Susan Arasmith.

Dr. Myrvik still looked weak after his weeks in the hospital and the additional weeks on bed rest at home. But he had recovered well. His posture in the old-style oak swivel chair behind his desk was straight, and the crisp tie and jacket offered a sense of strength.

"Detective." Myrvik acknowledged him with a nod, and waved a hand toward a chair.

"Thanks." Raumin seated himself.

"I presume that you're interested in verifying my switch of allegiance," Myrvik said.

Raumin wasn't accustomed to being surprised, particularly in these harsh times where he anticipated the unanticipated. But the professor's bluntness both startled and refreshed him. Startled, because most people could not so clearly identify the point of his visits, let alone come so swiftly to it. Refreshed, because it suggested a forthrightness that he could appreciate and deal with.

"That would be nice," Raumin answered, smiling slightly and settling into his chair. "You'll be on my team, and before I put the rest of my team at risk, I'd like to know where you stand."

"So far as the Senator knows, I'm still one of his people," Myrvik said. "I contacted O'Hara because I can no longer support him or his objectives. I'm embarrassed to say that I ever did. I can only plead to have been deceived. That's a hard thing for me to admit. I pride myself in my networking skills, and my ability to read people. But, in the Senator, I met my better. The Senator's a charismatic man.

"Also, I believe in his stated goal of securing this new power, whatever it is, into the hands of our government. But, apparently no law or ideal or even life is too great to sacrifice for his ends. That's recipe for a tyrant, not a leader."

"What can you offer us?" Raumin asked.

"If the Senator calls on me again, I can let you know," Myrvik replied. "If he doesn't, you have my expertise in remote sensing and surveillance technologies. You surely know of my work using Doppler shifting to listen to remote conversations, and my work with quantum sensors to detect gravitational disturbances indicative of large movements of personnel and equipment."

Raumin had read a brief report of Myrvik's work, but didn't understand it. All very scientific, no doubt. Incomprehensible. But surveillance was crucial to the success of a small revolutionary organization like ONE.

Raumin still wanted better assurance that Myrvik wasn't just a means for the Senator to infiltrate and destroy that fledgling organization.

"Such a striking shift of allegiance is somewhat unsettling. Can you help me understand it?"

Myrvik thought a few moments, then with a sigh asked, "Are you married, Detective?"

Raumin shook his head.

"Ever been?"

"No, never felt the need."

"Hmmm. Well, you might not understand then. I guess you could say that I did feel the 'need'. Still feel it. But my wife doesn't. Not anymore. At least not with me. She left me and took my kids with her. This past year has been difficult. I've been emotionally distraught, and even my behavior and character toward my colleagues has been affected. It's no excuse for my poor judgment, but it's a *reason* for it, at least partially."

Raumin waited for him to continue, but he did not. A faint smile lingered on the man's lips, almost as if to say, "that's what I've got, take it or leave it."

"You ask me to accept marital disharmony as reason for supporting attempted murder and backing a would-be dictator?" Raumin asked, a bit incredulous. "And what's changed? Are you now healed?"

Myrvik said no more. He only shrugged.

Raumin rose from his chair. "We'll be in touch if we need you." He took his leave.

The man's explanations were thin, Raumin thought as he returned to his car. But they were also bold and carried a hint of authenticity. He couldn't empathize from personal experience with the man's desertion by his wife. But he could understand the confused muddle the brain transformed to when deeply pained. Instinct led Raumin to believe him. And in these times of urgent haste, instinct was all he had time for.

Chapter 45

Their route tangled through the forest of buildings in such a twisting maze that Jonathan could not imagine anyone following them. Even though he knew the city well, he lost track in the darkness of exactly where they were. When the detective asked him to wear a blindfold for the last few miles, he doubted it was necessary, but complied.

They parked, and Raumin led him down a flight of stairs into a building. Raumin removed the blindfold inside a long, windowless hallway lit by yellow lights in small metal cages secured to the ceiling. It felt underground.

Raumin left him in a clean room furnished with several couches and chairs, a reading lamp, and a large mirror on one wall. Jonathan presumed the mirror to be a one-way window. It made sense, he supposed, to not expose members of the underground to identification while they questioned him. Although he wondered why they didn't simply use a video camera. Maybe they liked the more personal feel of proximity afforded by the window.

A woman entered shortly, pushing a wheeled cart with a small metal box and computer.

She smiled. "We have a few questions for you. Would you be willing to submit to a lie-detector test?"

Jonathan agreed, slightly offended but also comforted that this organization took such care to protect the group of people of whom he might soon be a part.

Or, at least they protected *some* of their people. The woman, probably some technician, was left vulnerable on the wrong side of the one-way window. If Jonathan were a spy for the other side, she would be the first to disappear into the bowels of some interrogation chamber.

The woman connected him to several wire leads coming from the machine. "A few more of us are watching behind the window," she said. "I hope you understand the need for caution and won't take offense. We have not only ourselves, but our mission to protect."

Jonathan nodded.

The woman seated herself in the chair opposite his. "There's no need to be nervous. Just tell us the truth. What's your name?"

"Jonathan Renner," he replied.

"Where do you work?" she continued.

"I'm a professor at Burns College here in L.A."

"Can you tell us, Jonathan, why you agree with us and our goals?"

Jonathan paused at that question. It was, so far as he understood the workings of a lie detector test, a terrible question, being far too vague and broad.

But it gave him a chance to address his many misgivings.

"I'm not sure I can agree with everything you stand for," he said. "But I believe there are serious problems with present U.S. policies. Problems that threaten our own freedom, and the stability of our relationship to another race, the Shimera. For the sake of those concerns, I can work with you on some things.

"Does that make sense?" he tacked on reflexively.

Many other vague and broad questions followed. Jonathan answered each truthfully, hoping he didn't undermine his credibility with these people. Or, perhaps, even put himself in danger.

When the interview was completed, the woman removed the electrodes from his skin as quickly as she'd applied them.

"Welcome to our group, Jonathan." she said. "I'm Jane O'Hara, if you didn't already recognize me. I direct the California branch of ONE. But you will be working under Raumin. You will report to him."

She left with the wheeled table, while Jonathan, fumbling to put his shirt back on, grappled with the realization that the flunky who tested him was one of the highest officers in the underground organization. She was, by rumor at least, the founder of it.

He felt a surge of loyalty toward this woman who put herself at risk before any of her people. Whatever happened, and however things turned out, she couldn't slip quietly back into her former life and former role. She kept no chips in reserve in case her plans failed, but committed herself entirely to her cause.

If that was a play to generate loyalty, it was one that Jonathan respected.

***

Zealous to commence his contribution to ONE, and impatient with delay, Jonathan drove to the CalTech campus the next day as soon as he finished teaching classes. He tempered his impatience with the understanding that the moil of revolution must progress slowly. But Jen, his friend whose entire life was set aside by the present circumstances, bore the burden of that sufferance. He chafed at delay for her sake.

Conversation with the female Shimera always tasted peculiar, because she communed with thoughts rather than words and because her succinct conversation seemed especially stiff and abrupt. His last meeting with the Shimera in Susan's lab had been particularly eerie. He'd encountered a younger version of her who'd never met him before.

As she had materialized in the room, a vague shimmer becoming gradually more concrete, he had recognized immediately that she floated higher from the floor and across the lab from her former location.

"Who are you?" she'd asked.

Her question had taken him aback. "Jonathan," he replied. "Jonathan Renner. We met before."

"It might have been before for you. But not for me. You'll have to catch me up on my future."

It had felt odd to have to explain to her who he was and what was going on when she had known so much more than he in their first two meetings. He'd alerted her to the events impending in his world that were destined to affect hers. He'd called her Shimera, no doubt when she first learned his name for her race. And he'd learned that her name was Wielei.

Jonathan reached Susan's lab, left open for him by Myrvik at Raumin's request. The 'older' version of Wielei appeared this time, as he'd hoped. He needed to explain the ongoing efforts of his people to stop the harm done to the Shimera world. Convince her that his people acted earnestly.

Wielei appeared very quiet today. Her voice came soberly into his mind. "What is to be done by your people?" she asked.

"We're taking steps to preempt any effort to travel in time again," Jonathan said. "We're prepared to go to war against our own people to prevent this. Please know that this is hard for us, and reflects our grave resolve. But, we don't know when to act, or where to act, because we don't know which actions or events cause damage in your world. We need you to tell us."

Wielei nodded. It was such a human gesture that it startled Jonathan. "We have watched you. And we understand your effort and your risk," she said. "I must tell you that part of what we feared can no longer be averted. That part is decided, and, from your perspective, it shall come to pass. Because of this, part of our world is gone permanently. It's a long trek to our loved ones now, around this hole in our world. And many died who lived in that time. I plead with you that those events still undecided not come to be.

"We know more than we did," she continued. "The events that harm us are those that distort time. You can work safely within your own time, but if you cheat time, or steal from time, or move in time, a part of our world is destroyed. Does this help you know how to proceed?"

Jonathan wasn't sure. He didn't understand it. But maybe others would.

"I hope it's enough," Jonathan said. "We'll be working to understand it, and you can let us know when actions threaten you."

"No, Jonathan. I cannot. You won't be back to this place where our lives can cross. Nor can I come to you. You may encounter others of my people, or you may not. But you will not meet me again here."

Jonathan nodded, listening but not understanding. What did she mean when she said that he would not meet with her again? Why not, and how was he supposed to know what to do?

"I can tell you this," she continued. "Our people have chosen not to use our most formidable weapons against you, regardless of the outcome for us. We found no way to exonerate ourselves from such a crime, even to save ourselves.

"But we have other weapons, and other means, to affect your world. Those of us who can come into this time will be watching, ready to support you if your war reaches this place on Earth."

Chapter 46

The vision came into my mind more vividly and with more detail than any that came before it. At first, I watched from ground level, as though through a window. The initial silence was broken with sudden noise and motion. I felt the earth tremble and saw it break open in great cracks and rifts. Buildings and bridges fell. The scene widened below me as though I rose up on wings. I looked on as people ran screaming from the destruction that cascaded around them.

Then the earth lapsed into silence again. More silent than at the beginning. Police stood guard everywhere. Military police. I saw no vehicles but theirs on any of the still-intact roads.

They secured the city methodically, regulating traffic and people on each street, at each grocery, and in each business. In my vision, I descended back to the ground and watched as the police searched for someone, through each building and in each hiding place where the homeless lived. I knew that they searched for me.

A newspaper, blowing in the empty wind, lodged at my feet. The headline read "Earthquake Devastates City." But the date grabbed me even more. It was just two days away.

When the vision ended, and I found myself once more back in the janitor's office with Kar-Tur, I trembled much as the earth had. I knew that I had seen things to come. I had seen a catastrophe turned into opportunity to strengthen government, which serves the strong and the many, at the expense of law, which protects the weak and the few. I was the weak and the few. I had to escape Los Angeles before this reality came to be.

The disruption promised by the earthquake invoked the need to escape. But it also provided opportunity to escape. I was growing weary of hiding, of having such limited mobility and living in constant fear of detection. I'd wanted for some time to visit Jonathan's site in Wyoming, to see if Susan had left something more for us, something that we'd missed. I couldn't believe that she, a scientist, would fail to leave behind a record explaining and documenting the work she must have done to understand her journey into the past. But I had, until now, found no safe means to leave L.A.

The turmoil of an earthquake would provide that means.

Kar-Tur also hoped to leave Los Angeles, to see if anything remained of his people in Wyoming. I interpreted his desire as a spiritual longing to say goodbye to his tribe in the place that they once shared.

Also, he was as much at risk as I was in a city under martial law. He might wish to flee the city with me.

I had grown accustomed to Kar-Tur's presence in my recent exile from home and university. I realized now that I *hoped* he would want to go with me.

I told him of my vision, and asked if he wanted to go to Wyoming.

"Yes, Tribefriend," he said. "Of course I will go with you to Wyoming."

His matter-of-fact tone, gently reprimanding my uncertainty in asking the question, made me feel good somehow.

He was seated on the small couch, and I went to sit beside him. "Why do you call me 'tribefriend'?" I asked. "You've been calling me 'tribewoman' until now." I watched him uncertainly, hoping I was not breaching some social taboo of his people.

"It's the way of my people to be open about our feelings," Kar-Tur replied. A faint smile turned his lips up on the edges, and he turned his eyes from mine toward the empty desk in Walt's office. "In that way, others always know where they stand with us, and can modify their own behaviors and feelings accordingly. They need not guess our regard for them, hoping or fearing what we might think."

He turned to look at me again, and caught my eyes into his, his voice taking on a depth and richness that made me realize he was sharing something with me that meant a great deal to him. "'Tribe' indicates my feelings of association with you, that I would not wish us to be separated. My people very much believe in the sanctity of tribal union, and that separation, except in death, is to be avoided. 'Tribewoman' indicates our bond in community, that I feel our lives are linked and that we are part of the same fellowship. 'Tribefriend' is a closer bond, a special bond, not only in tribe, but between you and me."

"Aha," I replied.

It warmed me to know of Kar-Tur's friendly feelings toward me. Remembering his names for me, and their progress, I realized that they reflected our expanding and changing relationship as we grew to know each other better through the trying times we experienced together. I felt somewhat ashamed of my harsh opinion of him in those first few weeks. But it was only natural that my feelings toward him would change as our acquaintance matured. My feelings were certainly different now.

"We must leave Los Angeles today, Tribefriend," I said. "We have a lot to do."

***

I sent an email to Cynthia, and through her to Jonathan, warning them of the earthquake my vision prophesied. I received a new message from Cynthia. One sentence in particular impinged on my distracted awareness.

> "J, I know that you want things to return to normal, but are you sure that simply waiting for others to take action is the correct course for you? I'm wondering if there might be some truth in the Senator's claims about your abilities. Maybe you are meant to do something with them."

But I was too busy with other concerns to reflect on this. I turned my attention to our own preparations. It didn't take long to pack our small store of food, toiletries, and clothing, into the duffle bags we had arrived with months ago. I looked around the now-empty janitor's closet that had been our home, making sure we'd left no trace of our time there. I felt a sense of melancholy loss even as I steeled myself for the next drop on our blind roller-coaster ride.

The ID Raumin acquired for Kar-Tur, and the false ID he got for me, gave us mobility. The AmRail trains served both Denver and Cheyenne from L.A. We could buy tickets with the fake IDs. But we needed cash. And that required using my true identity to get money from my bank account. I could go to a branch office where the tellers wouldn't know me, or I could use a cash machine, although a machine might balk at the percentage of my account I hoped to withdraw. Hopefully the earthquake would prevent my withdrawal from resulting in a quick pursuit of me. In any case, we'd soon be gone from L.A. and, unless they caught me in the bank, simply accessing my account shouldn't help them find me.

"I think, Tribefriend, that we should try the cash machine first," Kar-Tur suggested after we discussed the danger of exposing myself in a place where my true identity must be revealed. "It's less confining, and provides greater opportunity to escape should someone be waiting for us to take this very action."

I agreed. There was a cash machine for my bank just a few blocks from the office building we hid in. We walked there, moving casually to avoid standing out from other pedestrians. Trying not to show our nervousness, and with Kar-Tur watching for the approach of any suspiciously interested types, I keyed in my number and cash request. To my relief, the machine gladly relinquished nearly my entire account's balance. In another time and situation that would likely have been cause for concern rather than relief.

Our taxicab trip to the train station likewise took place without problems. We purchased tickets using our fake ID's and my cash and sat down in the station lobby to await our departure. It felt long, although it was only an hour. We boarded quietly, our presence drowned in the tide of humanity.

A sense of relief flooded me, gathering momentum with the accelerating train as it pulled from the station. I looked at Kar-Tur as the buildings and cars swept by the window with increasing speed. My relief must have shown on my face, because he gave a smile and said, "We made it."

Our relief came too soon. I felt the train shudder with the impact of the first seismic waves from the earthquake. I heard a rumbling and screaming as the wheels clutched the steel rail. I had the momentary sensation that I was on the tilt-a-whirl at the Fair, my body jerked suddenly one way then another.

The primary and secondary waves came upon us in quick

succession—proving we must not be far from the epicenter. I worried vaguely about the surface wave that must follow, but was too concerned with the turbulence of the moment to really fear it.

The surface wave swept across the desert like sea waves sweep across the ocean. I watched, fascinated, as the landscape rippled in the grip of the rolling earth that left the land behind it broken and hummocky.

The surface wave reached us and tossed the passenger car like a toy train on a snapped rug. Our momentum sent us airborne, and my stomach convulsed as gravity vanished during a moment of freefall. The silence of flight dissolved into the screech of metal as the passenger cars crashed into earth and each other with all the power that Newton's laws of motion could muster.

For a brief eyeblink our car remained upright, then tumbled sideways to its direction of motion. Somewhere in the melee, Kar-Tur grabbed me around the waist and secured his other hand to our cushioned seats. Somehow, incredibly, he held us there, keeping us from being bashed to death like a head of wheat in a combine's thresher. They should have provided seatbelts, I thought uselessly.

My face was close to Kar-Tur's as he held us there. His jaw tensed with the strain of his effort. His eyes burned with rage, as though he intended, through force of will to defeat both maleficent events and the universe itself to save us. His open emotion and anger didn't frighten me in that moment. I felt glad of the strength and vigor I once feared.

We came to rest at last, the screams and groans around us eerily muffled in comparison to the auditory melee of a moment before. The earthquake had come too soon. And we were too late in escaping L.A.

Chapter 47

Cynthia finished balancing her bank account, a task that had become increasingly stressful over the last few months as both savings and the relatively small insurance payment from Mike's death ran low. There was not a lot left, perhaps enough for a month or two, even with Adam working part time at McDonalds. Her new job writing for the newspaper editorial page was coming just in the nick of time.

She'd managed a few financial mini-coups since Mike died. A national publisher bought two of her short stories a month or so ago. She sold several editorials to the local paper, as well as a general interest science article. But freelancing was discouraging work, especially when crammed into the busy schedules of two teenagers. The predictable income afforded by a steady job, even if small in amount, would help to keep them on their feet.

She gladly turned her attention from numbers to writing. She ran her hands over the keyboard. She enjoyed the sensation of the keys at her fingers as much as she enjoyed the opportunity to renew her writing career. Rather whimsical how the fleeting joy of a sense of touch and the long-term impact of a source of income both played out as equal in her mind.

Most of her editorials so far had concerned human-interest stories: children's opportunities for education, poor people's access to social services, or other issues of justice and injustice. But the political winds rustled through her mind as much as everyone else's these days. The ideas of war and revolution, both bantered extensively in the recent social dialogue, bothered her. Because of her inside knowledge of government actions as pertained to Jen, she too questioned her leaders.

But that didn't mean she supported revolution.

She was a strictly law-abiding person. To her, laws were not options that you 'paid' for the right to break with fines. Nor were they guidelines to submit to so long as they were convenient. They were permanent and lasting agreements with society that only had meaning so long as they were not dismissed when dismissing them became personally beneficial.

She and Mike always complied with laws, even laws easily ignored, such as speed limits and traffic signs. She smiled a bit. They even obeyed the 'bump ahead' signs. Whenever they saw one, they would lean toward each other and gently bump their heads together.

A wave of melancholy swept over her. Used to. They used to bump heads. She wished Mike were here now to face these troubled times and make decisions with her.

A shock wave knocked over the cup of tea on the desk where she'd left it and nearly knocked her from her feet. Her disorientation with the first jolt lasted only an instant. She'd lived too long in L.A. to not know the feel of an earthquake. She shouted for Adam and Erin who were in their rooms upstairs. Stumbling with the dancing house, she ran as best she could to meet them at the bottom of the stairs. She could hear the scraping sound of the stove and refrigerator walking across the floor in the kitchen.

This was no small quake.

With a kid under each wing, she step-backstepped her way to the bathroom doorway, hoping the combination of pipes in the walls, the small room, and the doorframe would provide sufficient structural support to keep that part of the house safe. The roll of the floor increased, making it impossible to maintain their footing. They collapsed to the bathroom floor as the undulations continued, the earth-tempest leaving them momentarily seasick.

Cynthia heard a crash outside, which she supposed to be the collapse of the brick façade. The house sagged to one side, suggesting a portion of the foundation had failed.

It seemed like a long time, although Cynthia knew it must have been only seconds or minutes. But, at last, the temblor ceased.

They crept outside to look at the broken world. The street was split in several places. Four or five houses on the block had been destroyed, and several more, including theirs, had suffered severe damage. Looking farther into the distance, Cynthia saw that the downtown skyline was forever altered, missing two of its greatest towers. People wandered aimlessly in the street, having emerged from their houses like curious squirrels emerging from tree nests to survey broken trees after a storm.

She wasn't sure how safe or livable her own home would be now, but undoubtedly in the last few minutes many people had lost their homes entirely. Many had probably lost loved ones. Even so, she couldn't restrain a sudden burst of joy. She and her family were ok. She hadn't lost yet another member of her family. She held her children tightly against her.

***

The next two days were busy ones at the newspaper office. Significant effort went to finding a way to print, since their primary printing facility had been destroyed when the roof collapsed on it. And, addressing the earthquake and its impact on life in L.A. demanded extra online editions.

Jonathan stopped by the day of the quake to see if she and the kids were ok. That was a thoughtful gesture, and she appreciated it. Since then, he had stayed with the kids at her home when she had to work late hours—the house remained safe for habitation despite the foundation damage. Schools and universities were all closed, so Jonathan wasn't working.

She, on the other hand, found herself with more work than she could do. Her writing for the paper involved both the human drama of the tragedy, and the dialogue about the martial law that followed it. Preventing rampant crime in the devastated streets and businesses was indeed important. And providing general safety to citizens was the crucial purpose of government. But, to Cynthia, the implementation of martial law seemed so swift and efficient as to suggest it was planned or hoped for. It concerned her that these events came during such an already troubled and unsteady time.

Maybe she was just being cynical. Why should she criticize her government for being prepared and efficient? She would likely have criticized them even more harshly for their *failure* to be prepared or efficient. Jen's experiences with a suspect government subgroup need not imply that every government action was suspect.

But some part of Cynthia believed that the California Senator had capitalized on the tragedy to seize a power that he had long wanted. Why, for example, was the national military in control of the city rather than the state guard?

Also, the California Senator found too much political fodder in this misfortune for it to be coincidence. Already he was on TV and in the newspapers, including her own, talking of the senselessness of the destruction and how but for the recalcitrance of his opponents it could have been prevented. The government, he said, could have the power to control such events as this, to either prevent them or use them as need be.

The government, he said, could make its citizens truly safe, if only this new power could be harnessed, and those who opposed its harnessing could be ousted. Those who opposed him, he said, were indirectly responsible for the death and ruin caused by events that could and should be controlled.

"We can prevent these disasters," he said. "Let us."

Didn't anyone else hear the terror in that, echoing down through history? Oppression began with a promise of safety or plenty. Apparently others didn't see it that way. The Senator's popularity continued to expand. That too, should have sent warnings.

Every oppression began with a popular leader.

Chapter 48

After a day avoiding TV cameras, doctors, and other attention, and after two nights in motel rooms provided by AmRail, and after a bus ride to the nearest station with tracks not destroyed by the quake, Kar-Tur relaxed at last in the comfortable dining car of the train. The gentle clinking of drinking glasses and eating utensils contrasted sharply with the noise and strain of the past days. He had not felt such peace since leaving the home of Woman KarenRoden.

His stomach growled at the aroma of food, and he disciplined himself to eat slowly, with gentility, as his Tribefriend JenHewitt instructed was the way of her people. He feared that the time spent hiding in the office building had robbed him of most of the skill he had gained with knife and fork while at Woman KarenRoden's home, but he gamely struggled to use them well, proudly pointing out to Tribefriend JenHewitt how most of his herb-stuffed pork was eaten in small bites.

The glints of red in his Tribefriend's hair caught his eye as she sat across the table from him. He knew that many colors of hair embellished this new time, both natural and unnatural. The coal black color of his own people's hair was only one of many hues here. But when he first entered this world, it had been his Tribefriend's hair, with its brown sheen and sparkles of sunset, that he saw first. Her hair in particular remained striking to him.

She spoke, drawing him from his reverie. "Tribefriend, do you think I might be able to alter the events that are disrupting our lives? Change things, like the Senator says?"

She didn't look directly at him, but gazed on the landscape sliding past the train.

"I think that's possible, Tribefriend," Kar-Tur replied. "You have a special insight into another world, another place."

"Kar-Tur, what might happen if you taught me to *feel* into things, like you've talked about before? What could happen?"

"Are you wondering what might be possible?" he asked. "Or are you wondering how you might change inside?"

She appeared to lose interest then, recoiling from the promised discussion. "No, I'm not concerned about that," she said. "I was just wondering."

A measure of anger found its way into Kar-Tur's mind. So much might hinge on what she and he decided to do about this matter. Why wouldn't she talk it through with him? She still didn't trust him with her inner feelings. She still fled from that intimacy of *Tribefriend*.

The beautiful valleys and hills slipping past the window drew his eyes. They were green, yet spare. They had few trees, but the patches of grass were verdant. The valleys suited his ideas of perfection. Not opulent, but just enough.

His Tribefriend wasn't as open with him as he wished, not as emotionally candid as was common in his tribe, but she was more open now than she had been before. Maybe in the same way that every landscape need not be filled with trees, so every person need not be filled with openness to the same degree, or learn openness at the same rate.

He could be patient.

But he wondered if this world, this time, could afford that patience.

***

The last light of evening sprayed across the painted hills visible from the window of their sleeping-cabin. No longer simply spare, the landscape here was bare, but made beautiful by the colorful rock. Kar-Tur knew from his Tribefriend's geology lessons that these cyclical layers of rock, colored by ancient rivers and then exposed by the carving knife of wind and rain, told stories of a time far more distant than even his own people.

He thought to ask her about it, but saw that she prepared to retire for the night. She took the top bunk, leaving the lower one for him.

The rhythmic sounds of the train on its track soothed him. It was good to be *going*. He'd spent enough time in sedentary stillness in the office building. Motion was a release, a pleasure.

Whenever he finished one of his long, silent studies as seeker for his tribe, he always anticipated the time afterward when he could *go* with his people, *do* with them. He might hunt, carry meat or wood, or simply run. But it was the going, after so much stillness, which delighted him. After his long immobility in the tiny rooms of the large building in which he and his Tribefriend had hid, this time of movement felt good, like the times of going and doing with his tribe.

He missed his tribe. He wished he were not separated from them.

Thoughts of that loss brought to mind his fears of separation from his Tribefriend JenHewitt. In truth, he knew almost no one else in this time. She was his entire tribe.

However, despite his joy in her company and hope that they not be separated, he felt uncomfortable with the accommodations that this sleeping cabin provided. Considering that his Tribefriend was a woman and he a man untied to a woman, the accommodations were quite intimate, at least by the traditions of his people. He wasn't used to sleeping in the same space with her. When they were hiding in Tribeman WaltRoden's building, the two of them were able to sleep in separate custodial rooms.

But Kar-Tur understood the need to avoid attention. Tribefriend JenHewitt said that pretending to be husband and wife gave them 'cover'. The ID's that Detective Raumin acquired for them listed the same last name, a fact which Kar-Tur vaguely understood made them appear to be husband and wife. That was an odd and superficial marker for something of such import, he thought.

***

He awoke sometime in the night. It must have been near morning, since the half Moon hung high overhead. He rose, and watched the landscape slipping past the window for a time. The light from the Moon outlined the shadowy mountains, still capped with snow, against the darker sky. He listened to his Tribefriend breathing gently and felt warm in her presence. He enjoyed the motion of the train, the changing view, the sense of life experienced. After a while, when the sky began to brighten in the east, he returned to bed.

***

They changed trains in northern New Mexico. They had no

sleeping cabin on this new train, only seats in the passenger car. Kar-Tur knew he'd miss the other train, and the cabin he shared for a night with Tribefriend JenHewitt.

They changed trains again in Denver, and came into Cheyenne by evening of the next day.

Chapter 49

I had a plan when we reached Cheyenne. We needed flexible transportation. That meant a car, preferably with 4-wheel drive. Having ditched my phone, I had to buy a local newspaper for classified ads and scanned them for a match to our needs.

I could pay for the car in cash, not using my credit card as a rental would require. I might not even need to use my fake ID as long as the sellers allowed me to handle the registration change. And if they insisted on doing the paperwork, I could still use my false name on the registration.

Cheyenne was a small city, and we found an old 4-wheel drive pickup for sale within walking distance of the train station. We bought the vehicle, after assuring ourselves it would start at least once, and drove away with the unsigned registration form, promising to handle it. I *would* handle it, I comforted myself, salving my conscience. *Eventually*.

It was late, but the longer days of spring left sufficient light for us to see by. I was eager to start on the next leg of our journey and expected that Kar-Tur also would be impatient to see the place where he once lived.

"Shall we go first to where you used to live, or to Jonathan's dig site?" I asked.

"No, neither." His vehemence startled me. "It will be dark soon. We are tired. We'll stay here for the night."

"Aha." I hid my reaction to his intensity. I wondered how he marshaled such self-assurance. His face looked almost angry, and I found him frightening again, as I had at first.

What did I know of this man? Despite the months we'd spent together, I knew nothing of his background, whether he saved baby birds fallen from their nest or chased children out bedroom windows and beat them.

I knew him better than I once did. Had come to trust him. Call him Tribefriend. But his manner tapped into deep fears I couldn't stem. I wished my Tribefriend would be less abrupt.

We stopped at a motel and rented two rooms for the night. We arose early the next morning, before the sun. Using maps as well as topographic landmarks he remembered, Kar-Tur identified the approximate area his people had inhabited. We drove about twenty miles north of town to the creek along which he had once lived.

"It's very different now," he said as we approached his former home. "It's not as green. The river doesn't carry as much water, and the meanders aren't quite the same. I'm afraid I won't be able to find exactly where our summer homes stood."

We drove for a while, looking. In one place, we got out of the pickup and hiked around a hill that Kar-Tur thought he recognized.

Of course, we found no sign of Kar-Tur's people. That world, the very land he knew, was long since washed away to the sea.

I sat with Kar-Tur along the banks of the river for a time, striving to see what he must see, to look into another era with him. I watched for the great herds of camel and horses scampering across the prairie, and listened for laughter from homes filled with children.

I couldn't see that time. But I could stay with him while he said goodbye to his people and his world. And I did.

We rose to return to the pickup and were walking up a shallow slope toward the highway when I saw an odd shimmering appear in the air in front of us, like rising heat waves painted with reds and greens. I stopped and tried to focus on the light as it resolved into the shape of two beings, human in form. I knew these must be Shimera, beings like the one that killed Mike, Cynthia's husband. Beings like the one that Jonathan had communicated with in Susan's lab. Beings like those that Susan and Kar-Tur had inadvertently harmed when they travelled across time.

I tensed, not sure whether or not to flee. Beside me, I felt Kar-Tur ready himself as well, his knees flexing slightly, his posture alert. The eyes of the beings, bright sparks in their opalescent faces, turned toward Kar-Tur.

"You're one of those who traveled," one of the beings said. I heard the voice in my mind, and from Kar-Tur's expression, I guessed that he heard it too. "Why did you do this? Why harm us this way?"

Kar-Tur didn't speak for a moment, startled by their sudden appearance. "I didn't intend to harm you. I didn't even intend to travel to this time. It has separated me from my loved ones and my people. I, too, wish it could be undone."

The two beings no longer appeared to address us, but we still heard their voices in our minds. "That's what the other said as well," one said.

"Then perhaps it's true," replied the other.

And they vanished from sight.

***

The drive to Jonathan's site near Medicine Bow took much of the remainder of the day. We rode mostly in silence, seeming to share a sense of melancholy. The emptiness of the place that once held such life and joy for Kar-Tur sobered us.

"I wonder what suffering I caused the Shimera," Kar-Tur said at one point, as he reflected on the strange, brief encounter with the beings. "I didn't mean to harm them."

After a long silence, watching the prairie slide past and the mountains rise up ahead of us, he added, "I wish I might have found some sign of my people."

His hand lay on the seat beside me. I took mine from the steering wheel and covered his, letting it rest there quietly. There was nothing for me to say. No words could change his loss. I could only offer my friendship in exchange.

We arrived at the end of the gravel road in late afternoon. We drove the pick-up up the trail as far as we could, then hiked the rest of the way, reaching the site by evening.

The rocky outcrop seemed more somber than I remembered, perhaps because of the thickening sky, or perhaps because of my new knowledge that Susan lay buried there. A corner of Jonathan's blue tarp had blown free of its rock anchor over the winter and now flapped and moved against the ground with an eerie scratching sound. Kar-Tur and I grabbed it and peeled the tarp back from the fragile bones it protected.

I had no time for a thorough search of anything. We didn't dare remain for long, for fear that Jonathan's site was being watched, or that we'd been followed. And the sky hinted at inclement weather. We wouldn't want to be caught by a storm in such a remote place even with our four-wheel drive vehicle.

Even if we had more time, I wasn't prepared for a meaningful excavation, having brought neither tools nor expertise. Suddenly, I wondered why I was there at all.

But I knew I had to look for something more. Susan's message, 'Be a Friend,' was too brief and opaque to be her last or only communication to us. She was a scientist with discoveries to report. She'd have found a way to report them.

Falling to my knees, I examined the area of the excavation, searching for something more, a record of Susan's work, a testimony to her astonishing insight into the nature of nature.

The bones still lay imbedded in stone, only partially exposed by the incomplete excavation. Cavities in the soft shale marked where we'd taken out the broach and wooden cross, and where Jonathan had earlier removed the small radio that first drew our attention to the exceptional character of the find. Cracks from mud-shrinkage indicated where water leaking under the tarp had accumulated in the cavities and dried.

I had brought no tools to dig with, but took out my pocketknife to probe into the soft stone. I slid the knife through the mud-rock and felt it hit something solid just below where Susan's head lay. I scraped around it with my knife, exposing the corner of a large, flat stone, better-indurated than the softer rock which entombed Susan's remains.

With more clearing, I saw writing carved in the upper face of the stone, not in words, but mathematical expressions that squiggled their way across the stone. Susan's Magnum Opus.

I scraped more of the softer stone away, exposing as much of the harder rock beneath as I could without damaging the skeleton. More writing trickled thinly across the top of the stone, writing that looked like words. With the tip of my knife, I cleaned out the carvings, making the writing easier to read. I could only just make out part of what was written:

Derivation of...............
.... and detachable rivets in the temporal folding
................corridor to P of T.

I had no idea what it meant.

Kar-Tur called me from the writings of the distant past with a warning for the present. "Tribefriend, I'm concerned for the weather. We should go."

I looked up, my eyes searching the sky for the clues that Kar-Tur was likely far more practiced than I at noticing in this region. The high, wispy-white cirrus clouds had given way to frosty altostratus. The warm southeast wind had yielded to a cooling one from the northeast.

I had to agree with Kar-Tur. The sky looked stormy.

I looked again at the corner of the newly-excavated stone protruding from under Susan's head like a pillow. Answers were there. Perhaps answers to the questions that plagued us in the present time. Perhaps answers to questions I had yet to formulate.

But there was no time now to excavate the stone, even if I had the knowledge or skill to do it properly, which I did not. The stone was too large, and too integrally buried with the skeleton to allow simple removal.

I rose slowly from my find. There would be another day for this. Kar-Tur and I re-anchored the tarp, better than before, and began the hike back to our pickup.

I noticed the land around me, this place that Susan had chosen as her final resting place. The gray, lowering sky accentuated the remnant reds and golds that autumn vested in the grass and shrubs of the arid prairie. Even after winter sapped much of their color away, they still held a quiet, unpretentious beauty. What a lovely place, a peaceful cemetery, to spend the millennia waiting for us.

We reached the pickup in a light rain. I drove quickly down the rough pathway toward the road. Before we made it to the gravel road, the light rain changed to heavy, wet snow. I hesitated to continue on the steep trail for fear we'd slide over an embankment or otherwise get in some pickle we couldn't get out of even when the snow ended.

I parked the pickup and prepared to wait out the storm. We had two blankets, packed with us in L.A., one for each of us. Snow soon covered the windshield, causing the dim light of evening filtering into the cab to grow even dimmer. The falling light emphasized the chill air. As the temperature continued to fall, I began to shiver with the cold.

"Tribefriend, we should share our two blankets between us," Kar-Tur suggested. "We will both be warmer."

I hesitated a moment, unsure whether Kar-Tur had other motives for his invitation. Seeing my doubt, Kar-Tur continued, "My people also have rules for behavior between men and women, Tribefriend. You don't need to be afraid of me."

The cold grew uncomfortable and Kar-Tur's invitation appealing, both for the sake of warmth, and because, I had to confess, snuggling under a blanket sounded nice, even with this man who often frightened me and who came from a strange culture.

I drew myself against Kar-Tur, and we spread the two blankets above us. Soon I was warm and drowsy. As I fell asleep, I felt my head slide down to pillow in the crook of his neck, at which point I no longer felt inclined to move.

Chapter 50

Jonathan could see much of historic Washington from his position near the top of the Hyatt Regency, including nearly all of the Mall, with the Capitol Building dominating his view. Although rising less than a quarter mile away, the building had a grey cast to it, as though viewed through a smoggy haze. Jonathan wasn't sure if the effect was caused by atmospheric conditions or his own inner mindset.

When martial law was declared in L.A. after the earthquake, people noticed. When the mayor was assassinated because he insisted that martial law end, people grew uneasy. Once martial law was declared in Washington D.C., and the U.S. Congress was held hostage, everyone knew a coup was in progress. But by then, it was too late.

Ironic, Jonathan thought, that ONE had believed *they* were the subversive cadre preparing for a coup. At least they now had an organization in place to defend against this one.

The California Senator had brought in his own army, clearly trained for this very task. Oddly, the President still backed the Senator. He insisted that martial law was required to restore order in the country and secure the country against the new forces at work in the world.

Most people now saw him as a puppet, but about a quarter of the military remained loyal to the President. The rest prepared with the British troops for war against their fellow U.S. soldiers in an effort to retake Washington D.C. and reestablish legitimate government.

Communication with most of the U.S. Congress was cut off. Only the President and the California Senator's voices were still heard, along with a few others who hadn't been in D.C. at the time of the uprising and who had avoided the broader net cast by the Senator to immobilize national leaders. The sheer scale of the coup, coordinating an overnight capture of nearly every national government official and seizing effective control of the nation's capital, was breathtaking. However heinous it might be, it was also brilliant.

The Senator still insisted in his integrity, not quite admitting his attempt to seize power, but not denying it either. He continued to claim that the safety of the American people depended on his actions, and that the new power over nature needed to be harnessed by government. Jonathan believed the Senator was persuaded by his own rhetoric. Hopefully, few others were. The Senator's popularity had plummeted from the stratospheric high of just a few days ago. Although he had no doubt already used his burst of public approval for its intended purpose.

At least, his popularity had plunged among people Jonathan knew. But then, Jonathan's connections were limited mainly to people who had opposed the Senator even before these new events.

Historically, the Senator's argument that he acted for the safety of the nation was not unusual. All political persuasion was found in promises of money, services, and safety. How much money or how much safety were always the points of contention among the electorate. But America remained too entrenched in the tradition of personal freedom to think that *any* need for safety warranted the present action.

Or so Jonathan hoped.

Clearly, some people still believed in the Senator, or the present confrontation would not exist. Even though the forces advancing against the Senator's were overwhelmingly superior, the Senator still held the upper hand in D.C. where his troops prepared to defend against the invasion by U.S. and British forces. The need to be careful of civilian lives made retaking D.C. a difficult challenge. However, even that advantage didn't seem to account for the incomprehensible confidence exhibited by the Senator's troops. Exploring the reason for that confidence was what had brought Jonathan and Jack Myrvik here to D.C.

And to the top of the Hyatt Regency. Jonathan didn't like heights. As far as he was concerned, if people were meant to be high up, God wouldn't have made gravity.

He especially disliked dangling over the edges of roofs. The frail rope, tied to his harness and held by Jack Myrvik, made his precarious perch only slightly more secure. Jack claimed an even greater dislike of heights and generously volunteered to hold the safety rope while Jonathan secured the Doppler detector to the building.

Jack offered instructions as Jonathan aimed the detector's wide-angle sensor toward downtown D.C. where the Senator and his officers resided and where they hoped to pick up conversations about enemy plans and expectations. Fortunately for Jonathan's vertigo, this was the last of the detectors needed, or so Jack said. They'd installed six of them, providing for 3-D resolution and also allowing signals from greater distance to be distinguished from those originating nearer to the detectors.

Jonathan didn't pretend to understand Jack's wave-sorter. How could they listen in on thousands of conversations in the dozens of buildings the Senator and his advisors occupied? Jack's explanation of how he used the Doppler effect of light radiating from dust particles vibrating in the air didn't help much. Jonathan supposed it was an elegant way to observe conversations over a large area when you didn't know where crucial conversations were occurring. But sorting that mess of sound into intelligence seemed impossible.

Jonathan crept back up to the relative security of the roof, taking care not to over-test Jack's ability to keep him from falling. Then they slipped down the stairs to the top floor, relocking the roof access door with the key Raumin had acquired through his ONE contact in D.C. They took the elevator to the ground floor and returned on foot to the basement under the printing office, which they'd procured for their headquarters. They avoided the military police stationed at nearly every street corner by traveling back alleys and backyards, a skill they were well practiced at after spending two days sneaking into downtown from the outskirts of the city.

The basement allowed access both from the alleyway and the printing office, providing flexible entry for them, and an alternate way out if they had to escape. ONE operatives stationed in D.C. had furnished them with several computers powerful enough to run Jack's wave-sorter program. Jack had programmed his phone to download the signals from the detectors. Simple, but sufficient.

The room had no windows. Although that made sense so far as maintaining secrecy went, the single, bare light bulb left the room dark and shadowed. Jonathan always found himself standing in his own light. Fortunately, his main job consisted of watching two computer screens, which provided their own light.

The computers ran in parallel, each processing a different segment of the combined signals arriving from the detectors, filtering noise, and assembling possible conversations. The wave-sorter required human input, including help in recognizing which combinations of vibrations made sense and might be part of single human conversations and which were gibberish, reflecting pieces from unrelated conversations or noise in the city. Jonathan identified fragments that made sense.

To Jonathan, it seemed naïve to expect meaningful words to appear from dust vibrating in the middle of a city replete with background clatter and endless conversations useless to them. However, the computer fed him progressively less gibberish as it learned to identify useful or meaningful phrases. Fragments of conversation materialized from the noise, sorted and prioritized for his human mind to judge. Astonishingly, the wave-sorter became smarter even at separating conversations of the troops and leaders of the Senator's forces from irrelevant background conversation. As they spent less time in teaching it, Jonathan and Jack pored over the increasingly relevant conversations it reported to them.

One consistent idea emerged in conversations ranging from lowly privates to high military officers. The Senator's people expected their enemy to be completely obliterated.

How that might come to be was less clear. Jonathan and Jack searched long into the night among disjointed pieces of conversation floating in the air like seaweed in the ocean for a clue. They found a reference to a twenty-megaton explosion beamed from space. By satellite? *It didn't make sense.* No such weapon or technology existed. Only a nuclear bomb could release energy on that scale.

Jonathan suspected Jack's wave-sorter had assembled unrelated words, creating a seemingly-coherent scramble that was never part of any real conversation.

Jack asserted that wasn't so. His wave-sorter was a smart program, he said, learning from them which pieces were germane to their quest. The fragments of conversation were real. Somehow, the reference to a terrible weapon from space meant something. But they couldn't determine what.

By the end of the week, all they could recommend to their troops was to retake D.C. quickly before the weapon could be brought to bear.

Jonathan wished he could have contacted the Shimera before leaving L.A. Found out what they knew. Perhaps whatever gave the Senator's troops such confidence was related to the events that harmed the Shimera. Or perhaps the Shimera knew of some technology that could produce such an explosion.

Unfortunately, the basement housing Susan's lab had been demolished in the earthquake. When he went back to the building to talk to the Shimera after the earthquake, he had found it collapsed, rendering the room inaccessible. He had felt a shiver of comprehension, realizing that the Shimera had known ahead of time what was to come to pass.

Perhaps in time, it would be cleared. By then, it would be too late to matter to the fragile humans afloat in the present storm-tide of events.

Chapter 51

Kar-Tur marveled at the size of this great building and the roar reverberating through the walls from the immense birdlike airplanes parked beside it. He'd seen airplanes in the sky and noticed the winding, cloudlike trails they made there. But he'd had no idea they were so large.

His Tribefriend JenHewitt hoped to return to L.A. by airplane, thinking that the higher level of security at airports over train or bus stations might be to their advantage, and deciding against a long drive over the mountains where assassins might easily catch them alone. The changed political landscape, and the assassination of the L.A. mayor, presented a different set of constraints than those they faced when they left L.A. Although the higher level of security at the airport made it more likely that he and Tribefriend JenHewitt might be caught, it made it equally more likely they wouldn't be assassinated. Kar-Tur liked the idea both because being assassinated sounded like a bad thing, and because flying was a form of transportation he particularly wished to experience. He had always envied the power of the great eagles to rise on the invisible stairways of the sky.

The Denver airport certainly bustled more than the train station, although the abundance of empty seats in the terminal led Kar-Tur to suspect that even this level of activity was far below its capacity. They purchased tickets using the ID cards from Detective Raumin and then found the appropriate gate to wait for their flight.

Tribefriend JenHewitt withdrew for a few minutes to visit the facilities where people of this time relieved their bodily needs, leaving Kar-Tur alone with the crowd noise. Through the cluttered sound of the terminal, one particular message found its way to Kar-Tur's ears, coming from the TV set mounted to the ceiling in the gate area.

"Two terrorists are loose in the Denver area," it said. Kar-Tur looked at the TV to see his own image there along with that of his Tribefriend. "These two are extremely dangerous and must be found.

If you see them, or know of them, please contact the authorities."

Kar-Tur rose from his seat. They were not safe here. He must inform Tribefriend JenHewitt.

Before he had time to find or warn her, three men approached. Two stood back, aiming pistols at him. Though small, those weapons had great power, as he had seen from books that his Tribefriend had used in teaching him to speak, and from TV, and from his experience with the shooting at Man WaltRoden's house. The third man drew near with handcuffs like those he experienced when he first arrived in this time.

He couldn't escape them. If only one held a gun on him, he could have perhaps moved swiftly enough to disarm him. But he couldn't overpower two before he was shot.

But before the man with the handcuffs took more than a step toward him, one of the armed men crumpled to the floor. Tribefriend JenHewitt stood behind him with a seat from the toilet facilities in her hands. The two remaining men froze for a moment in astonishment and her second swing took out the man with the cuffs. Kar-Tur moved much too quickly for a man of this time to defend against, and knocked the third man unconscious to the floor.

He picked up the man's gun, sliding it under his shirt into the waistband of his pants. Two parents by the window hustled their children behind a row of seats, trying to put themselves between Kar-Tur and the children. Several men a few rows farther back were conferring, no doubt trying to decide what to do. Events had been too quick for people to react, but after the news report, everyone might be against them.

His Tribefriend dropped her weapon and grabbed his hand. Together they raced down the corridor until, rounding a bend, they found themselves momentarily alone. They slowed their pace, and stepped onto a moving walkway which carried them away from the increasing hullabaloo developing behind them where airport security had already begun to question witnesses and fan out to search.

They walked casually past the metal detectors, and made it out of the airport before the rapidly expanding search caught up to them or the airport was closed to prevent their escape.

Upon reaching their pickup, his Tribefriend said, "We have to stay away from populated areas, Kar-Tur. I know a place south of here, near Cañon City, where we can hide for days, or even weeks. But we need to get some food."

They tried to be both casual and quick at the grocery store. They bought some general supplies for wilderness cooking, including oil, flour, salt, and sugar, as well as some quick and nutritious meals requiring only water, including instant oatmeal, and some packets of ramen noodle soup. These were not unlike the convenient and easy foods that his Tribefriend had provided while they hid at Man WaltRoden's office in Los Angeles, although, to Kar-Tur's mind, food must surely be available at their destination, offered by the natural world even in this future time.

As they drove south, Kar-Tur reviewed his impressions of this woman he called Tribefriend. He liked and respected her more each day that he knew her. When she had fallen asleep beside him in the snowstorm, he had found her touch more disorienting than expected.

And today she had come to his rescue when she could have simply fled.

"You could have escaped safely while they handcuffed me," he said to her. "Thank you for coming to my aid, Tribemate JenHewitt."

Chapter 52

Two things vied for my attention as we turned southwest at Colorado Springs and drove toward Cañon City: the meaning of my newest visions and why Kar-Tur called me *Tribemate*.

My vision in the restroom at the airport had proved swiftly true, and provided only barely enough opportunity to prepare against the attempt to capture Kar-Tur. The veracity of that vision, as well as all my others, gave me confidence that this latest vision would also prove true, terrifying as that was.

I recognized this latest vision, having seen part of it before. The hummocky landscape, smoldering with scattered fires and stinking with burned rock and flesh, terrified me more than it did the first time I saw it, before I realized that my visions truly forecast the future. This time, the vision came with new information, new insight into the cause of that scene.

I must warn them. Tell them to get out. Get the soldiers out. Get everyone out.

I sensed that it came from another *time*. No wonder it destroyed the Shimera as well as our people.

I must find a way to contact Cynthia, and warn the world through her.

We drove in silence for a time, as I troubled over that terrible vision.

After a while, I summoned the courage to ask about my second concern. It seemed odd that I could worry about such a thing when so many people faced death, and our nation faced more turmoil than it had ever known. But I did.

"Kar-Tur," I began, "Why did you call me Tribemate? Do you think that I..." I hesitated, embarrassed and angry at what I had to ask. "Do you think you have some claim over me?"

Kar-Tur examined my face, probably seeing in it both my anger and embarrassment. Then he laughed, his eyes crinkling at the corners.

"No, Tribemate JenHewitt. That would be *Kar-mate*, and would reflect your claim over *me*, as I offered myself to you. Kar-mate derives from my incomplete name, *Kar*, reflecting my own personal incompletion, combined with *mate*, that which makes me complete.

"Tribemate, on the other hand, testifies to my great affection for you, and confidence in you, but does not imply that other relationship to which you refer. Tribemate is the closest of my people's community relationships. I call you Tribemate because I trust you completely, even with my life."

I pondered his answer for a time, unsure whether to be pleased at the trust he placed in me or embarrassed at my own presumption. I decided to be pleased.

We drove around in Cañon City for a time, looking for a place where I might access my email connection to Cynthia. There were plenty of prisons, I noticed with a shiver, hoping that didn't bode ill for my choice to come here.

We found a small community college on the west edge of town, nestled near the hog-backs where tilted rocks from the age of the dinosaurs angled up toward Skyline Drive. I found an internet connection there, available to students and accessible to the public, and sent my warning.

Then we parked along a street on the north side of town, and began walking up Garden Park Road, where I knew of caves nestled in the Fremont Limestone along Four Mile Creek. My cave man and I could hide there.

Chapter 53

Senator Jerry Roden, wrestled with the action he planned. His duty was to protect his people, to keep them safe. Not to harm them. But before he could protect them, he had to defeat his enemies, the enemies of his people. And that required war. War killed innocent people. Sometimes, it killed those he hoped to defend. If his childhood with his violent father taught him anything, it was to defend the vulnerable. Yet in this case, defending the world meant that vulnerable people might suffer.

Maybe he could warn them. Tell them to get out of the way. Then, those who believed in him, trusted him, could be saved.

He would do that.

His efforts to change the future had succeeded beyond his expectations. He'd set up a team of bright people, introspective people. Explained to them what was to come to pass, and showed them Susan's experiments that proved it *could* come to pass. He could feel their belief, palpably altering what could happen, what *would* happen.

The meteorite that they summoned upon Washington D.C. was already near enough to spot by telescope, if one knew where to look. His astronomers verified it to be on a collision course for Earth. That observation further strengthened the belief of his team. Their belief would make it fall where he decided.

He still had much to do to set the trap. He must get his own people out of Washington, and lure his foe in. It shouldn't be too hard to draw the enemy into DC. When his own army retreated, the antagonist would naturally advance. Some would remain outside the city of course. But he didn't need to kill them all. The very fact that even the heavens obeyed him would quickly dispel any further resistance to his leadership.

The timing for getting his own people out was trickier. They could move more quickly during the day, but it would take more than one period of daylight for everyone to evacuate. If he took too long, his men might be attacked outside the city where they weren't protected by the proximity of civilians. Or they might be caught in the basal surge of debris exploding away from the meteorite impact.

To this problem, he again applied his Belief Team. With extended daylight, his army could be out in twenty-four hours. His team could provide extended daylight. They would simply stop the Sun at midday.

He liked that touch, to stop the Earth's spinning, to hold the Sun still. Like Joshua, he would stop the Sun to lead his people into a promised land.

The Promised Land was the future. This war was for no less than the power to occupy that future. To choose it.

He would make it a future safe and peaceful beyond anything humanity had ever known. There would be no more crime, or war, or disaster. There would be no more angry, violent fathers beating their sons.

Chapter 54

Cynthia gathered up the wilted flowers left on the grave from Memorial Day. She noticed there were several arrangements other than her own. She knew about those left by Mike's sister, and her own parents. She wondered who had left the others.

The mound of earth above the grave had settled over the winter. She felt a sense of finality with that settling, not quite closure yet, but acceptance. The presence of his name on a tombstone began to seem real.

"Michael D. Brown
Loving father to Adam and Erin
Loving husband to Cynthia
Loving friend to many."

She ran her fingers over the stone, feeling the texture of the rough granite. The stone was strong and reliable, like Mike. Just a summer to go, and it would be a year since he died. Hard to believe. She wondered what Mike would do in the present circumstances.

Just what he always did, she supposed. The right thing regardless of personal cost.

She wondered, too, if she was doing as well. Did she speak out in her editorials, unafraid of the martial law? Did she speak boldly, not intimidated by the brutal assassination of the mayor when he had spoken boldly?

Like her, the mayor had not been part of ONE, but just a citizen who believed that, ultimately, his nation was on his side and he was on the side of his nation. He had stood in the open, before his city, and spoke. And he had died.

Jane O'Hara also spoke boldly. But more cynically doubting her own nation, she protected herself. She still lived.

Cynthia thought of her words to Jen, encouraging her to consider a more active part in national events. There was something special about Jen. She had an insight, a power that she was yet to develop and use fully. Her visionary prediction of the earthquake proved her potential. She had a responsibility, a duty, to use that power.

But didn't everyone have a power that could always be developed more fully and used more completely? Didn't Cynthia also have power? Power to write, power to do?

She considered whether she ought to take her own advice. Whether she should take a more active role in events, and not bury her head in her children and her writing. Should she do like Jonathan, and do as she advised Jen, and act?

The cemetery seemed so peacefully unaware of the trauma in the world. Even now, someone who was not diverted by civil war or natural disaster kept it mowed. Not everyone in society was consumed by its present turbulence and uncertainty. Some of them kept that society running. She took comfort in that.

Cynthia returned to her car, somewhat rejuvenated by her meditation at Mike's grave. And with a resolve to reconsider her part in the future.

Her frequent visits to the cemetery over the past months had helped her reconcile with Mike's death. She wished Susan had a grave for her to visit. There *was* a place where Susan's bones lay, Cynthia knew. But, for her, it was not a grave. Just a cold, ancient rock that would frighten more than comfort. Perhaps one day, though, she would go there.

On the way back home, Cynthia stopped by the library. She often used the computers there to contact Jen. She hoped it gave one extra level of security against their communication being discovered.

She worried how Jen was doing. She missed her and wondered how long Jen's exile must continue. She'd like to see her friend again. Talk to her. Give her a hug. Jen was the friend who'd been there for her when Mike died. The shared adventure and trouble of the past year had tightened their bond.

An email from Jen was waiting for her, the message direct and short. Cynthia feared that too much directness might make it easier for the Senator to find this address. There were programs, she knew, that could monitor email traffic, searching for key words or phrases that might reveal their communication to enemy ears. But she quickly realized that the message's risky directness reflected its urgency.

> C,
>
> You must get a message to R or J immediately. There is a trap being set in Washington. The army must not advance into it. In fact, the city must be evacuated. Everyone left in the city will die. Get them out. A meteorite will strike D.C. The entire city will be destroyed.
>
> J.

Cynthia read the message twice before she comprehended its significance. An entire city! It would take days to evacuate. Jen's message implied no such time available. She felt a surge of empathetic terror for the hundreds of thousands of lives at risk.

And Jonathan. Jonathan was in D.C. His life, too, was in danger.

She left the library, heading for the police station, hoping that Detective Raumin would be there when she arrived. She drove too fast, skipping through several stoplights as they turned red and cutting off other drivers as she wove through the traffic. She thought about Jonathan, wondering if he'd think that her reckless driving *made sense*. She smiled a little at his verbal quirk, warmed by the memory despite, or perhaps because of, the gravity of the threat to his life.

Raumin was in his office. The officer at the desk called him to the lobby. When he arrived, and saw her grave face, Raumin beckoned her into a private room with a large conference table and utilitarian chairs.

"What's wrong?" he asked.

"The forces in Washington are walking into a trap." She recounted the warning in Jen's email.

Raumin nodded as she finished. "Jonathan and Jack learned something about this, but didn't have enough information to figure it out. How did your friend find out?"

Cynthia paused. She didn't know how much Jonathan had shared with the detective about Jen's 'visions'. She didn't know if he knew about her prediction of the earthquake or not.

"Jen has been having visions," Cynthia said. "She sees into the future. That's how she's escaped the Senator's people for so long."

Cynthia saw the skepticism growing on the detective's face, and quickly added, "She foresaw the earthquake. She sent me an email before it happened. I think this should be taken seriously."

Raumin rubbed his face, a bit stubbly. "Well, it does coincide with other evidence that we have. And the Senator just announced that all civilians should leave the city. He's opened the roads for travel." The detective paused. "Forward her email about the earthquake to me. If I can confirm she sent it before the quake, I'll recommend we go with this warning from your friend. We can't risk so much loss of life. But, you realize, if it's not true, it could cost us this war. We're ready to take the city."

As they rose from the table, Cynthia remembered her resolve to become more active.

"What more can I do?" she asked.

"Just what you're doing," Raumin replied. "Speak out. Use your voice in the newspaper. In the end, if we defeat an enemy in combat, there will always be another enemy. But if we persuade enemies to be friends, we can win."

Chapter 55

As their helicopter approached D.C. at the end of the flight from Cincinnati, Raumin shouted some last instructions to Mendez over the roar of the rotors and the wind. "Once we land, we can't mess around. We don't know how much time we have. Get your two back to the chopper within two hours. This time of afternoon, they should be at the King Library. That's where we agreed they'd wait in case of unforeseen events. If they aren't there..." Raumin paused. "Well, search for them as best you can, but the chopper leaves in two hours. Be back."

Jane O'Hara had agreed to evacuate the D.C. area based on the intel from his operatives in DC as well as Jen Hewitt's warning. The confirmation that Hewitt had indeed predicted the L.A. earthquake had overcome the last of her skepticism—and Raumin's own—about an impending meteor strike in D.C.

Raumin wasn't content to simply hope his operatives in D.C. got the evacuation orders. He wanted to personally ensure his people got out safely. His four operatives hidden away in D.C., semi-cutoff from contact to reduce their chances of being caught, would likely not hear the warning to evacuate, or, if they heard, not realize it was meant for them as well.

He had mixed feelings about bringing Sarah Mendez with him. He had two groups of people in D.C. Alone, it would take him twice as long to locate both and evacuate them. It made sense for Mendez to go for one group, and he the other. However, some part of him hesitated to put Officer Mendez at such risk.

She was his best officer. Her reliability made him trust her to get his people out or die trying. Her ability reassured him that she wouldn't die trying.

Raumin checked the sun for a qualitative feel of time. Peculiar. They had prepared to leave Cincinatti about 3PM but, based on the high sun hanging due south, it now looked to be about noon. He checked his watch, which read 5PM. He must be more disoriented in the helicopter than he thought.

With the Senator's troops in full retreat out of the city, Raumin decided it was safe to bring the helicopter into the downtown area. As they approached the outskirts of town, Raumin saw that bumper-to-bumper traffic jammed the main arteries of the city. With both sides of the conflict ordering everyone out of town, few chose to remain. From the slow movement on the crowded highways, it would be a long time before many of the people reached safety.

Raumin instructed the pilot to set down in a small grassy park central to his and Mendez's destinations.

"Good luck, Detective," Mendez said as she turned to trot off.

"You too." Raumin checked his map of the city and ran toward the small print shop where Jonathan and Jack had been working. He was less sure of finding Jonathan and Jack 'at home' than the other two. They'd made no arrangements for what to do or where to meet in an emergency. But with the city evacuating, it made sense that they'd either evacuate as well, or return to the only place where ONE could find them and await instructions.

He thought of the meteorite and ran a bit faster. He wished he knew exactly how urgent the evacuation was. He wished he knew if he had hours to rescue his people and escape to safety, or only seconds and his efforts were futile. His scalp tingled at the thought of a meteorite bearing down on him. He knew that he might see it coming, a flash of light in the sky speeding ahead of the meteorite. But he would never hear it. It traveled faster than sound, faster than any shock wave in air or rock.

There might be others who would hear it, those far away from where it struck. But for him there would be only silence. His ears would be vaporized before the sound could reach them; his brain would be atomized before it could comprehend the sound.

It could come anytime. From what he had seen from the helicopter, all or nearly all of the Senator's forces had evacuated the city toward the north. The Senator could bring down this calamity in the next minute, without risking more than a fraction of his own troops.

At a speed of two hundred thousand kilometers per hour, less than a handful of seconds would pass from the time the meteor first began to glow in the sky until it had vaporized everything beneath it. Scarcely enough time to pray.

Raumin traversed the blocks to the print shop in a few minutes. He'd not been here before, and it took him a few minutes to locate the entrance to the basement in the side alleyway. He had no key, so he knocked loudly on the door.

No one answered. Another five precious minutes ticked by while Raumin picked the lock. Finally he walked in, only to find the basement empty. The bare light was on, casting dim shadows across the floor. The computers were running, monitors throwing a dim blue color into the darkness. But there was no message or clue to lead him to his two colleagues.

Raumin took out his short-wave radio and keyed in the number to Jonathan's device. Of course, nothing that used radio was truly secure, not even secure private short-range radios unlinked to the wireless grid. Risk of detection or not, he had no choice left but to try to contact them electronically. Chances were, the contact would not be picked up. Few if any of the Senator's troops remained in the city. The Senator had successfully demonstrated his power, his effective victory. What need was there now for him to worry about a few straggling enemy spies? Why should his people be monitoring radio waves now?

To Raumin's relief, Jonathan answered. "We're ok." His voice over the radio sounded breathless but unpanicked. "We got the warning and are on our way out of town. But we're not going to make it on foot. Can you pick us up at Arlington?"

"If we can, we will," Raumin promised.

He ran back to the chopper. Within a few minutes, Mendez joined him with the two other agents, and they took off.

Raumin spotted Jonathan and Jack waiting for them as the helicopter descended toward an open area at Arlington about twenty feet from a copse of trees. Shadows cast by the trees seemed short for the late hour, and Raumin again cast an eye toward the sun, which still seemed too high in the sky. The skids hit the ground with a soft bump, but before Raumin could jump out, a burst of machine gun fire sprayed the helicopter. Jonathan and Jack, already trotting toward the helicopter, dodged for cover.

So, their communication had been intercepted after all.

Quickly sheltering themselves behind the armor of the military chopper, he and Mendez returned fire.

Raumin saw only two men. The Senator must have left a handful of his troops behind to die, solely to handicap the very type of rescue they attempted. Strategic in a peculiar sort of way, serving to undermine morale as the Senator brought down the sky upon them. Almost wasteful strategy, Raumin thought, unnecessary and excessive. This must be what the comic-book word 'diabolical' was reserved for.

Caught between the crossfire from the chopper and from Jonathan and Jack, the two attackers held a disadvantage. They fell within a couple minutes.

Raumin approached the bodies warily. He found one man dead with a gunshot to his chest and the other unconscious but alive with a bloody gash where a bullet ricocheted off his skull. Raumin found that he couldn't just leave him. "Get him in the chopper, and let's go," he said.

As the pilot prepared to take off, Raumin noticed again that the sun still hung at noon. The time was 6:00pm. This certainly reflected more than simple disorientation.

The chopper carried them west of the city to where the largest contingent of their military forces gathered. Bulldozers had built up a large levee between their location and the city. Hundreds of earth-and-steel shelters sprinkled the area behind the levee, and more were being constructed.

The soldiers went about their tasks with a professional air, but Raumin felt an atmosphere of confusion and doubt stirring among them. There was also an element of fear. Why had they retreated when victory seemed imminent? Why was this large embankment necessary? Why were they building field nuclear strike shelters?

About three in the morning, Raumin found himself seated with Mendez and Myrvik by a fire in the military camp. They watched the sun go down and talked into the abnormally long night. Myrvik talked about his lost marriage. Raumin about old friends from his military days. Mendez about her foster son.

"I didn't know you were married," Raumin said, looking at Mendez.

Mendez looked down at her feet, probably wondering what would happen to her boy if she didn't return. "I'm not. I decided someone else out there might be alone, like me. I didn't need to marry to take away their loneliness, or my own. So, I took in a foster child. We've made a good family."

"It's good to be needed," Myrvik said. "Good to need someone."

Raumin nodded. He could relate. He still had his friends from the old days, but time and distance made them more acquaintance now than friend. And he had his friends at work. But part of him knew they were more colleagues than friends. He hadn't even known about Mendez's foster child, and he'd known her for years.

The simple relationships of everyday life had never seemed so important to Raumin as they did now, while the three of them waited together in the darkness, unable to sleep. Waited for an approaching Evil to try to obliterate those relationships into insignificance. It could never be allowed to succeed, he decided.

Raumin watched the fire dancing. Listened to it pop as expanding gases escaped their confinement in tiny explosions that sent sparks showering toward the black sky like little prayers. There was something peaceful in it. Eternal. He wasn't the first to sit and watch the fire. He wasn't the first to face danger or sorrow. He wasn't the first to hope for victory and a better tomorrow. He wasn't the first to have friends whom he cared for.

Nor would he be the last.

Many hours later, when the sun should have risen but hadn't yet, they saw a brilliant light burst into the eastern sky, streaking closer and growing brighter than the sun. Raumin watched for a fleeting moment until his eyes could no longer bear the light and he blinked away. It flashed through the sky, its native speed enhanced by the Earth's own orbit and its rotation, like a cheek turning sharply toward a slap. The time before dawn marked the time of highest impact speed and greatest destruction. He felt the heat burning against his skin.

They hurried toward the shelters built behind the levee. The ground began to roll just as they reached their assigned shelter. Scarcely able to keep their feet, he, Sarah, and Jack held each other up as they stumbled into the earth and steel structure. A powerful roar rattled the wall. Deep drums sounded from the Earth. A shrieking like sirens pierced the sky.

The basal surge exploded past them, and the dim light from the thin, just-risen moon winked out into utter blackness. Even behind the earthen embankment, their shelter trembled before the onslaught of wind-driven debris. Dust pounded its way through tiny cracks into the room where fifty of them huddled together. They piled clothing and any other material they could find over the cracks, hoping to diminish the choking dust. It went on and on. The long minutes seemed like hours. They stayed in the shelter long after the thundering roar ceased and until the dust had settled both inside and out.

***

The next day, Raumin flew as ONE representative with a group of military commanders to inspect the city. There was no city. The zone of complete destruction extended at least twenty miles from downtown. Beyond that, the level of destruction gradually diminished. Where the capital building once stood, and for a mile around it, lay a circular crater, just beginning to fill with blue-gray water seeping in from the Potomac through fractures in the crater rim.

The sun was a dark, deep red in a gray sky. It swept across the heavens like a frightened rabbit, or perhaps an angry panther. News came to them of ferocious tides and earthquakes stirred by the frantic spin of the Earth. The Sun, eager to catch up on its overdue sleep, and angered at its delay the day before, exacted its revenge.

How could ONE, or the nation, or the *entire world* oppose this Senator, to whom even the Sun and falling stars gave fealty?

Chapter 56

Kar-Tur and I sat in the dust of the cave at the edge of twilight, where sun seeping in from the sky outside met the deep darkness of the cavern. The cave we had chosen for our shelter opened to the surface in two locations, both well-hidden to the casual observer, but offering egress in case we needed to escape. One entrance opened onto the plateau above, the other onto the cliff face over the river. Indirect light from the opening in the cliff cast a pink warmth on the limestone around us.

We sat together at the edge of twilight and moved into the new reality we were only beginning to discover. I *felt* my way from that light and stone into a new world that I had never visited before, feeling the forces, atoms, galaxies, all wound together like a ball of twine. I picked at one of the strings, unraveling it so that I might examine it more closely, guided by Kar-Tur's mental hand on mine.

The strand was neither force nor matter, but *principle*, appearing solid, a law of nature made concrete. I couldn't change it, or destroy it, but I could *move* it, placing it where I wanted in the tangled twine. Or I could move it to another of the branching tangles that I saw scattered toward my horizon like Joshua trees in a flat desert.

I recognized this world, the same world that I knew through equations, principles, and experiments. A rational world, reasonable and predictable in its behavior. But I saw it in a new way. I was no longer examining it from afar, a stranger, a doctor measuring the patient's pulse. I *was* the pulse, walking as a participant in the very being of forces and matter. A part of the laws of nature that I had explored as a scientist.

This universe was the same as the one I knew, yet different. Like knowing a colleague from work, knowing how she behaves at work, and then visiting her home for the first time, seeing the photographs of her family, the way she decorates, the more personal way she converses, and realizing suddenly that she is more multi-dimensional than I realized before.

I understood more about the implications of Susan's experiments. I couldn't alter laws of nature. Rather, I could work with those laws. Nature wasn't my lackey obliged to do my bidding. Rather, nature provided structure, the framework for a house that my choice could paint and decorate. The more I understood of its structure, the better my own contributions to its ultimate design could be. The more I knew, the more I could choose. My own choice was *part of* the laws of nature.

I came back to the 'real' world to catch my breath, unable to stay focused on feeling into the nature of things for more than a couple of minutes. Even my well-disciplined thoughts sagged under the weight of this new contact with my universe. Given my experience with it, my respect for Kar-Tur's abilities grew. He seemed to go easily into that place, that *sense*, without any compelling need to come back to the more tangible world.

I rose, and wandered to the opening that overlooked the river. Echoes from the water below sighed back and forth across the canyon. As my attention returned to the physical world, I noticed again the odd color to the sky. A persistent haze altered the blue sky to yellow.

The haze, combined with the deep red sunsets beguiling the sky for the last several days, struck me as significant. Such color at sunset resulted from dust-enhanced dispersion of the blue colors from the sunlight. So much dust in the air was no doubt a consequence of the disaster in Washington. It must have already happened. I considered how long it would have taken the dust to circle the globe eastward with the prevailing westerlies to our location in Colorado. Only a few days, I estimated.

I remembered the exceptionally long day a week or so ago, with an unreasonably short day following. That, too, probably related to the disaster. Presently, my watch indicated the sun was again synchronous with clock-time, the shorter day simply compensating for the longer one.

So, my dark vision came true. I hoped that my warning came in time to save some. I wanted to return to town to see if Cynthia had sent me any news of the impact. How much was lost? Who survived?

Then, I realized that I might be able to *feel* into my questions. Learn about them through this new insight that Kar-Tur was teaching me. That would be a good practice of my growing abilities.

I returned to the twilight of the cave where Kar-Tur still waited. I explained what I hoped to find so he could guide me, and we returned to that world of sense.

I touched the day of the impact. Touched the past as easily as I touched a stone. It felt different from the strands I'd touched before. Dead somehow. I recoiled from it as from the cold stiffness of rigor mortis.

I found the long day and the short day. I felt rather than saw that the angular momentum of Earth was not removed, or destroyed, nor even transferred to another coexisting object. Rather, it was deferred into the future, loaned through time. The angular momentum from one day was moved to another day, stopping the Earth in one time, and accelerating it in the next.

I reached farther into the cold blackness of that place, dead in both space and time. I felt the icy touch of the meteorite itself. I felt the shift in time. The meteor had always been destined to strike the Earth. *Eventually*. But in a time of its own choosing. That choice was diverted by the Senator. The cataclysm was stolen from another time. Probabilities distorted. Energies whisked from one time to another.

With the Senator's *choice*, there was no asking nature's participation, but a wrenching of participation from it, a demanding insistence, dragging resistant events through both time and space. That's what had destroyed a part of the Shimera world. The demanding. The dragging through time. That's what I must avoid as I practiced to feel and choose in this new world.

***

Kar-Tur and I finished our practice a couple of hours before supper. Meals weren't so convenient now as I had been accustomed to in my former life. We had to plan ahead for them. We hunted and foraged or went hungry.

Kar-Tur set off toward the river to hunt for rabbits or squirrels or something, and I headed across the piñon-juniper desert in search of pine nuts and cactus. Yummy. Actually, fried in oil and with a bit of flour-and-crushed-pine-nut breading, the fleshy prickly pear branches weren't too bad.

The roles we assumed by default in our wilderness exile bothered me. I'd planned to show Kar-Tur the ways of a more enlightened civilization, one in which men and women worked as equals engaged in the same tasks. Now, I foraged and cooked while he hunted. How primeval.

But there was a sense of being equal partners.

Pine nuts were pretty scarce this time of year. I had found only a few when I heard another potential food source calling from a grove of piñon. An early cicada gave its piercing cry. I walked into the grove a ways. It smelled very piney in the hot sun.

I wondered if I could catch the insect. Some crunchy, breaded cicadas sounded tasty. With salt and pepper, of course. I was growing quite tired of cactus, and our noodle soup was long gone.

There was something about the tone of the cicada's call that made it hard to locate. I looked for several minutes for the source of the high buzz, but just the moment I found it, it flew away.

Its escape disappointed me. With a locust in hand, I would lack only some wild honey to be like John the Baptist. What a story to tell when I came back into the world as a spiritual wisewoman returning from her cloistered novitiate. I had always wanted to do something spiritually significant. Something that mattered on the grand scale of Biblical epic. My journey in the wilderness of Colorado felt very much like a retreat to the desert by some of the great mystics of the Bible. A time to prepare for great things to come.

I sheepishly reigned in that arrogant and dangerous notion. Dangerous not only for my spiritual journey, but also for this new journey I'd just begun into a new and frightening power. The Senator dealt with the universe, invoked its power, with a demanding arrogance that infected whatever he touched with cold death. I didn't want to practice that kind of faith.

I wondered about Kar-Tur's faith. I knew that he, too, had been a mystic of his people. Strange that I had never pursued that, given our shared spirituality. Not so strange, I supposed. It intimidated me to think of delving into a strong faith that must be so different from my own. He couldn't be Christian, since his life predated the birth of Christ by so many tens of thousands of years. Whatever his faith, I knew I couldn't simply dismiss it, or disdain it as pagan. Kar-Tur had proved himself too sincere, too deep in his insight into the inner world.

Honestly exploring another faith undermined my comfort in being surrounded by those of like belief. I hesitated to try my own faith in such a fire.

But I wanted to know of his faith. And, perhaps, he would like to know of mine. I made a mental note to pursue that.

We ate cactus. Again. Kar-Tur had caught a small fish, which added a little protein to our meal. We cooked at the cave mouth, waiting until after dark so the smoke wouldn't be noticed by neighbors. Hopefully. We used a shiny, reflective 'space blanket' purchased in Cañon City to deflect any infrared radiation that might be picked up by airplane or satellite.

After supper we talked for a time, and watched the stars burst upon us from the clear desert sky far from city lights. I retired with a greater sense of well-being than I'd felt for many months.

The next morning, we made a trip to town. We needed to move the pickup periodically anyway, since we didn't want it to appear to be abandoned. And the possibility of real "town food" almost made me giddy. We walked the miles to town briskly in the comfortable silence of friendship.

I enjoyed my scrambled egg brunch almost as much as my walk with Kar-Tur. Then, we went to see a movie, which was fun and relaxing, although the movie-adventure seemed pretty tame. Afterward, I checked my email for messages from Cynthia.

> Dear J,
> You were right. A meteorite has destroyed Washington D.C. It seems unbelievable. Thank you for your warning. It saved many people. Although many still died.
> J was one of those that you saved. He was in D.C.

I'm writing for the newspaper regularly now. There isn't much joy to write about. I always thought I'd write science articles, and I hoped that people would *pore* over my writings looking for understanding. Now, I can only hope that I move people to compassionate tears to *pour* over my writings. Taking a page from your book, J, I try to temper these troubled times with humor. I'm afraid, though, that I slide toward a philosophical irony rather than the silliness that you're so skilled at. I miss you, friend. Don't stay away. We can't defeat this power the Senator has. We need your help.

Love, C

I trembled at how close I'd come to losing another friend. Why and how had Jonathan ended up in D.C.? I hadn't even known that he was in danger. Fortunate, perhaps, since knowing would have distracted me when I needed to focus on getting myself and Kar-Tur to safety.

The phrase "We need your help" troubled me. What was that supposed to mean? What could I do? I already felt guilty for watching a movie, and for relaxing and enjoying the day, when so much sorrow stalked the world. Cynthia's email didn't help.

A brief shower swept upon us on the walk back. It was refreshing, but the fat water bombs falling in the dry road-dust spattered my legs with mud.

When we arrived back 'home', I decided a bath was in order. I took my things down a narrow deer trail to Four Mile Creek which ran through the canyon below our cave. The water was chilly, and even more invigorating than the rain shower had been.

I felt nervous that Kar-Tur might see me as I disrobed by the river. Did his people have taboos against watching a woman bathe? I realized suddenly, sheepishly, that the flush rising in my cheeks had very little to do with embarrassment at the idea.

I stepped into the river, and the cold water rising to my waist caused me to catch my breath. I glanced up at the mouth of the cave cut into the cliff face above me, hoping to catch Kar-Tur there, spying on me. But, the cave mouth was empty.

I dropped my gaze, disappointed, and ducked my head into the cold water. The world under the water was shadowy and hushed. For as long as I could hold my breath, I watched as the refracting light in the moving water warped and rippled the rocks along the bottom. When I raised my head, I checked the cliffside again. Still no Kar-Tur.

I cared for Kar-Tur. I'd grown to know him and, in knowing him, to value his friendship. But, was I interested in Kar-Tur with more than friendly interest? Or was I merely vain enough to want to attract male attention? What an odd emotional tangle, that I both hoped he'd be gentlemanly and not watch me, yet feared that his gentlemanliness reflected poorly on my desirability.

Or were my feelings more than the vanity of wanting to be attractive? Did I want Kar-Tur, *in particular*, to want me? Did I want *him*?

I put the thoughts from my mind. Like the refracted light from the stones along the river bottom, my perspective was probably warped, and I didn't want to risk Kar-Tur's friendship with my own silly fantasies or risk being hurt if I wanted more than he could give. Such thoughts didn't aid us in a solution to our current plight or in our obligations to our world, which were weighing on me more heavily with Cynthia's admonishment and my own ongoing reflections.

I had another reason, too, for not wanting to examine my feelings for Kar-Tur too closely. A reason tied to my growing sense of responsibility and the actions which that responsibility might compel me to take.

Actions that could take Kar-Tur from me forever.

From what Jonathan had told me and from what I could piece together, the Senator had learned of Susan's work, and all the potential that it implied, from a Shimera who had contacted him seeking revenge for the loss of loved ones. And the Shimera lost his loved ones because Kar-Tur and Susan had seared a pathway through time and space.

If Kar-Tur and Susan had not journeyed in time, then the Senator would not have learned of Susan's work, and the present trouble would not be. Many sorrows could be changed, and healed, if only Kar-Tur and Susan never made their journeys through time.

I thought of the meteorite that the Senator forced to strike the Earth before its time, and I wondered if an event that should never have happened could be undone. Could I return Kar-Tur to his own time, as though he had never traveled at all, and take away all the tragedy that had followed?

If so, I would never know Kar-Tur.

I sat on the shore after my bath, listening to the water gurgle and drying myself in the lowering sunlight. My thoughts went to the world of *sense* that Kar-Tur had shown me the day before. I wondered if I could feel my way there without his guidance. As a test, I felt for that pulse of life.

I found it, startled by my success, as I once again shared being with the forces and laws of nature. But, compared to yesterday, that world was dim and distant. The Joshua trees vanished into the obscurity of the remote terrain. Although darker, the new perspective gave me a wider understanding of this world of sense, like an Earthling seeing his or her home world from a distant galaxy and understanding it as though for the first time. The place that I saw yesterday as a great flat desert now appeared as only a small terrace in a far more immense landscape folded onto itself many times like a sheet of paper. The folding created a pattern, an image, like origami. I struggled to perceive the appearance of the image, but my mind refused to give it a concrete form.

The landscape reminded me of the words on the stone at Susan's grave about folding, and time, and the letters 'P of T'. I tried to remember what else she'd written, but it escaped me. Something about nails? Or screws?

The darkness of that place deepened as I stood there, the view gradually vanishing in the gloom. I wanted to see it more intimately, as I had with Kar-Tur. But the landscape reached too far into the distance for me to contemplate traversing it. As my sight faded further, I grew disoriented. Unable to see well enough to find my way, I quickly became lost in that place and had to withdraw.

As in Susan's experiments, the belief of two was exponentially stronger than that of one. The place of *sense* was both darker and more distant when I went there alone. I rose from my rest beside the river, and went to find Kar-Tur to see if we might share another lesson together before supper.

When I returned to the cave, Kar-Tur was sitting just inside the entrance that overlooked the river. I wondered how he could have missed seeing me bathing below. He had only to stand and walk a half-dozen steps and he could see the whole river. Suspicions roused within me, and I wondered why he should be reading in that particular spot.

I calmed myself, remembering that this was the best spot in the cave to read, where just enough light entered to see by, and where the limestone rubble and dry guano dust of the cave floor made a reasonably comfortable place to sit. He was reading one of the two books he had brought from Los Angeles, the one on prehistoric archaeology of Europe. He smiled when I sat down beside him.

"Where have you been?" he asked.

I started at his question, feeling a bit guilty at my own thoughts. "I just sat by the river for a while," I lied truthfully, a skill I prided myself in.

He nodded and resumed his reading.

I wondered why I didn't simply tell him the whole truth. If he hadn't seen me bathing, it didn't matter. If he *had* seen me, he knew that I was lying.

And anyway, my lack of openness probably revealed the very thing I didn't want to tell him, or myself.

Chapter 57

The morning sun peeked at Kar-Tur over the small mountain that lounged quietly to the east of their cave. Trees extended to the top, their branches breaking the red of the rising sun into many rays.

Kar-Tur enjoyed the solitude of the desert and the quiet roar of the river as he sat on the rough limestone cliff, his legs dangling toward the rocks and water far below. It gave him a chance to simply *be*, to examine himself and his thoughts.

He thought of his Tribemate JenHewitt. She treated him respectfully as a friend. Called him Tribemate and seemed to understand its meaning. Grew with him in the intimacy of friendship born under duress.

But did she care for him as he had grown to care for her? She didn't seem to. She held him at a distance, keeping her inner emotions aloof.

He had tried to find a way to talk to her about his feelings, to explore their growing intimacy, and where it might lead. But she had left no opening for that exploration.

When he had inadvertently seen her bathing, he'd found it both exciting and troubling. Exciting because it was exciting. Troubling because it was exciting. She was not only Tribemate to him, but something more.

Still, she gave him no encouragement in that feeling, nor opportunity to express it to her. When he'd asked her what she had been doing, hoping to open opportunity to either apologize or pursue his increasing interest in her, she had lied about it, preempting his efforts. She certainly offered a type of friendship, even intimacy, meaningful to her. But he realized that wasn't enough. He began to hope for something more.

The morning coolness felt good to Kar-Tur after so many hot days. It was good to be outside the cave where light and life burst with abundance. He liked the cave better than the office building, but the cave also grew more like a prison with each passing day. He enjoyed this time with his Tribemate, often spent in conversation, exploration, or in companionable silence. But he grew impatient with hiding.

More and more, his thoughts went to their joint work, their prospection into this new world of *sense*, and how they might use it to free themselves and their world from the enemy who kept them pinned in this place. His Tribemate also believed that this might be their purpose, their burden.

They had developed the habit, over the past days and weeks, of talking together in mornings. They talked of their different worlds and experiences. Of their shared passion for learning and their compassion for people. In afternoons, they practiced in the world of *sense*.

Seeing that the sun had reached the point in the sky where they often talked, Kar-Tur rose from his perch above the river, and returned to the cave, eager for the company of his friend and their morning conversation.

This morning, she asked him about his faith.

It pleased Kar-Tur to tell his Tribemate about his beliefs. It had been many months since he thought so carefully about the gods, and the search that had consumed his former life as seeker for his tribe. He told her of his people, their hope and fear, their puzzling over the meaning of life, his own search for deeper understanding.

Then he asked his Tribemate to speak of her beliefs.

She, too, was clearly a seeker for her tribe, although she divided her pursuits into two parts, seeking into the nature of existence and seeking into the nature of god--a division that Kar-Tur did not make. He listened to her beliefs with deep interest, considering them as part of his own search.

"Is this the belief of all your people?" he asked when she concluded.

His Tribemate thought for a moment before answering. "No. Many of my people have similar views, but many have very different views as well. Views range from those who see no spirit world at all to others who adopt elaborate superstitious beliefs that seem weird and extreme to me.

"Surely, there must have also been variations in beliefs among your people?" she asked.

Kar-Tur nodded. "Yes, that's so."

Kar-Tur considered his Tribemate's words. He and she shared a spiritual sense of the universe, a sense of its *beingness*. A sense that it was more like life than non-life. That it was more ordered and rational than disordered and irrational.

But her beliefs were so complex and intricate. If one scarcely comprehended the most basic concepts, that there was God and a spirit realm, then how sensible was it to manufacture ever deeper and subtler subordinate scenarios that one understood even less? Perhaps this was the inevitable consequence of ages of spiritual exploration, conquering the simple and surging onward toward the more complex.

He wasn't ready for it.

But he found her idea of a single God compelling. If the nature of existence was indeed Being, then it made sense that Being would be One. *Even if many*, that Being would still be one. Hadn't this present tribe discovered that humans themselves are simply colonies of smaller creatures, tiny living cells comprising a larger creature? Cells that the body fed and cared for through an elaborate architecture of conduits within itself?

Yet the individuals of this tribe considered each human to be a single being, even though made of many living things that each grew and reproduced and died in its own individual life.

How much more the Being of the universe must be one, caring for all parts of its identity through the elaborate architecture of creation or the spirit behind creation.

Kar-Tur also liked her discourse on the revealed invisible God who made himself known not through magical intervention but through the actions and words of people. He wondered to what degree these prophets she spoke of, and the visions they saw and foresaw, were born from a like insight, a like *sense*, to that which he and his Tribemate practiced. Was it the same? Or was it something different?

"Thank you for telling me about your faith, Tribemate," he said.

She smiled. "It's not always easy for me. But, I will keep trying."

That evening, they practiced in the world of sense, as they did each day before supper. To Kar-Tur, it seemed as if her efforts to be open with him had given her new and better control in the world of sense.

The solution to one key challenge had continued to elude them. If there was to be any use to this power outside of that strange, inner realm, and if they were to find a way to oppose the Senator, they had to be able to affect the normal world around them, and in a way that did not harm human or Shimera.

As they sat in their chosen spot in the twilight of the cave and journeyed into that world of *sense*, Kar-Tur focused with her on a package of air before them in the cave. Their test was to see if she could change the air enough to cause water to come from it like a storm cloud wrung water from the sky.

His experience in his long vigil at the fire allowed him to guide her and provide the strength of his own belief, a synergy that lit this world far brighter than any single mind could do. But she understood the forces of this world better than he, knew more of the laws that governed it, and her influence in this place was in proportion to her greater knowledge. He watched as she gently twined and untwined the fabric in ways he could not quite comprehend.

He felt her nudge the energy of the volume of air she examined. She moved particles, along with the energy that they carried--the material and power that he had seen in his long vigil at the fire--*choosing* each particle's location. She willed those with greater speed, with higher energy, to leave the volume. She replaced them with slower particles, lower energy, from outside the volume.

She drew each, not from time, but from place. Not commanding, but asking. Not *controlling* existence so much as *trusting* in it and working with it. A dance with nature.

Kar-Tur felt the packet of air grow cold as his Tribemate transferred energy from it. As it grew cold, its capacity to hold the water evaporated in it decreased. He opened his eyes upon the physical world and saw a little cloud floating in the air before his Tribemate. Raindrops fell from it as though from a miniature thunderstorm.

She squeezed the water out, condensing water from the dry desert air.

Kar-Tur looked into the eyes of his Tribemate as she rejoined him in the normal world and saw in her eyes his own excitement and hope.

A small feat, but a significant one. They both knew what success in altering the external world meant. It meant they could face the Senator, who wielded his will like a weapon, and stop him from destroying humanity and the Shimera. It meant that all things were possible, including freedom from their prison.

Chapter 58

Jonathan sat patiently cramped in the tiny crawl space of the air duct where he and Raumin had waited since long before the sharp increase in security that heralded the Senator's arrival. Twenty men and women were gathered in the conference room below them, awaiting the Senator. The small listening device and amplifier he pressed against the metal duct-wall extracted words from the murmur below.

"There's no way the rebels will attempt to capture L.A.," one voice said. "Not after what happened in D.C."

"They are all crazy," another voice disagreed. "There's no telling what they might do."

"I heard that the Shimera were prepared to help them," came a third voice. "If so, we might yet find ourselves outmatched."

"Not even the Shimera can defend against the kind of power that we can bring against them," the first voice responded. "And the British are wavering anyway. Even the American rebel troops are losing heart. The military law may be severe, but the longer we go without a major revolt, the more that people will accept it. Especially when they see that it really isn't all that bad. Peace and safety from both crime and catastrophe are pretty hard to oppose, even by those with grand theoretical ideas of democracy."

"Once things settle down, democracy can resume," another contributed. "They'll see that and lose interest in war."

Jonathan slowly lifted his left leg with his hands, taking care not to bang the drum-like metal shaft as he shifted it to another position. The rush of blood back into his leg made it tingle.

The American people *did* seem to be losing interest in resistance, just as the voices asserted. Jonathan caught Raumin's eye, wondering what he thought of the conversation.

Raumin shrugged and whispered against his ear, "Risking life in the fight to be free is the job of the few. The many must grow food, and build homes."

Still, it was discouraging. Could Americans who had lived for generations with the idea of freedom so quickly succumb to a god-king? It was true, the Senator offered prosperity and peace. Crime had dropped 90% in the weeks since the destruction of Washington D.C. when the Senator assumed full control of the country. And, of course, what was the chance of war when war meant such complete obliteration for his enemies?

L.A. was less enamored with the Senator than other parts of the country. They remained angry at the ongoing martial law. There was indeed little crime. But some might argue there was also little life.

Raumin beckoned Jonathan close again, then whispered, "I'm going down to the auditorium. The Senator may speak there first. Stay here and keep watch on his Belief Team. He'll certainly speak to them eventually."

Jonathan nodded, and watched Raumin slowly creep back down the long tunnel.

It was ten leg-shifts later that the Senator strode into the room. The murmurs fell silent.

The Senator began his speech with the pompous melodrama expected from one who doubted neither his authority nor his intrinsic *rightness*. One with the confident assurance of a god-king.

"This is what will come to pass," the senator addressed the room. "My hold on this nation grows. Soon that hold will extend to other nations as well. For a time, there will be less freedom, but that temporary loss will later on bring a great blessing. The short sacrifice of freedom will be for the sake of safety from crime, and for the sake of the greater freedom that can grow from that safety.

"Soon, our enemies must attack, or concede defeat. If they do not attack soon, there will be no support for them left. I believe that they will attack, and they will attack here, in L.A., where they still enjoy support from the people and where the Shimera will aid them.

"It's here that we will finally defeat them, and usher in the new world of peace. Here is where the tyranny of suffering and brutality imposed on humankind by both nature and humankind itself ultimately ends.

"When our enemies advance into L.A., and they will advance because they must, a meteor greater than that which struck D.C. will bear down upon them. There will be nothing left in Southern California but the pit symbolizing for all time the futility of opposing the new world that we now enter. All our opposition will be silenced, all war forever quieted.

"This is what you will bring here, in four days. You know it can be done. You've done it before. See to it."

Jonathan's hand shook as he keyed the recording of the speech into his secure communicator. He had to warn ONE of the Senator's plans.

But even knowing those plans, what could they do? The Senator was right. They must either attack now, or concede defeat. The window of opportunity slipped away from them. And ONE's morale was already low after the devastating events in Washington.

They could not win. They couldn't even mount significant opposition to this Senator. He was too powerful. ONE could not face him alone, nor with the U.S. army, nor with the British, nor even with the Shimera. The only way to face him was with his own power, his own methods.

Jen had to return. Whatever power she had that allowed her to see visions of the future, it must be related in some way to this power that the Senator wielded. Jonathan didn't believe in coincidence. Not in this case. Only she and Kar-Tur could face this man, this demon-god. Only they could counter his distortion of reality.

Jonathan typed in a message to Cynthia for Jen, a plea for Jen to return to L.A. Despite the risk that the message might be intercepted even though encrypted and secure, he had to send it now in case he failed to escape the building and couldn't see Cynthia in person.

Focused on his task, Jonathan stopped listening to the Senator and the conversations in the conference room below. Suddenly he heard his name, wrenching him back to awareness.

"I can see you there, Dr. Renner," the Senator said.

Jonathan nearly jumped out of his skin. The Senator couldn't possibly see him, could he? He looked around for some crack, some hole that might have revealed his position. He saw none.

"I didn't say that you could see me, Dr. Renner. I said that I can see you."

Shaken, Jonathan began to wonder if the man truly were a god. How could anyone possibly oppose someone who could see through solid walls? Who could call down the heavens on his enemies? Who seduced the world with his offer of ultimate peace and safety?

"Come out, Dr. Renner. Or I'll shoot you out."

Jonathan wasn't even close to the opening of the duct into the room below. Maybe the Senator was just guessing after all. Jonathan slowly unwound his legs and started creeping back the other way.

"Oh, come now, Doctor!" the Senator cried. Jonathan heard a shot and a bullet tore through the metal just inches ahead of him. "I said, come out, not run away!"

Reluctantly, Jonathan turned and approached the place where the air-vent opened into the room. Popping the cover loose, he dropped into the room and turned to face the Senator-become-god.

"How nice of you to drop in, Dr. Renner." The Senator smiled without humor. "Won't you stay with me for a while? I do believe you have some friends who might like to visit you, and I'd like to see them as well."

Chapter 59

Cynthia ran her fingers over the keyboard in her cramped home office, contrasting the familiar feel of the concave keypads with how alien the rest of the world seemed. With an increasing proportion of her work needing to be done from home, she'd converted Mike's walk-in closet to a small office. The lack of windows and tight space provided a sense of safety. Mostly illusory of course, but comforting enough to help her keep writing.

The martial law in L.A. had grown even more oppressive. For 'their own safety', no one was allowed to leave home outside of work hours without special authorization. Going to the library to communicate with Jen was no longer feasible, so Cynthia had to send her message from home, despite the risk.

Newsprint was censored. All communications were monitored, supposedly to prevent crime. Hopefully there was still too much email traffic for anyone to monitor it all.

She told Jen about Jonathan's arrested, or kidnapping, whichever you called it. Raumin thought he was still alive. Cynthia also conveyed Jonathan's belief, added to her own, that only Jen and Kar-Tur had the ability to face this powerful Senator because only they had a power of like kind.

She told Jen about the agent that O'Hara was sending to pick her and Kar-Tur up. Cynthia worried about betraying Jen's confidence, revealing their location to ONE, but there seemed to be no other option. The world needed her friend here, not in a cave in Colorado.

And Jen needed to be here to help her friend Jonathan. Cynthia hesitated a moment after writing that last, wondering if Jonathan would think it *made sense* to put others at risk for his sake. She felt a swell of affection for him, and hoped he was ok.

Perhaps a better question was why *she* thought it made sense to risk the life of the person who had become her closest friend after Mike and Susan died. Even if the Senator was overcome, an outcome seriously in doubt, was it worth Jen's life? Cynthia, of all people, valued relationships over politics or theoretical ideals. As long as she had her children, her friends, her work, did it *make sense* to risk more than she had already lost for a cause whose outcome was uncertain?

Many people even supported the Senator, a proportion that was again growing with each day. Was his dictatorship really as bad as she feared? Was it even fair to label it a *dictatorship*? Perhaps he really could deliver on his promise of safety from crime and war. In which case, she was summoning her friend to die for the cause of ensuring less safety. Did it make sense to risk those she loved when, in the end, the right course was still uncertain?

She squeezed her eyes shut, trying to think logically. A soft, musky quiet filled the closet office. She had moved Mike's clothes and things out to make room for her computer desk, but somehow the familiar scent of him still lingered.

My love, what should I do?

She thought of how he had, without a second's hesitation, thrown himself at a mysterious being of which he had known nothing except for the fact that it had just tried to kill someone.

It was one thing to throw oneself at danger, but did Cynthia have the right to put other people in danger? Conversely, did she have the right to shield her own friends at the expense of the lives of others? Even by her apolitical standards, the needs of all the friendships in the whole world exceeded her own friendships alone.

Cynthia opened her eyes and pressed Send.

Chapter 60

Senator Jerry Roden knew that only two people stood between him and complete rule. Once those two were gone, everyone would love him. No one would disobey him.

Then there would be peace. At last, as so many people had dreamed of through the ages, Earth would be one nation, one people. There would be no more war, no crime. He would take away the pain that one human caused another.

He could do more than that. Through this new power than grew in him, that he and his Belief Team practiced, there would be no more pestilence or natural disaster. He would even take away the pain that *God* left to vex humanity.

But, those two still lived, despite all his efforts. Lived and succeeded in remaining hidden from him, successfully hiding even in that other realm of *sense*.

Now he had a new weapon. He had their friend. He didn't really care about Dr. Renner. He didn't need him, or fear him. But through him, he could reach the man and the woman who, like himself, could *choose* the future. Those two must die so that his own will might prevail.

It couldn't work to have multiple choices for the future, and multiple people choosing. The world, the people of it, must settle upon a way for things to be. Otherwise, there would be constant turmoil. Nature would not know how to behave. Cosmos would degenerate to Chaos.

Jerry determined that people must settle on the way that *he* decided, unpolluted by these two interlopers.

He would build a trap for them, and the best way to do that was through the very thing they thought to be their strength. Jennifer Hewitt did indeed have a great power to foresee future events. Her visions had saved her more than once. But, compared to him, even after the recent breakthroughs he had felt her make, she was only a beginner in shaping the world of sense.

She would indeed learn that he had captured their friend. She would indeed find her way to Dr. Renner once she reached L.A. Given the strength of her visions, she and Kar-Tur might even fight their way into the building where he had hidden Dr. Renner and overcome the heavy guard he had posted.

But Hewitt would not foresee the explosives that he had left there.

As with all true deception, it was not the lie that was effective, but the partial truth. Already he had started building a blind spot into the architecture of the realm of *sense*, a part of his plan that Hewitt's visions would not see. He took care of the arrangements for the bomb himself, telling no one, and thus leaving no trace for her to find in the realm of *sense*. He had begun to build into the structure of her visions the belief that she and she alone had to decide what was to be done, because anyone who helped her would die. Which of course, was also true, although for reasons different from what she might imagine. And, finally, and most critically, he was building into her visions an amplified confidence, a certainty that the visions could not fail. Flush with her newfound power, Hewitt would be swayed to trust the partial truth too much, not imagining that he could hide something from her.

He knew that his own intellect towered over that of even his well-chosen Belief Team. And it towered over Jen Hewitt and her companion from the past. Their strength within that world of *sense* couldn't match his own. They could not uncover what he hid from them.

Not now, not when the entire world was with him. Who still doubted his ability to control even the universe itself? He'd brought down one meteorite on Earth, and now the very pervasive belief that it was possible made the second meteorite he planned much easier. The resistance to it was lower. Everyone knew that he controlled the very fabric of existence. Their very belief was on his side. Jen Hewitt and the man from the past could not overcome that advantage.

He would lay a trap for them in L.A. And there, they would die.

Chapter 61

When I poked my head from the entrance on the plateau, coming up for my traditional brisk walk in the cool of the morning, a woman I didn't know sat on a boulder a short distance away. Her presence startled me for a moment, and I considered darting back into the cave. But the woman had already spotted me.

Probably this was the agent that Cynthia's email had warned me of. I had mixed feelings about Cynthia revealing where Kar-Tur and I were hiding. In the end, I was glad she did. I wanted to help Jonathan. And, I was ready to take my place in the events that swirled our world into such a whirlwind.

An angry stubbornness had grown in me. Did this Senator think I would be passive forever? I'd withdrawn from danger for a time. Hid in quiet, hoping that things would grow better. But did this man believe I would just roll over to his whims indefinitely and go quietly to my death? If he thought so, he knew little of me despite his interrogation.

I walked toward the boulder, and the woman rose and came to meet me part way.

"Dr. Hewitt?" the woman asked.

"Well, not Dr. yet," I replied as we shook hands.

"Jane O'Hara sent me. Our forces are preparing to free Los Angeles, but, without protection from this power the Senator has, our chances of success are slim.

"Our agents John Raumin and Jonathan Renner believe you may be able to provide that protection. My instructions are to bring you to Los Angeles. I have a private plane in Cañon City. My car is parked on the road. May we go?"

Her brusque manner made me both comfortable and uncomfortable. I appreciated her business-like approach to the urgency of the situation. But I wasn't ready to go yet. I had to talk to Kar-Tur.

I hadn't told him about the email from Cynthia, thus already falling short of my new goal of openness. I was unwilling to dispel the wonderful air of companionship and intimacy that had grown between us in this desert place. I feared what he might think of my need to leave him to save my friends and my world. This wasn't his world, or his people. I was afraid he'd see my departure as a choice against him.

But, I had to say goodbye and not just slip away. I didn't know if I'd survive to see him again. Or if he would still exist in my world if I survived.

"Give me an hour," I said.

I returned to our cave to find Kar-Tur sitting by the fire, as he often did. The day was not cold, but he liked to watch the fire; it calmed his thoughts and strengthened him in his travels into the world of *sense*.

"Kar-Tur," I said quietly, laying a hand on his shoulder. "I have something I have to tell you."

He looked up at me, his eyes trusting. I sat down beside him, beside my Tribemate, my eyes going to the fire, searching to find for myself some of the comfort that he found there.

"My friend, Jonathan, has been kidnapped," I said. "I have to help my people overcome the Senator's forces and rescue him."

"Is Jonathan..." Kar-Tur paused. "Tribefriend?"

I thought for a moment. I wasn't comfortable evaluating my relationships the way Kar-Tur did so naturally and honestly. I feared hurting someone, or preempting a growing relationship that might someday be more. Or, as my more selfish and honest part asserted, I feared making myself too vulnerable among people that I knew, revealing too much, and in so doing, losing some opportunity or influence. But as Kar-Tur had explained, relation-name was not intended to judge or to secure influence. It wasn't a statement of value or worth. It wasn't even a complete statement of a relationship, only my own feelings, not those of any others.

Jonathan was my friend. I knew that. One of my dearest friends.

"He is Tribemate," I said.

Kar-Tur nodded in understanding and rose from the fire. "Then we will die for him. Let us go."

I stared up at him, startled by his quick and easy commitment.

My own life was mine to offer. But I was not happy with the idea that Kar-Tur should put his life at risk for my friend.

I had another reason, too, for not wanting his life at risk. I had resisted it. Denied it. But, I knew I loved him. I couldn't bear the thought of losing him. There was no need for us both to risk our lives.

"This isn't your tribe, Kar-Tur. You don't need to go with me."

"I *will* go with you," Kar-Tur insisted.

"They might kill you," I replied. "They're afraid of you."

"No more than of you. I will go with you."

"Aren't you afraid?" I asked.

"My people don't fear death so much as yours," Kar-Tur said. "One becomes more afraid of what one doesn't see. Death doesn't happen often in your world. My people have seen much more of it.

"What my people fear is separation while still living," Kar-Tur continued. "That to which your people have grown accustomed. I would not want to be separated from you, Tribemate."

I stood slowly, beginning to understand. He would rather die than have us separated. What an incredible group of people his tribe must have been, to value community over life itself.

Perhaps that was the way of his people and not mine. But it was a feeling that I could understand and share.

"Then we'll go together." I hesitated only the barest fraction of a second, considering what I might be called upon to do, the events or history that I might be destined to change in order to set time and the world right again, changes that might separate us forever. I considered that the events ahead of me might even take away my life, and with it my opportunity to say what I wanted to say. Taking his hand in mine, I added, "Jen-mate Kar-Tur."

He didn't respond for long seconds. My thoughts churned, wondering what was passing through his mind. Wondering what he thought of me and my brazen proposal. He knew that I knew the significance of his relationship-name "Jen-mate," and that I offered myself to him. I feared how he might judge my offer. But I had at last, as Kar-Tur wanted me to do, opened myself to him.

"Then we'll go together," Kar-Tur repeated after me, his strong fingers twining with mine. "Kar-mate JenHewitt."

Chapter 62

That he got the opportunity to take an airplane trip after all pleased Kar-Tur, although they took a much smaller plane than those he had seen in Denver. The prop plane brought them around the Rockies to L.A., taking many hours. It was evening when they approached a small municipal airport on the outskirts of the city. As they descended, Kar-Tur looked off to the west to see the sun hanging on the edge of the sea. It was the first time he'd ever seen the sea. It was as immense as maps claimed.

As they taxied across the runway toward where they planned to park the plane, his Kar-mate laid her hand on his knee and spoke. "I know where Jonathan is, Kar-Tur. I had another vision, my strongest yet. I know what we have to do, and have a plan, but we must go there now before they move him again."

Their pilot, O'Hara's agent, spoke up. "You need to come to ONE headquarters first. Tell Raumin and O'Hara what you know, then you can go with their support."

"No," she said. "There's no time. We must go now. Can you call for a taxi to pick us up?"

The agent called in the request, but still pleaded, "Ms. Hewitt, I'm responsible for you and your friend. Don't leave me like this."

"We must go now or it will be too late."

"At least let me contact Raumin and have him meet you. Where will you be?"

Kar-mate JenHewitt paused a moment, thinking. "It's essential that Raumin *not* meet us, or follow us. Do you understand that?"

The agent nodded.

"Jonathan is being held at the Symphony Hall. He'll be there until tomorrow morning when he'll be moved again. That might be a time to try to rescue him, should Kar-Tur and I fail today. But don't contact Raumin unless you hear that we failed. Do not tell him where we went before that, do you understand?"

The agent nodded again.

As they left the plane for the taxi, Kar-Tur worried about JenHewitt's insistence that Raumin not be contacted. It seemed unwise to be so self-assured and dismissive of potential support. If she feared that a communication might be intercepted and undermine their efforts, why not just say so? If she had a better plan, why not tell them of it?

The power his Kar-mate had newly found, arising from her understanding and faith, gave them reason for hope. But the support of friends and a shared plan seemed like good companions to faith and understanding.

Kar-Tur remembered what he had seen in the flames, what seemed forever ago now. Yes, all things were possible, and that meant both good and bad. And the bad was this: that good judgment and even good intent could be corrupted by unlimited power and pride.

A concert was in progress when they reached the Symphony Hall. Kar-Tur heard the sound wafting through the big wooden doors at the inner wall of the lobby area. As his Kar-mate cast her eyes around for the stairs going up to the room where Jonathan was held, Kar-Tur peeked into the room from which the sound came. He'd never seen so many people gathered in one place before. Toward the front, the musicians played their many varied instruments, not merely a group of individuals but *one tribe* as they worked together. The audience joined in that tribification, united by the music, participants in the creation of it.

Perhaps this clear example of the power of tribe might help his Kar-mate understand what he feared she was missing in charging into a dangerous place trusting only in her own vision.

"What a wonderful practice of community," Kar-Tur said as his Kar-mate came up beside him.

She tugged on his arm to hustle him along the corridor toward the stairs. When he didn't immediately move, she said, " I hadn't thought of it that way, but I guess music is about working together. We act in *concert*. A plan is well *orchestrated*. Some of our best words for working in unison are related to music."

She didn't seem to allow her mind to linger on the thought for long, and in a moment was pulling on his arm again, more insistently than before. This time, Kar-Tur reluctantly followed. Her thoughts were on her Tribemate Jonathan, on facing the Senator, and on her own vision of what must be done. She did not seem to understand what Kar-Tur had tried to tell her.

They met one of Raumin's officers on the stairs, Sarah Mendez. Kar-Tur saw the anger flash across Kar-mate JenHewitt's face. Anger at the airplane pilot for disobeying her. Anger at Officer Mendez for coming.

"You shouldn't be here," she said coldly. "If others come with us in what we have to do, they will die. We will all die. I have foreseen it."

"I am sorry, Ms. Hewitt," Mendez replied, taken aback by her intensity. "But Detective Raumin is concerned for you. He thinks this whole thing stinks of a trap. He's in the basement now looking for…..something."

"OK. Just stay away," his Kar-mate insisted.

"Very well. We're here if you need us."

Kar-mate JenHewitt seemed so sure of what was to come, sure of her course of action. Such confidence could lead one astray, as it had led him astray when he first discovered his power and travelled through time. As it had led the Senator astray in thinking he could save the world by shaping it to his own vision. Her peremptory treatment of the people who were trying to help did not seem at all like the person that he loved.

As they mounted the stairs, leaving Mendez behind, Kar-mate JenHewitt drew the gun that Kar-Tur had captured from the man in the airport. "The first of them are just ahead in the hallway," she said.

Kar-mate JenHewitt leaped into the hallway, shooting. She didn't appear to be a particularly good shot, but she seemed to know where to shoot ahead of time. She knew where her enemy would be. Watching her gave Kar-Tur advance notice as well. He charged the three men guarding a doorway. Observing the direction of their guns, he moved to avoid them, dodging from side to side faster than the relatively sluggish men of this time could swing their guns upon him. He felt confident of his ability to avoid being shot by them, watching where their guns pointed and moving away from the line of fire. But, given his Kar-mate's shooting abilities, he worried a bit more that he might catch a bullet from behind.

Despite Kar-Tur's concern for her marksmanship, one of the guards fell to her shooting, and the other two fell to Kar-Tur's swift fists.

Kar-Tur knew that they would not be able to surprise the occupants of the room. They must have heard the gunfire, and would be ready. He looked to JenHewitt for guidance, and she waved at the door. "Knock it in," she said.

"How many?" he asked.

"Ten."

Ten soldiers, fast and skilled. He and JenHewitt had only his own speed and strength and her precognition to compensate. Kar-Tur hoped she had more of a plan than she had shared, that her precognition was sound, and that her vision had not somehow been corrupted by the Senator.

"Where are they?" he asked her. She drew him a finger sketch on the doorway. After the ruckus in the hallway, the men inside were all in protected locations awaiting this very invasion. He wondered why she had resisted bringing reinforcements.

Kar-Tur burst through the wooden doorway, expecting to be riddled by bullets. To his surprise, the gunmen inside let them advance through the doorway unscathed. They seemed to be waiting. Perhaps they were waiting for the full contingent of attackers to invade the room, but there were no more of them to invade.

In the moments of respite, JenHewitt clicked off the light switch, casting the room into darkness. Kar-Tur's knowledge of where the guards were hiding gave him an advantage in the gloom. Leaping to their hiding spots, Kar-Tur dispatched one, then two in the first few seconds. JenHewitt shot another two before they began to return fire, shooting at the gun-flashes and noise around them.

Methodically Kar-Tur dispatched two more, slipping silently through the darkness from one to another. A third tried to use a flashlight, catching Kar-Tur in its beam for a moment, but revealing his own position even more quickly. Kar-Tur knocked him unconscious before he could fire his gun. Kar-Tur heard screams at JenHewitt's gunfire and presumed that others were being silenced as well.

JenHewitt turned the light back on. Jonathan sat in the back of the room, handcuffed to a table. JenHewitt rushed to him, and together the two of them lifted the heavy table just enough to slide the handcuff off the end of the leg.

But the two by the table, busy reassuring themselves of the other's safety, didn't see that a tenth man had slipped from a closet where he had hidden in the commotion and drew a bead on his Kar-mate. Kar-Tur lunged toward him, but the man saw him from the corner of his eye, and, in one swift move, turned on Kar-Tur and fired.

The bullet struck his shoulder like a flying boulder, killing his forward momentum and knocking him to the floor. Whirling, the man again aimed at JenHewitt. He fired, and Kar-Tur saw his Kar-mate, the one whom he loved, crumple with the impact.

With all his strength, Kar-Tur lunged from the floor toward the man, catapulting himself like a great cat leaping to the back of a mastodon. The force of Kar-Tur's assault crushed the man against the edge of the open closet door, snapping his back like a stick. The man fell into an odd twisted pile on the floor. Kar-Tur rose, his wounded shoulder dripping with blood, to see if his beloved still lived.

She was badly injured; blood seeped across her shirt from a wound in her chest. From the blood on her lips, Kar-Tur suspected that the bullet punctured a lung. But she was alive. Jonathan helped her to her feet.

"You shouldn't have come, Jen," Jonathan said. "This is just a trap. A trap for you and Kar-Tur. I overheard the Senator talking to one of the guards. The Senator and several guards have detonators to trigger a bomb planted in the building. He knows you're here and he's going to blow the building up."

JenHewitt frowned vaguely, not comprehending. "That isn't possible," she mumbled. "I didn't *see* that. It can't be so."

"The Senator was confident that you wouldn't see it." Jonathan said. "I heard him brag to his guards about how he hid it from you."

JenHewitt shook her head, disbelieving. She coughed and

staggered a bit despite Jonathan's support.

"Let's not tarry here, in any case," Kar-Tur said. "If we die, we die. But let's die trying to escape, not standing still awaiting it."

Kar-Tur took hold of his Kar-mate with his good arm, his other hanging uselessly at his side. Jonathan took her on the other side. Together they made it down the stairs. So good was the sound-proofing in the building that the concert still continued after the gunfight, rousing to a crescendo as they came into the lobby.

Raumin and Mendez were waiting for them there. Seeing Kar-Tur's injury, Raumin replaced him in supporting JenHewitt. "We have a car waiting outside," he said. "We need to get you both to the hospital."

Kar-Tur noticed that his Kar-mate remained subdued on the ride to the hospital. This was partly from her injury, of course. Her breathing was shallow and raspy and wouldn't likely support a lot of talking. But her somber expression made Kar-Tur suspect a deeper concern than her own injury.

"Raumin," she said. "What were you doing in the basement?"

"The Senator had a bomb there," he answered. "Big enough to take out most of the block. He knew you'd come for your friend. He didn't intend you to leave alive. We disabled it just before he sent the signal to detonate."

Kar-Tur's Kar-mate leaned against his good shoulder in the rear seat of the car. She whispered to him, conserving her diminishing strength and wind, but speaking almost as though to herself.

"Why didn't I see it, Kar-Tur? I was so sure that what I saw was real and complete. But, obviously, it wasn't. The Senator somehow influenced my visions, hiding things from me, even making me believe that if I let anyone help us they'd die. If he's so much stronger than me, how can I be of any help? ONE and the Shimera will depend on me to protect them, and I will fail."

Kar-Tur put his good arm around her shoulders, feeling warm at the touch between them. It felt good to be with his Kar-mate. Good to share this moment together, even in injury. Good that his Kar-mate's tribe were such skilled healers that he might expect his beloved to live. Good to be part of a tribe working together.

"Perhaps the Senator is stronger than any of us, Kar-mate," he said. "But because of our friends, we won today. Whatever else is true, it is our community and friendships that make us strong, and in that, we are stronger than the Senator."

Chapter 63

For better or worse, they'd begun the effort to free L.A., a first step toward freeing America. Raumin felt glad. However it turned out, they would have tried. History could never honestly cast them as cowards cowering before a dictator's threats. They would have done their part to stop this madman who set himself to conquer the world like some emperor of ancient times.

If they died, they died. Everyone died eventually anyway. But they would die doing what was right. And if, as the Senator proclaimed, only an empty crater would testify forever to the futility of their efforts, it would also testify to their courage and their convictions.

He looked at his watch. By now, the U.S. and British troops, under ONE leadership, were landing up and down the coast and converging on L.A. The Senator's troops would be congregating along that front to resist the invasion. As though to verify his time-piece, deep thundering explosions echoed to his ears from the sea.

Macabre, Raumin thought, how the Senator hadn't evacuated his troops as he had done in D.C. He must consider their use expended. Nor had he warned the city to evacuate. The Senator wanted a monument, a horrible monument of death, to his un-opposable power. His power to bring the sky down on his enemies.

Raumin huddled with his group of one hundred on the roof of the building, with the huge air handlers roaring around them, waiting for the signal to attack. Their own forces had dwindled since the events in D.C. Support had melted away, both public and military. They no longer held the numerical advantage over the Senator's army.

But, if they could flank the Senator's forces, and pin them against the sea, they could win this battle. With the main focus of the Senator's strength along the front at the coast, Raumin's hundred soldiers, along with dozens of other ONE groups scattered throughout L.A., could pour out into the thinned flank of the enemy and overcome them from behind. No well-defined lines of battle, no fronts or controlled territory. Just a confusing tangle of fighter-against-fighter, like the sword and chariot battles of the days of empire that the Senator hoped to reinstate.

And, they had the Shimera.

From his place on the roof, Raumin saw shimmers appearing all over L.A., in the streets, in the shadows, in the air, in the buildings. Wherever in space their being existed, the Shimera appeared, hovering in their places, their rifle-like weapons firing on any enemy within their zone of cognizance.

"Go!" Raumin shouted. "Go! Go!"

He and his one hundred raced down the stairs to join the battle in the streets or take their assigned places sniping from the roof. In the rush of battle, as his mind prepared to abandon reflection and consume itself with action, Raumin felt a peace in knowing that they were doing all that they could do. The remainder depended on Jen Hewitt and Kar-Tur, the man from the past. On those two alone rested their hope of shelter from the Senator's power to call the stars down upon them.

Chapter 64

It was good that Kar-Tur felt well enough to come to my room, since I didn't feel like getting out of bed at all, and all the IV's and other tubes dangling from me would have been embarrassing out in the hallway. After all, with the fate of the world resting in my care, the last think I wanted was to be *embarrassed*.

Or so I poked fun at my own pretensions.

I took Kar-Tur's hand as he sat on the bed beside me.

"Are you ready?" he asked.

I nodded. "Actually, I could use a couple months rest first. Would you mind?"

He smiled, and held my hand tighter. "We will do our best, Kar-mate. And we will do it together."

I knew that if I lay around thinking about it, I'd never get started on the job I had to do. Not if I let my reflective mind sail off in thought about those who depended on us, and what might happen to my world if we failed. Or what might happen to Kar-Tur if I succeeded. The time for thinking was past.

I took a final deep breath, and, with my Jen-mate, surged into that world of *sense*

The tangled strands of force and idea reached to the horizon. There was no sky. Everywhere I looked, forward and backward or up and down, I saw only horizon and Joshua tree-like tangles. Those, and Kar-Tur, who stood in that strange, minimalist landscape with me.

I knew that the Joshua trees represented my mind's efforts to make sense of that incomprehensible place, like dreams created sense from the random pulses sent to the brain in sleep. Human brains excelled at finding order in things.

But I liked having an image that made the ethereal world of *sense* concrete. I also liked that the image implied a life-like character to the underpinning laws of nature.

I wondered if Kar-Tur saw the Joshua trees, too. Or if he saw some other landscape more familiar to him.

I reached deeper into that world, gently unraveling the tangled threads, looking for the danger that was bearing down upon my world from another time. I found the dead strands where the previous meteorite had disrupted time and place. Looking behind them, as though on another branch of the Joshua tree, I found a second meteorite, also stolen from the future, rifting across time toward us.

I reached out for it, feeling its potential and threat. The threads of principle and purpose around it responded well to my hand, as though eager for my restoring touch. Gently I nudged that trans-time stone away, asking, working with the rules that nature established. And I set it back in its proper time, its energies returned to where they were meant to be.

Our troops, and the people of Southern California, were safe from that threat.

But, I had no time for elation. Although I still felt the warm glow of Kar-Tur's presence with me, I felt another presence as well. A powerful one, with a mind stronger than my own.

A dark cloud appeared on one of the many horizons around me. A glow like *goodness* appeared in the midst of the cloud, but a roiling blackness obscured it. As the cloud swept toward us across the Joshua trees, I saw the form of a man hovering within it.

The man had the appearance of a Greek God, fierce, powerful, beautiful. He carried a large sword, swiftly cutting across the tangled strands to reach us, not wasting time with raveling or unraveling them.

This was the Senator as he appeared in this world of *sense*. I knew that his was the brilliant mind whose force I felt.

He had not yet reached us when I began my second task. I didn't know what the Senator could do to us in this ethereal world. I didn't know whether he could kill us or stop our efforts. But I couldn't afford to wait and see. I had to do my part for the battle that ONE fought against the Senator's forces.

I found the strands representing the air above the Senator's army. As I'd done in our cave in Colorado, I pulled the heat from the threads, cooling them, bringing the water vapor to the point of condensation. Similar though it was to my efforts in the cave, I did it on a much larger scale, not a small packet of space a single foot on each side but miles of sky. My mind strained under the effort.

I felt Kar-Tur there with me, strengthening me with his belief and insight. Reaching out with me to move the strands of energy.

I felt the rain begin to fall.

The rain couldn't defeat the Senator's army, of course, even though it might inconvenience them. My goal was not to defeat them with rain, but to reveal that the magical forces the Senator once wielded now supported his enemies. The sky was no longer his to command.

In so doing, I hoped to defeat their will to fight on, win the war without bloodshed.

I returned my attention to the advance of the Senator-god. The cloud around him grew larger as he approached.

The Joshua trees did not extend unchanged to the horizon, as I'd thought before. Around the Senator and expanding outward from him, a ripple appeared in the fabric of this world of *sense*. Beyond the ripple, the Joshua trees were uniform in appearance with a precision, a symmetry, that the nearer trees lacked.

The ripple advanced and retreated between us, as though constantly adjusting to unseen forces. I realized that the ripple represented neither time nor place, but *potential*. Two distinct worlds existed on either side of that ripple, each world pressing against the other to compete for which would be. This was the place where possibilities were not yet decided, futures not yet set.

The movement of the ripple, forward and back, was the cumulative choice of all sentient minds. The scope of each world shifted as minds in concert moved one way or another in the fluctuation of choice. But only one of those worlds could prevail. One way would carry us into the future. That one way was not yet chosen.

The world I saw at a distance, which I presumed to be the Senator's choice for the future, seemed so perfect and exact. I hesitated a moment over what that might mean, unsure of myself. The nearer world was more flawed. Could it be that the Senator's future was better than the one I would choose? Was *I* the enemy of the future?

I spoke to Kar-Tur for the first time in this world of sense. "Do you think his world is better than what we pursue? Do we know what we're doing?"

His voice came to my mind, much like when the Shimera spoke to us. "I see good there, and the intent for good. But, something is missing. Variety. Creativity. Would you want a world with such sameness?"

I would not. But seeing the good that could be in that other world, its flawless peacefulness, I wondered if I acted for the good of all, or if I merely sought the world that I wanted.

I was willing to suffer crime for the sake of freedom, error for the sake of creativity. But did I have the right to make that choice for everyone?

The other side of the ripple, that other possible future, seemed darker to me, shadowed by the cloud that attended the Senator's image. I wondered if that darkness symbolized an evil in that future, despite its seeming perfection. But then, the darkness was simply my own interpretation of reality, my mind creating images out of that world of natural law and innate existence. Was the darkness truly an indication of evil, or merely an interpretation born from my own preferences?

I had no more time to ponder. The Senator swept upon us.

He cut with his sword at the cooled strands above his troops, the strands that brought the rain upon them, trying to reassert his control over the heavens. Kar-Tur and I repaired the strands as he cut at them, but our twining and untwining, gently working with the principles represented by those threads, was slow in comparison to his sword. His swift cuts *demanded* rather than *asked* the strand's cooperation with his plans. His intellect—the slashing sword-- gave him an advantage over us. I realized that we must eventually succumb to his swifter sword.

Nevertheless, for a time we repaired the strands of cooled air almost as quickly as he destroyed them, our efforts to maintain the rain stalemating the Senator's efforts to end it. There was one thing in our favor in this battle among the forces and essence of nature; the strands themselves were not static or inert. They grew naturally of their own accord, in such a way as to heal the rifts his sword struck. The natural growth countered the work of his sword in the fabric of the world of *sense*, but enhanced the changes that Kar-Tur and I worked with our twining and untwining. The more we twined, the more the natural character of the strands supported our efforts. His changes were swifter than ours, but if we could keep the strands alive for long enough, our slower approach would prevail, the way a geometric growth overtook an initially faster arithmetic one.

He must have seen this as well and changed his attack. I felt the strength of his intellect, stronger than mine, stronger than Kar-Tur's, surging in him. I felt him tap into even more strength--his Belief Team.

Only then did I remember the exponential growth in strength that came with numbers. I remembered how much brighter this world appeared when I had entered it with Kar-Tur. I remembered how much greater the effect had been in Susan's experiments when there were two believers rather than one.

As the first of the twenty joined him, the ripple between possible futures surged toward us, allowing the Senator's possible future to encompass a much greater part of the visible world. The Senator's strength expanded, along with the beauty of his image as a Greek god. His muscles bulged. His sword lengthened. I realized that a continued exponential increase in strength would soon make our resistance futile. Kar-Tur and I alone could not defeat the Senator and his twenty believers.

However, as more of the twenty joined him, the Senator's increase in strength did not continue to be exponential. Although two were much stronger than one, creating an initial exponential effect, with each additional believer the effect grew incrementally smaller, perhaps approaching an asymptotic maximum.

We still had a chance.

I focused even more diligently on repairing each strand as soon as the Senator-god cut it, feeling the new speed and power surging from his Belief Team, but seeing that their work was still resisted by the nature of the world of *sense* while ours was supported. As I concentrated on my healing work, I failed to notice that the Senator-god's eyes had left the strands and fallen on me. When I did notice, his sword arm was already drawn back and ready to strike. I heard Kar-Tur cry out, but too late.

The sword lanced out, and I felt the force of the Senator's intellect pierce me through the chest, an intellect that I knew I could never match. I fell backwards, away from the surreal world of sense into a place with nothing at all. Kar-Tur, the Joshua trees, even the god-like Senator shrank into a tiny point of light and vanished. I felt the life slipping from me as I fell and fell.

A pair of arms reached out to catch me. I could see nothing through the darkness that was overtaking me, but I knew that the arms belonged to Kar-Tur, and a sense of peace suffused me. There were worse ways to die than with the one you loved best.

I felt Kar-Tur lower me to what passed as ground. I was conscious enough to realize that I hadn't the strength to return to the real world. I was trapped here. I would die here.

In the real world, I'd have already lost consciousness with the drop in blood pressure in my brain. I wondered what form death took in this realm of *sense*.

I looked down to see if I bled in this place. Kar-Tur's hand was on my chest, covering the wound.

"The great cat can't harm you," he said.

What cat? I saw no cat. But I had no strength to speak.

I felt something, a stirring, a warmth that seemed to come from Kar-Tur's hand over my wound. I looked down at his hand, and, as I watched, the edges of the wound seemed to shrink away, disappearing under his hand.

"Kar-mate," he said. "It's not intellect that rules here, but *faith*. And that's where we're stronger. I *believe* we can win. That we are meant to win. Do you believe that as well?"

My mortal wound was almost healed. I rose, astonished, the power of the world of sense pouring into me with Kar-Tur's revelation. I *did* believe it.

I felt myself growing in strength and size, felt Kar-Tur's strength also pouring into me, through me. I grew until the Senator stood small beneath me, nearly lost in the tangle of Joshua trees at my feet, no longer a direct threat. He tested my strength briefly with his sword, but could not harm me, and withdrew.

From my larger vantage, the folded origami universe stretched around me again, brighter and closer than when I had seen it alone at the cave. In the brighter light, I saw the folds as places where unconnected parts of reality touched, creating relationship where none existed before. I saw many connections. Meetings between people who might not have met. Encounters between societies where technologies, art, and beliefs were shared. Places where events of the past affected the future. And places where the future affected the past.

Each fold created more than the sum of what individual segments had been before, as each fold became part of a larger emerging image. As before, my mind refused to give concrete form to that image, like an abstract idea in a dream that refuses to assume its role as an actor in the dream. I looked for birds, or ships, or hats in the origami pattern, but recognized nothing. I realized that the pattern's ambiguity resulted because what it was to become was not yet decided. The pattern represented creation still in progress. A living pattern still forming and transforming in response to the actions of its participants.

The ambiguity meant that the ongoing creation, the living origami, could be changed. I noticed that some of the folds looked new and still limber, as though easily unfolded. Others appeared stiffened, or welded into place, as though change were no longer easy. I saw bindings, like rivets, holding some sheets together.

I remembered Susan's comments concerning folds on the stone in Wyoming. And I remembered her reference to rivets in the folds. What else had she written about the rivets?

I strove to remember, and it came to me.

"Detachable rivets in the temporal folding" Susan wrote.

Detachable? Could the rivets holding the folds in place be removed? Could parts of the pattern be undone? Folds unraveled? Creations, connections, and relationships that *once were* become no more?

I had grown lost in my own thoughts, and paid insufficient

attention to my adversary, the Senator. A sudden wave of nausea drew me from my meditation and caused me to stagger slightly. The nausea arose from a sense of lightness, as though I had entered free fall, or became weightless.

I became aware of the Senator again, now only a very little god. I hadn't noticed him earlier because my attention was on much larger patterns than those where he worked. He worked near a small fold nested within many bigger ones, almost hidden by them. The Senator, seeing he could not threaten me directly, hacked away with his sword at one of the rivets in the many folds that undulated around us.

He broke through the rivet holding the small fold in place, and another wave of lightness swept over me. My arms and hands became transparent briefly before becoming solid again.

He was, I realized belatedly, breaking the folds in the fabric of reality that led to my own existence. Cutting away that pleat in creation where I came to be. Trying to destroy me before I ever existed.

The folds didn't immediately fall apart when he cut the rivet, but remembered their shape like stiff paper. That made sense, I thought. There had to be some stability to the pattern of things. A stability maintained perhaps by the mutual expectation, or common choice, of sentient beings. Otherwise all of reality would be in constant flux, unpredictable and changing, where even the past would transform at the whim of some new belief or thought. Something had to make the universe Cosmos and not Chaos.

It occurred to me that if the past were in constant flux, I might never know it. I would only remember whatever past was presently manifest.

The Senator inserted his sword into the fold to pry it apart, trying to smooth the wrinkle in reality that brought together the people and events that led to me. As he bent his shoulders to the task, I decided that my intellectual curiosity about the stability of the past did not outweigh my interest in preserving this part of it.

So, I intervened.

I brushed him away from the fold, like a cat from the table, and reinserted the rivet he'd cut. I looked down to find a riveting tool in my hand, able either to set or remove rivets. I used it to set the rivet again.

So the rivets were attachable as well as detachable. I wondered if that were part of Susan's full message.

I turned my attention again to the Senator. I couldn't allow him to run free in this place, detaching rivets at will. Disrupting who knew how much of reality.

I advanced toward him. But he knew he was weaker than Kar-Tur and I, even with his Belief Team behind him. He and his Belief Team fled from the world of *sense*.

The rain fell and fell on the Senator's army. From this place, I felt their fear, and the realization dawning within them that they had been abandoned. The realization that the tide of power passed from them. I knew they would surrender.

And I knew we'd won.

But won at great cost. A cost that included the death of an unknown number of Shimera. That included the destruction of Washington D.C. and the loss of thousands, perhaps tens of thousands of lives. A cost that included the loss of Kar-Tur and Susan to their loved ones.

I looked at the riveting tool in my hand. I could find the place where Kar-Tur and Susan inadvertently folded two different times and places together. Where humanity came together with the Shimera for the first time. Where so much sorrow and death began.

I could find that fold in the evolving origami of existence, and remove the rivet from it.

Slowly, the fold would unbend. It would take on a new pattern, a new shape, bringing different people, events and realities together.

The Senator would not learn of this world of *sense* prior to anyone else and thereby gain opportunity to seize its power. I would not be kidnapped and interrogated and spend months in flight and hiding. The death wrought in the Shimera world by Kar-Tur and Susan, and by the Senator wrenching the meteorite across time, would be no more. Washington D.C. would still stand, and thousands now dead would live again. Jonathan and Susan would have each other.

And I would never meet Kar-Tur.

Surely, that was a small price to pay to save the Shimera, and my own people, from so much suffering.

But at what other cost would I remove that rivet? What might be the future cost of friendships that would never be, or of friendships that would mature differently? What might be the future cost of never knowing the Shimera? What might be the cost of changing the progress of our exploration in the world of *sense*?

I couldn't know.

I *did* know that it would take away the one I loved. Take away even my memory of him.

If I could simply undo the pain so many had suffered, make the world uniformly better with no negative consequences, I could do it. But these folds were the fabric of creation. I didn't have sufficient wisdom to see what that creation might become, or where averting one tragedy might inadvertently cause some other loss even more terrible.

I found my Jen-mate, waiting for me among the Joshua trees of this strange world. I held him tight for a moment, reveling in our victory and in his touch. And then we returned to our own world together.

Chapter 65

Although Raumin used all his skill and connections trying to track him down, he could not find the man again. Senator Jerry Roden had slipped away. Where, no one knew. He'd left no trace. At least, no trace that Raumin could find.

Perhaps he was gone for good, Raumin thought. Perhaps he would be content with hiding in obscurity. Or, perhaps he had died in his efforts to escape. Raumin was not very hopeful on that point.

The governor had appointed Jane O'Hara to fill out Roden's Senatorial term and she had asked Raumin to go with her to New Washington, where the new capital was already under construction on the shores of Lake D.C. She'd offered him a significant appointment on her staff. She'd made Jack Myrvik a similar offer.

Jack planned to go. Said he'd enjoy a break from university life. Said he respected O'Hara and what she'd done when others were too afraid.

Raumin considered whether he should go with them to D.C. Like Mryvik, he respected the new Senator. And he would like working with Jack. They'd become friends during the last few months of turmoil and danger.

It could also be fun to try his hand in politics.

Work at the station was a mess these days. Police functions had been sharply disrupted by the martial law. Getting operations running smoothly again was going to take weeks if not months.

In addition, a number of officers had resigned, making the workload heavy for those remaining. Several more had been on opposite sides of the conflict, causing high stress levels in the station.

He wouldn't mind leaving some of that behind.

Raumin stopped by Jack Myrvik's apartment on the way home after work. It had become a habit of his the last few weeks since the war ended. His own home near the coast had been destroyed by artillery, and his new place didn't seem that much like home yet. It was nice to have someone to talk to for an hour.

Myrvik offered him a beer, which he accepted, and he took a seat on the sofa.

"Any luck with visitation rights?" he asked Myrvik, as he sipped his cold beverage.

"Yeah," he replied. "I think I'm going to get every other weekend. I may not even have to go to court. Attitudes have improved between us. Alice decided not to move to Dallas after all, at least if I keep alimony up. I think the past year has left her content to just stay where she knows people."

"Glad to hear it," Raumin said. "What do the kids think?"

"Well, they don't say much." Myrvik shrugged. "It's hard for them. And I understand that. It's OK with me if they don't want to talk about it."

Raumin nodded. "How will travel to D.C. affect your time with the kids?"

"I'll fly back every other weekend," Myrvik said. "I want to do that anyway. This is still home."

Raumin thought about that. What made this place home to Jack, he wondered? His kids? Or did he just like L.A.?

Was it *his* home? Or would he be equally happy in D.C.? He liked his community here. His work. His colleagues.

But was that enough to keep him here? Maybe he needed to shake himself up a bit. Try something new. It was good to not stay in one place or one job for too long.

"Think I should take O'Hara up on her offer?" Raumin asked.

"Yeah, I think so," Myrvik said. "These are exciting times. A lot is going to change in the next few years. I think you'd enjoy being part of it."

Raumin nodded thoughtfully. "Maybe so."

They talked a while longer, of the day's work, of the new world and the new nation. Of past adventures and future prospects.

Raumin went to work early the next morning, hoping to catch up on some of the backlog. No one else was there yet except Mendez, who always came and left early.

His thoughts were still on whether to take the job in D.C. It wasn't just about the job, he realized. It was about people.

While he had sat outside D.C., watching the fire and waiting for oblivion from the sky, it hadn't been his life's work that came to mind. Not his work with army intelligence. Not his years of service with the L.A. police. It was his friendships. Not that they were all that deep.

Maybe what he really needed was to get stirred from his interpersonal complacency. Maybe a new job in a new place could do that.

Raumin had no family. Why not go?

He told Officer Mendez what was on his mind, and asked what she thought.

"It would be a great opportunity for you." She paused. "You should go. Is there anyone to keep you here?"

Chapter 66

Jonathan looked down at Susan's grave. He couldn't bear to call it an excavation site anymore. The blue tarp had worked loose again, and one side lay shredded on the ground, victim of some windstorm of the past few months. Like life, it resisted constraint.

He wasn't sure whether he had come here to renew his work, discontinued these many months, or whether he simply needed to visit Susan's grave, to reconcile with his loss and say goodbye.

He stood there for a while, looking at her last resting place, the place she herself must have chosen all those ages ago, knowing as she chose it that the one she once loved would find her there.

He knew then why he was here. He was not yet ready to continue his work at this place. Maybe in a month. Maybe in a year. But not now. Now he was here to remember the first woman he truly loved. The woman who taught him that he, even he, could commit to someone fully, and solely.

His eyes looked beyond the grave to the mountains surrounding it. He wondered what they must have been like, all those years ago, when Susan knew this place.

Just beyond the skeleton, near what must have once been the shoreline of a lake long ago, Jonathan saw a glimmer of color in the air, shimmering. He started toward it, drawn by some hint of familiarity that he saw in the human-like form that began to take shape. It beckoned to him as he walked.

"Jonathan," it called.

How could any Shimera know him here? He was only known to a few of the Shimera in California. The Shimera here must certainly be far too distant to know or communicate what happened so far away.

"Jonathan," it called again. "It's Susan. Susan Arasmith. Do you remember me?"

Jonathan came to a stop beside the apparition and stared, trying to reconcile this ethereal shimmer with the woman he had known.

"You, you're Shimera," he said at last.

"Shimera?" she repeated. "A nice name. Descriptive.

"I wasn't able to return to you," she said, "because of the harm it would do to the People of Time, the ones you call the Shimera. But I can appear to you here, in this form, for a few minutes.

"I journeyed here to see if you ever again passed this way. I wanted to speak with you and tell you that I survived. But, of course, you already know that by now."

"Yes," Jonathan said. "We know."

"Many years have passed for me, Jonathan. I wanted you to know that I went on with my life, so that you might go on with yours.

"It is a good life," she said. "I've learned many things. Of the People of Time, the Shimera. Of our own roots and our destiny. I'm pleased.

"Tell me of my sister, Cynthia. Do you know anything of her?"

"Yes," Jonathan said. "She is well."

"I'm glad. I can't stay with you long. It's a strain to maintain both place and time. Please know that I have loved you and missed you these many years. Please tell the others also who know me. Tell them I've missed them dearly. All of you are the foundation of who I have become. Goodbye, old friend."

And she was gone.

Jonathan wanted to call her back. Talk to her of all his journeys, ask of all of hers. Why had he been struck so dumb? Why hadn't he told her that he loved her? Why hadn't he asked about her life and what she had done? Why hadn't he told her all the things that had transpired here, of what they had learned and overcome?

He knew then why he had not. The things of her life did not really impinge on his own except as a shadow. And his life did not truly touch hers. She and he were still tied together, somewhere, in the morass of time and space. Tied together in a way that molded their lives and the lives of many others. Tied together in a place and time that he would cherish always.

But now, in this time and place, a chasm lay between them.

Chapter 67

It felt strange to be at the restaurant by the sea where all these things began what seemed so long ago. Of the four of us, only Jonathan and I remembered that former evening, watching the moonlight twinkle on the sea, when we first talked about an impossible and wonderful discovery that set our footsteps toward adventure. So much had happened since then. So much pain and joy. So much friendship.

I thought about the message "Be a Friend" that Susan sent to me so long ago. Who would I be had I not been a friend to Kar-Tur? Where would our world be if we had not chosen friendship rather than war with the Shimera?

I wondered if those truly were the ones her message meant that I should befriend. I found it intriguing that I found the words "Be a Friend" on the ancient broach just before I first met Susan. If Jonathan and I had never befriended Susan, which of the events that followed would have vanished? What would have come to be instead?

I couldn't know. And there was no way to know for sure whom Susan's message directed us to befriend, or even who was meant to do the befriending. I was simply glad I was a friend.

I found it ironic that all these events had shown, through science, that faith was real, with real power. I had always hoped for some tangible proof of my religious beliefs, something I could point to and say to skeptics "See, there is evidence." Faith was the fulcrum of my religious belief. It was on faith that my intellect was balanced with feeling, that my concrete world was balanced with the spiritual. It was the foundation of my communion with an infinite Being.

It seemed, now that Faith was shown to be a True Force in nature, that this fact should count as evidence. Hadn't religious people always predicted that Faith was real, with real power? And wasn't accurate prediction considered valid proof, even in science?

But the very same events also provided a reason to *disbelieve*. It gave us a reason for faith to exist, even if there was no infinite Being of the universe. Instead of verifying and justifying the religion on which it was based, faith now promised a practical benefit that, in the eyes of many, explained why so many cultures and nations practiced faith in a God who never existed. To the skeptic, the practice of Faith, not the worship of God, gave them power.

So *my* faith was not proven. Perhaps it never could be. Perhaps there must always be a true Faith. A belief based on vision in the inner self, communing with spirit in a place the mundane human corpse cannot go.

After dinner, the four of us watched the endless waves roll into shore from a veranda that overlooked the beach. Jonathan told us of his conversation with Susan in Wyoming. Of how she appeared to be Shimera. He seemed quite upset, even saddened, by the encounter. I, on the other hand, couldn't help but see it as a joyous event. As I'm sure Susan intended it. To know her life went well, that it was productive, that she was happy in it, was a great joy for me. I would have envied her adventurous life had my own not looked so promising. Susan lived a good life, well entwined in the fabric of being itself. And, to ephemeral humans in a world of geological time, nothing more joyous could be said of anyone than that their fleeting time should have the meaning thus imparted.

I felt sure, once Jonathan thought about it, that he would know that as well.

I stood with Kar-Tur, my Jen-mate, looking out on the sea, wondering what lay ahead of us. I was excited at the prospect of facing that future, of facing it with my best friend, my comrade, my mate.

Cynthia saw that we were drawing together, wanting to be alone. She beckoned with her hand to Jonathan.

"Won't you take a walk with me down by the sea?" she asked. "And leave these two lovers alone?"

Kar-Tur and I watched them as they disappeared into the gathering darkness, walking side by side, their heads toward each other, engaged in conversation.

Made in the USA
Lexington, KY
10 September 2019